**THE HERO WAS TOO DAMNED LIKE
SOMEONE ELSE. BIG, EASY, ATHLETIC
WITH A NICE GOOD-TEMPERED
SMILE ...**

There was a sharp-edged beauty to his features
and his cleancut hairline that wasn't quite right
... But it wasn't wrong either.

Moke put it into words. 'But Dosh is dead,'
he said. 'Cass and I saw it. We were both there.'

There. The day Nimbus shot him and burned
his chest out in that set-up film that reduced us
from three to two and made me the kind of
public heroine no sane guy would ever want to
be ... Dosh. Who was Moke's lover, and mine.
Whose dying had been in my nostrils for nearly
two years of galactic wandering, because
whatever Mokey said, it was my fault ...

D0995577

ABOUT THE AUTHOR

Wilhelmina Baird was born in 1935 in Dunfermline, Fife, but was brought up in England. She took up teaching temporarily, while she tried to finish her MA thesis. However, her Open University teaching continued and the MA was sidelined. She describes herself as 'the classic taught everything-everywhere-can't-stand-still guy'. She dabbled in writing short stories and thrillers, but was published only once she retired from teaching and is still working at it. Her previous book, *Crashcourse*, is also available in Roc.

Wilhelmina Baird lives in France with two cats and a French-speaking computer.

CLIPJOINT

WILHELMINA BAIRD

ROC

Published by the Penguin Group
Penguin Books Ltd, 27 Wrights Lane, London W8 5TZ, England
Penguin Books USA Inc., 375 Hudson Street, New York, New York 10014, USA
Penguin Books Australia Ltd, Ringwood, Victoria, Australia
Penguin Books Canada Ltd, 10 Alcorn Avenue, Toronto, Ontario, Canada M4V 3B2
Penguin Books (NZ) Ltd, 182–190 Wairau Road, Auckland 10, New Zealand

Penguin Books Ltd, Registered Offices: Harmondsworth, Middlesex, England

First published in the USA by Ace Books 1994
First published in Great Britain in Roc 1996
1 3 5 7 9 10 8 6 4 2

Copyright © Joyce Hutchinson, 1994

 Roc is a trademark of Penguin Books Ltd

Printed in England by Clays Ltd, St Ives plc

ACKNOWLEDGMENTS

Thanks to my editor, Laura Anne Gilman, for her continued help and patience.

To M. Batail for the hours he spent teaching my computer to jump through hoops.

To Dennis Dodridge (again) and Helen (again) for the use of their Amstrad to get my old disks onto *something*, if only paper, and to Mme. Robin for enormous work on photocopies, both of which helped to save my sanity.

To Nick March, for generous publicity.

And to James, as always, for egging me on.

CLIPJOINT

Virginity. With its ravening gash three miles deep that slashes the main continent north to south with a river of sludge crawling through the bottom under snowfields of cloud. A killer mouth that sucks in everything, spawning monstrosities as it worms down to the Equatorial Ocean, a chemical soup lashed by hurricanes, mutating like yeast. UVs that microwave anything that moves even without the breaks in the cloud cover that happen alternate leap year Fridays. Hotter than a bathtub, as wet as a shower stall and everyone caked with designer sunscreen under their millionaire minimals. The river on Virginity.

Absolute paradise if you're an alga.

Moke and me are not and we were in the middle. The dump has one single advantage: the Virginites like monumental sculpture. Moke makes it. I make him make it and they pay both of us. The money bought the Theotokopolou bows I wore to the soirées where we wooed the money and a three-inch-deep puddle that contacted my butt on our costly terrace reduced them to mush and all it took was the death of the soul.

Our rented palace clawed the edge of the river and washed out into it through its cero foundations. The ex-garden was a rockhole already and we'd only been three months in occupation. The moss roots in cushions on the plascrete and multiplies faster than the domestics can rake it. Hell, it roots on the domestics. Sleep with open windows and you'll find it roots on anything. You can scratch yourself to death between three A.M. and morning. Some nights you feel there must be better ways to live.

"I seem to remember," Moke said sorrowfully, emerging from the shower in a toweling shirt just about covered his gluteus maximus, "we used to want this."

For the record, it *was* three A.M. and I'd a bruise on my butt. Theotokopolou was in the garbage. "You're sore because you got to see the General in the morning. It's nothing, guy. He wants something showy for his ninth green."

"He could try a sand trap. I can design him a sand trap he won't get out of in a thousand years."

"You're being spiteful."

"Anybody wants a golf course in this climate deserves to spend a thousand years in a sand trap. Golfers got no time for the arts anyhow, they're too busy counting their handicaps."

"When they've time to spare from their millions. That's where you and me come in, mec. We're taking part in the circulation of wealth by democratic free trade."

"What I'm doing personally is going nuts."

I sat on the couch and stretched my legs out over his knees. "Nice Mokey. One piece of splendor for the General's ninth green, please-please?"

He sighed. Pathetically. I can't stand it when Mokey gets pathetic. "Okay, Cass. But can I howl like a wolf while I'm doing it?"

At which moment Yell stuck his head through the sea green shimmer-curtain filling the arch into the living room and his hand after it. "You kids decent? Somebody feel like howling? Count me in. Cass, this came this afternoon. I put it on your desk but I guess you ain't been in there. You want it?"

"What is it, Yell?"

The hand waved at me, draped in green shimmer-curtain, mystic, wonderful, holding a small square package covered with Union Mail registration stamps.

"Looks like a letter bomb," Mokey said, digging his long skull into my shoulder and settling for either a sleep or a smooch, whichever came first. "Put it in a bucket of water, Yell, and if it doesn't blow up we'll read it tomorrow."

"Don't!" I yelped. I recognized some of those stamps. Real expensive hurry-up material. "Thanks, Yeller. Give it here and I'll take a look."

"It's bad luck, Cassandra," Moke said owlishly. That made it sleep he was curling up for. "When it goes off and blows both our heads off you're going to be sorry."

"Shut up and snore, Leonardo. Aunt Cassie wants to look at her nice parcel. Maybe someone's sent me a diamond ring."

"I'll buy you one in the morning. It's more likely someone's sent you a stick of dynamite."

"He's feeling put-on," I said to Yeller. "Does it smell of dynamite, spacer?"

"Not the kind that goes bang or I'd have put it somewhere safe myself. But it smells of trouble, Cass. You want me to lose it in the mail?"

"Uh-uh. How'd you know?"

"Instinct." He grinned and shaled the package across. "Open it if you like. I can lose it in the mail afterwards."

I caught it and his head and arm disappeared.

"Cassandra, you are going to regret this," Mokey said with sleepy disapproval. "Why don't we go to bed?"

"In a minute."

I turned the package over looking for a sender's address. There was an illegible scrawl of which the only word that stood out clearly was ASHTON. The stamps were Earth too, much canceled and overstamped with colored agency seals, which suggested it had followed us around. It looked as if it had originally been addressed to me at Moke's workshop on Never. So Eklund had forwarded it. Consequently it wasn't explosive because his security's formidable.

I unzipped the edges expecting paper and a shiny flat box with buzzing holofigures fell into my hand. They were wearing spacesuits and seemed to be massacring each other. The label was TROUBLE ON TOROS, with tiny faraway music, martial, the kind that goes with space battles, and mixed scents of ozone and musk.

"It's a vidcrystal," I told Mokey. "Someone wants to entertain us."

"Make them go away," he mumbled. "We don't watch vids. You got a conscientious objection. Who's Santa Claus?"

I fished around among the wrappings but that was it. One crystal in original case and the horse it rode in on. No name, address, shop-code, invoice.

"Some really shy guy. Unless he's got a bad memory. Writes his name so you can't read it and forgets the gift card."

"Throw it away, Cass."

I turned it over and over. Three-fifteen morning time and five thousand creds of dress that just went to the last roundup. I was wearing my panties and long hair in a lacquered pagoda with little bead fringes, and runnels of sweat trickled down my spine. An occasional blast of hot wet wind, inaudible through the house screens, still managed to vibrate the windows. I could practically hear the moss growing fatter on the terrace. Moke was snuffling on my shoulder. Yell, whose sleeping hours are mysterious, was making late-night snack noises in the kitchen, thinly audible through a hair-fault in the curtain. It felt like the end of the universe.

I snapped the box open and picked out the fresh glittering crystal. It was still in plastic that smoked when I touched it. I refused to think any longer. I slid it into my behind-the-ear socket.

A lot of black space with patterns of stars. A point of light growing in the distance, that became a red-hot meteor storm, that burst into flaming letters across the insides of my eyes, red and then blue, fading to violet and out. TROUBLE ON TOROS. More meteors that burst in bunches of dazzle like Fourth of July rockets announcing names, professions, accomplishments. Ozony smell with undertones of flowers and something that could have been cinnamon. A taste of strong coffee and the remains of what felt like apple pie. Space music, that electronic wailing goes with the Big Black the way coffee goes with apple pie.

So far so commonplace. I knew this story from the days when I was young and used to watch this garbage, before my life started getting serious. The guys are in the mess waiting around before the battle, establishing their sympathetic personalities, projecting the pathos of innocent boys eating their last meal before whatever awful thing the producer has in mind slithers in and falls on their heads. Locating the bad guy (who may or may not turn out to be a good guy) who squares off with the hero—the first sniff and the first wail and you know exactly where you're at. It's reassuring. Just the thing when you're tired.

I closed my eyes and watched the pictures on the inside of my head. The Ship. Huge, menacing, more naval than the Navy, covered with real military letters and badges, swanning through constellations like a whale among plankton, star reflections glinting off its sides. Mess room, right, and Our Boys, young, athletic, crewcut, horsing around the way film space-crews always do (and any admiral worth his salt would jam the whole pack in the pokey before you could say "insubordination"). Making doubtful jokes and acting macho in front of Our Girls, who're similar but got their bulges in different places.

One of the latter is fragile, sensitive, devoted to motherhood, home and duty, finds all this lack of professional seriousness offensive. Guys think she's a pain in the ass, what else, otherwise she doesn't get to show her True Grit in the last reel. She, obviously, is source of floral scent, improbable in the circumstances. She is obviously also source of a lot of trouble to come. I was her exec I'd send her to wash it off if I didn't positively clap her in irons but I'm allergic to the type. Did I say I'm a career burglar? Cute gets you dead.

And here's the mach, natch, grosser than the normal grunt, rubbing his designer unshave on Missy's ruby cheek, whiff of genuine armpit (never sure if that's supposed to turn us shemales on or off). She's too weak-kneed to slug him herself so her Loot gets to do it, better-looking girl than her, she's bound for the Big Spaceyard in the Sky.

And—music, musk, salt-taste, action!—here comes the hero.

I thought it might be possible I was goggling and making noises. I'd certainly bitten my tongue. The universe was shaking, I was shaking, Mokey was shaking me . . .

I came back to our cane-and-cretonne salon with a snap, the overheated plant-smells, the quiet perpetual vibration of the bubble above and the foundations below that gets into your bones without being noticed and drives you crazy, and I thought for a while I was going to throw up.

Moke was staring with terrified wild half-awake eyes and Yeller was leaning in from the kitchen with a half-eaten sandwich in his hand looking startled. I got a grip and tried to stop rattling. It was harder than you'd think.

After a minute I thought I'd got my voice at least under control. "Moke, take a look. Just the beginning till the entrance of the hero. And don't have hysterics, I've warned you."

He took it as if it was poisonous and slotted it cautiously where he jacks his heavy equipment. I watched him and saw his face concentrate, look puzzled—and change.

"Pass it to Yeller."

And we all sat around, half-dressed, half-fed, half-awake, blearing at each other like dummies.

The hero was too damned like someone else. Big, easy, athletic with a nice good-tempered smile, a way of moving, a habit of throwing his arms around people's shoulders when he wanted to comfort them. His yellow hair, buttercup color, fell enticingly over his brow.

The eyes beneath were strange. The left was gray-green, the right clear hazel. It gave something off-center to his look that was attractive and unsettling at the same time. There was a sharp-edged beauty to his features and his clearcut hairline that wasn't quite right. His shoulders were a shade broader and his hips narrower than I remembered, with a greyhound sleekness. It wasn't quite right. But it wasn't wrong either.

Moke put it into words. "But Dosh is dead," he said. "Cass and I saw it. We were both there."

There. The day Nimbus shot him and burned his chest out in that set-up film that reduced us from three to two and made me the kind of public heroine no sane guy would ever want to be. While Yell was in hospital dying because he got in the way of the wrong machination and it ran him over. Dosh. Who was Moke's lover, and mine. Whose dying had been in my nostrils for nearly two years of galactic wandering, because whatever Mokey said, it was my fault. Who was the major reason neither of us ever watched vids.

I picked up the box and looked it over. I didn't think I wanted to see any part of that film a second time. *Trouble on Toros. Starring Dein . . .*

• • •

I'd never heard of Dein in my life. But I could see I was going to. We all were. And the General was going to have to get another mug to put arty sculpture on his golf course. Maybe he'd be better with a sandtrap at that.

I certainly hoped so, because it was all he was getting. Moke was halfway into his packing already.

We'd been away from Ashton too long. Especially on Never, where the air's clear and the sun shines and the green grass is growing all around. Even if it's only five klicks by three.

Back earthside, the street was gray and the air was gray and the buildings were gray and it looked like a set for *Son of Terminator*. The only colorful note was the stink and that was rich enough to have been painted by Turner. I'd never noticed how Ashton stank when we lived there. I kicked a can—there were plenty—and got guck on my boot.

"Yech," I said.

"Huh?" Mokey doesn't share the same universe as the rest of us. He was probably meditating on how a heap of gucky cans would look soldered in a pyramid if you dropped a steam shovel on top of them, and whether the result would look better with or without a coat of plastic primaries.

"I said yech," I said.

"Uh. What happened to Hallway?"

"Why?"

I'd been looking at my boot. I looked at the street. It was as happy as a set of old dentures but a gap stared in the middle like a missing tooth. The old thrift shop hadn't exactly disappeared, it had fallen in. An accordion

9

of walls and floors lay like layer cake sliced with decor like cream-and-jam filling. The house-side next door rose three floors up marzipaned with peeling paint.

The yard behind was filled with rubble, a derelict copt dumped on top. The steel door of Hall's hardware hospital was punched in like a bulldozer had tried to flatten it. Broken glass diamonds winked in the windows. Sooty slashes crisscrossed the cinderblock. It must have been one righteous riot.

Righteous riots happen in Ashton but not around Hallway. He's neat and tidy with clean hands and a distaste for disorder. He also arms the major street gangs and they aren't dumb enough to wreck him often. There are other reasons he has immunity, all called Swordfish. I wiped my boot on a tissue and made it evaporate. "Any blood?"

Moke gave me one of his bleaker stares. "You want to go and look?"

The ruins of the thrift shop were like walking a tightrope over Niagara. Shifting lath in curled breakers with masonry sticking up like rocks. I could see what was left of their stock in the sediment, dirty skirts in stale glitter and shoes with fossil teeth. A drowned teddy bear with terminal injuries was beached on the step.

The yard was white water. We hung on the copt's fuselage and balanced bricks slid and re-formed in waves under our feet. Broken ankle country. I use my ankles.

The side door was half-open. That was a plus. When it worked it had an electronic control which without you're not getting in. I'm small and Moke's skinny and we sucked in our bellies and kissed off our clothes. It's a good thing he makes money.

The lab didn't exist. There had been a bench, cabinets and the operating table where Hall did open-heart surgery on sick machines. The cli-controlled mainframe, his little deck for five-finger exercises, the usual setup for stealing current and mostly, Hallway.

Glass sprinkled the dirty boards like spilled sugar. Yellow gouges cut across where someone had dragged equipment. The ceiling fitments hung by their wires and a steel table was crushed like a beetle. Glinty specks that could have been chips were stamped in the floor. But whether the damage was hurry, rage, or just efficiency wasn't on the label. There was no blood. There wasn't much anything.

It felt like a funeral. I've known the Strip since I was fourteen and Hallway's lived there most of my life. People you know don't have the right to evaporate. It's wrong, a gap in the order of things.

"Well, now we know," Moke said.

"What, Martin?"

"He went himself. The place is stripped, not blasted."

"Mokey. I been sending Hall cards every week and he hasn't answered. Suppose he's in jail? When did this happen?"

"Month or so back, by the look of the wood. What would Swordfish do while they were jailing Hallway?"

"Nuke em. Or . . ." I know Sword. He wouldn't stand still while he could pull a trigger.

"Don't panic, we've a town center. If Sword went down he'd take it with him. Let's go ask Eustace."

"Cops showing sharpness and zeal," Eustace said, polishing the piece of counter in front of him. He does it when he won't look at you. "They were also sore at Cassandra. It got down to sonic cannon."

The Gilded Dog hadn't changed, but we were early. We caught weird habits in the big black spaces, like getting up while it was still daylight. So there weren't any brunchers eating vodkas off the mahogany. The goldfish bowl overhead had been put back by Moke but the gyrators of all three sexes were home in bed. With each other, the patrons, or whoever. I blinked. Mokey'd said Sword was ready with the sonics when the cops and I had our little run-in but I'd left solo. "He didn't use them."

"Did a coupla months later. After you left. Guy you know disagreed with the police chief and the Central Square precinct house went and fell in. Right down to the thirteenth sub-basement. So they got sore."

"That's a reason for bulldozing Hallway?"

"I guess he supplied the cannon," Moke said reasonably. "Where'd he go, Eus?"

"You think I buy Naval artillery?" Eustace grumbled. "Stick around, the spies are out." I should have known that. "You want the special?"

Eustace has this thing for Mokey. Behind his meaty face lies an artistic soul. Moke has a thing of his own, unluckily; the Dog's food turns his stomach. Textured prote. Hell, that's class. Most of Ashton food's recycled. Unless you're Ari and live in the burbs. Or Gooder and grow it illegally in boxes.

"Great," I said, sincerely sincere. "Two and two beers, Eus. Can we sit in the corner?"

"You better. There's guys in here don't know you."

I suddenly remembered this was the Strip. And I was on it, without weapons. It's wild what money does to you. I'd spent two years in designer gauzes and forgotten to feel naked without a dartgun. My bag wasn't big enough to hold a rifle. Hell, my eyeliner was in Mokey's pocket. I got a sudden attack of prickles. We needed Hallway badly.

The Dog filled up with the darkness, painted faces shut and bolted. Nobody talks to anybody here, Eustace runs a respectable dive. The tarts are all well-behaved and gunfights are held in the street. Make trouble and the clients lynch you. The first gilded person who waggles its behind in Eustace's bowl started in around midnight and the blue neon that has whiteouts had its first seizure. Bowl lights do it, the power grid isn't what it might be. Chemical smoke scarved near the ceiling and Moke started to choke in his beer. He's cool on joints but the wilder mutes give him hay fever.

We had textured prote Stroganoff, pie with real dried reconstituted apple, three coffees each, and a beer or four. Then the doors crashed and something long and lean and brown came in on all fours. It was ribbed in a whippety way but that was its only relation to sea sand. That was a city boy. Ashton city. I spilt my drink. Nobody else moved a whisker.

It rose on its paws to grab a lemonade and poured it down like a good dog. Its teeth weren't exactly normal. It leered around the edge of its tumbler and winked lewdly.

"Oh, God. Dribble."

"He's grown," Moke noticed. Give the man a cigar. Last time I saw it it looked like a five-year-old but nobody was going to mistake this for a baby. It was pushing six feet and hung like a donkey. The rest looked like a half-melted taper, arms and legs dangling. It ran with its behind in the air and it drooled. It couldn't help it, its teeth would have scared a shark.

It gargled the last of its drink and lolloped over. It still took the way that would upset the maximum people, especially shes, especially skirted. I poised my boot. It skidded on its haunches two feet off and let me admire its enamel.

"You were going to kick me," it said accusingly.

"Only if you slobber on my ankle, you three yards of tapeworm."

It widened the gap in its head in a charming grin. The horrible thing always was cute as hell.

"I wouldn't," it said piously. Its hazel eyes were large, limpid and human. Its voice must have broken because it had stopped sounding like a dog-whistle, its register had dropped to Callas's high notes. It might have been seventeen, though it's hard to tell with genetic mutes. It made a dart and backed off, tongue lolling, strings of slaver hanging from its jaws. "I wanted to slobber on your knee."

I felt in my purse for disposables and wiped off my pants. "Let's understand each other, Rover. There's just one reason I haven't killed you."

"You don't have a gun," it yelped joyously.

"Correct. But"—I snapped eight inches of honed blade out of my sleeve and stuck it under its nose—"I do have a knife. If you don't want to be neutered, don't do that again."

It gave a happy giggle, also down a semitone. These days it was only agonizing. When it was young it could clear the room with a snicker; it had to be a godsend to ENT specialists all over the district. "I like you. Always liked you. You look Hallway?" Its grammar's always been fractured, I figure it's deliberate.

"If you can contain yourself so long."

It gave a frisk. With its equipment and no pants it was totally obscene. It had another lunge to slobber on Mokey's hand and scampered for the door. Moke wiped his hand on his pants. He's a nice guy. I'd have scalped it.

"I guess it likes you too," I said. "Shall we go?"

We covered street at a fast lope after his vanishing ass. The wildlife was out and my back was crawling. A rich off-planet tan and no artillery. In these parts it's a reason for calling the white-coats. Moke caught my wrist. "Slow down, Cass, he does it on purpose. Let's look in a couple of windows."

"If you want to. I never got mugged here before. If it happened in front of Dribble I could die of shame."

A pair of froth-haired kids in glimmering fluorescents veered towards us and I slid the ya back to my palm. Indeterminate sex, flossed orange pyramids above the forehead that raised them to near-seven-footers. Loops of chain joined their ears to their noses. Surviving on the Strip takes a strong stomach. The slightly more fragile had a glittery crystal threaded through its lower lip.

"Hey, mister." Tenor.

"Are you Martin Faber?" Contralto. Making a pair, he, she and them.

"Yeah." Moke was cautious. He always is when people ask that question, most of them want his autograph.

"Can we have your autograph?" the contralto asked, breathless.

"We're from the Central School of Art and Design," the tenor counterpointed. "We think your stuff's marvelous."

"Uh." Moke was dusky. He can take anything but praise. "You got some paper?"

"Do my arm, please?" husked the contralto. "I got a tattoo pen."

She had. She'd seventeen celebrated signatures already. I figured she'd also have a bill at the cosmeticist as soon as she was old enough to know better.

"You sure you want this?" Moke asked, holding the pen like a live scorpion.

"Oh, yes," she breathed with passion. "As soon as it's filled I'm getting it flayed to bind my autobiography."

Moke found a space and gritted his teeth. A dark line of blood followed the point over her skin. She grinned beatifically. "Thanks. We look at your construct in the Museum Sundays."

"Will you do my back?" the male half appealed, almost as emotional, hauling his shirt up over his shoulderblades.

"You going to turn into a binding too?" I asked. Kids were sure as hell getting weirder.

"No." He tried not to wince. "Exhibiting myself on Open Day. Then I'll keep them. Some of them'll get valuable."

"Storing up treasure for the future."

"Sculpting's harder," he admitted. "Day someone asks for mine I'll have them removed and frame them."

Mokey sighed, rubbing his fingers. "If you have time."

Dribble glowered from a doorway. "You guys wanting Hallway or not?"

The kids disappeared, holding hands and swinging chains. "We want Hallway. White man walk at reasonable pace or I fork his tongue for him."

"That's okay then," he said, and swaggered off. He can talk quite normal when he wants to. Allowing for his teeth.

He was taking us way off the Strip. Hall's never gone for major frontage, you know him or you don't. The decor worried me.

"Hey, Doggy-bag, we going someplace or this your evening ramble?"

He'd just cocked his leg on a wall and was exchanging hisses with a local cat. He looked at me with limpid innocence. "We go."

"Since when was Hallway a Gooder?"

"Since Sword knock down precinct house," he fluted happily. "Hall like quiet life. Peaceful smells here."

I guess so. Gooders are the Unemployed who work at living normal lives in abnormal environments. Or the opposite, depending on what you think is normal.

Like neat streets. Painted doors. Numbers that run in sequence. A closed bakery smelling of bread made with flour. Green oildrums with clipped bay trees outside a health-food restaurant. Window boxes along a housefront. Brown brick apartment-blocks with swept stairs and lights behind the transoms.

They have vigilante patrols who love their work and nobody messes with them. Gooders can get unbelievably nasty. Considering what they say about us.

Dribble braked by a closed store with empty veg racks and dropped on his haunches. "Hall. Knock and wait."

I looked at Mokey. Full Gooder-land and no patrols yet, which meant there would be soonest. I wasn't sure I wanted to trade explanations with vigos even with Art cards. Their trigger fingers tend to be faster than their brains. He shrugged and banged on the glass. The blind was drawn on the other side.

"Mokey, it's after two."

"You're turning respectable. Boy says knock."

"Do I get to kill him if he's being funny?"

"Me?" Dribble whined, injured.

A light came on behind the shade. "Whaddya want?" a blurred voice yelled. "You know it's after two?"

I got to shrug. "Knock three times and ask for Joe?"

Dribble grinned. Dinnertime in mid-Pacific. "Tell name."

"Cassandra Blaine," I yelled. "Looking for a friend."

"Wait," the voice grumbled.

We waited. Mokey leaned against the wall, Dribble scratched and I practiced knife draws. Matched footsteps crunched around the corner, several sets in rhythm. The music of Sam Brownes and boots with nails in. They came nearer.

The front of the squad was pointing our way, six hunks in field green with oiled gun barrels, when the door scraped open. A surly square guy prodded at his shirttails. His fluffed hair was haloed in a weak light bulb.

"Come in if you're coming. Got better things to do than stand here. Don't know why you folks can't operate in daylight."

We came and he slammed the door. Wouldn't have surprised me if the squad had crashed on in but they kept tramping. Maybe the guy was a friend. Never know where you are with Gooders.

It was a greengrocery with apples and turnips and boxes
waiting for morning market. An old-fashioned till stood on
the counter. Umps aren't allowed to have money except
what the state hands out in credit Fridays. They get around
it. Like making their own.

"Out back," the grump said. "Ain't taking you. Use the
back bell next time, I gotta work." He squinted a blood-
rimmed eye Moke's way. "Ain't I seen you someplace?"
He snagged his profile with a nail in mourning. "Weird
leggy stuff painted red."

"Some of it's plain," Moke said.

"And some of it's blue," I helped.

"Takes all kinds," the grump opined. He flounced behind
a curtain and heavily up echoing stairs to wherever he had
his kennel. Dribble giggled like descending razors and
bounded under the staircase. Where there was a door, a
cellar, light and Hallway.

Hall's a Luney, which means seven-three, skinny,
stooped and clean as a pharmacist. The stoop's kindness,
he lives with little people. He has red hair, mild blue eyes
and believes in pacifism. I don't know why he sells arms for
a living but he does and they work because he's an idealist.
He split in a grin like a country sunrise and bent double.
That brought his cheek to kissing level and I obliged and
blubbered slightly. I'd thought he was dead back there for
a minute. Mokey shook hands and we stood making good
vibrations. Dribble panted like he'd invented us.

"Hear you'd trouble."

"Nothing serious. We saw it coming." Innocent china
stare. His gear was ranged just like the old place. "Time
for a change, they had my address. It's quiet here. Are
you okay?"

"You got my postcards?"

"Sure. I've a friend in the sorting office." He has friends
everywhere. A lot of them got to work on battlecruisers and

have the morals of screamer monkeys. "Nice collection. Looks like you've been all over."

"Better believe it. Just in from Virginity. Yech. We were pesticided coming and going but I could still sneeze and turn to soup."

He smiled nicely. "Take Moke out back, Drib, he can look at my rock collection. Help yourself to a drink, Mokey. He sticks with lemonade, orders."

"You want to talk to Cass. Rocks any good?"

"Couple of nice ones. Could get you quantity, the guy's a friend."

Moke needs no other bribery. He and Dribble loped off, Lady and the Tramp, cut for partners. Hallway turned his mild eye. "Have a good time, Cass?"

"So-so. Fucking soirées, tiaras and taradiddle. Moke's okay, commissions as fast as he can handle, money to our ears but *bo-ring*. You can't imagine."

"You could have sent Sword a postcard."

"No, I couldn't. What's to say? Dear Sword, wish you were here, love and kisses, P.S. if I die I'll call you."

"That might have done."

"He'd have come running."

"Probably," he said with gravity.

"You're kidding. He doesn't need me."

"You're sure."

"Sure I am. When did Sword need anyone?"

It was a quality in the silence. A sense of things that exist and aren't visible. I whipped around and caught air shifting beside the bench. Not even a shift but the smallest ripple in the surface of reality. Like a ghost makes. Or a guy in a coolsuit slow-breathing. I dived at it.

Swordfish had his hip on the edge of the table and his long legs stretched out in front of him. Another ripple said uncrossing ankles. I slammed on his rib cage and we breathed at each other. The last ten ticks before the explosion.

I laddered my hands up invisible ridges. Now I knew, his shadow lay on the wall behind him like Peter Pan's that needed sewing on again. "Sword. Say something."

Held breath. Then his voice, tired and scratchy, velvet worn threadbare. "What's to say? Are you and Moke happy?"

"Yes. No. Maybe. Pick one."

"Got any kids yet?"

"Six. Maybe seven, I lost count. *Sitting Woman* and *Looking at Stars* before we left, and one on Averroes Moke called *Spare Ribs and Mutton Bone* but the Council didn't know so they paid him. Then there was a lump for a private collection that was sort of free-form, it sat in a park and the ducks shat on it. And an inquiry from Hampton-of-Argos . . ."

"I wasn't asking about Moke's career, I see the vids. I can even read. I was asking if he's your husband."

"He's my twin brother. We live with a gap. There used to be three of us."

"Have you thought there might be something pathological in the way you make guys into brothers? Does he think he's your twin?"

"I don't know. I guess we were mourning. We live together. I like him."

"Jesus. I bet he sings hymns to the dawn."

"Is this revenge for not getting a postcard?"

"When I revenge myself people know it. You sent Hall a million postcards and not one said, pass this to Swordfish."

"Every one said, pass this to Swordfish," Hallway said. "I did. Maybe I shouldn't have."

"Maybe you should."

"I wasn't thinking of you, Cass. I was thinking of him."

"Nice." I rubbed my fingers on silky fabric. "I love a welcome. May I peck your cheek?"

"No." A hand like a power vise twisted into my pagoda and scattered beads. His kind can break your neck without trying. My nails scratched on his suit. "What cheek? You've seen me. I'd an idea you didn't want to see it again."

"That was two years back."

"Did you think I'd changed?"

I took in as much air as a stretched neck let me. "You need to fix your filters, I can smell your breath. Spearmint and something. Apples."

He let go, exasperated. Unraveled coils straggled down my back. "I sent that damned crystal because I thought you might be mourning. Maybe you want to know about this guy. I've two pieces of advice. One, if you're poking at Coelacanth again get some artillery. Two, get your hair cut. Didn't Razor teach you anything?"

"Yeah. He taught me not to mess with hypes."

"It doesn't take a hype to grab a bim by the curls. But that gets you a third piece of advice, free. Don't mess with me. I kill for a living."

"Gee. True profundity. Gratis."

He moved so fast I didn't see it coming. When he let go I was gasping like a flounder. "A peck on the cheek? From me? Don't drive me to extremes, Cass. Incest may be your thing, it isn't mine."

"You're not my goddamned brother."

"I know," he said, and left.

"He's kind of antsy," I told Hallway. I was trying not to rub the bruises.

"Yes. I almost wish you hadn't come back. Nothing personal. What can I get you in the way of cannons?"

"One of these days I'll kill that fucker."

"You just might. Did you hear why he blasted the precinct?"

"No."

"The chief of police got oiled at a public dinner and said you were a less than lady of unimproved morals. It got on the vids. We nearly had a war."

"What stopped you? He's stiff on the off-switch."

"The guy apologized. After a while."

"That's why you don't want me back? Someone else could say something nasty? Christ. Guys say that three times a day."

He raised his shoulders. "He's my friend, Cass. I got him cooled on the stuff you children pulled at the ice rink, when he'd had time to get over it."

"Sorry. I was afraid he'd get bad exposure."

"From the film? You just aren't there, kid. Some of these guys are so perverse they see the backs of their heads when they look in the mirror. He was the hottest property since Jack the Ripper. He'd offers of four starring roles in horror pics, from Coelacanth plus three other companies. Women wanted to marry him. Rich women. The ones who longed to hold him to their bosoms and heal his scars and the ones who wanted him just as he was. One wrote him over and over, passionate dirty letters with vids to prove it."

"Wow. What were the vids like?"

His cheeks pinked. "Don't ask."

"He could heal his scars for himself."

"He does what he wants to."

"Then why the hell blame me?"

"Don't ask that, either. I got a nice late-model rifle, self-sighting, lightest thing you ever handled. Come take a look."

Moke and Dribble were sitting either side of a kitchen table playing dominoes. Was the first time I knew Dribble could sit, much less play any game but scare-the-lady. Mokey took my hand. "Sword give you a hard time?"

"You knew he was there."

"Figured he had to be. And he's the only guy regularly makes you cry."

"Him? He ain't even human." I snuffled on his tan velvet shoulder. "Moke, do you feel like my brother?"

"No. It's a defense mechanism. Come play dominoes."

"Do you wish you'd kids?"

"Sure. I've just never been in the right place at the right time. Take seven."

"Sword drives me apeshit."

"Uh-huh. Nine years and you still don't know how he thinks."

"He doesn't think, he ticks. Like Dribble. A deck with a gift for humor. He believes annoying me's funny."

Dribble whined and Moke patted him as if he was a kid. It's bad for the brat, gives him ideas. "Yeah. That's why he follows you around risking his neck."

"His neck's invulnerable. He likes breaking things. I want to play dominoes."

"If you think it'll make him go away."

"What do you mean, the right place?"

He sighed. "Which of us has been taking precautions? Any seven and no peeking."

I started picking tiles. Guys are a weird animal. Some are so weird you practically meet them coming around the other side.

I don't know why it's me has to know them.

Dein's agent was a foxy lady in emerald leather that covered her closer than her skin and showed thighs much too long to be the ones she was born with. It went fine with her re-gened black hair and showed her eyes were too pale for her taste in clothes.

She greeted Mokey with such passionate enthusiasm I hoped she wasn't going to whip out a tattoo-pen and ask for his autograph. He'd signed three more corpses on the way and it was getting to him. But I guess it was her normal routine for celebrated males. Me she ignored, which is a mistake. Moke's terrified of man-eating women, it's one reason I'm his manager.

"He's not working at the moment," she confided huskily. To Mokey, of course. "A production hitch—they're rewriting part of the script. So you'll find him at home. He has a house in the satellites. May I arrange a yacht?"

"Thanks, but we have transport." I showed her enamel. "Coordinates'll do. If you'd tell him we're coming."

"You wouldn't like a film-company pilot?" she asked Moke.

"I couldn't insult Yeller," I told her.

She took a slip of gilt-impressed cerocard from a little box on her desk and wrote on it in a dashing scrawl with a gold stylo. It was weighed down by an emerald the size

24

of the Ritz, and I was surprised her delicate claw could cope. Maybe it was hollow, like home with the Borgias. "That'll find him. I'll call him right away, I'm sure he'd love to see you. He's very esthetic."

"Extremely. Especially around the eyes. You still write coordinates on cards? How exquisitely old-fashioned. We just got back from the colonies, where they disc 'em. Brash, boring and practical. It's nice the old planet keeps its sense of style."

That put her in a dilemma. If she answered she'd have to notice I existed. If she didn't, she didn't get to slay me. She compromised on giving Moke a three-cornered smile designed to leave him brain-damaged. I don't know what would have happened if it had connected, but since he was too busy being honestly worried about (a) what we were going to say to Dosh if it was him, and (b) whether Hallway really could get him a three-ton pink granite boulder, he didn't notice.

Moke's a trial to foxy ladies. That's another reason I'm his manager.

"What the hell's this?" Yell said when he saw it.

"It's reputed to be the coordinates of a sat. Don't let it worry you, it's called Divine and it'll be on the chart."

"You could sell it to a chemical company," he said. "I bet it explodes if you fill it."

Divine was one of the little globes that dot the sky around our celestial equator and would give the pygmies something to look at nights if any of them still survived. They're all incredibly expensive, which makes our mentor Hans-Bjorn's terraformed asteroid Never the authentic product of old Ari money and his five klicks by three nearly infinity. As sats go.

Divine didn't go nearly so far. But it had a dumb charm. A house and grounds curved around a core of self-generating grav-units on solar power, a genuine view of the sky, and with a horizon you probably got used to after the first few centuries. Since it didn't have either Never's size or its terraform artist, said sky was black, but it was all-hell spacious.

Me, I feel vertiginous having the swimming pool over the terminator, but it's a matter of taste. Their decorator had done his best with a midget forest of weeny trees, vaguely Edo, that cushioned the shock by reducing the vistas. They also had a lot of raked gravel and horizontal junipers in stone boxes. Esthetic to the point of suffering.

The house floors were built flat off the ground, which is one solution to the problem and does stop the coffee table sliding onto the baseboards in the night. It also means the house has to be what you might call faceted, so every time you move from one room to another you step onto a different plane and reorient, but you can't have everything.

Our yacht took up so much of their pad you could just about see her nose from the upper windows with a ray of sunlight blinding off her forward antenna. We crunched over a ziggy path too narrow for Moke's sneakers, doing my pin-heels no good at all. The ground loomed in front of us like a permanent uphill and went on feeling level. Alice would have loved it. I am not she.

Moke's head broke suddenly into sunlight, and then mine. Our feet went on being in shadow for another three or four steps. The terrace was in full sun, laid out with striped loungers and classy redwood furniture. And on the terrace was the Man.

Boy. Actors have this quality of looking smaller and more fragile for real than on-screen. Dein was the exception. He didn't really have the muscles of Arnold Schwarzenegger. Maybe for real Arnold Schwarzenegger didn't have the muscles of Arnold Schwarzenegger. Or otherwise, of course. That aside he was six-four in his socks, yellow-blond, bronzed and one eighteen-carat sweetie.

What he also was, was mad. At a guess. Unless he was cultivating the Byronic look, which with actors isn't impossible. I'd settle for mad. I got the feeling the foxy lady hadn't consulted her client before she signed away his leisure time.

"Do I know you?" he said.

I stopped like I'd collected a bucket of water in the eye. I'd just decided the guy was a stranger. If he was, he'd no right to speak to me in Dosh's deep lazy voice, however mad.

"I don't know," I said. "Do you?"

"No." That was definitive. He didn't know us. He didn't want to know us. He'd like it fine if we sold him our insurance and got the hell off his property sometime in the next five minutes, so he could go back to doing whatever he'd been doing, or not, before we woke him up.

I'm acquainted with quandaries and this one was prime. How do you ask someone, "Excuse me, are you the guy I went to bed with every night for three years the year before last?" It doesn't sound right.

"Hi," Moke said, stepping into in the breach. Breaches are his natural home, he doesn't notice them. "Martin Faber, I carve rocks. We saw your film. *Trouble on Toros*?"

"Yeah?" He didn't sound impressed. There was no damn reason he should, especially since we'd never watched more than the first five minutes and if he set us a test paper we'd fail.

"I got three tons of pink granite," Moke said wistfully. "That is, I will have. Would look great right there."

"Thanks, I can't afford it." Frankly hostile. "Did you want anything else?"

One thing was sure, the guy never knew Mokey. Anyone who did knows he doesn't sell bills. If he says something would look great right there it's because that's where he wants to put it. You don't have to pay him. If he wants it bad enough he'll pay you. It's another reason he needs a business manager. Dosh loved Moke. He thought he was the sunrise and the sunset and the best thing since Michelangelo. He would have plucked his eyes out before he looked at him like trash. This one was giving us the eye like the skip was around the back, all we had to do was go jump in it.

"Trouble, honey?"

Bucket number two. I took a breath and came up gasping. Looking like Dein it was natural he had a lady under contract. What was dumb was I hadn't expected her. I had absolutely totally never thought of it. Until she stepped out of the louvered redwood doors and took his arm, in three dimensions and full color, and told me my old lover was finally, completely dead.

You could see why he was mad. The loose house-gown, freshly-combed hair, new makeup, air of innocent candor all said bed, recent, interrupted in progress. She was taking it better than he was but women get philosophical. She was small, rounded, cuddly and had hair the color of a late sunset. Her green eyes matched the robe and she looked like she might be friendly if she hadn't been defending her mate.

"A pair of guys selling rocks. Told 'em we can't afford it."

"A pair of admirers," I said, trying for gentle reproach. It doesn't come natural. "We're not selling rocks. Moke got carried away, he does. I think he got an attack of Edo. We came to say we thought your husband's films were great and he saw some gravel called to his artistic soul. We're bothering you, we'll split."

The lady was the more gracious. "No, come and have a beer. You'll have to forgive Dein, they're in a contract fight, he's usually nicer. It's nearly his birthday. Maybe he'd like a rock. Why don't we talk?"

"Three tons?" Dein asked derisively. "You could buy me a necktie. Everyone buys people neckties."

"Nobody ever bought me a necktie," I said. "This rock comes with holes courtesy of the world's greatest living rock-hole digger. We'd love a beer. If he doesn't want a rock maybe I can find him a pebble. Three tons is Moke's lower end, below that he can't see them."

The atmosphere thawed to around the melting point of methane and we sat in striped loungers while Rose Red went for beer. Which she fetched personally on a tray featuring Mickey Mouse in a vintage motor vehicle. Which said they had no taste, a lot of taste or were in love. Her other half went on glowering in a minor key.

"You in films too?" I asked as she stripped caps.

"If you like bad comedies." She sounded like she didn't rate her art alongside Sarah Bernhardt. "Aurora. I'm the heroine gets tied to the monorail tracks as the train's coming down. I don't play them that well. You have to be dumb to get tied to monorail tracks."

She didn't sound dumb.

"Not adventures?" Moke's okay if they're just attractive. This one didn't vix.

She made a face. "I'm not physical enough. Just the dumb lady gets rescued by the guy with muscles. If you play adventures you need to be athletic. I haven't the temperament. They do earn more."

"Not enough to buy rocks," Dein said with vigor. "Remember the mortgage?"

"Shut up." Cute but not dumb at all. "Who's buying this birthday present? Go bully someone else or I'll get you a doghouse. Let's talk rocks."

We talked rocks.

• • •

"Thought you were staying the week," Yell said. "I quit after the third beer, didn't want to get you a ticket. If I'd known, I'd time for three more . . ." He got a look at my face. "No good, huh?"

"Thought you were off alcohol."

"This ain't alcohol, Cassandra, it's beer. Be reasonable. What's the answer?"

"We don't know, Yell. The guy doesn't know us, period. He doesn't know Moke, he doesn't know me. If you'd come he wouldn't have known you."

"Not surprising. Nobody knows me anymore."

Back in Dosh's day Yell was the noseless spaced-out wino under our steps. He's had surgery since.

"He has a lady," Moke said. Apprehensive.

"Red hair, one careful owner."

"But she's buying my new rock," he added with a look I recognized. Hungry, with laser drills in it.

"In spite of the fact it's going to clash."

"You didn't get anywhere," Yell diagnosed.

"Correct. Only our paymaster took a liking to the garden and promised them a rock he hasn't got."

"I think I better take you kids home. I'm not sure travel agrees with you."

He had a point. I was beginning to doubt it myself.

"Yeah, well," Hallway said. "Got some stuff from the files, less than you'd expect. Guy's name's Ottery, Franklin Rhodes, from a low Art district in the south burbs. Father an actor too, mother a singer. A sister plays alto sax in an early music group. Last relative. Rest of the family's dead."

"Yeah? What happened?"

"Copt crash. Boy was in school, girl was at the Conservatoire in Tokyo. Plain accident far as I can see. Kids seem to have fallen out after the funeral. Girl stayed around and married, boy went on the road in touring rep. Probably not much money left after tax. Surfaced four-five years ago in the chorus of *Strings!* at the Willway Theater and lucked out. Second lead got sick and Ottery inherited. That was four years ago. Played spacer for about a year and was scouted."

"By Coelacanth."

"Correct. Supported in one of their space epics, same deal as *Strings!,* cheapie thriller with uniforms, then got the lead in a jungle pic. For Marchand."

"Not Coelacanth?"

"Nope, but these deals happen. It's his lady's company. I've looked at the jungle one, it's not bad. Modest success, anyhow. Then *Trouble on Toros.* He's contracted for another space pic, big production number. Divine's his regular address, on mortgage, guess neither of them's big billing yet. Lady isn't his wife but she's known in second-rate comedies, clean bill. He's never been married, no listed kids. Period."

"So Dein's Whatever Ottery."

"Not necessarily."

"Not?"

"Not. People do change company, but there's something funny about this change. The original contract with Coelacanth's listed, for instance, but I can't get a copy from Central Information. All legit contracts are supposed to be on file. The space epic's the same. It was made, it's listed. Out of print, no copies available."

"Central Library's got to have one," Moke said. "Copyright law."

"Uh-huh," Hallway said. "They haven't. They're sorry, there's a gap in the files. They tell me it happens with minor stuff, it gets dumped sometimes."

"Possible," I said doubtfully.

"Sure. The publicity stills got dumped too, and that's not so common. Not when the guy's a working actor with an agent. People tend to keep their past triumphs. Especially when they're only four years old. What's least common of all's *Strings!* It's still playing at the Willway but if you want cast holos you can only get the current cast, no retrospectives. In clear, there aren't any pictures of Franklin Ottery before his jungle pic two years ago. His identity file shows Dein. But I got the sister."

He punched the projector button.

Small skinny greyhound with eyes the color of washed denim. The holo swiveled. Straight hair, almost white, to her hips. Narrow face, thin mouth, pointed chin. Her resemblance to Dein was nil.

"Takes after his daddy. Or whatever."

He silently worked the projector twice more. Mature woman, more silvery, the same clever narrow face and light eyes. A slender dark guy with the face actors like, so neutral it makes up into any character at all. Eyes gray, fine brows, look of gentle intellect. He probably played Doctor Phibes and Jack the Ripper.

"Look at their ears," Hallway said. We did, dutifully. They looked a lot like ears. "Attached lobes," he said with patience. "Like the daughter. Dein's are free."

"He doesn't look like any of them," I allowed.

"Doesn't prove anything, you get sports. But the gray-brown eye thing's unusual. It almost always comes from one fair parent, one dark. This family's light for generations."

"Surgery," Moke said.

"Sissy's are quite pretty," I said.

Hallway snorted. "Guess where Dein was the night Dosh got killed."

"Tell."

"In surgery, my prophetess. A little appendix problem. Which got sorted out at an expensive clinic."

"Coincidence?" Moke asked unhappily.

"Sword hates coincidences."

So does Moke. He calls it Occam's Razor. My principle's the old one. Too many coincidences are enemy action. And I could guess the name of the enemy. After all, I been a film star, if that's what you call getting run over by a film in full career. That film killed Dosh. It was made by Coelacanth.

"A restructural clinic for wealthy Aris," Hallway said. "Don't you think that's an odd place to have an appendectomy?"

"I guess he has one beautiful appendix."

"You mean we don't know a thing," Moke concluded.

"Don't forget dear little Socrates, Mokey."

"Uh-huh?"

"It isn't not knowing that's important, it's knowing that you don't know."

"Great."

It was Dosh used to say I couldn't read.

"Unless the lady Aurora's known him for a good long time," Hall added. "Preferably from infancy."

"She hasn't."

"Then we're stuck with Socrates."

"Great," I said.

We spent the evening glooming around our hotel room. It was an okay hotel room, but I remembered a time in our innocent youth when we didn't know what to do with the buttons. Now we did. It was ourselves we didn't know what to do with.

"I could call room service and order smoked salmon and pink champagne."

Moke lay flat on the billowy mattress and looked at the ceiling. He was wearing red jocks with gilt stitching and a few gray smears where the glue didn't wash out last time he got inspiration before he'd time to put his pants on. Apart from the jocks he hadn't changed in two years. He looked exactly the same on a patched-together bed-pad in our old loft.

"We could go to the Dog and eat tortured dead soya beans," he said. He sounded white, like a Chinese funeral.

I went and sat on his stomach.

"Moke. Things are bad. The only time I knew you to eat Eustace's prote willingly was the time the house burned down."

"What do we do, Cass? I thought when we saw him we'd know. Well, I don't."

"Me neither."

"And it matters."

"Yes. Sword knew when he sent me that crystal. Because if Dosh is dead, I killed him. Okay." I saw his mouth open. "We won't start again. What happened, happened because I interfered. We won't argue whose fault it was, I agree there's no answer and it doesn't help. All I know is, if Dosh isn't dead, I didn't kill him. And not having killed Doshky matters to me."

"It matters to me, too, Cass," he murmured. "If only because it stops you sleeping nights. But I did love him myself. Not like he wanted and maybe that's what gripes me. But I did. I'd give a lot to know he was okay. And we don't. Still."

"Right. So tonight we get drunk, here or at Eustace's, whichever, and tomorrow we think of something clever. Damn it, you're a genius."

"Oh, I know something clever now. I'd just rather cut short on the fight."

"What fight?"

He lifted a ratty off-blond head. You can take Moke to Dimitri, you can take him anywhere, it doesn't make any difference.

"The one we got to have before we go and ask Sword for help."

"No!" I yelled. "No, no and no!"

"Right," he agreed. "That one."

I'd got my mouth open on another string of negatives when a polite burp interrupted. We looked at each other in wild surmise. If hotels on different planets would coordinate their signals you'd have a chance of knowing if the current one was room service, telephone, fire alarm or just a glitch in the central heating.

The burp repeated with visual aid. There was a red blinking light under the interphone. Our rule is whoever's on top gets it. I got glumly off his stomach and plowed over a couple of hectares of fake goat, reaching for a robe on the way. It was his but anyone calls me in my bedroom when I'm glooming deserves what they get.

"Cassandra Blaine," I growled.

The holo-image that flowed right in and took possession is what I hate most about interphones. It's always when you're standing barefoot in the middle of the rug wearing someone else's robe and this morning's makeup some highpowered guy has his newly regilded Barbie secretary call you. And she always makes such a big thing of not noticing, you'd brain her with a blunt instrument if she was there. Which of course she isn't. Just her damned smug expensively perfumed holo-image.

"Miss Blaine?" she fluted. Even the flute was golden, or at least gilt. "A personal call from Mr. Cordovan."

"I don't know any Mr. Cordovan," I started to say, when it came to me I did. Not willingly, but definite. "Put him through."

I don't claim I was Hostess of the Month about it.

"Miss Blaine," the bronze man boomed in his bronze gong voice, holoing in like he'd just made us a present of the place. I knew him all right. Jason Cordovan, head of Coelacanth Studios. The very same guys killed Dosh, employed his murderess and thought all they had to do was buy me. "Nice to see you back."

I didn't reply, the sentiment not being mutual. I gave Moke's belt a vicious tug and waited for what Coelacanth wanted to communicate. I didn't expect to like it. I'm still waiting for something to like about Coelacanth, but not with energy.

"I hope you enjoyed the Colonies?" he went right on booming. His bronze lip quirked a sixteenth of an inch and his bronze brow lifted the same amount, just to show they could. I was impressed as hell.

"Is there a point?"

"You're here. That's the point," he said. Like a Buddhist temple in a high wind but less sanctified. "I thought you'd stay away. The lifetime's ambition? Since you've come back, I'll repeat my proposition. Now you've had time to cool down and really think. Our offer's still open. Coelacanth Studios can use you. Of course, we'd have to lower the price. Your face hasn't been seen for a while and people forget so quickly. But I can still give you something extremely advantageous."

"Certainly, Mr. Cordovan. There's one very advantageous thing you can give me right now."

He looked at me like he had a flush to the ace and only his ten showing, his head slightly cocked, with that small bronze smile. I was being honored. Poor Nimbus hadn't managed to make him smile at all. He's the type only smiles when people don't care.

"The freedom of my bedroom. I wouldn't work for you then, I won't work for you now and I don't ever expect to work for you in future. Good night, Mr. Cordovan."

The bronze lips tightened minutely but he continued to smile.

"I was afraid you might say that. But you can change your mind anytime. Can I say one thing to you? I have my company's interests to look after. I'm sure you wouldn't want to meddle again. The results were so very disagreeable, weren't they? I hope we understand each other, Miss

Blaine. If not, I'm sure we soon will. Give Mr. Faber my compliments. I do wish you both a peaceful and pleasant stay. Good night."

I swung around on Moke, furious. "What makes that overgrown horse-wallow think he can call me up any time at all and insinuate at me in my own room? Fuck it, the place is uninhabitable, it stinks of that plastic doll's plastic scent. Okay, the Dog and combed soya. Bastard's put me right off my salmon."

"Give me my robe back and I'll take a shower," he said, getting himself lazily off the bed in sections, which is the Moke method.

"Okay, just don't take all night. I'm hungry."

He caught it in midair and yawned slowly towards the bathroom. I went to the dressing table to have another look at Dimitri's slaughter of my hair. Razor would have been proud of me, but it would be a long time before I wore any more lacquered pagodas. I held a pearl chandelier up to my ear and considered the effect.

The flare of white incandescence took both of us by surprise. Moke stopped in the bathroom doorway, his lean face blank. I half turned from the mirror, clawing for my darter before I realized we were alone.

It was white phosphorus and it had been cozily tucked under the quilt. We stood together and watched the bedclothes burn. It was only when the fumes started to get to us and the smoke alarm began shrilling we thought of calling the lobby to say we had a problem.

They got us another room almost right away and our departure for the Dog was delayed maybe half an hour. The fire department was still working when we left.

"But, Miss Blaine," the manager whimpered, running out after me like a distracted collie, "have you any idea what could have caused such a conflagration?" If you're going to be manager of a major hotel you got to know major words. Like conflagration. I think they get bonuses every time they use one.

"Sorry. I really gotta quit smoking in bed."

But as Moke and I waited for our traxie we held hands and shivered.

Twenty seconds previous that was right where his behind had been.

"Congratulations," Swordfish said bitterly. "I take my eyes off you for five minutes and you get under a phosphor-bomb. I don't suppose, Cassandra, you've heard of the virtues of tact and finesse? You couldn't have told the man he was a great and fascinating personality and you're dedicated to sculpture?"

From ghostly indications he was sitting cross-legged on Hallway's work-bench. Hall's as clean as a surgeon and he was going to have to disinfect that.

"How was I to know he was going to call me up and blow my head off?"

"Dear child. He told you, didn't he? You're lucky it was a warning shot. If he'd been serious you could have got hurt."

"Moke was damned nearly roasted."

"I doubt it. If that was on a timer he couldn't be sure he'd get you. You were leaving. Five minutes and he'd have missed. Serious people set time bombs for the small hours of the morning. I'd say it was a plain radio-controlled detonator and he fired when you were out of range. He may have been looking. I'd have had you bugged."

"Serious guys have such cute little minds."

"Serious guys. You've forgotten who you are, Cass.

Too much rich living. I can't guard you twenty-four hours a day. Not without help."

"And don't ask what that means," Moke advised.

"It means sharing her bed," Swordfish said viciously. "The idea gives her urticaria."

"I'm scratching already."

"We called four times last night," Hallway said. "You were out. Marchand Films is in the Commercial Directory. It's a subsidiary of Coelacanth."

"Oh, boy. Dein still works for Cordovan."

"Doesn't he know?"

"He believes he's contracted to Marchand."

"Hard luck."

"I'm interested in why," Sword said. "Cordovan doesn't need to drop bombs just because you're here, even if he got a mouthful of Cass's famous grace and delicacy. I haven't killed her yet. Sounds like visiting Dein's against his principles."

"Bet it was that restructured secretary."

"Probably. Something smells. Franklin Ottery was in *Strings!* He existed on stage for a couple of years while Doshchenko was alive and whoring."

I growled. He ignored me, which is normal.

"Dein's on record since. Someone better go to the theater, see if he'd friends in the cast. If no one's resorted to mass murder."

"Moke's liable to die of allergic reaction. Lying brings him out in a rash. If he doesn't give colored rocks to all the actors because he likes the shape of the stage."

"I'll do them a set'll win them a Gorby," Moke said. "What's it about?"

"The conquest of the final frontier by a bunch of guys in blue hairstyles, you wouldn't like it. I was thinking of you, sweet thing. Hypocrisy being your natural state. I'll find you an escort. Go put some clothes on."

"What do these look like, wiseass?"

Sword looked at them with attention.

"Indecent," he said.

Avoid the question, Why me? It saves a lot of grief.

I came out of the hotel dressed for theater in lime pants, yellow shirt and glitter around the edges. Since the business was Sword's and he hadn't ordered artillery I left my tools at home. The guy gets nasty.

There was a white sports copt on the roof plus a guy gave me an instant crick in the neck.

"Hi," he yelled from roughly seven feet up. "Want a lift? MacLaren DeLorn, only man in the world with two names and four capital letters, my father's fault, guess you've heard that line, shall we go?"

I racked my head back. I'd seen him last at Countess Cara's party couple of years ago. What I hadn't known was he knew Sword. Come to that, didn't know anyone knew Sword and survived unless they were genetically mutated. Maybe he was. He was also cute, which is not par for the breed. I wasn't sure I was supposed to know him. I was being someone else at the time.

"Hi. Where you going?"

"Willway Theater, aren't you? I've friends of friends in the cast so another friend of a friend volunteered me to tour you. I spent my last incarnation as a war hero, an overrated occupation. Nowadays I make up for it by devoting myself to life, liberty and the pursuit of coward-ice. Are you cowardly?"

"Sometimes."

"Great. Now's your chance. I'm driving."

He wasn't kidding. The copt took off at an angle that made Sword's lieutenant Wings look like a careful driver, and he's the craziest bastard ever made the traffic ordi-nances into basketware. We hit the zoom laser and started skipping zones like a rock over water.

"What branch of heroism did you major in?" I asked for something to do, clutching the edge of the shagged leather seat. My belly trailed a mile or so behind me wailing for its mother.

"Getting shot," he said cheerfully, missing a heavy Kenoba full of yelling kids by a sixteenth of an inch and leaving them making obscene signs.

"I mean what service, or whatever?"

"Third alien war out at Resurrection, hunter-killer pilot for the Navy. Don't ask what I did, I forget. In civilized societies they almost certainly lock you up for it."

"You quit?"

"Got my ticket, lovely. There's only two ways you leave the Navy if you're a hunter-killer pilot. Either they sort through the bits working out which is you and which is your plane and re-glue them, or they hold a service where you reverted to interstellar dust. In my case they got a few bits were really me. By chance. The two don't look very different at that stage. But they also got some were really my plane, which was lucky because it's the more intelligent of the two."

"Oh."

"I know that tone. You want to know if I'm sane. Certainly I am. I've a green card certifies I'm absolutely normal a good deal of almost every day."

We'd come to a distant rooftop a long way below with a distant pad the size of a postage stamp. He made a screaming turn, whined down on it like a kamikaze, and dropped the copt delicately in the middle.

"Here you are. Did you enjoy it?"

"No. I meant to do some shopping on the way back and harps weren't on my list. If you don't mind I'll take a traxie. Unless you could get the human bit to fly the copt next time."

"That was the human bit. The mechanical bit flies fast."

We walked the bared-brick corridor like a Great Dane parading the next-door chihuahua. He had an amiable slouch, long eyelashes and a cute grin.

"How's . . ." I began, and remembered I wasn't supposed to know his friend Haver. Another film actor, stuntman, drug addict and full-time charmer. The time I met him.

"How's . . . ?" He bent double and looked into my eyes like he was crystal-gazing.

"Has this been running long?"

"Nearly six years. Haven't you seen it? If I'd known I'd have taken you and we could have got sick on chocolates."

"Sounds great. Do they have paper bags behind the seat or do you wash your shoes on the way out?"

"Paper bags. That's *Strings!* If the audience doesn't get vertigo they change the male lead and shoot the FX director. Hope you don't mind makeup."

He was walking down a rubber-floored corridor lined with doors and I was doing the hundred-meter dash alongside. It stank. Of rubber, plastic, Face. Makeup. I admire actors. They've got to have bellies like industrial storage flasks. Me, I don't mind, it just gives me heaves. Guess who knew that when he sent me.

"It's a talent," he said. I hate thought-readers. "Dressing rooms next floor down. I know a couple of friendly aliens and with any luck they won't have their jeans on."

The elevator dropped us into a pushing crowd with caricatures for faces. They were all talking at once. Mostly to bellyache, by the sound.

"Stage-play," Lorn said. I really do hate that. "It's kind of gross, not like holo. My friend's friend's in here, if nobody's husband's caught up yet."

His friend's friend's door hadn't stars, just scratched blue paint. He opened it the simple way with a kick and we fell in on top of six or seven guys, all elbowing each other around and trying to wiggle out of different Faces and into different jeans and shirts in front of the same mirror. Three were aliens with extra legs and tails, two wore white spacesuits patched like a jeans factory and one looked like a dolphin.

"This show I gotta see."

"You've got to be the last remaining person in Ashton still hasn't." He did a loom over the most spangled alien, which hadn't got at the mirror yet though it was kicking hard. "How. White man walk with forked tail."

The alien tore at his snout, which peeled off. There was a cute redhead underneath with green eyes and the skin they get when they don't freckle. If Lorn hadn't been a foot above he'd have been tall. Dein was lucky to have a bareface part. This one would have looked okay on a film-set, discounting the metallic paint around the eyes. His tail was in working order and he used it on Lorn's ribs.

"Big Chief doesn't get any smaller. Long time, flyboy. Don't suppose you want something, by any chance?"

"What could make you think that?" Sweet injured innocence. "No, but my squaw does."

"You got a squaw?" The redhead came over faint. "How did that happen? Has she seen her analyst?"

"I borrowed her. Friend of a friend."

"Figures. Hard luck." The redhead offered me a paw skinned with green scales and ending in claws like meathooks. Rubber, luckily. "This guy hasn't any friends, only friends of friends. I sometimes think that's sinister. Luke Trent, second lead in this turkey. Two nights a week I get to play Captain and wear a fishbowl on my head. You seen it?"

"Sorry."

"Don't apologize. Stick around a year or two and you could miss it entirely, then you can come watch me play Hamlet."

"It's a deal."

He smiled, sweet, glittery and stinking of plastic. "What can I do for you?"

"Tell me about a friend."

"Uh huh. A friend of a friend?"

"Guy called Ottery. Franklin Ottery? Heard he started here and got hooked by a film scout."

The milky skin had gone skim-colored. The green paint stared. "Frank Ottery. Sure."

My belly knotted. Dein wasn't Dosh. My boy was still dead.

"I knew him. Went to the party." He had an actor's voice-control but he was working at it. "I do believe I was jealous. Read, jealous as hell. A good friend?"

"Goodish." I was working too. "Nice guy. Lucky."

"Sure. For two weeks."

"Two weeks?"

"I think that's how long it took them to kill him."

Lorn grabbed my elbow. Going down. The redhead's forehead had ridged.

"Shouldn't have said that. A real good friend, huh?"

The dolphin whipped underwear off a chair and Lorn folded me onto it. I shook my head feeling like I'd hit major water. "Called himself Dein?"

Luke Trent's mouth opened and some pink came back under the resin.

"Hey. Wrong guy. Frank was a nice kid but he never grew up to be Dein. White-blond, blue eyes, light and slender. Missed Dein's size by half a foot. Doesn't matter much in vids. Had talent. Called himself Karel or something on film. One of Coelacanth's lesser epics. Their fucking mockup ship exploded. Coelacanth habit. Bits of guy all over. They used the scene, they always do. R.I.P. in the credits. Dein showed up in a jungle pic a few months later. He's okay but Frank he ain't. I shared a dressing room with Frank. He's dead."

He wrestled his face and got the grin back. "Remind

me not to be a film star. Those jungle guys must've nearly drowned."

Lorn was serious, a great whooping crane talking to a sparrow. "They couldn't have put the bits together? Leg, arm, regen, add height, end up Dein?"

The redhead tried sitting on the table, got tangled in his tail and coiled it over an arm. "It would've had to be radical. Guy's whole skeleton's different. Plus eyes and hair and the shape of the skull. He doesn't even move the same. But, hell, what do I know? They put you back."

"They missed their chance to turn me out human."

"Whose fault was that?"

"My old man's, at a guess," Lorn said mildly. "I'm not sure I had a tongue. Come along, Cassandra, you're looking sea-colored. It's the smell of actor. Thanks a lot, Belagana. Uh, Luke?"

"Uh huh?"

"Don't boast we were asking. Someone let off fire-works in Cinderella's bedroom last night. I wouldn't like you to need radical surgery."

"Now what are you into?" He made dangling paws from the wrist. "If anyone asks I'll tell 'em you're in love with me. How's that?"

They parted with mutual insults and Lorn let me sprint beside him to the roof.

"Satisfied, lovely?"

"Yes and no. No and yes."

"Very clear. Shall I call you a traxie, or would you like me to take you back to your hotel? I can be fearfully well-conducted."

"Is that a promise?"

"Oh, absolutely."

"Your friend's cute," I said, as we piddled up toward the middle-speed lane like a lame dowager and a green laser-line began to reel out on the panel.

"Luke? Nice guy. Good actor. Classics don't pay so he's spent six years as an alien. Boring."

"Bet he has a girlfriend."

"That's not fair," he protested. "You're supposed to lust after the guy you're with, not his friend. Especially if cute. Are you lusting after me?" He turned around to gaze long and sorrowfully into my eyes. "I didn't think you were."

"You promised to be well-conducted."

"I was talking about the copt."

"So was I. You could look where you're going."

"But, Cinderella, that's what this green line's for. If you'd let me drive I could do you clever tricks. Since you won't I've hooked into the city guide network and it's going home on its own. It's what you do when you want to make out on the way."

"You get a lot of practice?"

"Me?" More injured innocence. "Where do they make girls my size?"

"Where they made you?"

"That's my sister. It's illegal."

"I bet she has a thin time," I was saying, when the copt's nose took an abrupt lurch.

"Very thin," he said absently. "It runs in the family, but she doesn't eat nearly enough either."

"What are you doing?"

Outraged yelp. The peaceful green line had sputtered out and a steady red LED was glaring in its place. The spurt of acceleration that went with it threw me back violently inside my seatbelt.

A second later I recognized the sharp *whup* that had just spanged over the canopy. It was a disruptor bolt, and a whole lot too close.

"Taking evasive action."

He was still absent, and extremely peaceable. The copt

wasn't. We were still in the middle-speed lane and he was zipping in and out of traffic like he was driving a bumper car. I could see colored streaks with terrified eyes in them blur past us. A shrill siren began to ululate from the control panel.

"What's that?"

"The cops don't like the way I drive. I can see my daddy's going to have to explain I'm brain-damaged again."

I took a nervous look behind. The cityscape was disappearing as if we were falling off a mountain and a lot of multicolored dots with wide eyes fell backward along with it. All except one. There was a big gray copt right behind taking the same zigzags we were, and it wasn't getting smaller.

Then a black muzzle poked through the canopy and I saw the blue flash a fraction of a second before another *whup* even closer.

"This is getting annoying," Lorn said.

He sounded as if he'd just swallowed a handful of Valium. I wondered if his war traumas left him going to sleep where he sat under fire. If they did I'd better think fast about taking over, and at the speed I wasn't exactly dying of enthusiasm. Apart from him having to weigh at least twice what I did. I slid my eyes sideways. He wasn't asleep. The dreamy eyes under the girl's lashes were fixed on the red display that stuttered across his foreshield and his narrow mouth was shaped in a smile of relaxed concentration.

"They're fast," I said.

"Yep. Ought to be a law against civil copts with souped-up engines. In fact, I believe there is." He took another violent swerve that threw me sideways against the straps and ducked neatly under a long slow vehicle. It looked a lot too much like a school bus. "If we go on like this someone's getting hurt. We can't shake them in the open. Let's get some cover."

He sounded like he was making personal notes. I didn't mind. I'd rather not carry out small talk in the middle of a war, on the whole. The copt dropped in that whining kamikaze dive and rooftops jumped at us. I tried not to shut my eyes and felt cornices scrape my eyeballs.

"What's the matter, Cinders? You've an objection to dying with your boots on?"

"Yes, if they've stilt heels."

"I'll put you spares in the back for next time."

A slit in the buildings about the size of a hyphen shot toward us and he sliced the copt through. It was an uptown street, a fashionable shopping mall, and it was paved with upturned faces.

"Uh-oh. No improvement."

Another *whup* made him right. The gray gunship was still on our tail and if anything closing. A helping of decorative carving peeled off a roof in front of us and began a slow fall into the street. Comparatively speaking. Lorn swung in a right-angled turn into a side street, then rapidly zigged through two more.

We were still uptown and the gray copt was still leaning on us. I didn't hear the next blast but I saw another wedge of building fall. It took the corner neatly off an office block and left blank-faced people sitting at desks inside staring out at the sky as if they didn't believe it.

Our own crate slid sideways into a narrower alley, shrieked over a low roof that it missed by maybe four inches and spun back on its trail. I knew the technique but not the circumstances. He was trying to get behind them. It makes a lot of sense if you're stalking a guy at ground level, and for all I know for hunting-killing in open space. I wasn't sure of its applications in a town center, in an overstressed sports copt meant for looking dashing in, without a tool to our names. Unless I threw my shoes at them.

"Lorn, you need cannon."

He didn't quite turn me a blissful smile. He really was looking where he was going.

"Don't worry about it, Cinderella. I got all I need in my head."

Which, as I remembered, was brain-damaged. It wasn't a happy idea. I sat on it. It wiggled.

The alleys below were getting narrower and more crooked, with less room for maneuver every turn. I could almost feel brown brick scraping my elbow. I hung on to the edge of the panel with white nails and wished I'd told Moke good-bye. I wished a lot of things. I wished I wasn't wearing lime-green pants because if this went on it was going to show. If there was enough left to identify. I thought about figures of speech involving glue. I've never liked fancy grammar.

"Here we go."

We screeched around another turn and came out into a street I thought I'd seen several corners back. The gray copt was halfway down it doing a slow search-pattern side to side. Lorn came down on it like the angel with the sword, his nose directed straight at its stern tubes. They had perhaps three-fifths of a second to see him. They did, just too late, and panicked.

The pilot tried to lift the copt's nose as Lorn lifted his own exactly enough to skim across the gray fuselage, then, realizing we were coming over the top, hauled it frantically back down.

The big copt bucked like a bronco, lost its grav, slid out of control and crashed against the side of the nearest building. Over my shoulder I could see burning fragments tumbling into the street.

"There you are, Cinderella," Lorn remarked, slowing down to a virtuous putter and pulling calmly up toward the middle-speed laser path. "You don't need cannon at all if you know your position. Poor reflexes. I expect better from a hired gun."

"What would you have done if he'd faced you out?"

"Missed him. We had twenty-five centimeters in hand."

"That much."

"It's all you need, princess."

"And more dead guys. It's really a talent."

"It's what I was trained for. You've no idea what it cost. Be grateful to the nice Navy." He took in my face—I don't know what color it was outside but it felt candle-colored inside, and not the Christmas kind—and got sweet again. "Those big bastards have very solid passenger boxes, Cassandra. I'll be surprised if they're more than shaken. They'll come back and shoot you up another day, don't worry."

That was all I needed.

"Let's go home." He looked relaxed by the exercise.

"I wish I didn't have lime-green pants on."

"Don't let it worry you. It happens to all novice pilots in their first battle."

"Remind me to make this battle my last."

"Of course. I say that myself every time."

I cowered inside my yellow shirt like a bad puppy.

I'd stopped feeling theatrical entirely.

"Quick reactions. Delicate little creature, Mr. Cordovan. Like a sea anemone. Draws in when prodded and digests small fish. I think DeLorn had better see his friend Trent gets an attack of Shakespeare soon. An interplanetary tour might do his health good."

Swordfish was on the floor. I thought he sat on the bench to make us feel inferior. I was wrong. He was just as nasty at ground level.

"Can he? Seems sweet but nutty to me."

He grunted. "There's a Northwest National Theater troupe leaving for Asterios Monday. One thing Aris do well is pull strings. Mr. Trent may be playing Horatio."

"Slender, light, white-blond," Hallway said. "Like the sister." He was thinking, his eyes vague.

"Apparently. There go the miracles of modern surgery, in which case one asks why Coelacanth didn't choose a big yellow-haired guy in the first place. How's the hospital?"

"I may have something. Dein first shows getting his appendicitis fixed at a restructural clinic. Coelacanth were filming just outside Moon orbit. Normal for cheapies. Seven cryo-capsules were delivered at the City hold facility a few days before you blew that film, Cass. Ties in with Trent's story about a drone that exploded. They'd keep the remains for the next of kin. Five were claimed, leaving two on hold. The night Dosh died, someone sent for one and took it away."

"Family?"

"Not signed for by family. Transit firm. I've tracked the delivery. Wound up at our clinic."

"So it was Ottery and they remade him."

"After he'd been on hold for nearly a week?"

"They found out his family was rich."

"None of these guys had what Aris call rich families or they wouldn't have got blown up. There was another delivery around the same time. Another cryo-capsule. With police escort, on account of the traffic was backed up around Highfield. Caused by you. Neither subsequently seen again. Dein signed out two weeks later."

"Where you get this stuff, Hall?"

"Here and there. The second capsule's in police files. Took me a minute or two to break in. I can't get any further here. The clinic's private files are on a personal."

"Great," I said. Personals are my job.

"The girl wonder," Sword said. He sounded less than stunned. "But we could take a look. How's their security?"

"Diligent," Hallway said. "Be careful."

"My life's work. I'm going out. Wash while I'm gone, Hippolyta. I may need you later."

Moke and I lay on our bed in our most recent luxury hidey-hole and gazed at the ceiling while Yell clattered in the kitchen. Yell was brought up engineering warp-drives so he understands the coffee machine. At least Moke gazed. I was hopping like a flea on a waffle iron.

I'm always nervous before an operation but I'd given up blue angel when we landed with Eklund. Coming to dinner stoned every night looks bad. I'd have given a lot for a couple of high-class packets right then.

It was another of Swordfish's uptown apartments with decorator decor and enough buttons I think even Yeller hadn't figured them all out yet. There was also a wall-to-wall holoscreen and Mokey was fiddling with it between inspecting the patterns in the plaster.

"Will you knock that off, Moke? You're driving me crazy."

"Likewise," he said, shifting channels. "Have you thought of taking a trank? It's like sharing a trampoline with a troupe of performing ponies."

"Thanks. Wait a minute, stick with that, will you?"

He came down from the ceiling to see what he'd caught. It was a news program. If you play up and down the channels you're bound to hit one, they run them twenty-four hours a day. I don't know why, Ashton ain't that interesting.

". . . offices of major holovid studios Coelacanth. A powerful explosive device partially destroyed the building and slightly injured two employees. The police are following up leads on the crime, which is the latest in the series of unidentified . . ."

I doubled up and rolled around on the squelchy comforter.

I knew that decor. The fire was munching on the furred jungle of Jason Cordovan's private office and it was shriveling like supper in a Boy Scout camp. Phosphorus if I've ever seen it. Unidentified? That hit was signed Swordfish in letters a yard high.

"That'll teach them to disrupt virtuous citizens minding their own business in the rush hour. I thought Sword was bored again."

"I didn't. He's most dangerous when he doesn't say anything. Hadn't you noticed?"

I kicked my feet some more and quit having tics.

I felt better already.

• • •

"Right," Swordfish said. There was a shifting of coolsuits around our apartment and weights on the bed that were heavier or lighter than humans ought to be. Mokey had his knees drawn up to make room. He was the only guy visible but the blurring lines of the furniture would give you motion sickness. I was a suit, though I had my hood back for Moke.

"Place is defended like a military base. Advanced life-detectors and random field-code changes, according to Hall. Wings and I took some pups out this afternoon and we can add flying mickeys and automated dog-scythes with combat gas. At a guess."

Pups are miniature mechanicals with sneaky little spy functions. Sword and Wings must have been two busy guys.

"Claims to be owned by Doctors Murmansk and Yaki-mura, psychosurgeon and cosmeticist. From the copts, exclusive covers it. Maybe ten patients in suites like the Ruiz-Sheraton. Cosmetic mostly, male and female. Lower floor reception. More than oriental splendor, someone's paying. Second, private suites and nurses' station, operating block and recovery on third. Fourth is admin, Cass, that's where you want. Fifth has its own elevators. You'll get a look anyhow, it's where you get in. Ground's impossible. Their front door's four inches of cerosteel in sliding grooves with another four of tropical hardwood fore and aft. You could let off dynamite to the tune of Greensleeves. I left cams on the two docs."

"Heating?"

"Closed system with internal recirculation."

Um. Not what I'd recommend for a hospital but maybe their surgical hygiene was good. It's death to burglars.

"Yeah, that makes it the roof."

I hate roof entries. One day I'm going to find something about this job I like.

"This is a diversion. The object's to let Cass in and give her worktime. No heroics, no smart initiatives. We keep them occupied. When you get the signal you leave. Anyone captured's on their own. Questions?"

Silence.

"What about me?" Moke said desolately. He'd wanted to come and got turned down.

Sword's bared eyes swung. "Go see Hall. He'll keep you amused."

"Okay, Yell and me'll take our gear over. Lux apts upset my stomach. Maybe he can find me a cellar."

"And take it easy, Cass," Sword said wearily. "If you get assassinated I'll kill you."

"Thanks," I said. "Does this job have a disability pension?"

"Sure," Swordfish said. "Fuck up and I disable you. Move, guys, let's go."

We moved.

Riverside's beyond the edge of town, south of the smart upper-Ari districts in virgin countryside. An old haggard virgin with wrinkles, but it has grass and trees. Of a sort. The expressway stops at the 'burbs. I hate countryside. Too fucking much of it goes around on too many legs.

Sword makes expeditions on foot. Coolsuits guarantee limited invisibility and they're hard to track. Anyone can see hostile copts coming and it gives them time to call the police. His guys infiltrate.

We smoked down the walkways as far as Riverside and came off at a copt-park, a monorail terminus and a mall of exclusive boutiques shut for the night. The 'burb stretched away, linked to the main dome by chains of beads enclosing mansions, a school, a health club and the local conference center.

There was no one about but I could hear the soft whistle of a police copt making rounds among millionaire

real estate. I did think we had a mile or five of rough
grass and scrub in front, and it was going to be a long
stumbling way. A coolsuit isn't a charm against breaking
your ankle.

The group was flowing west and I flowed with it. The
bright beads receded and we came out on grass near the
edge of a highway. Below on the road cops were sitting
in a lighted guardhouse playing cards and hoping for
business. They like to stop cars. Up where we were the
countryside was in darkness, barely lit by a clouded moon,
but I could make out the ten feet of bare earth that marks
the edge of the force-field. It circled away northward into
shadow.

Blurred forms made the jump, not-too-human figures
rimmed with blue as they cut the field, a soft clink showing where each of them landed. Last time I did this I
messed up. My legs were tense. It's not far at all. The
alarm just goes off in every precinct house in town if you
touch earth passing.

A hard hand caught my elbow. I braced and wasted my
time. We landed five feet the other side without breaking step.

"Okay," Sword's voice said above my head. "Hit tarmac
around the turn, about three hundred yards. Wings and
Hilt are in charge. Keep together or you've got a long
walk."

A military transport truck under a camouflage tarp was
at the roadside where your ordinary commuter passes too
fast to look. When we arrived the tarp was off and most of
the group inside. Sword shoved me into the cab and came
up fast and easy by my side. Someone else followed and
we banged knees. I restrained curses. So did he.

"Wings?"

"Yeah." Hoarse snarl from my elbow.

"Okay behind?"

"Any time you like."

Sword's invisible hand let in the clutch and the big slider skimmed silently onto the road.

"Now listen, Cass," he said, as the rotors got up to speed and we reached cruising height. "We're going to make noise. Just get in and out, we'll look after ourselves. We've a copt there and Wings'll wait for you at the foot of the wall. The rest of us'll come across country if we have to. We want you and the chips in one piece or the operation's shot. Got it?"

"Yeah. I promise not to bite Wings even when he deserves it. You're making overheads tonight."

"We'll get them back."

The highway reeled out under us, illuminated central strip brightening as our nose approached and fading behind as we hissed past. The moonlight was brighter outside the dome but not enough to show topography. Low ragged clouds drooped, their bellies lead-colored. Brush flashed in our direction-beams, ghostly and dead.

Two solid bodies pressed on my elbows and neither even had a silhouette as their suits coped with shifting radiance. The cab looked empty. Almost but not quite. It was full of voiceless breathing. I looked down at my own knees and couldn't see them.

Sword turned the slider off the road in mid-country and cut the engine.

"Okay, people, we walk. If we're lucky, rendezvous here. If not, use your legs. It's what they're for."

Unseen feet thumped softly down. Someone grabbed my hand and pulled me towards the highway.

"Clinic's over the ridge. Nasty place, Cass, wait for my all-clear. And have your gun jacked. You don't want to converse with their mechanicals."

I'd met flying mickeys before, the little mobile camera units that report on intruders and squirt acid in your face while they wait for the troops. Automated dog-scythes were new but I wasn't anxious to get acquainted.

"Interesting security for a hospital."

"Real up-to-date guys."

The coolsuits were spreading out. Not more than half a dozen, a small diversionary expedition. An occasional shape showed up against the skyline, bent low and trailing blunt cylinders. Feet brushed past in the rough grass. I knew the routine, circle and make noise from the rear. The artillery looked heavy.

"You expecting trouble?"

"I'm about to make it."

The dome opened under a torch-sized resonator and left a hole big enough for Swordfish, me and Wings, in that order, to slide through. Sword's a pretty slider for his size. "We got entry codes this afternoon. They change at night but Hall hopes they're cracked. If not, the trouble starts now. Otherwise we've two minutes advance."

Something drifted out of the bushes in front and Wings froze it. Sword added the jinx. It's better than destruction, it delays alarm. I saw it dimly and made a note. Automated dog-scythe, yeah. About the size of a German mastiff with whip-jointed blades, three a side. He hadn't mentioned it also had jaws.

"Remember, it spits gas. We think nerve but it could be worse. Had to pull some pups back when one of the doctors came in. His copt's armored and he carries a blocker."

"Jeez. Doesn't look like they even trust themselves."

"They could be right. One's gone home, other was working on modeling diagrams when last seen. They're still covered by cams. Neither's doing anything interesting."

We scooted over shaved grass and up to a ceroglass wall. Wings made a foray to freeze another blade thing and we played statues as a buzzing sphere came around the side of the building at head height. It whistled past and around the corner, its swiveling camera-eye catching moonlight.

"Thought they had life-detectors?" I hissed.

"They have, but not in the mickeys. The screen. We've cut the siren but there's nothing we can do about visuals. There's got to be a red light blinking somewhere and any moment someone's going to notice. Up you go. There's a skylight on the roof. If you meet anyone shoot them."

I grunted and jacked in my rifle. I don't like climbing with functional artillery but God disposes. I took two steps up the wall, and stuck as the dome behind flashed and shorted out with a noise like the death of a power station. That's probably what it was. The instantaneous black shapes of Sword and Wings below stayed frozen for a moment and then were off fast and low in different directions. I still thought the armaments were heavy. I've never seen Sword carry anything more macho than a disruptor and I'd have sworn he had a sonic bazooka on his shoulder. Looked like they meant to make noise loudly.

The ceroglass was slick and I'd say antiburglar coated. Hallway'd given me suckers and they sucked, but only just. It had a lot in common with walking on butter. I wasn't going to have a problem leaving. If I lived so long.

My jacked laser had its own night vision and automatic target program, and the sighting brackets gave red corners to my field of view. I looked from side to side, trying to keep fast and smooth. My size and weight help in this kind of job. I'm small, light and skinny. Even Hallway's suckers wouldn't have supported a man on that surface. I had to shin like a monkey, moving arms and legs like swimming crawl, to get a grip higher up with hands and feet before I slid back down.

About fifteen meters up I half heard a sound like a flustered bumblebee and my right hand lifted faster than I'd time to register. That's automatic targeting and why I don't like it. You can shoot your best friend before you know what you've done if you aren't careful. A mickey stared right in my eye, close enough for me to see the glittering nozzle come out like a wasp sting. A flash and it evaporated. Its acid spray evaporated with it. I was lucky I had eye filters because the choking smoke made me cough through my suit. The rifle dropped back to surveillance mode, I made up the five meters I'd slid down and went on shinning.

Really nasty people. Who has mickeys halfway up a thirty-meter wall? I was suspicious of this skylight.

I shed suckers on the roof edge, put them into a thigh pocket and surveyed the garden. It was noisy. It sounded like a full-grown Naval battle. I wished I had ear plugs. I hoped Sword knew what he was doing. One of these days he's going to meet something bigger. Like a great white shark. If there was one in the garden now, I wouldn't be surprised. And we were getting cops damned soon. The flashes had to be showing in Ashton.

I took off across the roof at a run, my laser pulling my head around as it scanned. No guards, no blade-things, no more visible mickeys. Smoothly laid leads, parapet, a sort of big glass doghouse. Too simple. Much.

I looked at it from a distance. My preferred entry's air ducts but I don't despise skylights. I despised this one. I fished in my thigh pocket. Soda-mint. You'd be surprised what burglars use. I lobbed it to hit the doghouse.

It didn't. About a foot above it burst into a bright glare and burned like a gnat in a candle. That could have been Cassandra. Or, to put it differently, these fuckers had a high-intensity force-field protecting their skylight and that's the kind of security you expect at either a government arms factory or an Ari wedding, but sure as hell nothing between.

That called for strong measures. Hall's diffident but he covers possibilities.

I sure hoped he'd covered this one. An innocent gray disk like a washer with a hole in the middle. It either banged or fizzled since that's what Hallway gadgets do. Half of them explode, the other half stop other people's garbage exploding. It landed in the middle of the field like the soda-mint and proceeded to burn to a crisp. I was disappointed. I'd hoped it would do something different. Like bore a hole, maybe.

Only burning to a crisp was taking time. A lot of time. It went on burning and burning.

It took me a while to get it. The field was trying to destroy it and failing. The more it burned the more energy it used and the more energy the field put out to contain it the more it burned. The light was getting the blue-white glare of Moke's welding-torch. The field flickered. I saw blue sparks at the edge of the frame that became uncertain wavering lightnings. The little washer blazed up for an instant like a minor sun, and went out. It fell on the glass with a quiet chink and melted through.

I got over there. The skylight was black and partly melted, even the frame sagging like a very old doghouse for a very old dog. The glass was too opaqued with burning to show what was beneath, except for a round hole with sharp-cut edges where the disk had fallen. A thin curl of smoke came out and rose lazily into the sky to join the layers of bitter-smelling mist that were accumulating above the garden.

I grabbed my cutter. We hadn't come to burn the place down, particularly if there were sick people in there, and especially before I'd got the records out. I slashed a reckless circle—the glass was too far gone to be worth delicacy—suckered it off and dropped it on the leads. Then

I let myself through. The frame member I used to belay my rope was warm and not the strongest support I've ever had, but it didn't actually melt the fiber. That's all I ask.

We were in.

There was a laboratory underneath and it was the bench that was burning. That was one righteous disk. It had fallen right through the foot-thick teak slab and was busy sinking into the floor. I crawled under the table to poke the muzzle of my rifle in the hole and concluded it had met insulation six inches down and was cooling. It was a lot thinner but unbowed. With any luck it wouldn't fall through the ceiling and land on some sick guy's head. The teak and the plastic floor tiles were smoking but it didn't look like they were going to flame.

I felt better. I don't really do massacres.

The lab looked interesting. I filed it and made for the door. Locked. Since we weren't being discreet tonight, I burned it. The place was full of smoke anyhow. I fished my caftan out and slung the billowing gauze over my head. See what the cameras made of me now. Then I inflated my platforms and pushed outside.

A corridor, empty. The staff should be out staving off sonic bazookas. If they weren't hiding under the bed. I know what I'd have done. The night-sight of the jacked laser gave me vision in the dark. Disadvantage was the dim safety-bulbs of the corridor blazed in it like arc lamps. I squinted against them and resisted the urge to pull the jack. I'd need sight when I found the offices.

There were paired soft-entries ahead outlined in red with up-down arrows. I shouldered through and drifted to the floor below. Another soft-entry, another corridor. This ought to be administration. I catfooted along it. If I was running this joint I'd have a guard here by now. I turned the laser to stun and prodded at doors.

There were plenty, fine woods with gilt edgings. I wasn't anxious to burn out locks, let them think we'd come for the lab. But I didn't have all night.

The first three were open. That almost always means nothing inside. Every so often you meet a wiseass read "The Purloined Letter" who's put the family jewels in one, so you have to go into them all. It takes forever and from the vibration we hadn't got it.

You could have bet there'd be decks in every office. The ones in the unlocked rooms were slaved to something bigger and switched out at source. There had to be a main memory bank, unless these were the guys I've been waiting for who put it on chip and file it with their sandwiches. My experience of guys is the smarter the dumber. This lot thought they were red hot.

Door four was locked. Most doctors are orthodox and tidy-minded. I was happy Murmansk and Yakimura didn't want to stand out. Hall had given me a self-programing analyzer handled anything but top-security handplates, and it handled this. It flickered a warning halfway for an anti-theft circuit, which is one of his private improvements, and stood still while I bypassed.

Paydirt. The big industrial deck had to have access to the main file bank and it looked like they had lots of files. I slotted a cruncher and waited for access codes. I didn't expect it to be hard. In hospitals everyone needs access.

After five minutes with the screen still flickering letters and figures, I was wondering. Maybe this rated the outlay. Because it shouldn't have been so hard and believe me, this gear ain't cheap. Not even with Hall for a friend.

Even Ari skinjobs scarcely need military security.

I was getting desperate when it locked and settled. In and waiting. I usually sort files. I hadn't time. I took a handful of chips from my thigh pouch and got stripping.

I was soaked with sweat by the end. Each chip went into a plastic sac and each sac back into the envelope. They'd been hardworking guys. I'd stripped maybe fifteen chips and I was getting nervous. There was still nobody around and I didn't like it. I wondered who their patients were.

I popped the last chip, closed down the machine and checked my gear was sealed. A look around the carpet, guys get caught leaving genotype traces. Then the door backward. Lock. Bypass off. Check corridor. Head for elevator and . . .

The woman rustled around the corner just as I was splitting the soft-entry. She had braided corn hair, a sunlamp complexion and ploddy white bucks under her blouse. She could have been a nurse. If so, she shouldn't have been carrying a snub-nosed blaster with automatic firing and an hour's worth of magazine. I dived through, whipping my caftan around to give an impression of whiteness, waved a hand like I had urgent business and hit it for the attic.

I stood rigid outside the upper entry, zigged gauze billowing in the draft from broken door and window. They had fire stairs. If she was smart she'd come up them. If she was even smarter she'd send for the Navy. If she was half-smart she'd take the elevator. If she kept me waiting I'd have to shoot her some other time.

She was ordinary smart. Maybe the white blur had suckered her. She threw back the fire door, stuck her snubbed muzzle around it and prepared to hose down the corridor. My automatic sight snicked onto her with an electronic yelp of joy and laid her out flat before she touched the trigger. Great. Our body-legging credentials were growing. And the lady had three hours' sleep ahead.

The ones you meet are those you aren't expecting. A medium-sized Oriental with tired eyes behind horn-rimmed granddad lenses. Some people find them reassuring. He didn't have a gun, just a set of rolled blueprints and an expression even dumber than mine. We looked at each other with our mouths open.

I growled through my resonator, "Dr. Yakimura, I presume," and tranked him. He lay down and went to sleep. He looked like he needed it.

I ran to the lab and gave myself two minutes. The place was a rejuve clinic. Vats of human tissue. Some in sheets and lumps, some cloning into internal organs. It's easier to grow them externally and replace them than regen onsite because they're complex. They regen limbs and skin.

I nearly missed the private store because the door was flush with the wall with no handle. My sighting prog got it. I prodded, got nowhere, and blasted.

As soon as I walked in I knew it was going to take longer than two minutes. The armorglass cases filled with cloudy liquid came in different sizes, a lot of them smaller then they ought to be. For complete bodies. We've an ordinance against fetus trading. Others had corpses in a state oughtn't to be in a storeroom. You're likewise not allowed to keep them on life support with half their bits missing unless you're actually working on a remake.

Exhibit A was in a corner. It had worse then bits missing, it looked blasted and half its skull was gone. Though not by blast, because the face and head were otherwise intact. Guess he'd been a good-looking boy once. Slender, lightweight, white-blond. He had a date on his label. Two years old.

My rifle had a memory facility and I set it to register. I hosed my sight around the place good. With a shot of Yakimura on his back in the corridor for reference.

Then I got the hell out.

• • •

The noise was extreme.

Down was what I'd thought it would be. Delete butter. I zoomed like a kid on a helter-skelter and it was all I could do to lean on my suckers before I bent my neck terminally. I hit turf hard enough to knock my breath out and had a panic over the chips. But it was only my skin was broken. Lucky. Sword doesn't mind a little gangrene but he'd be mad if I lost the records.

I looked around and got one of these lonely feelings. Where the dome had been was a blackened ring with trees and bushes smoldering inside. The place was fogged with smoke and bitter with the sharp ozone scent of laser-fire. It looked like Sword had been using his sonics on the copt-park because there were a lot of bits of metal about shaped like bits of copt. I guess the guys were around the back. I still had my hearing.

A couple of police copts were buzzing vaguely overhead and more sirens wailed in the distance. A bladed dog-thing came staggering past with its blades snapped, like an eccentric garden-tool.

A red glow under a column of black smoke over the rise said the slider had joined its fathers. Wings would be lucky if he saw me. And contrarywise. A good pair of filters or a laser sighting-program usually gives you a misted outline even of a coolsuit. In the shifting lights of cop beacons complicated by reflections from the slick ceroglass wall I couldn't see anyone. I thought there were people in the garden but not Sword's, because they wore smoke-overalls. I thought there was debris about, most of it mechanical. As far as I could tell the only guy around was me.

I stood feeling dumb. I had to contact Wings or the jerk would wait forever. All I didn't know was how to do it. Maybe I'd slid down the wrong bit of wall. Coolsuits are stupid like that. If you haven't a way to identify your troops you can be half a yard from a guy and neither of you know it.

I was thinking it would be simplest to skin my hood and make like a foghorn when a hand grabbed my collar and yanked me toward a stand of laurels by the pad. The leaves were cooked and so were the copts behind. One had exploded and taken a piece of ornamental wall with it. A lonely canopy lay upside down like a discarded chrysalis.

"That our transport?"

He didn't stop to snarl. Police copts were pouring in, the first drifting down to land, wailing as they came. He hauled me by the neck toward the back where an octagonal swimming pool was burning like the Olympic Flame. Either they had a new kind of water or somebody'd ignited it with a Hallway special.

We detoured and came out in a stretch of parkland, burned in patches to the line of the fused-out dome, that stretched towards marshes behind. The shadow of the hospital wall blacked out the ground, and even with nightsight I'd trouble defining the grass. Areas of earth heated by fire and burning edges of tussock flared in my scope like pieces of sun.

Hard fingers dragged me to a clump of bushes that made a hiatus of shadow on the gray turf. We'd come maybe five hundred yards. He jerked my arm, meaning knees, and dropped on his belly at my side, looking through the interlocked stems at moving copts. I could hear him breathe. He was in better shape than me. He didn't even pant.

We lay there half an hour, give or take a century. I leaned on him. Wings and I suffer from hate on sight, it's been following us around for years. He was rude, he was invisible, his suit was absolutely neutral and he didn't like me. But if we were going to stay there all night I wanted to lean on someone.

The clinic quieted. The copts stopped circling like disturbed wasps and settled out front where the crews could yack together and count up the damage. The ones who had been flying search-patterns over the countryside looking for Sword had quit. They knew already it was a good way to waste a night.

Sooner or later they'd come evaluate the damage around the back, then someone with a life-detector just might fall over us.

"Hey. If we're walking we better start?"

"Hold on."

He let me drop and snaked off into the marshland. I followed his track three yards before I lost him. I admit the boy's a nice mover. We just have this thing.

A wait lasting another century. A police copt whistled up over the roof and I was afraid they were going to start serious search-patterns but it spun in a fancy swerve over my head and swung off back to Ashton, probably to report to someone. I bet it was important. I sat on the grass several eons more, nursing my laser and wondering what the hell I was doing there. I get these moments of philosophy.

My hero was back, lips to my ear, barely audible.

"Let's go before someone sends in a holovision crew. Keep down."

I squirmed. It was a decent belly-walk, maybe fifty yards. Into a bog-hole. Water squelched under my suit. Then we were in the bottom and a fine skeletal shadow stood like a Chinese drawing in the rushes.

"Transport."

I squinted at the wire puzzle overhead. It was a delicate sports ultralite, the kind can be folded and carried on a man's back over rough terrain, with blunt transparent wings. It had as much substance as a dragonfly and would fly as quietly.

"Not fast, but fairly sure. Strap in. She's sensitive to air currents."

I slid a leg over the fragile sling that took the place of a seat and groped for the harness. The thing swayed every time I moved and when he put his weight on the other side I thought it was going to fall flat on its face and disappear into the mud. It stayed balanced. His arm stretched to check my clips and I heard the clink of his. Then the motor woke to a hum so soft and low it wouldn't have disturbed a guard-mute at five yards.

The little thing quivered, shifted and slipped into the air. We rose like a moth under the dying moon with the last embers of the garden glowing ruby beneath us, caught a current that lifted us into the fringes of cloud and hummed off for Ashton making no more noise than an owl.

"Everyone okay?" I whispered. "Took time. Is Sword mad?"

"About as sane as usual," his warm velvet voice murmured in my ear. "Got the chips, I hope. Or I'm damn well going to have to take you back."

I breathed, with control. "I been sitting on you?"

"Yep. Lucky you're lightweight, this toy plane carries two and I count as one and a half. Thought I'd leave margin for error. Save our feet."

"Wings isn't hurt?"

"Nope. He has a desire for command so I'm letting him command the withdrawal. That way he gets the blisters. Anyhow, it's my ultra. Wings is a copt man. Shouldn't have let them blow it." He sounded cheerfully callous.

"Bastard. You don't have to sneer."

"At Wings? He's one tough competent boy. Keep telling you so. It's you doesn't like him."

"He doesn't like me. I think he's jealous."

"Just embarrassed. Be nice to him and see."

"He'll bite me and I'll get tetanus."

"Much more likely to be the other way around. What the hell d' you mean by smooching all over me if you thought I was him?"

"I smooch over anyone when I'm lonely."

"Look at pretty Ashton," he said savagely. "It's nice in the dark."

I looked down. Chains of light and white laser-lanes and spaceport floods jeweled the coast from north to south as far as you could see.

It seemed a pity so many people were in the act of dying down there right now.

Like every night.

I leaned against Sword and looked at the streaks of dawn over the sea and wondered what was wrong with us.

And what, if anything, you could do about it.

Whatever it was, it was going to take a tougher guy than me to do it.

Moke looked at his hands. His face was a symphony in off-green and shot blood, his knuckles white.

"I went to the burbs. Didn't feel like sitting. Markus Lopez, power-back for the Sabertooths. He happened to be at home, strained ligament. His two little kids were with him. Skinny white-blonds. Antonia Ottery Lopez had a concert in Mdina but he expected her back on the evening shuttle. Gram came while I was there."

His red eyes lifted. The lines by his nose were the color of bad cheese. "Lady hasn't seen or heard from her brother in seven years. She wanted him to stay in school, he walked out. But she knew he'd done okay and was pleased. Been spending time on her own career. She fell apart on stage this afternoon in the middle of a Getz number."

"He means fell apart," Hallway said. His freckles stood out like burn-scars. I'd never noticed he had them. "Face and hands disintegrated and her scalp came off. Then her feet at the ankle. What's left's in hospital. Whole area's under quarantine. There's a news blackout but some guy with an illegal peeper got the pictures on holo before the blinds came down. I saw it."

"She was fine this morning," Moke said. "The kids are aged three and five. Markus weighs two hundred and eighty pounds and when I left they were trying to give

73

him sedation. I called the medic."

"God." I had to sit down abruptly. "Did we do that?"

"No." Sword's eyes burned my neck. "The next time you set about thinking the universe cares for your whims I'm going to beat you till you can't stand."

"But we did," Moke whispered toward bloodless fingers.

"I'm not going to tolerate hysteria," Swordfish said evenly. "Cass has her own pictures and they're not pretty either. Hall, make with the projector. We won't help any of them by yelping."

Hallway dragged himself upright. He walked like he was broken.

"Body-legging country." Sword was on the studio couch with a dent in the pillow suggesting hands behind head.

"Yeah," Hall said, tired. "Especially plus the chips. Current cases'll do. Suite One, elderly male, sounds high Ari. Aged a hundred sixty-seven, wore out his rejuve and his fourth heart. They've just done a transplant by donor, young male, who was alive until the exchange. It's explicitly forbidden. Only cloned material may be used in transplants. Special permission can be given. Not recorded."

"Who was the young male?" I asked.

Sword's invisible stare turned. "You're kidding. Boys and girls disappear every day, on the Strip and off it. Some of their parents sell them. He's dead now."

"Suite Five. Middle-aged female with brain damage. Drugs, at a guess. Damaged sector due to be replaced with regenned tissue from accident victim, source not recorded. Forbidden ditto, no license likewise. The lady's apparently drooling but there's no obvious reason she can't survive until they've legally cloned her own."

"Except probably she's a film coming up where drool isn't in the script," Sword said.

"That or a party. Suite Eight, pregnancy. There are severe fetal defects plus a family history of miscarriage. The child's to be removed for repairs tomorrow. The donor fetus is on hold. No identity for the source-fetus but a payment was made."

"Mother or mack, I wonder?" Swordfish said. "Pregnant girls disappear on the Strip too."

"Most of the records are for cosmetic treatments. This lot are on official record as one facelift, one eyelid fold, and a ventral tuck. And that's as far as I've got up to date."

"Do we know who they are?"

"Yes, if you recognize top families. Does it matter?"

"Won't do a lot of good to get the clients, Cass," Sword said. "Guy gives a service, people pay. Desperate people don't ask questions. We want the suppliers."

"Are they recorded?"

"Not here. They have double books, obviously. Cosmetic records go through IR."

So that was what they took home nights.

"Do we know about the doctors? How about your cams?" Moke asked.

"Murmansk and Yakimura," Sword supplied. "I put one on each. Yakimura was working at the clinic, Cass laid him out there. We got that on film. He's the cosmeticist, I guess they've got to do some authentic business if only for cover. Murmansk's the psychosurgeon and senior partner. Went home early, been there ever since. Private lab at his house. Has a license for experimentation. Couldn't get a good look, windows are poled. Cam's waiting around, he's still there."

"Careless of them to keep Ottery's body."

"Or careful," Sword said. "Depends who's paying and what for, doesn't it?"

"So what do we do now?" Moke asked.

Swordfish and Hallway both looked at him. At least

Hall did and I thought Sword's head was turned.

"Send the files to the public prosecutor. Anonymously."

"After Hall's read them. We look first. Maybe there's something we ought to know."

"Real public-spirited guys," I said. "We know Dein isn't Ottery but we still don't know who he is."

Swordfish lay back on the couch. "I'd quite like to talk to Murmansk. Right now I need sleep."

"And when you're through pigging?"

"Maybe we can go search a sandwich box."

It was dark again. I seemed permanently around at the wrong end of the day. I guess old habits are hard to shake. We were out at Riverside for the second time, running the length of the chain of beads that marked the development.

Yeller flew our hired copt sedately and Moke sat in front in evening velvet and ruffles trying to look like he didn't mind.

The radio crackled as we approached the last-but-one bead containing the conference center.

"Identification."

Yell reached for the tag. "Wright Allen, for Mr. Martin Faber. Mr. Faber's speaking at the Arts Society meeting tonight. His business manager Miss Blaine's doing the slides. Request landing space."

They looked us over. I sat upright in back in my silver chain cocktail overall and looked like there was a bad smell. There was. I had Swordfish flattened invisibly against the side door and Dribble on the carpet under my feet. The little bastard was drooling lasciviously on my ankles and I was sitting on my kick until the cops couldn't hear the yelp.

"Granted," the radio said curtly, and cut out.

I let the kick go, Dribble yelped, and Mokey turned a

pathetic face. "Do I have to?"

"Yes," Sword said. "It's dark and crowded, nobody's going to notice Cass isn't there. Show them pretty slides and talk plenty of garbage, then answer a lot of questions. Until she gets back. Then we go home. Right?"

"Yell'll hold your hand," I told him consolingly.

"I'll put his slides in order, anyhow," Yell said. "Spell me when you get back and with any luck it'll look as if you've been there all the time. Just don't bring me any corpses, I'm overloaded already."

"We'll compensate," Swordfish said. "If we bring you a corpse Dribble can walk home. It'll teach him to keep his tongue to himself."

Yeller laughed and Dribble whined piteously. So did Moke. Give them time and they were going to turn into a great double act.

The conference center was full to the doors and Mokey got the recognition he hates. I walked with my hand under his elbow smiling graciously and Yell carried the slide-box.

We twisted Moke's arm into sitting at the front and Yell and me went to the projection room to fuss. After we'd done it enough to get noticed I had an urgent natural function and hip-swayed to the Ladies. I stripped off fast, threw on my suit and slid out the cubicle and the door. Self-closing doors are a great help to guys in coolsuits. It's nice to know science is still doing its best in the cause of crime.

Outside I sprinted. A whimper between two copts said Sword and Dribble were on hand and Sword was working on Dribble's social education. With him it means kicking the little brute's behind every time he shoves his nose up someone's crotch. I think he should leave it to Moke. He specializes in children and animals and Dribble's both.

"Hi, guys. We going?"

Sword's blurred shadow slid out from the fuselage and Dribble followed on all fours, belly to the ground. If he met anyone it was going to be hysterics in spades— he's not one of nature's happier thoughts—but we were headed away.

The pad was planted with rhododendrons and other delicious things which also ease the lives of the criminal classes. I followed Dribble's slinking silhouette and crawled through branches to bare grass. We seemed to be alone. Bright patches of light and shade gave us perfect coolsuit cover and the macaw chatter of artlovers came from the far side. They sounded happily self-absorbed.

Swordfish isn't exactly normal. His implants give him vision at inhuman frequencies and he acts as test pilot for Hall's weirder devices. He found the edge of the bead and made us a hole. We slid out onto acid-nourished grass.

"How many domes?"

"Only two if we cut through. This guy's rich."

"Great. Hope they haven't pets, I hate leaving a trail of dead dogs. Upsets the kids."

"Sentiment," Sword said.

"I'm squeamish."

"Nature ain't. Move, pup, and don't fraternize."

That was a thought. I'd supposed Dribble fancied humans but he could be catholic. With him it's difficult to tell which half's leading.

We cantered the few hundred yards to the neighboring shield. Three houses around a central wood with jogging paths. Rich, but not crazy rich. We cut across a garden with glimmering pool, windows lit behind polarizing shades. There was a dog, a floppy kind of collie out for its nightly round. Dribble touched noses and we parted on good terms. It didn't bark but it looked the kind licks burglars' hands wherever it finds them.

We jogged the wood to the other side and over another garden with elaborate beds and a cat. It hissed and shot up the nearest tree. Dribble took off two steps before Sword's foot connected. He rolled in silence, collected himself and licked with injured dignity. Unhappily his anatomy lets him do that.

The exit was in another smelly thicket and I had to bite on a sneeze. Flower beds don't agree with me. I managed to fall outside first. Sword didn't kick me but I felt him controlling himself. I snarled on principle.

The next dome held a single isolated house which says big, big money. Doctors rate as Techs and only Ari industrials get space to themselves. Unless you're a guy does the right kind of service for Ari industrials. I thought I might dislike Murmansk.

Swordfish approached with caution. He tested the shield before he used his torch and did some work with a scope.

"Suspicious bastard. More advanced life-detection. We're going to have bloodshed. Jack up. Dribble, keep behind. Some people think I'm responsible for you."

Dribble obeyed, snuffling.

"And keep your nose out of Cass's hind end or the blood'll be yours." Three seconds too late.

I kicked him myself. He swallowed it. There are things Sword's better not to know.

The shrubbery grew right to the shield-edge, which can mean mantraps. A wide swath of shaved lawn, gray in the diffused light, separated it from the house. That can mean a desire to see what's coming.

Not reassuring.

My jacked-in rifle showed Sword moving through the trees, the beam from his scope sweeping ground and foliage in front. He braked suddenly and put out a hand. Dribble hunts by nose so he'd stopped already.

Sword beckoned and I slid up beside him. Force lines in

front. He raised the scope slowly to let me see the barrier rose all of twelve feet.

"Uh-oh," I whispered.

"Uh-huh. I can jump it. You can't. How's your vaulting?"

"Pole? You got to be kidding."

"Grav-trampoline. Dribble can make it, but I want you."

"Right. It's my business, dammit."

"You're adult," he hissed back. "Though it doesn't always show."

"I'm too crushed to jump."

"Not yet, but you will be."

Guys always want the last word. I saved time by shutting up and looking submissive. Dribble had settled back on his haunches in case we meant to have a really showy fight. When we didn't he looked resigned.

Swordfish drew back as far as the vegetation would let him, got in three strides and took off with calculated power. He rolled at the top of his jump, pulled up his legs and landed on his feet at the other side.

"You next," he whispered from across the screen. "The tramp's in front of you. Three or four strides, land in the middle and give yourself less impulsion than you think you need. Enough for what you'd rate at three feet. Only keep your legs up or you'll touch the edge of the field. And don't break your neck in the branches. Come on."

I looked at the glowing rectangle without dancing a jig. It's the sort of thing you'd like three or four weeks to practice. I suppose it showed Sword's confidence. I wished he had less.

I backed off, took the four steps I had room for and loped up. I hit it squarely with both feet, took a little bounce and went up like a rocket. It was as well he'd mentioned the branches. It was pure luck I didn't break my neck. I grabbed instinctively, pivoted on my hands like Tarzan and managed to direct my swing in Sword's direction before I did a complete circle.

"Clown," he snarled, snatching me out of the air. "Could you do that on purpose?"

"So give me warning. If you want circus tricks I gotta practice. We're not all as weird as you."

He didn't bother to reply. Dribble came across with a neat standing hop but it wasn't fair. He had four paws.

"Let's hope there aren't any more or I'm going to have to go back for the tramp." Sword was advancing an inch at a time, scope in hand. "Uh-huh. This one's the broad jump. You can do this, Cassandra. About twelve feet. Give me your hand."

I guess Sword was made to be a trial to people like Murmansk. Guys aren't supposed to be able to hop these obstacles. His enhancements are illegal. Sometimes I see why. Dribble made a doggy bound and landed on our feet. His tongue was lolling. If he'd had a tail he'd have wagged it.

"Why hasn't he a tail?"

"Ask Moke the next time you see him," Sword snarled. "The little brute wanted one but I vetoed it. You and he go together. You're both infantile and not quite human. Clown around any more and I'm putting you both on leash."

Dribble and I fell in behind, subdued.

The shrubbery gave way to manicured lawn. We paused on the edge and looked around.

"We've got to have registered in the house, so there's some kind of reception," Swordfish whispered. "Watch it."

We didn't have to watch long. These weren't real mute hounds, just enhanced pit bulls three feet high at the shoulder with jaws like bear traps. There were four of them and they ran silent and in fan formation. I had automatic targeting and Sword had vision. God knows what Dribble had. Insanity, maybe. He uttered a yelp of joy and bounded to meet them.

I hadn't time to watch, though I hoped Sword was running protection. I used the laser on the one coming for my throat and threw myself aside to miss the still hurtling body as it crashed past my ear. When I picked myself up with not more than a dozen fresh bruises there were two corpses on the lawn with their necks at bad angles and Dribble was sitting a few yards away chewing happily on the throat of the fourth. It didn't look in good shape. He, oddly enough, did.

My respect for him went from negative right into positive. I swear the damned thing weighed twice what he did. I was the only guy who'd been wimp enough to shoot. I was going to have to eat more spinach.

"Shall we go?" Sword gave Dribble another prod with his toe to recall him to duty, and Dribble hastily dropped the remains and lolloped after us.

The house was dark. It was all rounded angles and big sweeps of glass bay with silky steel between. I guess Murmansk must have picked the design for the clinic, unless he got them as a job lot, because they resembled each other a lot.

"You're sure he's in?"

"Our cam saw him moving around inside this afternoon and he hasn't come out. So he's still in there or there's a secret passage. I don't take my oath there ain't, I just doubt it. Someone let the dogs loose."

"Maybe they were loose on principle."

"Then they got clever with the cam. Besides, I heard a latch click. It could be on remote but someone let it go."

"Are we expecting cops?"

"I think not. Last night attracted attention. This guy's into something up to his neck and I doubt if he wants too much uniformed help, they could open the wrong door.

He may have private security but they have to get here. What we do now is go in."

We walked up to the carved slab, Dribble frolicking at our heels. It was broad, heavy and looked like a door. Ironwood from the grain. And probably sandwiched with steel. It had a handplate lock.

"Damn. My gadget doesn't do handplates."

"That's okay. Mine does."

He hooked a lever from his upper pocket, slid it under the edge of the plate to a creak of stressed metal, you aren't supposed to treat handplates like that, and leaned on it. The plate flipped off like a tiddlywink and clattered on the step. That left the works on display. He wrapped his hand in insulating sheet before he shelled them out so he'd been here before. They came with a shower of sparks and a most melodious twang.

I wasn't too surprised. I've seen Swordfish crush diamonds in his bare hand and after that handplates don't astonish me. I did wonder what his lever was made of, but no doubt the same stuff as his muscles. They have great materials on battleships these days. Sword's a one-man battleship, heavy cruiser class. You'd have to ask Hallway about the gear. Not that he'd tell you.

"When reason fails, try brutality," he said pushing the door open. "If you don't mind, Cassandra, I'll go first."

We made a nice procession. Mr. Noah, Mrs. Noah and the family dog, Dribble being in one of his all-fours phases. The hall was rounded at the angles, softly carpeted and empty. Several doors opened off it. Swordfish tried them one by one without panic. They were all dark and uninhabited. We looked at each other. Or I looked at him and I thought his head turned.

"I got a feeling," I said.

"Yeah, so've I. Still don't believe in secret passages, but he's here somewhere."

"Like the priest's hole."

"Right. Dribble, seek. And when you've sought keep your damned prying nose out, this guy goes bang."

Dribble panted happily and pushed his wet drool into the cushions of a luxurious couch in old-rose shagged suede. I hoped Murmansk was as nasty as we thought because he was going to have to replace that. Anything touches Dribble has to be disinfected. Then he cast around a bit, ass in the air, and wandered into the hall.

"Can he tell where the guy is? The place must stink of him."

"Sure. Why I brought him. I generally leave the kids at home."

Dribble ran twice around the hall with his snout to the ground and took a sudden turn out back.

"Uh-huh," Sword said. "What do you bet on a basement?"

"Not a cent. Anything else would surprise me."

Out back a corridor led to the kitchen. More buttons than a shirt factory, and a routine domestic in rest-mode.

"He wants us to think he's out," Sword murmured. "I hate people who underrate my intelligence. Where's the door, Dribble?"

Dribble was on a circuit of the floor, so truly dog I was almost surprised when he spoke.

"Behind refrigerator. In, not out yet. You look."

"Okay. Stand back."

He ran the scope over it while I peered beneath his elbow. Behind the refrigerator the line showed clearly with its rectangle of lock.

"Another handplate, or is he confident?"

He felt around. The guy was confident. It opened with a snap when he touched it. Steps led down behind the swung-out machinery.

"Dribble, stay here and whistle if anything happens. Don't go to sleep and don't be heroic. All we want's warning." He jerked his head. "Okay, girl."

He shifted the gun from his faster-than-light hand back to the supernatural one, bent his head and stepped inside. I gripped my laser and followed.

The steps led down a good-sized flight with a turn in the middle and came out on a square landing floored with plastic tiles. The port of a service elevator opened to one side.

Sword shrugged. "Kid's talented, not clairvoyant, he scented on the guy. Meant for goods, would you say?"

There was a door in front of us. He tapped politely and walked in. It's wiser when you think the answer may be high-frequency radiation.

Inside was a laboratory-cum-study with bench and library furniture, and there was a guy in it, a medium-sized square guy with a well-fed complexion and reassuring silvery hair. I bet his bedside manner was terrific. Just like Baron Frankenstein's.

He didn't have a gun. He had a little gas-cylinder, a mouth and nose mask and a jumpy look. But he was prepared to be high-horsed first.

"What's the meaning of this?" he said.

If I knew Sword he was about to find out.

Trouble with gas-cylinders is you need to see what you're firing at. Murmansk couldn't. He knew someone had come in. He didn't know who or in what direction.

Sword and I get moments of telepathy. He was in front with my nose looking past his elbow. His gun was shielded by his hip and mine by his body. He moved right as I moved left, freeing both our artillery, and I slapped my control to stun in midstride.

People who don't know Sword underestimate his reach. You've got to have met him to know he's well-proportioned—too long all over. He moved faster than Murmansk and simply took the cylinder out of his hand. Then he nipped together the edges of the nozzle and folded it into a seal.

"Nice little thing," he said. "Do you think it's lethal?"

"Could be. Why don't one of us borrow the guy's mask and try it? I bet he's got a fume cabinet."

"It's an idea. Can't be fatal on skin or he'd be protected, so it's respiratory. Why don't I take him and see? It should have a window, so you can watch. Irresponsible with a child in the house. Man's a monster in human shape."

"As opposed to Dribble, who's a human in monster shape."

"You're getting to like him."

"Three of you," Murmansk said. He looked nervous, but not as nervous as he should have. "I hope the third's careful. I've delicate equipment."

"I hope so," Sword agreed. "I'm looking forward to trying it. Starting with the fume cupboard."

"Here?"

A clear bubble big enough to hold a corpse-sized table with lots of sleeves, body ports, manipulating arms and other toys not owned by the average taxpayer. It had a mini-airlock.

Swordfish hooked the tip of a finger under the straps of the mask, flipped and fitted it on his own head. It looked bizarre but threatening. Like *It Came from Outer Space* and wasn't going back nearly as fast as it might.

"Okay," he said. "March."

Murmansk laughed. "Now, let's not be foolish. I don't know what you want but there's no need for pranks. Call your colleague and let's have a calm adult discussion. I'm sure we can reach a solution."

"He thinks we're pranking," I said. Not adding the next guy has a calm adult anything with Dribble will be the first.

"So he does. He also thinks we don't know he's waiting for reserves."

He pushed Murmansk towards the fume cupboard. The doctor resisted.

"If you want money the safe's upstairs, I'll give you the combination. But if you're who I think, maybe we can talk."

"He's a humorist. First he tries to gas us then he wants a conference."

"While the cavalry comes galloping, galloping, galloping."

"Cupboard's quicker."

"Wait," Murmansk said rapidly. "We can talk. I need to know your terms and the quality of your goods. I never interfere in professional quarrels. If the territory's yours I'm willing to deal with you."

"He started thinking we were safebreakers, now he thinks we sell bits of people. I'm insulted."

"So'm I. It's lucky we left Dribble upstairs."

"Very. I'm supposed to be giving the brat a moral education. This kind of talk'll give him bad ideas."

"Shall we gas him now?"

"I think we'd better. Before he debauches the youth of the city."

"Who's listening at the door if I know anything about him."

"He'd better not be," Sword said grimly. "I left him to guard our rear."

We listened to a soft receding scamper that disappeared upstairs.

"Evil-minded brat," his master concluded. "Open the lock, partner."

I did. If he really gassed the guy I was going to be pissed off but it's as well not to interrupt Sword when he's busy.

Murmansk looked slightly worried. I guess the cavalry weren't all that close.

"Don't be unintelligent," he said, his voice climbing a tone or two as he tried to shrug his luxey knit jacket out of Sword's hand. "I've high-placed friends, very high-placed friends. I'm willing to talk to you in spite of the damage you've done already but my patience isn't endless. I advise you to consider your actions carefully."

"He knows guys," I said, with admiration. "Trapeze artists."

"So he says. What he doesn't know is me."

"I bet he's going to."

"Right." Sword heaved, or so I deduced, since Murmansk flew about three feet into the air and came down in the entry to the lock. He had another try at twisting out of the grasp on his collar and didn't get anywhere.

"There's no need for violence," he said with something that was trying to be dignity. "It's natural I should protect myself. One of your group injured my partner. The gas isn't lethal in small quantities. It would have disabled you, which is what you'd do yourselves. If it isn't vented quickly it can damage your lungs. You've no reason to harm me. I'm doing my best to cooperate."

"Shall we damage his lungs?"

"I wonder where he's going to vent it. This city has a pollution problem."

"That's because guys like him keep venting lung-damagement into the public air supply. Okay, let's torture him instead."

"If you want. What you got in mind?"

"Well." Swordfish hauled Murmansk over to a steel-and-leather desk chair to match a steel-and-leather desk and plonked him in it.

Murmansk sat with a whooshing expulsion of breath like a balloon going down. He was gray and his thick silvery hair was ruffled.

Sword has that effect on people.

"The guy's a doctor so he should have surgical materials. Tape, bandages? Have a look, Loot. I'm getting tired of holding him, his after-shave's making me quaky."

I opened cupboards at random. They were full of bottles and boxes, packets, packages and little racks of colored ampoules. I found elastic bandage and passed it.

"Self-adhesive. That do?"

"I'd rather it was him-adhesive but we'll manage."

Murmansk wriggled furiously as Swordfish bandaged. I could have told him it was a waste of time. I've never got anywhere with Sword and with me he doesn't even try to be rough.

"Just what do you want?" he asked breathlessly. His lips were blue. "You can't be here for entertainment.

In any case, I warn you I've called my security service. They'll be here almost at once."

"Let's hope they aren't. I don't want to play Little Big Horn. I'm one of the Indians." Sword sounded as if he'd just turned on the holo and found a soap opera. Bored, but not terminally. "We're a deputation from the city and people of Ashton. We represent the Public Prosecutor and since he's not clever he needs all the help he can get."

"Public Prosecutor?" Murmansk was trying to be scornful. "We're an entirely legal organization. Our operations are on the net as the law requires. If I've made a mistake it's because your infantile vandalism made me think you dangerous."

"And now you know we're wooly lambs. It's odd you wanted to talk business. Body-legging business. Or was I mistaken?"

Murmansk sneered. "What body-legging? All I know is you broke into my house and threatened me."

"When you were simply getting ready to combat-gas us in a concealed cellar like any ordinary honest citizen."

"I know it's inconvenient, but my other half went into your lab with a recorder and taped all you've got. I believe she did meet your partner. She was nice to him, she has a sympathetic soul. The tapes don't look good."

"I'm a respected member of the medical establishment. Do you think the Public Prosecutor's going to listen to a group of petty criminals?"

"Actually," Swordfish murmured, "the guy who did my implants was also a respected member of the medical establishment. It's no use denying the tapes, we've played them. Loot here stripped out your personal in her spare time. I'd say we've a proven case. Illegal experiments and body-legging. But we aren't vindictive. I don't see any reason to punish your clients. Do you, woman?"

"Nope. My aims were more specific."

"Maybe we could talk about the specific aims of my mate."

"If the lady were to define her aims," Murmansk said. His color was improving and he was getting back his little chipper air. He tossed his silver pompadour trying to get it back to where his hairdresser put it.

"He's waiting for the cavalry."

"Then we'll have to speed up. Trouble is, doc, we don't trust you. Rational discussion's a waste of time because you aren't rational. Limits us."

Swordfish wandered absently between the steel-and-leather desk, the fine teak work bench and the operating table with a battery of dead floods above on the other side of the room. It had the hood of a complex air-extractor capping it like a snuffer. I didn't think I wanted to be one of the doctor's patients.

"I wonder what these are for," Sword said, reaching into a cupboard. He took down several cardboard drums and spilled a cocktail of derms into the palm of his glove. It went derm-colored. "Shall we try them and see?"

"We could," I said doubtfully. "He might just pass out and wake up with his brains scrambled."

"But would it make him happy? And would it amuse us? I don't like him."

Murmansk looked apprehensive. "Be careful. Some of those medicines are dangerous. You don't know what you're meddling with."

"Right. That's what's amusing. Or—" Sword reached down a glass bottle with a paper label. It was filled with clear liquid and sealed with a rubber diaphragm. "Look here, my child. It's got the base coordinates of the Universe written on it in Greek. And you get to put it in with a real hypodermic." He held it up glittering. "I've never seen one before except on vids. The kind where they die screaming. In a vein? We could try. Maybe we'll get a big bang."

Murmansk had gone waxy yellow. "Put it back," he said thinly. "That's modified Hansen's disease."

Sword went rigid. "Hansen's disease?"

I saw Moke in green and red and Hallway walking like his spine was hinged. "Modified."

"I wonder what it does. Or do we know?"

"I think we know rather well."

"Maybe I'd better put him in the fume cupboard after all. Sounded like this stuff infects fast. Go wait outside. This could be nasty."

Sword's warm velvet voice can sound like something you get on the late late show leaves you coaxing the children down from the curtains. He'd lifted his filters. Murmansk looked into his naked gray eyes and believed him. I believed him. The bottle glittered in the light like a complex crystal.

"Sword . . ."

"Outside, woman."

Murmansk was sweating. The skin of his forehead under the rich silver hair was tight and pearled with dew. A drop gathered at the edge of his scalp and ran down the side of his face to the angle of his jaw where it disappeared wetly into his collar.

I thought again about Hall and Mokey and went.

I sat on the bottom step for a long time and waited. The door stayed closed. It was soundproof. Dribble stayed upstairs. Swordfish's educational methods had to be working. To some degree.

After a long time Sword came out, filters down. He moved like he was tired.

"Did you—?"

"Sorry, Cass. I did not. Stuff's too damned dangerous. We could have had an epidemic, starting with me. What I did was convince the good doctor I was willing to."

"He cracked?"

"From side to side. He's liable to have seven years' bad luck, starting now."

"He did—that—to Antonia Lopez?"

"He sold it to a guy who bought it. It's how he makes money. He's also sold it to other guys. Such as the Government."

"I guess that figures."

"Who did you think was paying? He was coy about his client. Or really didn't know him. I leaned fairly hard."

"But why, Sword?"

"You want a laugh?"

"Can you give me one?"

"No." He sat beside me and leaned sharp elbows on his knees. "It's no way funny. But it's how it had to be. Coelacanth were actually interested in Doshchenko as more than a plaything. So when Nimbus laid him out they slammed the remains in cryo while you and Moke were leaving by the back, and whipped him out to old pal Murmansk. Or more probably Yakimura, who's the restructural guy. And he remade him."

"Using bits of Ottery."

"Murmansk used the bits of Ottery. I know you don't like me to say this, Cass, but the guy was a prostitute. And they had a respectable Art on hold with terminal injuries and no family. So Murmansk, who does the psych bits, remade his mind. Out of Ottery's memories. Dein's not Doshchenko except the corpse and the stem-brain. It's the cortex makes character, and there Doshchenko's gone. What's left's a kind of Ottery amalgam. Neither one nor the other."

"Could Ottery have lived?" I asked with difficulty.

"If anyone had cared enough. If his sister had known. But they didn't know he had a sister. Until recently. The memory-transplant killed him, in any case. That's why the doc's keeping the body, obviously. Doesn't trust his paymaster."

"Particularly since what happened to Antonia."

"It would sober a man who loved his skin less. It's sobered me."

Pause. He put his arm around me.

"There's more, Cass."

"Still?"

"Cordovan was set to make you a present of Dein if you accepted his film offer. But you turned it down so he kept quiet. Murmansk called you a stupid whore for not taking the chance. He doesn't know who you are, of course."

"Uh." I shuddered, looked for a reaction and found a quagmire. I'd mourned Dosh for two years and all the time Cordovan had been laughing. While Moke and me cried. Dumb guy, stupid whore. The world's full of us.

Sword dug long fingers into the back of my neck. I was getting around to sniveling when a whistle like nails on a blackboard cut my eardrums. I jumped. Sword dropped the hand to his gun. He was pointing like a hound dog.

"Cavalry. Out, Cass. Get Dribble and hit country if you can. If not, be with you."

"What're you doing?"

"Bastard passed out. I need to clear things up a bit. We need him. Move!" He gave me a shove.

I moved.

"Where boss?" Dribble fluted, sticking his head through the refrigerator.

"Clearing up. Who's out there?"

"Two copts, four or five guys each. Not police."

"Figures. Doc was expecting friends. Can we take the garden?"

"Me, yes. Got dogs. Go talk to."

"Hey, come back here!"

But he'd gone like a bare brown streak. A moment later I heard a medley of barking and snarling like dinner in the pound. Angry yells mingled with it and the sound of laser fire. Something canine squealed and the riot redoubled. Then it moved yelping and howling into the distance.

Someone outside was cursing and several pairs of boots scraped the brick by the door. I moved to a window and peered. No sign of either Dribble or dogs, though something darkly glistening smeared the bricks near the grass. He was right about the two copts and the guys.

I could only see three out front but they were enough. Dark jumps, ski helmets and automatic weapons. All the signs of private security. The others would be around the back or maybe covering from the bushes. Nobody could doubt we'd come in. Sword's methods work but they aren't discreet. If there were really eight to ten we could have a little trouble getting out.

Quick breath warmed my ear and Sword's hand leaned over onto the sill.

"Rover's gone. Took a pack of dogs. Says four or five guys per copt."

"He'll outrun them. Guys are ours."

"That's good?"

"Unless any of them knows my doctor. What's in your pockets, prophetess?"

"One gas grenade, one frag. And my tools, but they aren't going to help unless you want to walk on the ceiling."

"Think maybe I'll walk on the roof. Got a couple of incendiaries myself, but give me your frag, I can throw farther. Lie flat left of the door and keep your head down. When I give the word I want random laser-fire to the right. Like you're running across the lawn, got it? When they look away get up the stairs fast. Meet you on the landing."

I flopped. Sword knelt at the other side, disruptor raised. The guys outside were still pissing around. It looked like Dribble's maneuvers with the dogs had upset them. They weren't sure if we were still in there or not. And Sword's habits with handplates don't take the place of a welcome mat. I cuddled my rifle.

"Count three and go. Now."

On one he gave the door a shove with his gun muzzle that shuddered it inward, on two he loosed a random volley across the steps, and on three he lobbed the grenade out into the garden. It struck in the bushes and hung. I let off the laser in the opposite direction, gave it a good spray, and turned for the stairs like a rabbit.

Sword followed. More like a weasel. The grenade went off maybe five seconds later and showered the front of the house with shrapnel and blasted leaves. The guys outside were flat, gloves over their helmets, but I could hear the bits clattering off the roof. Glass shattered.

"Okay. You and I left by the front door. They've figured we're suited but they won't die of surprise. Like I said, if anybody went to the same doctor I did he also knows we're still here and things're getting serious. If not, which I'm relying on, we stay peaceably upstairs until they feel brave enough to come investigate. Then we leave and go home. Suit you?"

"Master suite or guestroom?"

"Let's see if there's a Mrs. Murmansk first," he suggested ironically. "She may care."

We slid along a corridor done up in mossy silk-pile, my sighting brackets outlining everything in super tri-D like an old-fashioned stereoscope. A pair of pink-painted double doors picked out in gold were closed. Sword laid his ear against the panel. He shook his head and jerked a thumb forward.

The next door was single and got the same routine. He opened it gently, relaxed, and pointed in. This one had to belong to a teenager who had to be in college but wasn't right now in bed. I made a face at the pennants, which looked like the last hours of the Alamo, and a multi-keyboard synth, short of incisors. When the owner came home it wasn't going to be pleased. The window faced forward and fractured glass glittered everywhere.

"Madam's whimpering under her pillow by the sound. If she gets rash and comes out try saying boo. She could have hidden reserves but I doubt it. I'll be back. Oh, and give me your gasser. I may use it."

"Try not to break anything. You're getting us a bad name."

"I'll be considerate."

He went. I guess he found a use for Hall's craftwork. I leaned on the windowsill avoiding the sharper edges of glass and looked down at three guys prodding among the bushes like they expected a minefield. I kept an ear out for Mrs. Doc but she didn't show. The echo of a soft plop came from somewhere behind and a brilliant flare lit up the night leaving me with violent after-images. Something distant began to crackle. A smell of smoke drifted over the house mixed with a stench I didn't want to know.

Sword arrived silently beside me. He got his elbows on the sill in time to see two of the three guys pick up their guns and leave at the double.

"Q.E.D.," he said. "Got suckers?"

"You think I'm an amateur. But only four. Think we can make it on hands only?"

"Thanks, but it's what, twenty feet? Kit up and come after me. When you hit ground make for the trees and remember the tank traps."

"Could I forget?"

"Knowing you, yes."

He went over the sill in a one-handed vault and vanished. I didn't wait to see what dimension he ended up in. I slid over the jagged frame and did the second-fastest sucker-job of my life toward the good doctor's azaleas. In theory I was invisible but that didn't stop me expecting a shot between the shoulder blades.

It didn't come. When I squelched into the decor Guy Three was on the ground communing with nature and my little friend Swordfish had evaporated. Again. For well over six-and-a-half feet of overenhanced bone and muscle he hazes off like smoke.

I dived into what was left of the trees and catted across. Without Sword's scope I couldn't be sure where the field was so I had to keep stopping and heaving bits of twig into the darkness. I'd just located the first zip of blue flame when he arrived noiselessly at my elbow and nearly scared me out of my skin.

"I wish you'd knock. Where you been?"

"Taking bits out of their copts. They're busy around the back trying to stop Papa Murmansk's garage going up in smoke, except the two who're beating the bushes for the guy who lets off gas bombs. Give me your hand."

He took it without waiting for my adult consent and hopped me over the field. When we got to the faint square of tramp on the far side of the screen he flipped across, threw the tramp back and stood with folded arms like Crazy Horse meditating the fate of the paleface.

"Okay, you've had practice. Get it right."

The lovely boy. I was feeling as if I'd been through a mangle. Since it wasn't any use telling him so I glumly backed off, took four lumbering steps, and bounced. Maybe because I hadn't any hope I sailed over like a gull and landed on my feet. Don't imagine he was impressed. Crazy Horse still being full of whatever it is animates lunatics, he went back for the tramp and packed it in his kangaroo.

"Wouldn't like them to trace it. Okay, we're through."

"In principle. What you bet the neighbors are on their lawns watching the fireworks?"

"I hope so. Means they aren't going to see another damned thing."

• • •

He was right. We slid out of the Murmansk dome, arrived in the smelly things back of the second house, skirted a babble of guys in luxury nightwear all staring eagerly at the sky, hissed at the cat and jogged through the little wood. There was a second gathering yacking their heads off with their neighbors—which stopped them noticing their dog barking at us—and we landed back in no-man's-land in sight of the Conference Center without killing anyone.

"Sword, I'm pooped. Do you really think I'm going to get back into silver mail and stilt sandals and look like a cocktail party?"

"Sure. You've been working your fingers to the bone over a hot projector all night. Come on, kid, we've exactly a hundred yards to go."

He was lying. But he did give me a hand to pull, let us both in, and slide us among the copts. There was nobody about. Even the doorman was sitting in his booth with his back turned.

"Thank God for coffee breaks."

"See you in."

And he did, right to the door of the Ladies. The doorman went on drinking coffee. When I came out five minutes later in silver chain he looked slightly surprised, but I guess anything happens at upper-class Arts bashes. I'd say I kept him from his supper doughnut four whole seconds.

I limped into the projection booth and found Yell looking impassive, which is as close as he gets to panic. Moke was explaining something about plastic values and fidelity to natural form to a guy with a honking voice. He was so earnestly patient you could tell he was long gone and talking in his sleep.

Yell lit up at me like a shipwrecked mariner seeing a sail, a sail and made one white flash with the projector.

Moke cracked a full-wattage smile and astounded the type
with the honk, who probably hadn't been smiled at since
his mama quit buttoning his panties. He babbled, "Thank
you, that's the last question," and left the stage as if he'd
won the lottery.

Two minutes later we were collapsed in a heap at the
back of the hall taking nips out of Yell's private flask
and failing to listen to a lady explaining plastic values
and fidelity to natural form as expressed in her collection
of antique lace doilies. For a guy who's off the sauce
Yell makes a lot of provision. I decided not to quarrel
about it.

"Cassie, don't ever do that again," Moke whimpered,
trying to climb in my lap. "I've been answering imbecile
questions for three million years until I'd started to believe
my own answers. If I go on like this I'm going to end up
a critic."

"Seventy-eight minutes," Yell said, looking at his wrist.
"It's okay, Cass, we've had the plastic qualities and fidelity to nature of the paintings of El Greco while you were
gone. Moke's slaughtered 'em. How's Sword?"

There's a connection of ideas there if you look for it.

We got to the copt after twenty minutes' applause, and
a load of learned garbage Moke was luckily too well-lit
to hear. Yell's flask was a lot emptier than it had been.
All around evening suits were babbling happily to dinner
dresses. By contrast the back of the copt was peacefully
silent. It worried me.

I leaned over and looked down.

"Hi," Dribble fluted, lifting one eyelid slightly. "Don't
wake up boss."

I leaned down further. "You okay, Fido?"

"Me?" He yawned, showing ivory fangs and a throat
as deep as the San Andreas Fault. "Sure. Had nice game
with cop doggies. Ran around and around and led 'em

into poodle hotel." His grin was probably, in his terms, sweetly childlike. "Made beautiful big noise. Poodle hotel people very cross with cop-dog people. I think they going to get lots of big litters mixed puppies."

"Loathsome brat."

I grabbed him by the nearest hairy ear, hauled him to my level and planted a kiss on one of the drier parts of his cheek. When I let go it had gone scarlet.

"Thanks, Lassie. Remind me to buy you a bone. Clever little bastard."

He wriggled happily. "Soon you get to like me nearly's much as Sword."

"God forbid."

I'd figured on staying in front to comfort Moke but either Dribble was mistaken or Sword was foxing. As I made to sit an invisible hand grabbed the back strap of my chain overall and hauled me bodily onto what felt like knees. Then he draped long arms around my neck and really went to sleep. It didn't make any special difference. Moke was unconscious too.

Me and Yell were the only guys still awake. We exchanged sympathetic looks in the mirror.

After a bit he passed me his flask and I raised it to gulp. Sword's mystic hand caught it in midair like the Lady of the Lake taking off with Excalibur and emptied the last inch through a temporary slit over his mouth. It's the first time I've ever seen him drink in public. Then he hiccupped and passed out.

"Big white chief slewed," I said to Yell.

"In that case," he said, "I'll make you a prophecy. Big white chief may not be ordinary guy, but tomorrow morning he's gonna have one real ordinary headache."

"Wrong," Sword said from the depths of his slumbers. "You any idea what alcohol does to my metabolism? Tomorrow I'm going to have a headache you never thought of."

•   •   •

Then he settled down to absentmindedly cracking my ribs and we all breathed heavily.

Well, I guess Yeller was awake.

He got us home, anyhow.

"I hate it," Moke said. "Dein was Dosh and now he's a second-hand Ottery and you want to leave it alone? Haven't you guys any moral sense?"

He was Moke-normal this morning, worn-out jeans, T-shirt belonged either to Yell or Hallway since it didn't fit him, bare feet, his cheekbones gravelly with powder that could have been pink granite dust. I guess it was a reaction to three hours in an evening suit. He'd been waiting for me to wake up and tell him the story, and now he'd heard it, it was sticking in his throat.

"He's alive, Moke," Hallway said.

"Alive and happy," Sword said. "What would be so moral about breaking him up, Martin?"

Mokey had tears on his spiky blond lashes. "It's a lie, that's what. Dosh was in love with me, he was generous and kind. Now he's some kind of a doll with Coelacanth pulling his strings and he doesn't even know. We got to tell him."

"He won't believe it, Moke. He knows he's Dein. And they did it partly because he was a hooker. How's Aurora going to relate to that? She thinks he's a nice Art boy too."

"If she loves him she won't care. You didn't. And you're letting Coelacanth walk away? They let you expose Nimbus knowing the guy you did it for was alive, and they killed

103

her to stop her saying so. They could have prevented it. They didn't. I guess the film came out more interesting that way."

"Now, that's another question." If Swordfish had a headache he was living it in silence. "Two. One, can we leave Coelacanth alone? Two, how badly does Cass need this guy?"

"I never had him, Sword. I wanted him but he didn't want me. He was nice to me because he was like that. It's over. As soon as I saw Aurora I knew."

Moke looked at the floor as if the gray insutiles had some fascinating texture he'd never noticed before.

"Coelacanth created Nimbus."

"She may have had something to do with creating herself," Hallway said. "Nobody's got to be like that."

"Haven't you the smallest pity left, Cass?"

"I think that's the unkindest thing I ever heard you say. Yes, but I think Sword's right. Maybe we can only make trouble."

"And I think you didn't hear me," Swordfish said. "Doshchenko isn't in there anymore. The guy's Dein. He doesn't remember you. He'll never remember you. Doshchenko's dead."

"Not for me he isn't."

"Coelacanth values him," I said. "It's what Dosh wanted."

"He never wanted this. How many people do they have to kill before it counts?"

"We can't change the world, Genius. Or I can't. Takes all the running I can do to keep the Strip in the same place."

"I was working," Moke said tiredly. "I'm going to work some more."

And he padded off to the next-door cellar where he was drilling a rock or rolling in glue, I wasn't sure which. From his pants it could have been either. His head was lowered over red eyes. He looked alone and dejected.

Sure he couldn't forgive us. He isn't stubborn or stupid, he understood just fine. It's how you see things. For Sword, Dosh was gone. For me, there was enough left for me to think he was alive at some level and I thought he was happy. I also thought for me it was finally over. For Moke he was plain still there. Even if he was only a stem-brain. Even if the crocodile wasn't rational and would never know him, he knew it. He'd loved it when it was a man and he wasn't going to abandon it now. Not if it killed him. Our desert genius.

And the biggest traitor was me. Sword doesn't count, they never did get on. I had some grit in the eyes myself.

"Poor Mokey," I said. "He was hit when Dein didn't know him. Harder than me, and that's funny because he wasn't in love with Dosh and I was. I guess he isn't the getting-over kind."

"I'm acquainted with the state. What do you say, Hall?"

"It's insoluble. You're both right. If you interfere you could spoil all Dein's got. But Coelacanth smells and I don't see a way out."

"So what do we do?"

"Nothing, Cass. If you leave things alone they've a habit of coming out themselves."

They did.

The noon newscast came first. A medium-sized item:

DEATH OF SOCIETY DOCTOR

Murmansk's body, apparently overcome by fumes, had been found in the basement of his burned-out house. His wife was critically ill and in a coma. Neighbors had seen smoke, flames, and flashes, and a gang battle was suspected, they didn't say what about. It was also possible a chemical experiment had gone wrong, Murmansk being a distinguished man of science.

I looked at Swordfish, or where I thought I'd find him.

"Not guilty. My incendiaries went in the bushes. We left the lady in her room and Murmansk had thrown a faint but he was alive. I didn't want the cavalry to find him in too big a mess. So I put things back, broke a couple of cabinets like the Body-leggers' Revenge, and left. I wanted him for the Public Prosecutor. If he'd followed through, a few big heads might have rolled, Murmansk knew stuff. I doubt if it'll happen now. Murmansk had the evidence. What do you bet things have changed at the clinic too?"

"You mean somebody's got around to burying Ottery."

"I'd suppose so. Him and a couple of other incriminating details."

"Why Mrs.?"

"She was there. These guys make a clean sweep. It's a principle."

"I love principles. How safe's Yakimura?"

"Let's hope he has the sense to take a holiday. A long holiday far away."

He hadn't. That hit the news late afternoon.

DOC TWO IN SPACEYARD SMASH

By a tragic coincidence Murmansk's partner had stepped in front of a heavy slider that hadn't been able to stop. Death was instantaneous. His services would be much missed at the Riverside Clinic where . . .

Nobody bothered to explain why a serious medic had been cruising around the entry to the spaceyards where heavyweight sliders have a habit of coming out of dock gates too fast.

"Some people'll believe anything," Swordfish said. "Did

I tell you I persuaded Murmansk to give me a little piece of paper?"

"Yeah? With what?"

"The base coordinates of the Universe, press Delete. Sent 'em to Mdina. Tell you later if they work. He didn't know, it's experimental." I could feel his shark grin. "Why do you think I left him alive?"

Yell brought the second item home. He works for Moke and me, especially Moke, but he isn't a slave. When we don't need him he's free and nobody asks what he does with his time.

He doesn't get drunk since he had his liver fixed but his other urges are normal. Or that's my impression. A procession of ladies, most human, many female and a lot surprisingly attractive, troop in and out of his quarters. He's a good-looking guy and he wasted a long time under our steps.

So it didn't surprise us when he dropped into Hall's cellar with a bim. It's true Hall's cellar was getting a bit like Grand Central Station but Hall was being nice about it. What did surprise me was the bim. Yell exercises a lot of good taste. Normally.

"Meet Caronne. Have a piece of floor, doll."

"Thanks a lot," she said in a gravelly voice. "What is this, a freaks' convention?"

The personnel at that moment was me, Hall, Dribble, Swordfish who as usual wasn't visible, and Mokey much smeared with clay, who was. We all and severally took offense except Hallway who grinned, and Moke who doesn't recognize insults.

I got to make it clear the lady wasn't the local Harvest Queen. Yell's in his forties and she was giving him seven-to-twenty-five. Which wouldn't have mattered if she hadn't been disfigured with it. I'd say the mess that used to be the right-hand side of her face had been acid and a decent cosmetician would have regenned her eye or removed it altogether. I doubt if she could see anything with it but it was visible to other people. Like it should have belonged to a baked fish.

The rest was lank, flabby and wearing puce satin with peeling spangles and black leg-warmers that didn't make her look like a dancer. I'd have said her hair was a wig. If it wasn't she had just cause to sue her hairdresser. She'd done her best with a couple of kilos of terra-cotta correction stick and it hadn't corrected her. I figured nothing could, short of either major regeneration or death.

"Hi," I said guardedly. "Want a drink?"

"Sure," she graveled, running her remaining eye up and down me like there was some kind of contest. "Vodka."

"I got beer and beer," Hallway said.

"Okay, I'll have beer."

Her perfume must have cost five cents an ounce and I guess she'd bathed in it. Sword, whose heightened senses can make life difficult, sneezed and stood up.

"Hey, hold it," said Yell, who's got enough used to our friends to read shifts of reality. "You don't want to leave yet, Sword. Give the lady a beer. I spent time finding her."

"You could have brought the whole truck," Sword said. "Genius has some garbage to dispose of himself while you're here."

"If you're going to be insulting . . ." the harpy said, tossing her purple dreadlocks.

"Don't listen, doll. Have some snake oil," Yell consoled, passing a can.

"That ain't garbage, it's his latest work in progress." I'm always willing to keep the peace. It's unlucky the chance seldom comes my way.

"Tell us why we're going to be so happy to make the lady's acquaintance, Yell," Hallway said.

"Apart from her personal charm," Sword added.

Dribble sniggered and inchwormed closer to the hem of her skirt. Sword and I kicked simultaneously, which produced an injured howl and a complaint it wasn't fair. It also rolled him onto my feet since Sword kicks harder. Moke, who'd gone for glasses, came back in time to stop the fight.

"Hey, guys," Yeller said. "I told you, I went to trouble. The lady's a friend of some old friends."

"Which?"

Medusa tossed her hair some more and took a pull from her can. Then she asked suspiciously, "You got bugs?"

"Only a couple of roaches," Hallway said. "It's old property. The electronics I take care of myself. Up to date we're bug-free."

She gazed ungraciously around, pulling on her can and squinting at us over the rim. "Who's the guy in the suit?"

"Ignore him. He's not really here."

"Yeah. I met that kind. Lost skin to 'em."

"Not to me," Sword said. "I'm not a pimp, I'm a demolition expert. I've better things to do than lay discipline on thieving whores. If you're going to talk either do it or wash. I didn't bring nose filters."

She considered us some more. "If I do it's for him," she said defiantly, jerking her head at Yeller. "I'm taking his word for the rest of the circus."

"His word's good," Moke said.

"Okay. He says you guys got a quarrel with Coelacanth."

"You could say," I said.

"Right. So've I. Two, though one's too old to interest anyone."

"Like?"

She turned me her one bloodshot eye. It had been brown and maybe nice. These days it worked too hard for too little return.

"Like my sister. What's your beef?"

"Guy we knew."

"Dead?"

"That's the problem. He is and he ain't if you see what I mean."

"No, but I believe it. My sister's dead. Got another beer, Luney?"

"Sure," Hallway said. "Same or different?"

"Doesn't matter so long's it's alcoholic. Don't suppose any you freaks got a joint?"

Moke fished in his jeans and found a bent relic with some scented fronds draggling out. He passed it over, held her the miniature welding-torch he was using on his latest masterpiece and settled on his hams. She gave him a casual nod.

"Guess you kids're too young to remember Angie Merton."

Oh, boy. We were. But our parents hadn't been. The girl who got ditched from the holovid show when she made the mistake of lusting for the guy she was currently laying. The illegal tape sold millions, the guy cleaned up, and Angie took to the hills. We'd heard it.

"Boyfriend dirted her?" Being tactful.

She snorted. "Sure, he cocked his leg all over her. But that wasn't it. How you suppose he got that pirate tape?"

"Word was he stole it."

"Sure he did. With the door left unlocked and the caretaker out having coffee and everything but a luminous sign saying Open Here. They could've had that for all I know. Guess who got ten percent."

That was new. "The vid studio?"

"You could say. Cordovan was head honcho in my time, he was still learning the trade in hers. But they've always been the same. It made no difference to Angie. She took the electric carver from the kitchen and used it on her throat."

I shivered. Not so long before young Nimbus quit jun-

gle adventures and started tapping for blood in person.
"She was your sister?"

"Yeah," Medusa growled around her can. "She was
fifteen years older, believe it or not. I only look three million. I musta been seventeen. Just starting myself. Made
an impression." She took another long swallow. "But not
enough of one, I guess."

"You were an actress?"

"Astounding, ain't it? Yeah, I was an actress, pretty
face. Guess who for. I knew Angie'd been sold out but
not who by. Till it happened to me. Maybe they give
special prices for families."

"Coelacanth?"

"Right. Made three-four nice pictures. Thought I was
set up. Had a starring role coming and all things bright
and beautiful."

She touched her cheek. "Then I got into one of their
damned horror pics and the villainess threw a bottle of
acid in my face. It was supposed be water. It wasn't. You
heard they like realism?"

That brought a silence. Even from Dribble who'd been
doing the slow dog-slide skirtwards when he thought Sword
wasn't looking.

"They didn't fix it?"

"Does it look like they did? No, pretty-face, I wasn't
high enough on the totem pole. I got basic first aid from
a friendly Tech, after they finished filming the writhing
and screaming. Then they sent me home and terminated
my contract. I guess part of the fault was mine but they
helped me hope. I had a fancy house on mortgage, a copt
wasn't paid for, a wardrobe from here to there, all set for
my big scenes. When the vultures had gone I'd nothing
left for surgery. I went to a Gooder para-med and he did
what he could. It may not look much but you shoulda
seen it before."

"And now she works the spaceyards," Yell added.

"Which is where I found her. I'd heard she was around a year or so back so I figured maybe she still was. Thought you'd like to be acquainted. Miss Jeannette Merton."

"Caronne to you. Cordovan's vindictive. Don't like people talking about him."

"I can understand that," Sword said. "One day somebody's going to say something nasty."

"Yeah. Well, it ain't gonna be me. I haven't such a great life but it's all I've got. Satisfied?"

"If they are or not, we're going out to dinner," Yell said. "Promised it to Jeanne if she'd come home with me. Okay?"

"Me and Cass're going to dinner too," Moke said. He'd been acting hurt all afternoon, which always makes him feel even worse than me because he's nicer. "I was nasty to her. Anyhow it's my turn. She played with Sword yesterday."

Swordfish snorted. But he was sprawled on the floor with his legs outstretched, his elbows bent behind his head, and he didn't bother to answer. The attitude said thought. I don't much like it when Sword thinks.

His thoughts have this habit of exploding.

Moke and I spent several happy courses at The Bent Duck in town where they've a real chef, real food and an air-circulation system stops you smelling the other guy's fish in your tournedos Rossini. The decor's sparkly without being indecent and their floor show's the season's big dancers, occasionally in person, and a house illusionist does almost all of it with his hands.

Tonight's rostrum was Signis in one of his more athletic moods looking like he'd made the conquest of gravity under his own power, and the Great Mudlow filling the place with multicolored doves. We stayed a long time giggling and applauding and by the time we went home we were speaking again.

Neither of us brought up Jeannette Merton but I guess we were thinking about her. Between numbers.

We were dressed for moderate festivity, which is Mokey's way of being sorry; black leather gaucho pants with silver conches in his case and a silver sheath slit to the armpits and stilty boots in mine. So we took a traxie home, it being bad business to walk around the Strip in that get-up after dark unless you've a forty-five-pounder in your back pocket. Neither of us had, it spoils the set of your clothes.

We came down in the elevator, still giggling, swung around the chromed handgrip deciding who got to spoil their hair in the soft-entry, and finished by falling into the corridor in a heap. I readjusted my wig with dignity. Ever since Sword got heavy about my hair if I want a pagoda it got to be fake, which is why I wanted Moke to do the hard bit. His is his own.

We hesitated outside the door.

"You think Yeller's out?" he asked.

"Wouldn't be surprised. Got a key?"

"Uh-huh. Wouldn't mind a coffee."

He unlocked the handplate, printed it, and led the way. I was still sorting the beads of my pagoda so I was a step or two behind. I had a hand out to close the door when Moke giggled and made to raise his arm.

"That tickles."

"Moke! Freeze!"

My yelp of terror paralyzed him, his hand half-raised to his face. There was blood on his wrist, his cheek, his neck. The leg of his black gauchos was sliced through in a clean slash like a razor-cut and had fallen open to show a few inches of tanned shinbone marked by a red line just beginning to drip.

I turned my eyeballs down. My arm was striped with parallels of fine blood, thin as spider silk. It didn't even hurt. Yet.

"What is it?" He was tense but steady.

"Don't move. Don't even breathe if you can help it. It's monofil and we're entangled. Some clever bastard hung a mesh right where it would fall on our heads as we came in. Put pressure on and it'll take you off in slices. Fucker's invisible in ordinary light so you can't see it until it's too late."

"What can't it cut?" he asked, cool and quiet.

"Depends on the pressure. Metal or glass, maybe, if there's no whip in it. But try to move and you're going to lose whatever it's touching."

"Like an arm or a leg. I get the point. Can you see what's on me from there?"

"Blood. It's on me too. I can't move either."

"Information's all I want. I'm told graft procedures are pretty good these days."

"Don't laugh, damn you. I wish I had some fucking filters. It's a kind of irregular spiderweb, a wide-linked net. It was meant to fall on us as we walked and cut us to pieces, only we came in too slow. Whoever moves first carves up the other. I can see a reflection in parts. You've a loop around your neck lying on your shoulders and a strand across your left forearm. I can't see the other side. There's more wafting about the floor. If you take a step you get your legs in it."

"What happens if you heat it?"

I thought. "I don't know. It's got to burn, it's thin enough, but I don't know the temperature. Could be high."

"Is the loop going to take my left arm off if I put my hand in my pocket?"

"No. If you move carefully it'll lift. But there could be more."

"Then we'll go by results. Let's watch. If I move real slow we should see before I lose my head."

"Move damned slow. I like you."

He drifted his left arm a millimeter at a time. I saw the

rainbow filament lift and touch a knuckle, leaving another line of oozing red. He was trying to keep the arc narrow to get to his pants pocket in the shortest space.

I was starting to cramp, poised in midstride balanced unevenly between stilt heels, one arm out like a hat stand. A glittering strand showed between us. I hoped we wouldn't jerk it tight and cut someone's head off.

"Watch it. There's a loop cutting your sleeve. Don't come farther back."

"Damn. I liked that shirt." He froze the elbow and continued to lower his forearm slowly. His hand had almost reached the pocket.

"Logically," he said, pausing in a statue pose, "if this is one net it'll stretch if we move apart. If we move together it should slack off."

"In theory. But if you've a loop hooked on something you lose it if it tightens."

"It fell from above. So we should have loose swags between us. Let's edge, Cass. Easy."

I clenched my teeth, shifted the weight off my rear foot onto the front and began to move the back imperceptibly forward, waiting for my leg to drop off. A bloody stripe opened on my shoulder and I bit down on a jerk of panic. Moke was sliding backward the same way. Like a couple of modern dancers playing mime.

A red-hot bar burned the muscle of my calf and cauterized my leg from toe to thigh. I willed it not to tic. After a million seconds while I stood rigid it eased to an ache and I glided again.

The gap narrowed, from three feet to maybe eighteen inches, fourteen, ten. Another flash and I saw he was right. The net was slackening.

"Stop," he said. "I think I can get in my pocket. Let me know if I lose a finger."

His hand slid over the leather. His fingers were slick with blood but I couldn't see new cuts. It touched the edge, parted it, felt inside. I let my own arm drop, watching for stripes. Rainbow fiber dripped from my fingers. Down. I almost relaxed.

Moke's hand was back with something like a jeweler's screwdriver.

"Mini-welder. Got it for the bead-work on Ol' Bird-Eyes."

The thing he'd used on Caronne's cigarette.

"Cuts up to high-ceramic. I'll try it on the bits I can see. If it works we're advancing. Stand still and pray."

The end of the rod shot a minute blade of blue-white flame. He made passes in space and a little fragment of air lit to brilliance, drew into a bright bead, and fell away.

"It melts." He sounded more cheerful. "If we could see it." Pause. "If we sprayed it with something, would it stop being monofil? I mean, would it get thick enough to see?"

"I don't know. It's a single molecule, a kind of extended polymer. Sort of cero-metal. So I'd guess slick. But if the guck was sticky enough . . ."

"Trust me. Henry!"

That's an Eklund trick. It's the name of this real snot pilot who patronizes us to death, and Hans-Bjorn revenges himself quietly by calling all his household domestics the same. Now Moke does too. The nearest came bustling up spidering with all its limbs, making a hopeful subservient buzz.

"Stop right there. Henry, in my workroom, that's to say the guestroom bath, you'll find a can of red plastic paint and a spray gun. Can you recognize red plastic paint?"

"Yes, sir."

"Then you'll fill the spray gun with the paint, test the nozzle—I use the mirror-wall—and come back here with it. You'd better bring the small heat-wand out of my toolkit too."

"The master has instructed me in the past to leave his tool kit alone."

"He's now instructing you to get his small heat-wand out of it. The smallest. Now, please."

"Yes, sir."

And it spidered off.

"Just as well these bastards haven't any sense of humor," Moke said. "A real person would die laughing."

"Or just die. I take it our clothes are about to get spoiled."

"Oh, and our hair and everything. Protect your eyes, Cass. You'll need them again."

Henry got back with a clutch of tools in its spider claws. It didn't surprise me to see the paint was blue. They're not hot on colors.

"Thank you, Henry. Now turn the spray nozzle to fine-jet. No, the other way. That's right. And now mistress and I wish to be sprayed. All over, including particularly the space around and between us. Keep spraying until I tell you to stop. Go ahead."

"Your clothes will be spoiled, sir," Henry buzzed.

"I feel like spoiling my clothes today, Henry."

"Yes, sir."

I closed my eyes as the gucky mist reached out toward us. It dewed our faces, our skin, our clothes, our hair. I got a lungful of stink and tried to screw my nose as tight as my eyes. Breathing was one unhealthy activity.

"Stop," Moke gasped, muffled, just as I thought I was going to turn blue independently and start drowning.

I opened my eyes a slit. The web was outlined in clotted blue beads. So was the door, the carpet, a lot of of the hall outside and us. We looked like a clown act toward the end of the intermission.

"Thank you, Henry," Mokey said. He and Eklund are the only guys I know who thank mechanicals. "Hand me my heat-wand now and be very careful not to step on this blue mesh. Then move well back. I can't use a naked flame, Cass," he added. "Paint flares when it's wet. Stand still another minute and I'll get rid of this stuff."

He did. Now that the filament was visible, the white-hot rod shriveled it where it touched. There was a lot of tarry black smoke and a devilish smell but neither of us was complaining. He got rid of his, burned off what was still hanging from an almost invisible pin in the ceiling and started cutting me loose.

When he'd finished we stood and looked at each other.

"It's lucky it's a wig, Cass."

"Blue suits you, Moke. Especially the hair. You should do it more often. Does anything take this goo off?"

"Sure. I got solvent in the bathroom."

"Great. Let's go and swim in it."

We'd got about as clean as we were going to before Yell came back. We still had interesting ingrained lines in the crevices of our necks and ears and under our hair and fingernails and we stank of disinfectant and nuskin. We'd sent Henry to turn on the extractor and clean up whatever it could around the entrance. Yell stood in the doorway and looked at us.

"Decorating?" he said.

Moke held up a nuskined hand with a fresh red line across the back. "Thinking about detonating. Jason Cordovan's getting up my nose."

"Uh-oh," Yell said. "I'd have sworn it was paint. So where do we go now, maestro?"

"I think Moke's about to go bang. He doesn't often so he's a lot of powder to spare. It wouldn't surprise me if he's nearly as noisy as Swordfish."

"Don't know why I work for you guys," Yell said sadly. "All I ever wanted was a quiet life. Shall I take cover right away or d'you want me to make coffee first?"

"If I wasn't painted blue in rude places I'd embrace you passionately."

"Always some excuse," he said. "I'll fix the machine. What do I tell the janitor when he comes to complain in the morning?"

"Tell him we're moving," Moke said. "We don't like the quality of his monofil."

Yell paused.

"Maybe we could move now."

"Not till I've had coffee," Moke said. "If any more bad guys come around just strike a match. We'll probably lose the whole building."

"Great," Yell muttered. "Remind me to buy a rosary."

And he crept out like he was walking on dynamite.

Mokey and I cuddled in a mutual stench. Now he'd quit being heroic I could feel him trembling under the quilt. There's nothing like dying in someone's company to convince you you need them. I trembled back for luck.

The apartment stank like a paint factory. It was enough to give Sword a sneezing fit.

Hell, it had given me one already.

We got our gear together and left just after daylight.
Mokey left a note of apology and a blank check for the
management claiming we'd had an accident. It doesn't
read too good in the society columns to say you sprayed
blue paint all over the hall because some guy keeps trying
to kill you. They're apt to conclude you deserve it.

"It's only money," he said.

We thought of the days money was so precious we'd
almost rather wade through monofil and neither of us
smiled.

Hallway let in us calmly. "You out of a home again or
did Moke get bored with the neighbors?"

"Both. Don't suppose you got Gooder friends with
cellar space to let who don't mind the smell of plastic?"

"And getting blown up every couple of days?" I added.

"Maybe I'd better not tell them. If we're quiet could
we delay the next blow-up? Sword's getting nervy."

Even the idea of Sword's nerves is bad news.

"We'll try, Hall. We don't do it on purpose."

Yeller sat on our baggage and looked sardonic. "It's a
talent. There's a catalyst somewhere. We spent two years
in the big deep and this never happened once."

"Likewise. Cass spent two years away and the local
mayhem level stayed normal too. Got a neighbor with a
workshop in his backyard and a service apartment above.

It's utilitarian but you could paint it. Don't start any fires, people think I'm quiet."

"Ain't us, Hall."

"Yeah, it's your friends. I'll talk to him. My contact in the sorting office passed on a card, Cass. Since your address got to be fluid."

He fished in spotless coveralls and dug out a sealed spacemail envelope with SatService stamps.

"Hans-Bjorn?" Moke asked, looking over my shoulder.

"Not his writing. Do we know an Ainsworth at Stat One?"

"It's the inner-ring collection point," Hallway said. "You know anyone in the sats apart from Eklund?"

I ripped. "Signed Aurora. Dein's pre-acid sunrise? She wants me to call in the Marchand film lot at Overdale. Guess she's working. Maybe she's rethought her rock, the boyfriend didn't like us. You want to see the film industry from the outside?"

"Marchand's Coelacanth in drag."

"Then their studio's probably the safest place," Hallway said. "They're not going to blow you up in public. Why don't you two go while Yell and I move your gear?"

"Right," Yell agreed. "Let the working men work. Get."

"Who's going to drive?" Moke asked with desolation. It isn't nerves. He likes to have Yell on hand in case he finds a cliff he wants taken home.

"You got licenses. Let Cass work for her living."

"Sure, why not?"

"Every time she does we both get killed."

"Coward."

"Yup," Mokey said. "Call it experience."

I drove the copt in the end and Moke sat beside me doing designs on his little lap-slate. He had his last-but-one commission to finish, code-name Ol' Bird-Eyes. So one of us wasn't wasting his time.

"Can't be here," he said, coming up for air and peering out the windshield. He was sore about the landing on account of he'd got to a crucial part of OB-E's anatomy, but we both knew we'd nearly had a bad fight and we were being nice to each other.

"Lady's coordinates. You going to sit there and finish your whatever-it-is or you going to come sign autographs?"

"On paper. Skin I've had. These kids're decadent."

"All kids are decadent, it's part of kidhood. These guys are actors and actors don't tattoo their hides 'cause tomorrow they got to be filmed raw. Let's go ask where the action is."

"I don't see any action. If someone's about to kill us again I hope you got a number for Sword."

"I'm tooled myself. Don't look incredulous, I spent eighteen years in this city before I met you. Truth is you'd rather create humps and make holes in them. Bring your nasty slate, you can do it while I talk to Lady Sunrise."

I wasn't enchanted either. It wasn't on land, which makes me queasy unless there're teak planks underneath me with a guy in a captain's hat managing them. This was a platform that looked like an abandoned drilling rig with acres of rusty plates, decaying cranes and a superstructure that looked like it wasn't staying super long. The copt-pad had newly repainted landing marks and a bunch of tarp-covered lumps, but nothing else suggested life.

We jumped down onto rust and looked around. Someone hailed far away and I saw a chilly-looking guy in a padded suit and flapped cap poking his head out of a hole in the cliff above.

"Hey! This is private property."

"We're private citizens. This wreck belong to Marchand?"

"Yeah. Stay there, I'm coming down."

He did. The long way, by several staircases and ladders. By the time he got there we'd worked out the deep-freeze clothing. There was a sharp breeze on the water and it was colder than hell's kidneys. All around us a greasy black swell heaved to the gray horizon and a lot of dismal-looking seabirds did dismal-sounding wails and other birdlike things. The platform's rust was plenty splattered already so I guess they'd been doing it a long time.

"Marchand Studios," the padded guy said when he got to our level. "You got clearance?"

I held out Aurora's letter and he glommed it like he thought I'd made it in the back room. His face was red with cold and his breath smelled like a blowtorch.

"Uh-huh," he said. "They're below. Call you a bell. 'Less you want to wait for 'em, and God knows how long that'll be."

Moke and I looked at the black greasy water.

"Sure," I said. "I always wanted to see the floor of the Atlantic. What we waiting for?"

The bell was something like a submarine and something like half a warehouse strung on a cable. It looked watertight. It looked people-tight too. I nearly changed my mind. This time Moke got resolute, having quit his slate as well as frozen his ass off, so we walked in pretending we didn't care. The guy screwed up the ports. Then it swayed and squealed into the molasses.

"I hope this was a good idea," I said.

Moke said, "So do I."

I'd started to wish I hadn't had breakfast when we hit bottom. The lock doors creaked back slowly and I waited for the water that creeps to your knees, then your waist, then your neck, just before the hero breaks in and saves you. Except we'd left Sword at home.

What gushed in was warm damp air and a smell of tropical lagoons. We staggered to the entrance and out onto the lot.

Which was covered in sand. There were coconut palms out of old issues of *National Geographic* and people in blue paint with flowers in their hair. A couple of unlikely-looking canoes were drawn up on the shore of a paddling-pool that reached to the horizon with a wave machine in the distance. Wreaths of steam rose off the fizzy turquoise water and rubber starfish and other exotic beach furniture were washing about in the shallows.

The real sea, blacker and oilier, was above our heads, curved around like the inside of a tennis ball and swirling gritty currents full of lumpy things and jellied things and other excrescences the opposite side of the sugar-blue sky the studio lights were busy faking. The natural bottom looked like it was covered with gooey black mud with stuff sticking out I didn't want to get acquainted with.

I guess there's a reason guys go under the real sea to film a fake sea but don't ask me what, I don't make films.

The nearest blue people were swapping derms from a bottle the size of a candy jar and drinking coffee out of plastic cups. Somewhere beyond them a floating platform swooped a camera-crew up and down the face of a glass cliff where a forest of swaying weed was being threaded by striped and spotted neon fish. They didn't look real, which maybe meant they were.

Human shapes were doing a water ballet around a guy shaped like a hippopotamus with enough hair and beard to stuff an emperor-size sofa and a trident as big as a bazooka. Behind us was half a throne room with furniture based on seashells, and wind machines to float people's hair. It was all they had shy a scale or two so they all had a lot. A couple had taken it off the better to derm up and they had ordinary scalps and foreheads underneath. It made them look sort of surrealistic.

Moke was interested. I figured the next work was going to have labyrinthine whorls or melting watches, depending on how they hit him.

I hailed a mermaid, male from the chest arrangements. The rest was wreathed in glass-fiber with silver threads. "You know Aurora?"

"Sure," he said, looking up from beating wampum or maybe plaiting copra, I'm not up on sub-Atlantic customs. "She's due to be tied to a rock and eaten by a sea monster so I guess she's in her dressing room."

"Oh," I said. "Does she agree with its digestion?"

He had a cute smile. "You kidding? She's the hero-ine."

"Uh-huh. How'd she get in that state?"

He shrugged. "I only work here. Annoyed her daddy the Emperor of Atlantis at a guess. It's okay, Yardell's going to cut it open with his magic sword before she suffocates. At least that's the theory."

"That must be a comfort to her."

More pretty teeth. "Heroine almost never dies in comedies. Dressing room's thataway." He hiked his thumb to the rear.

We squinched toward the coconut grove and found polarized bubbles clinging together out of camera range. A blue guy in bits of aluminum armor was sitting in a lounger outside one under a headset that leaked threads of music. He opened narrow black-rimmed eyes when I touched him.

"Aurora?" I mouthed.

He gave me a slanted smile was meant to wet my pants and pointed next door. Since he didn't take the headset off I stayed dry. A cutlass as long as a vaulting pole was leaning on his dome so he was probably Yardell, the guy who was saving Aurora's life. I hoped his music had finished before he went on or he wasn't going to hear her scream.

The sun-lady was in a hammock under a sunlamp, in blue scales and swags of pearl jewelry that floated like a rogue drift-net. Dein was with her, looking macho. You could tell he wasn't in it because he was wearing white jeans and a T-shirt and was basically human-colored.

Knowing part of him was Dosh made me feel funny. But his particolored eyes were a stranger's. My guy's were cornflower blue and I was never going to see them again. Beautiful dead Dosh who would never ever be really alive. I could see now he belonged to the past, where we weren't. I wanted a sign from Moke but he had his wooden-Indian face on and wouldn't look at me.

I took his cold hand and Dein and Aurora looked at us like people do when they think it's a lovers' quarrel. After a moment he gave me a little squeeze and put my fingers under his elbow, which is Mokese for not to worry.

Aurora said, "Hi. We hoped you'd come."

She sounded tight, like she was overwound.

Dein said, "Have a beer. Dammit, we're rich. Have one each."

It was an improvement on last time anyhow.

"You still waiting around?" I asked him.

He sounded tight too. "I believe the big chiefs just about worked out whether the alien princess kills me or I kill her. Soon's it's agreed we can get on and have the terminal bonfire. That's what matters."

It was a space epic. Right. "Wasn't it in the script?"

"Script?" he said bitterly. "Maranna's Princess and she pulls more weight than I do. So her agent's holding out for she gets to do the tear-spilling. He figures guys don't spill well. Read she doesn't want to die before the credits. Hell, I'm a great sniveler. You should see me. I make Niagara look like a down-pipe."

"Studio politics," Aurora said. "But it isn't fair. They did agree. Dein loves her madly, he kills her thinking she's her brother, and he and Bub exchange blood over her ashes, swearing eternal friendship and equal rights for humans. She can't exchange blood with her own brother, it wouldn't be rational."

Dein made a glum face. "If she gets her way she kills me thinking I'm Bub and he and she snivel together and both promise equal rights. Her agent says it's more subtle. It also gets her the credit sequence to herself."

"If they're like that I wouldn't vote for either of them," I said. "Haven't they read the history of equal rights legislation?"

"We'll know Monday," Aurora said. Humming like a telegraph wire. "I'm due to get eaten alive in ten minutes if they aren't running late again. Don't ask why, I'm not sure. I think I behaved in some particularly imbecile way to my father the Emperor of Atlantis, and like any loving father he always has his daughters eaten alive when there's a family disagreement."

"You're getting saved by the gonzo next door with the taste for grand opera?"

"That's my prince. He also likes beautiful boys but he's fairly reliable with a sword, he used to play Shake-speare. At least I hope so. Film before last he had a fight with his boyfriend and was so busy being suicidal he nearly forgot to cut me loose before the Roc got me."

"It wasn't Wagner?" Dein asked. They were all knife-edges today.

"*The Marriage of Figaro* by the sound."

"Great. I've a chance of survival. He only plays that when the new boy's warm, willing and faithful." The dawn princess adjusted two gauze veils without helping a lot. They were transparent and short. "Come and talk to me. If Yardell's slow maybe you can intervene in the nick of time. It's been needed."

"Can't I?" Dein asked wistfully with his hands full of beer cans.

"They won't let me on-set with you. Stay and get drunk like a well-brought-up hero."

"They want to talk like girls," Moke said.

"Okay, let's talk like boys."

"I'm dismally faithful."

"Yeah," I said. "He only ever deceives me with a couple of tons of scrap-metal or half a mountain. Don't drink all the beer, sounds like the girls might need reviving."

"When he says like boys he means spaceball. They always do," Aurora said. She walked off clanking her pearls.

"Thanks for coming," she said as we scrunched through palms. "You were in a Coelacanth adventure. Dein dug it out. He thought he knew you."

Oh. I wasn't sure I'd tell Moke that.

"It was an accident."

"But you've met them."

"You could say. You're contracted to Marchand."

She tugged at her veils. "Dein just got word about his film. It isn't just the script that's changed. Jason Cordovan's directing. For some reason that scares him."

Yes, I saw that. The stem-brain's a long way down but it's what people mean when they say the heart has its reasons.

"It'd scare me. But I thought Dein was a pet of his."

She looked blank. "Oh, why? I don't think they've met. But Maranna worries me. She accepted the original script and now she's making trouble. She's not a troublesome person."

"I thought contract squabbles were kind of normal. Excuse me. It's the scoobidoo."

"It's okay. They happen. But I guess you know the scandal over Nimbus, you were in it. With that man. Gross." She shuddered. "Hope you've lost him. But it's not all that's gone wrong. There's stuff happening behind the scenes. Word is Coelacanth's losing market and they could be on line for a takeover. They need to pull something big soon."

"You mean blood and guts and bits of people all over."
I remembered Sword's hope Luke Trent meant to play
Horatio somewhere else.

"You've heard of it. That's just what I mean."

"Is Maranna—" I paused. Murderous sounds kind of
bald. "Ambitious?"

She stood still and dug a little dry pit in the sand with
the toe of a pearl-studded sandal. "She isn't Nimbus.
But she's a long-standing pro with a career, she isn't
getting younger, and I've heard she has gambling debts
and IR trouble. There's a bit of real needle in this quarrel.
I mean about who's the main star. And the script has
guns in it."

"You mean they could end up playing *High Noon*."

Her face was veiled in her blue-silver wig. "It's happened. With Coelacanth."

"Don't I know it. Can't Dein and Maranna sort it out
between them? After all, unless the guns are rigged, *High
Noon* depends on who draws fastest. She can't want to be
shootee."

"That's what's bothering me. We thought the same, so
Dein tried to call her last night. She slammed the phone
down. We didn't know why. Then we read the scandal
column this morning and it's a dirty fight in public. He
didn't know. They were friends last week."

"Yeah. Artistic temperaments fall out. You think she
may know she's the one whose gun's loaded."

"I don't like to say that."

"But it's what you're scared of."

She pulled her foot out of the hole, which had got quite
deep, and whirled her veils towards the seashore. The
hole filled right in like it had never existed.

"Damn. I'm on. Sorry, I'm neurotic. Old age. It's probably paranoia."

I stood among the fake palms and watched her being
arranged on a rock crusted with oysters as big as

dinnerplates. A couple of techs draped her in silvered chains would have moored a nuclear sub and the blue guy with the sofa stuffing came and ranted. That took twenty minutes, especially when they'd done it twice.

Several more blue guys blew on shells that made noises like the death of a cow and the sea monster reared up behind the wave-machine and bore down on all of them.

It wasn't a bad sea monster. They used to fake them miniature and now they like them full-size so the heroine can be cut out for real. It came coiling out of the dome-ceiling while blue people screamed in all directions and the unlikely canoes got lifted by a special effort of the wave machine and disappeared with a whoosh into a useful hollow in the dunes.

It opened a mouth like a factory gate with teeth I hoped were rubber and snapped shut on Aurora. Who made large gestures of despair and screamed like Fay Wray only contralto.

Yardell's love-life must have been in good shape because he appeared on cue toting the cutlass and did the carving. My respect for his muscles went up a thousand percent. The monster flopped and writhed all over the set soaking absolutely everybody and sicked Aurora up. She stood on the wet sand rearranging her hair and daintily wiping lime-green Jell-O off her pearls. I remembered this was a comedy.

Her Atlantean father wrang out his fiberglass and the hero pranced over for a kiss. On the way he slipped in the Jell-O and fell on his face in a rock pool. I wasn't sure if either of these events was in the script but both guys used a lot of language I didn't figure comedy audiences commonly heard. Whichever, it all got itself on film, then a guy in satin running shorts and a baseball cap appeared with a bullhorn and made them all do it again.

By the end everybody was getting kind of bad-tempered. Yardell's swings with the vaulting-pole were slowing off and I thought Aurora looked gray under her makeup though it was so blue to begin with it was hard to be sure. The only guy kept right on coming back was the monster and it was having a ball.

I stuck around in case she really needed to be rescued but maybe she was being actressy because her costar went on coming through. Though by the end his language was getting so metaphorical I figured they had to be making the sound tape separately. This story about limp wrists is a fiction. You ever see a dancer couldn't lift a hundred-pound girl over his head and twirl her like a baton?

What they all did get was wet. Extremely. So did I and a lot of the techs and the bubble holding the camera-crew.

I knew one thing by the time they'd finished. Aurora was blue in the lips. Yardell was lying flat out on wet sand with red grazes bleeding through his scales where he'd made contact with the rock pool, since if it hadn't been in the script to start with they'd liked it enough to keep it. The Emperor had shed his whiskers and a lot of Face with the help of a pair of girls in white overalls and was sprawling like a starfish. Not rubber, more dead. He was a youngish guy whose face was red and white in patches and he was losing enough sweat to refill the ocean if they needed it. They all looked beat. And that was one scene.

I didn't think she was paranoid.

We limped wetly to the bubble where Dein handed out beer and towels. Moke had been controlling his urge toward desperate honesty because they were speaking and the heap of beer cans was almost sculptural.

"Whoo!" Aurora said. "Every time I make a film I swear it's the last."

"Close your eyes and think of the mortgage," Dein said, rubbing her back.

I hauled Moke upright. "Gotta go. But we've an interest in Divine too. Moke's thinking pink granite and he hates his works to be wasted. See you around."

Aurora gave me a pale smile. I traded her its mate. Any one of the guys in that scene could have got killed over and over and nobody could have proved a thing. Nimbus had done as she liked for sixteen years and it took Swordfish to catch up with her.

I had a bad, bad feeling.

The air was cold after the damp heat below and the oily swells weren't improved by red streaks of sunset. Our copt was in place and the cold guy didn't bother to see us out, he just waved from behind the window of his hidey-hole. He looked like he was absorbing more cold-repellent. I hoped they relieved him sometimes or he was going to end up with cirrhosis.

Moke didn't say much in the bell or as we took off into the cindery crimson sky. I didn't either. I felt like we were walking on glass.

He didn't even take out his slate and that meant he had real bad stuff on his mind. I shut up and waited for it to hatch. It could be Tyrannosaurus rex.

It was, but not Moke's. We were cudding silently together when the trans bipped. A face molded in bronze came up with a minute smile at the corners of its lips as a sign it was based on humanity. It had as much expression as a statue, remembering Moke does stuff in plaster stares you in the eye and communicates.

"Miss Blaine?" Jason Cordovan's rich cordial voice gonged. "I hope your visit was interesting? I'm glad you didn't have trouble with the bell. It gets stuck between floors sometimes. As it were."

"I'm sure it does. But since you weren't on-set we felt quite safe. What can I do for you?"

"You can go home, my dear Cassandra. May I call you Cassandra?" He didn't give me time to say no. "Where you both have such long full lives. Unless you'd like to change your mind about my offer?"

He raised a bronze brow. I shook my head.

"I feared as much. You may have forgotten but I did once have a whole list of crimes canceled for each of you. They're still on file. It would be a pity if the police dug them up. Since you're respectable people with careers these days."

His metal lids narrowed. "Perhaps you don't understand how much a scandal would hurt you. Especially Mr. Faber. I'd hate it, since I'm one of his sincerest admirers. You will think carefully, won't you?"

And the trans went blank.

We sat dumb for a moment while Moke's eyes reflected the sunset and my hands went through the motions of flying the copt.

"If I were you, Mokey, I wouldn't give him an autograph."

"Nobody's asked lately."

"Actors. They don't get 'em, they give 'em."

"But I might just give an autograph to him," he went on as if I hadn't spoken. "With a tattoo pen. I think I have the urge."

Cordovan should start worrying, because Moke doesn't talk like that.

Blessed are the righteous because they're the only guys in the world really slaughter you when they get their dander up, and they don't even feel bad.

They know you deserve it.

The loft was at the back of a whole-food bakery kept by a mournful type who looked like a schoolmaster. He ran the kind of eye I seem to bring out in Gooders over my red leather jump and another over Moke's jeans. I could have told him they were the Moke best, the ones he visits film stars in, and the rest were worse.

Moke smiled at him like Moke and he dissolved into something human. The boy has that effect on people.

"There are friends of yours upstairs," he said, drooping like a beagle. "They seem odd people. I hope you don't give parties."

That ruled out Hallway who claimed to know the guy and Yeller who can look normal when he has to. I had clairvoyant vibrations featuring Swordfish and any number of his closer acquaintances.

"Never," I said firmly. "Martin works and I watch in the hope of catching the habit. We're very quiet, neither one of us is a screamer."

"My equipment's a bit noisy," Moke said, giving me one of the looks I'm always getting from guys, I don't know why. "But I mostly work during the day."

That's flatly untrue, he works whenever the spirit takes him and it has a preference for three in the morning. But I don't think he knows; when he's in the middle of something he could be levitating halfway up a cyclone and he wouldn't notice. "I'm welding right now, you won't hear it out front."

The beagle smiled sadly. "I hope you'll be comfortable. It's utilitarian, my son used it for a bike repair shop but he's moved away now he's married." The way he said it he could have been announcing the guy's funeral. "If you'd like bread I bake it myself. Fresh hydroponic corn, stone-ground. We take tokens."

"And we give them," I said heartily, making a note to ask Hallway what they were and where you got them. "Martin adores bread. We're really grateful. Shame about your son."

Mokey dragged me away. "She hasn't had anything to eat all day. She gets delirious, I think it's being hyper-thyroid. If you've any bread now . . ."

The beagle got a load of Moke's breath and almost smiled. "Your friends took it up." That was a relief. Maybe next time we'd have tokens. "We do home-brew beer as well."

"Great. We'll have a crate or however it comes." Moke was on full candlepower, which dims the lights for miles around and dazzles even Gooders. "Maybe we better check on these characters upstairs."

Well, at least the place smelled nice.

The yard behind was uncannily clean and had a wire bin down one side full of sleeping parakeets. When the beagle opened the door a couple woke up and squawked. The other side had a narrow strip of dirt looming with staked hollyhocks. You could tell the guy was a nature nut. Me, parakeets make me sneeze nearly as bad as overgrown pogo sticks but I could tell Moke wasn't in the mood.

The loft was up a flight of rickety wooden stairs over the door of the workshop and had batten blinds on the windows which is real Gooder territory. Elsewhere you only find them in museums. Thin lines of light crawled out between the battens, which meant somebody was up there. I'd have done a cautious approach but the steps creaked so bad we might as well have been preceded by a swing band. We squeaked up in chorus and tried the door.

"Hi," Dribble fluted from the middle of a medium-luxurious bed-pad. I made a note Yell was sleeping there, at least until we got the bug-operatives in. "We wait you hours, we eat all bread."

"That's a hanging offense," I snarled. "Get off of Yeller's bed, you insult in the face of nature, and if there's really no food I'm having you."

"That's your bed, Cass, mine's in the broom cupboard," Yell said from a battered basket-chair by an equally battered table. "We can't have him till tomorrow, I ain't laid in a spit. Got you some steaks."

"Steak steak?" Mokey asked hopefully.

"Combed prote," Yell said. "But you can hardly tell the difference."

"I suppose it's no use asking where you've been," Swordfish's voice said from the other side where the basket-chair's twin sagged dangerously. All the signs were they'd been playing gin rummy. "Another half hour and I'd have had the troops out."

"It's how time passes when you're having fun."

Since they had the sitting space sewn up between them I chose a cleanish corner and parked on the floor.

"Aurora thinks Coelacanth's fixing to kill Dein, and Cordovan means to put Moke and me in jail if we don't go home right away. I don't know what he means home. Hell, I was born here."

There was a short pause.

"I think they'd better eat," Sword said softly at the end of it. "Maybe they'll make sense afterward. Otherwise I'm fixing to kill a couple of guys myself."

"Sure, Tiger. In the meantime get your dog off Moke's bed. He could catch something. Oh, and the landlord downstairs is complaining already. He doesn't like our friends. You guys are going to have to find another way in if you insist on making house calls."

"I'm sure Moke's infection-free," Sword said. "Anyhow he hasn't slept in it yet so Dribble's quite safe. I didn't know you two had separate rooms."

"It's a new regime. Since Rover drooled on the old one."

"Get off Cassandra's bed, Dribble, or we'll never hear the end of it," Swordfish said wearily. "Yell, make some food, for the love of God. I want to hear about assassination plots and the children aren't rational."

"I'm absolutely rational. I can tell I'm going to love this place. We haven't had anywhere like it since our warehouse burned down. But you missed on the ambience. There aren't any packing cases. You got to have packing cases or it ain't authentic."

Swordfish made a snarling noise and Yeller started slapping prote on the grill.

"Don't know why we need Razor," I said a little while later, propping my boots on the panel. "You're a contract killer, all you got to do is kill them. He'll think I'm incompetent."

"He always was perceptive," Swordfish agreed, taking a foot off the controls long enough to kick my boots to the floor.

"So where's the problem?"

"You think I'm Superman, that's the problem," he snarled. "What do you want me to do, make the earth spin backward and start being yesterday? Sure I could take Cordovan. What you haven't got hold of is Cordovan isn't a person, he's a species. The guy's obnoxious but he's only Coelacanth's front man. You kill him today, there'll

be another tomorrow just like him. And tomorrow, like
clay ducks. Shoot 'em down and they keep on coming.
You don't exactly want Cordovan, you want to take down
Coelacanth. And that, my girl, is heavy business. If you're
into overthrowing empires I'm a street gunman. It takes
bigger material than me to dismantle the government."

"Sword. It's the first time I heard there was anything
you couldn't do."

"That's because you've never been outside my league
before. One reason I survive is I know my limitations. For
advice on the impossible we go to the old man. If there's a
way, he knows it. Anyhow, dammit, he's your stepfather."

"And yours."

"I visit him. He's been asking about you."

I looked down. "I guess I don't see him on a farm."

"Tough. You put people in compartments and won't let
them out. Then you call them inconsistent if they move
off the chalk lines."

"Unfair."

"Is it? Why didn't you write to me? Do you think Razor
doesn't want to see his daughter?"

"You gave me the long good-bye."

"And you took it."

"Yeah? Why's everything my fault? When did you
need your hand held?"

A smoldering silence.

"You're a snob," he said at last, muffled.

"If you say so. And you're the ultimate democrat."

I stared furiously out the bubble. Withered burned-
looking countryside streaked below covered with white-
brown grass and leathery scrub. Vivid green patches kid-
ded you there was life. It ain't true. It's moss and lichen,
likes the rain now the temperatures are high, and it's
resistant to acid and weeks-long cloud cover. They say
there was forest but if there was it's gone. I seen pictures.
I guess it was pretty.

The hydroponics houses caught the light first, a reflection on the horizon like clear water. Then the higher dome that enclosed the house, green behind the swirl of the field.

I never had been to see Razor. Not here, where the old chief was spending his retirement growing corn and beans and the inevitable soya makes prote for the city. He was boss before he raised Swordfish to succeed him. He was still boss for me. The grim old man with his clipped beard and thin smile and the oil-black eyes made people shift when he looked at them.

Who picked me up thieving when I was fourteen and saved me from the cops and taught me what he knew. Or some of it. And gave me his stepson for a teacher. My family. Until Razor retired and Sword and his pack went to ground and I met Dosh at a dance, feeling deprived. And he offered me a piece of the loft he shared with his friend Moke and I found Moke loved me better. Before Coelacanth changed everything.

Razor came into Ashton sometimes and when he did we went on the town. He took me to restaurants and we walked the streets and talked old times. We sent cards to each other. He was my stepfather. I never wanted to see him in overalls. He had been war-chief. Call it snobbery.

Sword swung the copt in over the house and the dome opened up like it had no defenses. Maybe it hadn't. Though out in the backlands there are guys even loot farmers. We came down beside a long building with a porch, surrounded by grass and big trees, fronting a stream dammed into a swimming hole. An open-fronted barn held machinery and a couple of copts with the name MORLAND stenciled in yellow and a Farmers' Cooperative star.

From the front you could hear the slosh of the purification plant around a shrub screen. On the other side hydroponics tubes curved away into distance, the pulse of pumps giving the place an arterial sound. A huge lazy shepherd lumped to its feet as we came up and slouched off the porch. Swordfish bared a hand and it licked it and sauntered casually away. It acted like visitors didn't bother it.

"Not much of a guard."

"He doesn't need it," Sword said.

Razor came down the steps in his usual black jeans and shirt with his finger in a book.

"Cassandra? Why have you made me wait a hundred years?"

I hugged him. Naturally he knew I'd come because I wanted something. One of his talents is not making you feel guilty. He just kills you or doesn't.

"My daughter's here and my son's invisible. Just like the old days. Do you drink anything as commonplace as beer now, Cass, or do I have to get out the bottles from the Farmer's Meeting?"

"Just pour."

"Yeah, right. Well sit, children. I take it this is a pow-wow. Do I dig up my war axe at once or are we going to smoke first?"

He had nice porch furniture, a workmanlike icebox, a table the right height, a rug for the dog. A box of thin cigars was on a stool. A crystal glass somebody'd made by hand for lots of bucks stood on the table with dregs looked and smelled pure malt.

"Where's the soil?"

"Why did I waste my time? You don't do hydroponics with plow horses, you ignorant brat. You do it by computer. I take a kart around the houses once a day for exercise. Peaceful."

"Yeah," Swordfish said. He'd stretched his length in a sling chair and unzipped enough suit to pour beer in. Clean ivory glinted in the gap. There was an ironic edge to his tone. "Old wolf's got nothing to do but read romances and think of writing his memoirs."

"Not entirely. Twenty-three guys in various parts of the government pay me a steady income to keep my memoirs to myself. I fend 'em off from time to time. And pirates. I keep busy."

So the dome wasn't undefended. His security was good. It always was.

"You've written them," Swordfish diagnosed.

"Self-defense. Day someone assassinates me the networks get to know where the corpses are. So what's the problem?" Mild interest.

"Suppose I tell it," Sword said. The disembodied hand held the beer up to the light. "She gets emotional."

"He wasn't your lover."

"Way I heard it he wasn't quite yours either. For that I may even forgive him. In a century. If he stays dead."

Sword heaved his feet up on the table and considered the beer some more. From the signs. Then he found his pace. I always wondered where Swordfish learned to report. Not if from guys in uniforms, just which.

Razor listened with his head bent back looking at the sky. The dome was slightly tinted, maybe for the crops. It made it look sunnier than it was.

"Well. You won't believe this but I studied law. Gooder law, what you can learn in the college down the road. I believed force was a weak man's solution. I still do in theory. In practice I ended up in jail for defending Ump clients who had the bad taste to be right. That's when I learned force is what you sometimes have to use to make the other guy listen long enough to hear your point of view. Some time after that I learned there are some guys just don't know how to listen. That's when I became a razor. Occam's, I've always hoped. I think it's time to go back to law."

"Law?" I squeaked. I could hear me. "The courts here'll award the case to Cordovan tied in pink silk bows and me and Moke'll never come out. He pays the salaries of half the police department."

"Sure. He says go and they goeth and come and they cometh. I wasn't thinking of home law, brat. The International Court made the film industry clean its act up already. There's no compulsion; they kill actors in absolute freedom and local sovereignty and lose the right to trade with civilized people, or they act reasonable and join the world. It's a proposition they understand. Simple and clear."

"You know someone with a taste for death? Lawyers are Techs. Anyone takes this'll never work again."

"What's wrong with me?"

I blinked.

"Why not?" He smiled peaceably. "Nobody's boycotting me, I grow the only oranges on the northern seaboard. But I need a case. Your friend Dein can't testify, he's been psychosurgically effaced. If he'd submit to examination we could show effacement but not how it happened. It would be proof of a criminal act but you'd need to show the film company responsible. They'll put it on the clinic. Or even on Dein. Could he prove he didn't choose to change identities, considering who he was? Your medics are dead."

"Right," Sword said. "Genotype would show he's Doshchenko, but there's only our word he knew us. His father buried him. He's over."

"Too true," I said. "Dein believes in his Ottery memories but if they face him with the cast of *Strings!* they'll say he's a fake. The trauma would be horrible and you can bet Cordovan would play it in six sharps. But even if Moke was right and we told him everything and hoped he'd come through, he could still end up looking a cheat."

"If Cordovan doesn't have him killed first," Sword murmured.

"Quite so." I got a shiver.

"The same for you and Moke. Cordovan's threatened you twice, but on private nets. I don't suppose you were recording?"

"No, dammit. A hotel room, a hired copt. I didn't know the guy knew where we were."

"His intelligence is competent," Swordfish said. "I thought they were covered both times."

"And they haven't complained. That was a mistake, Cass. You should have squalled like an alleycat."

"Sure, I know that now. But we didn't see any reason he should be after us."

"Until the body-legging operation started to come out, he probably wasn't. Now you're witnesses. Watch your rear, girl. Cordovan's threat to get your counts taken off the file's pretty certainly genuine." He reflected. "Which leaves Yell's friend Caronne. Her sister's a nasty story but the woman's dead. So it's hearsay. But Caronne's own testimony's real."

"She's scared."

"I don't blame her. But I can protect her. Get her, Cass, and I'll see she's safe. Talk to her, girl. She's another woman. Tell her about Dein, tell her anything. Just bring her to me."

"Can try."

"There's my small friend MacLaren DeLorn," Swordfish said dreamily. "The rich, sweet, nutty one. Sounds like a candy bar."

"Shut up. He is a candy bar."

"Great. In that case I'll get my chocolate-cream hero to talk to some of his cutesy friends. He knows people in theater and movies. Who knows what may come mincing out along with the honey and the real milky bubbles?"

"Sword, you can be uniquely offensive."

"He does it on purpose," Razor said. "It's a defense mechanism. You want dinner?"

"Steak steak?"

"Prote. The best. You won't be able to tell the difference."

"Sword doesn't eat in public. He never did."

"Then he'll have to eat by himself. I'll fix the grill."

We had fruit salad for dinner and Moke wasn't going to forgive me, the only thing he likes better than melon is green figs. You get them off-planet. Here it's Ari merchandise. I'm not sure you don't get booked just for holding.

The hot tube was as big as a subway tunnel with special glass for regulating the ultraviolets and fluorescent sticks slung from the upper curve. Razor let us use a couple of karts on the understanding we didn't race them. I thought he was going Gooder until I found what speed he thought wasn't racing. That tube did cover a lot of country.

The sloshing of pumps was louder inside but muffled by hot wet air like breaking the sound barrier down the lining of an aorta. When I see too many plants at one time I get this claustrophobic feeling, like maybe they're secretly growing the kind of pods have little blank humans in them waiting for you to get too close to go *whap!* and turn into nasty green people with monotonous voices.

The place stank of chemical fertilizer, citrus and algae. The algae grows on the surface and has to be skimmed off and somethinged. Razor wasn't too eager to say what, which made me think us guys in the lower end of the Strip probably eat it. We met a couple of his industrials on the way, prodding and snipping like oversized lobsters. They were much the same color, which makes sense with his driving habits. They were towing skips, one ripe fruit, one garbage.

Halfway down, the tube sided on a silo as big as a gasometer. A cascade of brownish slurry poured out of it into a pool at the bottom where the liquid sank out of sight, I supposed into the troughs that fed the plant growth. The edges of the fall were overgrown with hanging beards of green mossy stuff. Someone, I guess Razor, had planted orchids in it, and the trails of fleshy blossom rioted down to meet their reflections in the disturbed pool. It smelled. Of overripe meat and green decay.

On the opposite side a big squat thing like a mechanical octopus was swallowing another pool of slime-green sludge and chopped vegetation. From time to time an industrial would come trundling down, chomp its cart of leaves and twigs to mush, and spew them in. It smelled even greener than the waterfall, like you could bite it off and chew it.

We stopped to admire the floral arrangements and I sneezed. Stench does that.

"Doing business, boss-man," Swordfish said. He picked an orange off a nearby tree and put it absently in his pocket. To eat alone.

"He's running contraband."

Razor was examining leaves. "Pretend you haven't noticed. I'm okay. People got to eat."

"Even Sword."

"He's a lot of carcass to support. Plus his metabolism. You seen what he has to swallow after an operation to get his blood sugars right? Yeah, things are okay. But there's trouble coming, I can smell it. You noticed the city getting weirder?"

"It's been weird all my life," Sword said. "Still is. There's a lot of death. Bodies in the bay. But there always were."

"But maybe not with the same identities." Razor scratched the line of his jaw under clipped hair. "You seen dead guys in mohair suits before? There's a corporate war on. You've only seen the edges. It's why I'm listening. People are going under and some have big names. Coelacanth could be fighting for its life. When that happens things get dirty."

"Aurora said they needed a hit."

"Smart girl. They got to succeed or be swallowed. I heard a whisper too. It's a multibillion-cred business. Cordovan's a working director but he has shares. There are guys losing money in other fields who wouldn't mind diversifying. Big guys. And to fight you got to be big too. If the firm goes down Cordovan goes with it, and one good scandal could blow the works. You should understand, Cass. You made a living passing dynamite."

I shrugged. "Ari business. They've always slaughtered each other. It's when they start slaughtering us they piss me off."

"Maybe you aren't alone. All Umps live on the edge. It's surprising how far you can make people bend. But it's a can of worms down there. If anyone took the lid off we could find ourselves with wiggly invertebrates all over the furniture."

"Uh-huh," Sword said. "I stay on the tightrope. Balance of power. But it's a juggling act. I've got the same feeling. Something's going to give. Tomorrow, a thousand years. Sometime."

Razor shook his head. "Neither one nor the other. But there's a smell."

"Alien trouble stirring too," Sword said. "Those bastards come back every fourteen, fifteen years. You noticed that?"

"If you say so."

"I do. I've been counting."

"All we need. But I've got it in my nose. Smell of thunder. It's why I want this. Apart from a moral objection to guys who kill Cassandra. A judgment in the International Court could balance things. Or unbalance them. I'd like to see which."

"Bloody old man."

"Always was, Cass. I've an interest in your lives. I'm at an age for evaluating harvests."

Sword took his orange out of his pocket and started absent-mindedly to peel it. After a bit I guess it came to him he couldn't eat it since he doesn't and he tossed it to me. I'm not proud. I split it and stuffed segments. It was good.

"I'm thinking of getting out."

Razor stopped in the act of rearranging a spray of orchid and very deliberately turned to look at him.

"That so?" Neutral.

"Yeah." Sword was even more neutral. "Hell, I'm over thirty. Reflexes're slowing. Wings is young and hot and hungry. I been thinking about handing over."

"I was in charge at seventy-nine," Razor said, most neutral of all. "Figured it took that long to learn the trade."

"Yeah, well. I been fighting half my life. Almost exactly."

Razor shook his head. "And what you going to do next, boy? Don't see you curling ladies' hair."

"Hadn't thought."

"Ah. You hadn't thought."

He turned back to the orchids. From the rustling, Sword was doing more mayhem on an orange tree.

I was rigid. I couldn't imagine Ashton without Swordfish. But then my imagination's not too lively. It took me a damned long time to imagine it without Razor.

"Well, that settles it. If Wings is running things I'm taking off for the big black. Before he writes his own contract. On me."

"I keep telling you he's okay, Cass. It's in your mind."

"Sure. It'll be on my tombstone. 'It was all in her mind.' "

Razor slung a leg over the rim of his kart. "Sun's going down. Sword, if you're taking an orange help yourself but quit messing that tree around." He tossed a yellow globe that disappeared into the air and swung the wheel. "Race you home."

Weird times, yeah. Razor never contradicts himself.

He won easily, of course.

On the way back to the house I caught my foot on something just above soil level in the shrubbery and nearly fell on my face. Sword caught my arm.

"You keep manholes among the magnolias?"

Razor glanced over his shoulder. "Sure. Good earth. Be surprised what it grows."

It was one damned big manhole and my kick had done something to the lid because it was sliding back into the ground. The pit beneath was wide and deep. About the depth of a naval heavy duty heat-seeker with functional warhead.

He leaned back to work the manual lever that closed it. The electronic controls would be in the house. He didn't say anything else and neither did I.

But I did wonder just what it was he was protecting himself against. And I hoped it didn't mean to try his defenses.

Because if it did we could have a full-scale war.

The old man came out to the pad with the lazy shepherd lounging by his side and leaned against the door.

"I hope one of yous thought the best way to settle the Dein problem might be an explosion. Bang. Happens to sats. Very hard afterward to say what caused it. Meteorite, old core-reactor, guy got depressed and messed with the gravitronics, who knows? Nice place there?"

A current of cold air ran the length of my backbone.

"May not be anyone home. They're working."

"Uh-huh. Might be an idea not to weekend. Keep their little feet on the ground. Would be a waste to have the boy vaporized before I get around to saving his ass. You could keep an eye on the studio too. In case."

• • •

I sat on my side of the copt braced in my harness and looked out at darkness on the other side of the canopy. What I mostly saw was a reflection of myself looking like a bad day in the boneyard.

I'd seen my stepfather and he was kind, constructive, and practical. It wasn't my business what he kept in silos in his garden. Because there was no way there was only one. Swordfish the death angel was talking retirement. At thirty. Because he was getting too slow.

It was like reaching in the fusebox and putting your hand on a live wire. Thirty? When I was fourteen and he was teaching me to shoot I'd thought he was as old as the sphinx. He'd been twenty-one. Sword had no right to have an age. I hated even the thought. It gave him what he'd never had. Mortality.

I hadn't felt this gray since the day my mother slung me in the street for lifting from stores to pay my blue angel and I'd found myself loose, not knowing where to go next but afraid of the hole the future made. Hell, there wasn't one. Razor handed me a family before I'd even had time to get raped.

I felt like I was suddenly losing it all over again. Me and my old lady'd never got on together anyhow. The hole called tomorrow was bigger and blacker this time around.

Today felt like the board saying the end was nigh.

I felt somehow it was.

Even a basket between my feet with a bucket of green figs that was going to make Mokey's night wasn't filling my life with sunshine, and I like Moke.

I was miserable as hell.

I didn't even want to know why.

The Roaring Forties was in full roar and with them it's only full insulation and being two stories below street level keeps them from being raided for disturbing the peace every night of the week.

People who have joints below street level get them one of three ways. They inherit them from someone had a legitimate commerce there, they have them built special, or they make their own arrangements. The Roaring Forties was in the third class. They'd gotten hold of an old subway station on a disused branch line, stripped it out, blocked the tunnel both ends with thinnish cinder-block, and made what was left into two layers of medium-rare debauchery.

You got down to it through a funhouse-type door. It opened onto a curving slide shot the patrons in various states of messed-up dress, depending on whether they'd been there before or not, into the middle of a heap of cushions in the reception area. If you were unlucky and the guys previous had kicked and screamed more than usual you could land on rubber tiles taught you not to do it again. Any woman who'd been there once wore pants next time. Gazing up the skirts of ladies in transparent streamers was a local amusement. There was a working escalator to get you back out.

All of this depended on convincing the doorman you

could afford them, preferably by slipping him a largish piece of folding credit. The escalator came out a different way so as not to spoil the fun by letting smartass guys keep their shirts tucked in by walking down. It had a one-way exit at the top that looked after itself.

Another part of the entertainment was coming out totally slewed into a black side alley and finding the local muggers waiting. On the nights the two club bouncers were slow coming on the job. They never functioned before midnight so anyone with the bad taste to leave early got what they deserved.

Since we'd been there Mokey, Yell, Caronne, and me arrived as decently as you can in the Forties, spacing our slides so nobody landed on anybody else's head and spoiling the apes' entertainment by yelling like we were enjoying it. The slide dumped us on our butts in front of the hat-check counter. That's a euphemism. It's where the management collects as much ironmongery they can either locate or the clients are willing to give up.

Since we were only out for a respectable night's decadence Yell and I checked our tools, Moke demonstrated he hadn't any and Caronne showed her teeth. Which were long and possibly reinforced. When she did I worked out why she gargled with dime perfume. Her breath stank.

I guess they were her only means of defense, because she was wearing pink satin tights would have shamed a ballet-dancer. They showed her legs didn't rate it and stopped just short of her belly button. Which was ornamented with an artificial blue roselet with a glass sapphire. The tout ensemble was topped by an azure bolero in spray-on fuzz made it clear she should have either had surgery or worn a bra. If she had a ya I hated to think where she was hiding it. Or anything else.

Mine was in its usual place when I'm sleeveless, which is down my pants leg. They don't strip-search lady patrons, on the assumption they may have to defend themselves.

Sometimes they do the guys. You'd be astonished what they've been known to find.

I had tight jeans in wet-look leather and a silver mesh singlet so as not to look like competition. I wanted to make a good impression. You don't corrupt a bim if you start by making her mad at your clothes. It's true I'd added crystal chandeliers with matching bracelets, but a guy has her image to protect.

Moke and Yell were dressed like guys. I'd overridden Moke's protests and forced a blue crinkle-silk shirt over his party jeans, the ones with the ass covered, and Yell had got into a gray silk jump voluntarily. We were modest and correct. Well, three of us. We got the fourth through on sufferance and a larger than usual tip.

When we'd picked ourselves up and disposed of the burning-irons we got to put ourselves around a table not too close to the band and order drinks at ludicrous prices.

The Forties has this simple-minded approach to decor. They paint the whole place matte black with a polished chrome edge to the band platform, dim the lights and turn a spot on the entry every time someone comes down. Apart from that they have dimly colored cones in the ceiling rotate at random throwing red, green and purple shafts here and there, which does make sure you don't see what you paid to be poisoned with.

The band's the latest deuterium rock makes you think sometimes if the end of the world's nigh it mightn't be a bad thing. Since the walls are fragile you get an echo like something big was coming down the tunnel occasionally scares the patrons out of what minds they have left after the juice and the drummer. The musicians love it.

That's the upper level. The roulette, psychic poker and other games of manipulated chance are downstairs along with the men's and women's johns. Since most of the guys who come up and down are blued to the eyeballs, the floors are joined by a plain staircase with wide treads and a thick carpet. It minimizes the death toll.

Some creature of indeterminate sex and great grace and beauty passed out menus the size of the Great World Atlas and waited undulating. It's possible the Forties' menus have something printed on them, I wouldn't know. It could be pornographic pictures. I've never seen anyone open one. If you care about your eyesight it's not worth the trouble.

"Steak, four, rare," Yell said.

It's what everyone says with slight variations. The Forties is one of the few non-Ari places gets real steak steak, which means House has a hand. There's no point holding your nose, House has a hand in most things. The graceful entity took the four World Atlases back and swayed off.

"Class," Caronne said with appreciation.

Seemed to me she'd sure fallen. She would have found this dive too low to look at once. Things are relative. It was the highest class place we knew she was likely to be let in and maybe she hadn't tasted steak in a while. Come to think of it, neither had we.

We got our steaks, big and smoking, and a bottle of imported wine. Then sweet soufflé and another bottle, different. Caronne giggled. I thought her working eye had got watchful. Where she came from guys didn't buy bims like her this stuff unless they wanted something. Looked to me she was waiting to hear what.

In the meantime she had another glass and pretended to fall over Yell when he took her on the floor. Drunk she wasn't. There's very little you can do to deuterium rock but make small steps on the spot, and she was making them without faltering. It's true Yell brings out the urge but genuinely drunk girls can't even when they want to.

Moke looked at me.

"She ain't drunk and she don't trust us," I said. "Let's dance."

"She'll be laughing if she has a doctored liver," he said gloomily. Moke dances with the same loose precision he does everything, which means he's a lot neater on his feet than he looks, but he grudges the time you waste doing it. When you could be at home torturing metal.

"She hasn't. If she could've afforded surgery she'd've used it on her face. Wouldn't you?"

"Um," he said. Which meant in his case probably not, unless he found the eye inconvenient. "She'd make an interesting study. I gotta do a sketch when she's free."

I snapped my fingers. It isn't one of the regular movements but it takes the place of the light bulb over your head.

"What about bribery? How's the bank account?"

"You're business manager."

"And you're the guy buys seven tons of marble here, a bigger laser-cutter there, half a dozen dancing-boys to stand in indecent poses while you render them in welded hosepipes someplace else and I get the bill at the end of the month. When I don't fall over the boys in the corridor. Confess to auntie what passing toys you've bought in the last three weeks and I'll tell you if we can afford bribes."

"One pink granite boulder," he said with the wistfully innocent look means he'd have liked three. "I been lecturing like anything to pay for it."

"So you have, Moke. You're a sweet thing. Okay, as a last resort. Who cares if we spend the next six months on Gooder bread? You got enough granite to keep you happy for weeks."

He brightened. "If you bribe her quickly can we go home?"

"Martin, dancing is supposed to be a social pleasure. You're introverted."

"No, I got a headache."

Now he mentioned it so had I.

"Okay. Smile nicely. If the pretty lady lets herself be bribed we can go home practically right away."

The riot died temporarily and Yell led Caronne back to the table. Moke dug a tunnel and we got back ourselves with minor abrasions.

"Right," Caronne said when we were all on matte black stools. "Am I drunk enough for whatever you guys want or are we having another bottle?"

I like a woman comes to the point. "Let's have another bottle anyhow. Listen, bim, we need you. Coelacanth killed my boyfriend. Well, not quite. He's alive and breaking hearts but he doesn't know us. Problem is they may mean to kill him again. They already killed some other guys and they've tried Moke and me. My stepfather says international law. But we've no witnesses. Except you."

She fixed her one eye on me like the beam from a lighthouse. Its dead bloody mate squinted roughly the same way.

"Don't bother with the bottle, pretty-face, I'm leaving. I'm sorry about your problem, I see it's hard, but far's I'm concerned it's yours. I paid my dues. Told you, I only got one life and I'm economizing. Sorry, Yell. Nice knowing you."

"Hey, listen," I said grasping her wrist. "My stepfather's strong medicine. He's offering protection. Go to him and he'll hold off an army."

"Yeah. All I gotta do's live long enough to get there." She shook my hand off. "No deal."

"Caronne. You need surgery. Moke and me've got money. Go to Razor and we'll pay for your face and your eye and everything. We'll pay everything we've got. This guy matters."

She leaned down over the table.

"Listen, pretty, I appreciate the offer. I'd sure as hell like to take it. But the answer's still no. It's not much use being beautiful in hell. Sorry, kid. Get your stepfather to protect the guy is my advice. If he can. You may find none of yous as tough as you think." She looked around. "Shit, where's the Ladies'? All this drink's bad for me."

"Downstairs. You want me to come?"

"So you can argue some more? Don't bother, doll. I'll find it."

She strode over the carpet, her tights flashing on the black background. Her ass was flabby too. I'd sure as hell upset her. She'd forgotten to wiggle.

"She's real frightened."

"Good try, Cass," Yeller said. "I thought it mightn't work. She's one shaky lady. Why don't we broach that other bottle? Then I'll take my vid-star home. Hell, can't let her out into the alley alone, wouldn't be gentlemanly."

He waved for the waiteress and ordered something sparkly. "Hope she spends a minute on her makeup. If she wants to rush off I wouldn't mind a glass first. Cass?"

"Thanks." I was depressed. In Caronne's place I might have said the same. But she'd brought us to another blank. "Maybe Razor could convince her."

"You can try, kid. Wouldn't surprise me if her next move's to go to ground and you won't find her with bloodhounds."

Logical. It was also what I'd do in her place.

"Pass your glass." Yell glanced at the staircase. "Is there another way out?"

"Not that I know of." I glanced too. She'd had time to do whatever, including a complete lube and respray. Drunken bums of both sexes were rolling up and down but not Caronne. "You think she got sick? I'd better go look. I think you two might be conspicuous. Don't drink my champagne."

I went down the stairs to the room below and politely didn't stare at the guys getting clipped. It ain't nice to sneer at the unfortunate. I guess they had a noise-baffle halfway down because the ambience was a lot quieter. Just the soft click and murmur of credit rolling into the management's pockets. The clientele was glitzier too. The kinds of necklets and finger-jewels made the muggers' wait worthwhile.

The Ladies' was to one side behind a tactful Japanese maze, maybe to discourage the demons who were shooting craps across the room in velvet suits and chain bracelets. The door parted noiselessly as I came up after a brief pause to verify sex. Life here's difficult for transsexuals. Since they're genetically male they have to carry passcards. I got in to reasonable light, vulgar black tiles and enough mirrors to furnish a seraglio.

The powder room was empty apart from a row of velvet stools and the ritual courtesy creams and face-wipes laid out on the counter. Which confirmed what I'd thought. The lovely Caronne had eaten and drunk too much and was sadly throwing it up somewhere. I was kind of sorry. It's a shame to have your evening spoiled every which way.

I went in through the hot-air curtain that separated the sights and sounds of the powder room from the business end, if you'll pardon the expression, and found a row of cubicles with ebony doors outlined in gilt and even more mirrors. I guess there got to be bims want to watch themselves shit. I never caught the habit.

I was a bit alarmed not hearing the sound of vomiting. It isn't what you regret as a rule but if she wasn't barfing she was pretty certainly spaced and I wasn't sure I was strong enough to haul her to air single-handed. She was bigger and heavier than me and I didn't like the idea of calling attention to ourselves by getting in a hostess to rescue her.

I walked down the row trying doors. It did occur to me it was cold and drafty considering how the joint prides itself on its tacky luxury, and there was a musty smell. I suppose the patrons got to get sick often but I reckoned their airconditioning was missing a beat.

The cubicles were empty. Someone had thrown up in one all over the black plumbing and the built-in hot spray was trying to cope in lack of a responsible backside and was making a pool on the terrazzo. Someone else had left brassy hairs in one of their basins and a dryer was still humming. No Caronne. The door by the end wall was closed. I banged.

"Caronne? You okay?"

No answer. Damned bim had to've really hit the big black velvet. Locked on the inside. I hammered some more. "Hey, Caronne?"

The draft and the musty smell were stronger this end. There was an aeration unit in the wall above and I held my hand to it. The air coming out was warm, almost hot. Funny. I took another look at the door. The Forties is one of those places allows for all varieties of human perversity, as they ought to considering their clients, and it came right down to the floor. There was a gap of maybe a foot at the top to let the air circulate but not enough to let anyone through. I looked at it without enthusiasm. The damned door was high.

"Caronne! Come on, bim, snap out of it. If I gotta get the management we're in the street the hard way. Wakey-wakey, it's me. Unlock the fucking door, huh?"

Still no answer. But with those damned cinder-block walls my voice had one hell of a weird echo. Like *The Curse of the Mummy's Tomb* or something. I took another look at the door and sighed. If she'd dropped dead on us or like that we were in trouble. Way she looked there was no way of knowing what she had on the inside.

I dumped my bag, hooked my hands on the upper edge of the frame and muscled up until my head touched the ceiling. I couldn't even get my forearms over the wood, there wasn't room. What I did manage was get my eye level high enough to squint inside.

There was nobody in the cubicle. And there was no side wall to speak of either. The blocks had been burned out to a height of about five feet and a width of about three leaving an opening on stinking musty blackness. Which explained the draft and smell. The floor of the cubicle was littered with broken lumps of cinder-block, a lot of them sooted, and they'd been crushed into the tiles by heavy feet.

Not hers. It'd crossed my mind for a moment she might be frightened enough to find her own way out, but that hole was a laser cutter working from outside and she'd been wearing sandals with heels as high and pointed as six-inch nails. I had a very nasty feeling indeed. Maybe it had started being bad luck even to be seen with us.

I dropped down, backed off and kicked the door hard over the lock. It's a trick never fails on vid. In my case it jarred my leg all the way to my backbone, left an ugly dint in the ebony and didn't shift a thing. Damn. And I'd handed in my shooter upstairs.

I paused for thought, and had the illumination there had to be a way of opening doors from outside because drunken customers must pass out often and they could hardly demolish the place every time. Hence the fancy gilt facing at lock height. I prodded around, found a nobble and tried pushing. Then twisting. Then spoiling my nail polish trying to get under. Finally I got mad and hit it with the heel of my shoe and whether that was the technique or I just happened to spring the mechanism the door swung suddenly back.

I looked at the hole. I thought I ought to go back and tell Moke and Yell. I thought I ought to go back and ask for my iron at the hat-check. I thought if I did either of those things we were going to be up to the ears in management and meantime Caronne was getting farther and farther away and by the time we'd finished arguing we'd never see her again. If she was still alive.

I stepped into the cubicle, crunching on crumbs of cinder-block, locked the door before the next guy started yelling cop and poked my head out the opening.

Blackness. Smell of ancient disused places, dust and damp and old degraded engine oil, lichen, algae, every slimy and disgusting thing.

The drop to the tracks was maybe six feet. I turned on my belly and scraped down it, doing my pants a lot of no good. My sandals weren't made for hikes in a horror film either—though I notice the sandals of horror-film heroines never are. I likewise grazed my palms on the rough edges, which didn't surprise me.

There were a couple of inches of felted grease between the rails and I landed in it. It got between my sandal-straps and squirmed sensuously around my toes. Great. I just love adventures. I sent a hold message to my stomach and started down the track.

The first few yards were lighted by the soft pinky fittings of the Forties' toilets, made to persuade raddled ladies they don't look as bad as they do. After that it got inky. Luckily there wasn't much choice of way. The Forties was built over the station so what was left was tunnel. I thought it curved though it was hard to tell in the dark but whatever, it went one way ahead and I had the rails under my feet. Where I could fall over them every time I forgot about my heels.

I tried crossing to the edge and found some fool had lined the sides of the track with road-metal which wasn't hard to walk on, it was impossible. I crossed back and went on stumbling.

It was lucky I did because after a bit I came to a fork in the rail and the remains of an old points system rusted to hell and sticky with something I didn't want to investigate. I stood and breathed. A cold draft was coming from the right, which meant somewhere that line led to the open. The air from the other was still.

Decision time. Had the goons, whoever they were, taken Caronne down the open side where there had to be another station sooner or later, or the closed one where there might be God knew what? I'd no idea. I flipped a mental coin, influenced by a sense my stomach wasn't staying on hold too much longer, and made for the open. If I was wrong we were going to be sorry. Hell, we were damned certainly going to be sorry anyhow.

The felted dirt wasn't so thick here. From time to time I could hear my heels click on the surface under the rails. The click bounced backward and forward in the arch of the tunnel, magnified. Somewhere in front water was dripping. All we were short of was Dracula. No doubt he was due on any minute. I did wonder what I was doing here.

Oh, yeah, rescuing Caronne. Right. Cassandra the girl hero.

I hoped the damned goons meant to stand still to let her be rescued. Better still I hoped she was living and conscious. Because between us, two pairs of spike heels and her teeth, we might just impress them. I mean, they might even oblige us by laughing themselves to death.

Then I heard another echo, faint, from in front. The dripping had fooled me. I'd thought it was all water. Some of it wasn't. Someone in boots that clinked, saying metal reinforcements, was walking ahead.

I stopped dead, stretching my ears so hard my scalp moved back, and waited to know which way: going or coming. The bastard was walking carefully, for several seconds I couldn't hear anything but the intermittent plop of drops in a pool. Then another clink and a slight scrape. Going.

Right. Now was the time for all good women to tell their bellies where to go. Because I couldn't afford any more noise. If these guys hadn't heard me they'd better not start. I wasn't going to make much of a fight. My best hope was just to follow and try to drum up some sort of help as soon as I saw where we were going. Even a cop would do. I bent down and unstrapped my sandals.

The surface was slimy and viscous with occasional sharp lumps and nodules. I limped as fast as I could barefoot between the rails in the footsteps of clinking-boots and whoever was with him. Because they weren't sending one guy on a kidnap mission. These kinds of heroes don't like to be alone even when they're facing one not-so-young woman with one eye and half a face. Hell, there might have been two of us and we'd have said boo to them.

The dripping had been getting louder. I found my leading foot in cold water floored with slime and a big cold drop splashed down the back of my mesh singlet. I'd been regretting that for a while. It's not exactly combat material and the air was cold. I bit on a shiver, nearly slid and pulled myself together. My guys were still in front.

I nearly missed the station. When I came out of the tunnel I felt rather than saw the wider darkness that stretched off to the side. Then I heard the faint clink-scrape of metal-soled boots to the left. Platform. I limped over the rails, bruising my shins, and came up against the rim.

The bastard was high. It took another hefty muscling job and more damage to my pants to get up it. I stood on the edge, sandals in my hand, and sniffed and listened.

There was certainly an exit ahead. Maybe several. I couldn't see a thing. I groped into the dark trying to localize the cool wind that came down from above and stretching after that distant withdrawing clink of boots. My hand met tiles, rusted metal that had maybe once been a vending machine, rotted wood that touched my fingers not quite in time to stop me stubbing my toe on what was left of a bench. I didn't quite swear.

The clink was receding to the right. There was a draft that way too. I guessed the guys were wearing filters because they hadn't any light. I'd have given a lot to have the same. I felt my way, hands and feet, until the tiles turned a corner and a blast of air said exit.

More groping. Another tunnel but smooth-floored, turning upward. I took that one at a painful lame-footed sprint. There had to be a stair or something at the end.

There was. It fooled me at first. Cold, ridged metal treads and the boot-clink, metal on metal much clearer, high and parallel above. Until it came to me I was on a frozen escalator, one of two that had run up and down. The rail was gritty with dust and lumped with powdery extrusions of degraded plastic. I took hold of it anyhow, it speeded the climbing. The guys ahead were moving fast and I was having trouble stifling my breath. It sounded to me like a forge bellows in full blow.

Then the stairs flattened in an echoey hall with glints of colored neon jittering between the cracks of a broken barricade. Red and blue ripples trickled over the dirty rubble-strewn floor, canting ticket booths, a rusted turnstile. I climbed over the barrier, balancing my sandals, and made for the gap.

Mistake. You always get what you deserve in the end.

"Well, hell," a man's voice said in front of me. "If we haven't got the both of them."

And he let off a gas-bomb in my face.

Moke was walking away down a lighted corridor. I could see his torn jeans with plaster-dust on the knees, T-shirt pulled out on a couple of inches of bony spine, his lank hair held in place by a twisted band. His bare feet slapped lightly on the tiles, pad, pad, pad.

There was danger up ahead, I could feel it in my guts, and he was walking right into it. I tried to yell but my voice had got stuck and nothing came out but a choking whisper. I twisted my throat, breath whistling, looking for a howl, and all the time he was walking farther and farther away.

I unglued my feet and started to run, a slow syrup-footed plod that stuck to the floor. The corridor walls went by, very slowly. I went on moving my mouth soundlessly and he walked on without turning his head.

We came out suddenly on the edge of a cliff, a right-angled wall as sharp as the side of a box with absolute blackness in front. He was only a couple of steps ahead now, still walking, as if he didn't see the gap, like for him the emptiness didn't exist. He took a step, and another. His foot came to the brink and for a moment I wondered if he was going to walk out into air like Tom and Jerry.

At the last moment his eyes snapped down and he tried to catch himself. I saw him sway. All my muscles cramped. Somewhere in the distance I felt it burn and

164

didn't care. I dived frantically for his shirt.

And missed.

Then I was lying flat on my belly with the edge digging into my hipbones and I could see him a bare arm's length below. He was clinging by his fingertips to a crack hardly wider than a nail paring, feet braced against the wet stone, gazing up with intelligent green eyes. His look was calm and analytical like he was working out some abstract problem in spatial relationships. Beneath him a black gap dropped away into infinity. A million miles below I could hear the sound of rushing water and I knew it was the sick living torrent of Virginity that smothered whatever fell into it.

I wriggled forward and leaned over, arms and shoulders dangling into shadow. He was almost within touching distance and I strained toward him trying to catch his hand before that dangerous grip could slip. He braced an elbow on the face and edged a dirty-nailed hand toward mine, his feet scraping.

Our fingertips almost met, I thought we were going to make it. And then as he touched me his feet gave way and the hand reaching for mine slid, clutching for a hold where there was none. My heart closed and I felt my breathing stop.

But the hand was too long. It was ghost-white with ridged scars outlining the bones and it clawed at the rock-face with unhuman strength. The wall was smooth as a slate and the nails scratched and tore and slipped away in a long curve, leaving a white scratch like chalk across the layer of slime that covered the glassy surface.

I was looking down into Swordfish's ruined face. His painfully human mouth with its humorous lips was half-open as if he meant to say something and his bare eyes looked up at me, fixed in an expression I couldn't understand. But before he could speak his other hand slipped too and he slid away silently into the gulf, disappearing into darkness, his eyes still turned up to mine with that dumb message.

I saw him go, down and down, while I leaned after him with my arms out, my throat wrenched in a scream. Stretching until my tendons cracked, as if it would do any good, trying to will him back as I'd once willed Dosh, and knowing it wasn't going to help. Nothing helped. It hadn't then, either. He was gone and I would never know what he'd wanted to say. It seemed very important. Sword . . .

Violent winds tore at me, or maybe it was only tears that made the rock pitch and sway, throwing me off too, shaking me loose. Shaking . . .

A hand was wrenching my shoulder.

"Hey, wake up!"

Another shake and a slap, so lost in time and space I only heard it happen like there were layers of felt between me and my skin. My head rocked and a slash of pain sawed my skull. Then the voice got through and I tried to ungum my eyes and make sense of it.

It was a gravelly growl underlaid by something bright and metallic. The face that went with it was a grotesque clown-mask, garishly painted and leering. Then my eyes settled and I saw Caronne, purple dreadlocks over her spoiled cheek, her working eye so blurred with red the white and the iris seemed to have run together into a fusion of blood. The eyelid over the useless ball had a persistent tic as if it was trying to see where there was no eye left to see with. Her mouth was drawn back over discolored teeth.

"Cassandra! Wake up!"

" 'S okay," I said hoarsely.

Or tried to. My mouth felt like wood, my tongue semi-paralyzed. My throat might have been filled with sawdust.

"Don't hit me, I got here."

"Thank God for that."

She knelt back. The purple wig swung away from her face and showed it bare and rotted like something you'd expect on a slab with a tag tied on its toe. Her burned cheek had lost a lot of its coverstick and the skin beneath was shiny and mottled, scarcely enough of it to cover the bones. The other had a huge purple bruise the exact shape of four fingers and a thumb. A crust of blackened blood oozed over a puffy swelling at the corner of her mouth.

She'd lost the roselet with sapphire and her tights were torn. Fleshy thighs showed through the rip, stippled with gravel and dark points of blood on top of a blue-green lump of graze. A lot of her azure fluff had worn off and her left breast sagged, a hanging brown nipple like a winter rose hip furred with mold.

Her breath still stank and her armpits stank worse. A smell like a circus: wild animal, sweat and decay. Her one eye was furious and concerned at the same time. She looked scared out of her mind. Except the one glint of sanity that was working at slapping me back to the cold world we were getting to share.

"Are you awake?"

"As much as I'm going to be." I sat up, got a rasp of pain that divided my skull like a hacksaw and regretted it. "Ouch. What happened?"

"You followed me, shithead," she snarled. "If you had to stick your nose in, couldn't you've called the fucking cops or something?"

"Hadn't time."

"Imbecilic half-grown bim. Thought you were fucking dead. Not that it's going to make any difference," she added with a slurring grate in her throat. "Only I didn't fancy sharing a cell with a corpse."

"Bastards gassed me. Where are we?"

"Search me, doll. Gassed me too, I reckon, though I did see 'em coming. Didn't do much good. Got me this." She put her hand to the swelling on her lip. "Got dragged in the john at the Forties, passed out, woke up here. With you. You were making noises in your sleep like you were choking to death. Scared the hell outta me."

"Oh. Thought I was screaming my head off." I scrubbed at eyes that felt like they'd been grated. "Wow. Wish I'd made it, wouldn't mind being headless. Don't suppose the boyfriends left any water?"

"You think this is a hotel? There's kind of a washbowl, looks like it been dry half a century. Probably runs roaches. Want a breath freshener?"

Breath freshener. World's full of optimists, you meet one every day.

"Don't know I got any spit left."

"Try it. It's better 'n death." She ran a finger under her tights band. A strip of foil sealed over green gels flipped out. "Here. Like a mountain brook, you should watch the commercials."

I took a menthol-smelling disc. I hoped the menth wasn't going to give me heaves before the gel got me sucks. It was going to be a close race.

"Thanks." She at least got points for trying.

I swallowed hard and ended by getting a grudging drop of saliva in the well of my tongue. At the expense of having my whole ENT system gudged with mint stink. My head still felt like someone had operated on it with a chainsaw and slapped it back together with bolts like Frankenstein.

I was sprawled on a heap of shaled plaster on a filth-grained floor with my back against a wall. Most of the plaster must have come from the wall, though some was from the ceiling and it looked like further precipitation was expected.

The walls were close, high and had been painted pink. The ceiling had a cornice that sagged like the wreck of a wedding cake. The small barred window high up was so dirty and hung with cobwebs it was hard to tell if it was dark outside or not. The paint that was left was patterned with puffs of fungoid mush that looked catching.

I rolled my head to the side and saw a door with warped ply springing away from stained base-layers.

"No good," Caronne said. "Barred on the outside. Even I tried that."

I rolled back and turned just my eyeballs. Even that hurt. It felt like somebody'd lined my eyesockets with sandpaper.

The place reminded me of something and I was trying to think what. The ruins of what had been a curtained wardrobe in one corner, washbowl opposite with greened brass spigots and a dried-out plug stranded on the edge. It looked as old as the pharaohs and drier than the Sahara. The verdigrised S-bend under it would have done as a warning for plague. A brighter pink shape on the main wall was the ghost of a dressing table. A swaying snake of frayed cable trailed above with bare blackened wires.

"Window's useless. Wonder what's outside."

"Couple of guys with disruptors?" She wasn't even interested. "You hear something?"

I listened. No traffic, no footsteps. A faraway gnat whine could have been midnight traxies shooting the lanes above the Strip. Or not. Outside was dead as the tomb. Not natural. The place had to be a long way from civilization. Or underground. Or something.

"It's godawful quiet."

"Outside, yeah. Try that way."

I retuned my ears. Something funny. A running-water noise like an old-fashioned cistern that wouldn't stop flushing. Ancient empty pipes that gulped and gurgled. And someplace farther off a grinding mechanical hum.

Old machinery that pounded, a lot of walls away.

"Factory?"

"Uh-huh. What you think they're making?"

I thought I'd rather not know.

Plaster casts for skeletons. Papier mâché masks for freakshows. The materials for the House of Wax.

The place was lit with a modern ceiling-plate, new. The light was white, flat and shadowless. The pounding missed a beat and it dimmed as the thump-and-gurgle paused then brightened again. The pounding picked up where it left off.

Now I'd started hearing, seemed to me I could feel it in the boards. A steady not quite regular vibration that shivered up and rattled my ankle bones.

"What you figure these guys want?"

Her gummed red eye squinted. The jaw beneath was trying to shake but she was biting down.

"I wouldn't bet they want to crown us Miss Universe. They got glittery tiaras and velvet cloaks out there they gonna surprise me."

"Just wondered why they bothered to carry us. When they could've fried us on the spot."

"Real interesting. I know one thing, doll, whatever they got going we ain't going to like it."

I tried unfolding my skeleton. It was an experience. Not my best. I got acquainted with the blisters when my feet hit the floor. Major. But it was a higher viewpoint.

What was left of my pants was scraped raw and tinted this season's newest mud-color. My singlet was torn. Some guy with a sense of humor had slung my sandals after me which would have been more meaningful as a sweet thought if one of them hadn't been short a heel.

I leaned on diseased plaster and began unhooking my chandeliers. They were bent anyhow. I dropped them on the floor and unlooped bracelets on top. Caronne stared.

"Razor's first rule. Go by the book and pray."

I hauled the singlet over my head. That left me in torn pants and my skin. I'm fairly flat-chested. Luckily.

"What's in the book, doll?"

"Same rules made me lose my hair. Nothing to get hold of. Nothing dangles. Nothing can get pulled and hurt you. Nothing for a handle. Hair, jewelry, loose clothes. Especially earrings they can tear out and necklaces they can choke you with."

I limped over and poked in the dry sink.

"Want something?"

"Grease. Soap. Anything at all slides. If it's dirty that's fine by me. I'm not baring my titties for their erotic enjoyment."

She smiled mirthlessly. "I can help, if you ain't too particular."

"I ain't particular at all."

"Okay." She dragged blue-nailed hands over her ruined face and brought them down smeared with terra-cotta. "Help yourself, honey."

Under the smudged color her skin was drum-tight and shiny. Shriveled white patches clustered it in folds. Her hands were skinny as claws, a splatter-pattern of white blotches strewn across the backs. I swallowed something evil while she rubbed them over my nipples, plastering my chest and shoulders with pink and ocher dazzle-streaks.

"Keep still and you can have the rest of the circus. Don't figure I'm going to have much use for it."

Her eye shadow and lipstick went on the back and it was the first time I'd been grateful she was painted like the front of a sailing-ship.

"Uh. Not too tasty. I'd want to rinse before eating."

Her bare face was the mask of a plain, deformed old woman, twisted into a clown grin. Her one ruby eye glared above like a traffic light.

"Sorry. I didn't think we could do this to you just by knowing you. Goddammit, you refused."

"These ain't sane people, doll. Save yourself if you can. You're a kid, none of this is your fault." Her jaw muscles lumped. "You're damn right I refused. But I begun to think where we are now it don't matter whether I say yes, no or some day. So I'll tell you a little thing could be of use if you ever get out of here."

"Hey, listen. There's your future . . ."

"No, baby. Something's telling me all my future's in the past. Maybe yours ain't. I'm tellin' you anyhow." She leaned closer, her eye intent. "I hadn't that much to say, I wasn't in the councils of the big men. But there was a lady was. Same one threw this in my face."

It took me a moment to see her ghastly grimace was a smile. "Teeter-totter. One up, one down. Made her fortune and retired. I did hear her retirement wasn't entirely voluntary. Whatever, she's around and working. With money behind her. Cordovan's an old friend, she's spent the odd night in his bed. A lot of damned odd nights if I know 'em. Name's Halo. Ask around the spaceyards. If anybody knows what went on in that rotten outfit she's it. She was in the middle. It's the best I can do, babe. Make 'em pay for me."

She'd once been a rich, beautiful lady. I looked at her and she looked at me, three red eyes. She grabbed me in one swift hug like she might have been my mother, except my mother wasn't a hugger. Then we sat down side by side against the wall and waited for the executioners.

We waited a long time. All through that thump-gurgle went on and on. Until a sudden quality of the atmosphere woke me from a half-sleep and I realized it had stopped. Caronne was upright, her withered face tight. Then a sound I recognized. The clink of metal-reinforced boot soles on a hard floor.

I stood up. My headache had died back to a dull tension behind the eyes but my blisters flared to raw life and my muscles were stiff and reluctant. I was hungry, too. Caronne's circus face was underlaid by gray lines of fatigue, her lids swollen. Her bruised cheek had puffed and developed tones of purple and green. Her mouth was an overripe fig, leaking gum.

Bars crashed on the other side of the door and clinking-boots came shouldering in. It took me one look to figure that scenario. I know the Pack and I'm used to their mutation. It has uses. It's even a necessary qualification. This specimen was private enterprise.

He was six-and-a-half feet high and five wide and what passed for his face would have made a baboon look like Mars by Botticelli. Enough hair sprouted from his nose and ears to stuff a mattress. His hands were the size of shovels and you could have used his boots to sail down the Mississippi. The yellow ivory fangs that overhung his lower lip had started out on a male walrus. Double econo-my size. To make up for it his mean little red-brown eyes looked like he'd had them second-hand from a weasel.

He hulked in the doorway filling it from side to side and let us admire his wet red grin. Then he reached out a pair of arms long enough to brush his knees and grabbed a shoulder apiece.

There wasn't any question of not going. Our problem was getting our feet to touch the floor. Maybe he didn't know his own strength. Maybe he was the tooth fairy. His grip nearly wrenched my shoulder out of its socket.

Caronne made a stifled sound. I thought she'd have liked to moan. I also thought she couldn't, because she couldn't open her mouth any more. I was biting on the inside of my own cheek.

The corridor had something familiar about it too. Dark and narrow with doors down either side. Broken ceiling littered the floor. Some of the doors had rotted away.

They opened on dark smelly caves.

I cut my feet some more on sharp edges of lath and turned my head so the animal wouldn't see my eyes water. He saw. His grin widened. The pink tights snagged on a bolt and ripped with a silky nail-turning snick. An oozing scratch opened the length of Caronne's thigh and she made a strangled mew. His grin opened so wide I thought the top of his head might drop off. She bit on her tongue and tried to keep her pin heels straight. At least she had shoes.

We stumbled in rubble. The animal just waded through leaving great broad tracks like something prehistoric had passed here. He turned his feet out like a duck.

The corridor bent and and a glare of arcing brilliance cut my eyeballs. Some surface that reflected like a mirror, dazzling like a pavement of diamonds. A high blurred darkness soared beyond.

Sure. A pink room with a wardrobe for your skating dresses and a dressing table with light bulbs around the mirror. Thump-gurgle. Ice. The old rink where Swordfish had lain on a show for Nimbus after she killed Doshky. They'd been laying it on again. For us. At which moment we got to the performers' entrance where me and Moke had once slid out shivering, and the animal swung his long ropy arms and threw us both out right into the middle.

I'd watched Nimbus fly out of that tunnel windmilling. This time my feet hit the ice and they were bare and short of skin. Cold knifed up through my soles and took my breath away. I did a spell of flying blind, my eyes squeezed against the arclights blurred by tears of shock, staying vertical by climbing practice and a good set of semicircular canals.

Bare feet aren't the world's best substitute for skates but they did keep me from falling on my face. Caronne with her nail heels hadn't a chance. She tobogganed past me on her belly, her face contorted, her hands clawed crookedly trying to brake. I slide-footed after and tried to catch her.

A shovel-sized paw shut down on my upper arm and slung me like an apache dancer. The fucker thought he was giving me a fall but me and Dosh used to practice apache dancing. I spun around and dropped into a long kid-glide that carried me half across the rink. I like ice. Preferably when I'm wearing skates, it's true.

Things generally have an up and a down. Down, the cold was springing my bare upper half into goosebumps, but it anesthetised my feet. That up was powerful.

I ended with a bump against solid legs in laced hunting boots and spilled back on my hind end. And got a good look at what we were sharing our ice with. We were the focus of a semicircle of lumps. Big half-human hulks gene-muted to crosses of half a zoo that did no credit to either species. Not one smaller than the side of a shithouse and most smelling much worse. Drooling through feral grins. A couple had bulges in their pants could have been the normal state of their equipment only I didn't think so.

It's dreary the way guys do what you expect.

"Dear Cassandra." Bronze gong voice. "Help the lady up."

I got my arms grabbed by a pair of oversized goons, one so furry to you couldn't tell if he was truly a mute or just first cousin to a wolfskin coat, and the other decorated with dewlaps would have looked good on a water buffalo. They made a production of standing me between them. Real tough stuff. I tried not to swoon with ecstasy.

I already had a collection of blue finger-marks and their gallant attentions didn't help. They jerked me around to face the lights but I couldn't see Jason. He wasn't in the judges' box. The voice had come from higher up among the tiers of seats. The arcs blazed in my eyes and brought out sweat on my scalp. My feet were freezing.

"That's better. Cassandra, you're an enormous help to me. Your scene with Nimbus was such a success I'm sure this will be popular too. I needn't bother to explain, you're much too intelligent to need it. And audiences bore so easily if they're kept waiting. So I'll clear the way for the action." His voice paused, while he faked thinking about it. "A little suspense first, perhaps?"

No need to ask what that meant. His zoo was skating around in circles that spiraled in on Caronne.

"We need to make it clear, don't we, that treachery doesn't pay?" he purred, like a pipe organ in low register.

"Good thinking. But you sure your overmuscled geeks got the stamina? Have they been having their cornflakes?"

"Very good. When the villain's voice is dubbed in the effect will be splendid. You never disappoint me."

"Great. I sure hope I can say the same for you, I'm very exacting. I been accustomed to humans. Ain't never been perverted by a horsehair sofa."

"We'll do our best."

"Oh. Is that the royal we or are you weighing in personal? I mean, I'd love to have everyone see you on vid with your pants down—this is on vid, huh?—but like I said I got into the habit of people. Guy people. You wouldn't want to disappoint the fans. By the way, I didn't get 'villain's voice.' Thought we had it."

Infinitesimal pause.

"We're wasting time," he said sharply. "Get on with it."

Caronne was lying where she'd fallen, her knees slightly drawn up, absolutely still like a small animal that hopes not to be noticed if it only doesn't move. Two of the spiraling hulks had got to her level. They loomed over and grabbed her elbows. She got jerked up like a straw doll. It shook a little yelp of pain out of her like the squeak of a hurt puppy.

Number One grabbed at her breasts and started clawing away handfuls of azure fluff. His black-rimmed nails left red tracks on her skin. Two went for the waistband of her tights. He thought it was fun to snap the elastic on her belly a couple of times before he got around to tearing them to shreds and throwing them over the scenery. Real machismo's awesome. I tried not to vomit.

Without her clothes you could see the life she'd been working through for thirty years. Her stomach and thighs were stretch-marked like she'd been fatter and changed her mind. Her breasts dangled with dark everted nipples. She nearly lost her wig with the jerk. It slid way back so we got to see why she wore it.

Underneath she had cropped hair, wispy, thin and mostly gray with shiny scalp showing through. The acid burns went up almost to her crown at one side and her skin there was puckered in patches, ragged lines of bristle growing through. The goon who'd been defuzzing her caught hold of the purple rug and yanked it right off. He held it up triumphantly like a scalp then let it drop on the ice. It lay curled like a dead kitten.

That's when she started screaming. She opened her mouth so wide I expected to hear her jaw crack and shrieked like an animal, a long wild howl that raised the hair on my neck. It reopened the cut at the corner of her mouth and blood slavered down her chin. She jerked at her arms, didn't get anywhere since she had a goon attached to each, and caught a raucous rasping breath for the next scream.

I tugged at mine. They might as well have been set in cement. The rest of the pack were getting excited. Their eyes glittered in the lights and wet lips rubbed together eagerly. My two must've been feeling left out. Furry, the one on the right, had started to move his filthy crotch up and down against my shoulder and I could feel his hard-on swelling under the fabric of his pants. His mate snuffled with a noise like squelching mud.

The one who liked to play games with tights fumbled at the fly of his gents' suiting, special ape-size. His sausage fingers were too clumsy for the zipper but he finally got there and let it fall around his ankles. There was a gust of fetid air with a strong perfume of athletic socks and a vision of hairy legs gnarled with wriggling veins. But his attributes would have given a brood mare hysteria.

"Jeannette!" I yelled. Dewlap jammed his stinking paw over my mouth. I bit it but it was well-tanned leather with a damned bad taste. Caronne tried to turn her head.

Pantless hesitated and looked up into the lights with the half-intelligent expression of the little dog on old phonographs. For a second his grip was relaxed, but she seemed too scared to react. She went on thrashing and moaning, trying feebly to kick. Her thin ankles flapped in the rags of her tights and her feet skidded uselessly. Then I caught a glint from that red eye. She was in there okay, and intelligent and sane. I'd forgotten she was an actress. Her lips formed the word "Go."

His Master's Voice hadn't bothered to speak. Little Dog got his nerve back. He let himself fall heavily on top of her and cut her off in mid-shriek. His two mates went on holding her arms. It was maybe too late already, his weight had almost certainly caved in her ribs. I bit down on a yell shriller than hers.

My two were gasping over my head. Furry had rubbed himself to lava-point and was making pig-noises and jerking like he was on strings. Dewlap gawped with eyes like holes in a furnace while drool ran slobbering down his muzzle.

Me, I was brought up by Razor. The book first, last, and always. Jeannette Merton had played dead to give me a chance. I slid my fingers down the band of my pants while my guards jerked and moaned in their personal fits of self-expression and found the handle of my ya.

I caught a handful of chest-hair on one side and a hanging sack of flab on the other and jerked. The ice was slippery and neither one was in a state to expect it. The one on the left got the full length of my ya in his eye. It isn't esthetic but very few people walk away. Takes a more specialized nervous system than either of them had. The other just got my heel where he was feeling happiest, in a backward mule-kick that had a small weight, a big fury and a long, accelerating swing behind it. He shrieked and let go.

"Good," Swordfish said gently from the rink entrance. "Now let's cool off and talk."

The geek who'd been waiting his turn at Caronne reached toward his belt, which with Sword is a mistake. He was dead with the laser in his hand before he even started to fall.

That flash covered another. I only heard the gurgle. Sword's second shot took the smartass's head off but it was too late. Caronne was lying as limp and curled as the dead-kitten heap of her purple wig, a wisp of smoke rising from the ruin where her chest had been.

The whole tableau froze.

I heard a whimper and thought it was me. I took a skidding step.

"Stand still, Cassandra," Swordfish said. His voice was still gentle. "I don't waste charge on bought meat. I want a word with the boss-man."

I thought he was closer. I saw a ripple by the body of the nearer of the two dead geeks and movement as he raised his hand. I expected his face but what he did was reverse the polarity of his suit, turning it to a black outline of nothing against the starry glitter. The prow of his nose raised the fabric of the hood and his long outline was sharp and tense.

"Cordovan? I've a message for you." Of course. Cordovan wasn't there. He wouldn't risk his bronze hide in a place things could go wrong.

"Last time someone took out a contract on Cassandra I brought her his head. He's got forty years to go and a personality-refit. I've given you one warning, in white phosphorus. It didn't take. This time I'm going to kill you. That's a promise."

I wouldn't like to have Swordfish promise to kill me. He's one hell of a guy for doing like he says.

The Voice hadn't time to answer, even if it meant to. Sword snapped his fingers and the spots went out leaving the rink in darkness. I thought the scuttling I could hear all around was the sound of rats, leaving. Sword can see in the dark and anyone looks at him and doesn't know it deserves what they're about to collect. An arm that could have belonged to Don Juan's father-in-law swung around my waist and scooped me into the air. It was a good move. My feet felt like marble. He turned rapidly and moved fast for the exit.

"Jeannette?" I whispered.

"Dead," he said. "And I don't think she's coming back."

The rising chill stopped like a curtain as we got to the tunnel and a blast of stale warm air blew in my face. It was black in the passage but his feet crunched lightly over the rubble in a sure line. I could almost see his cold eyes shine in the darkness.

"I suppose you need a medic for frostbite," he said in the impersonal voice means he's mad at me again.

I leaned up and wrapped my arms around his neck.

"I'm real glad you didn't fall in the river."

His head stayed high, meaning he didn't choose to honor me with his gaze.

"One day I may know what you're talking about. This isn't it."

He was really mad.

• • •

Damn. Now I was never going to know what he'd been wanting to say.

And Caronne, limp dead kitten, was behind us congealing slowly and she'd never tell anyone what she'd been wanting to say either. Except a name and a location she'd left with me. So I could do something for her after she was dead.

Sometimes I don't feel clever at all.

My feet began to wake up in the copt and I regretted it. I sat on Sword's knee and sniveled. He wrapped an arm around my back but he didn't say a word.

That made it an all-time mad. He usually speaks to me after half an hour or so.

He sat on the end of the bed pad as the medic used his hand regenerator, a black brooding shadow, and I'd no trouble understanding his eyes. A cold front over Iceland. He looked like if you seeded him with silver nitrate he'd rain lightning.

"I'm still glad you didn't fall in the river."

"She's delirious," he said to the medic.

"It's probably an allergic reaction to the gas," the medic said. "She'll be all right in the morning."

That's guys. They understand everything. Ask one.

"Okay," I snarled. "I'm not glad. I wish you had fallen in. You'd give indigestion to the fucking fish."

"Giving guys indigestion's what I do," he said coldly.

"I wish you'd go away. You're giving it to me."

He went on sitting.

Moke brought soup and I ate it feeling green and yellow and blue all over. Inside and out. I held the spoon and added salt. My own.

"She wanted to help me."

"Yeah," Sword said. "She was more grown up than

you. Which isn't difficult. I've a pleasure coming. I get to kill a guy."

"Cassie," Moke said, "tell the man thank you. It took us hours to get them to look in the lavatory and then we had to skip before they called the cops. They seemed to think we'd made the hole ourselves. Yell wanted to go after you but I went for Sword. If he hadn't come faster than light they'd have got you both. I think Caronne had lived too hard too long. Maybe she did something she wanted."

"Thank you," I said. Politely.

Swordfish looked at me like I ought to be in a jar.

"Are you in love with her?" he asked Mokey.

"Sure."

"God help you."

Moke looked at Sword. Diagnostic, like an interesting problem in tensile strength. Sword *is* an interesting problem in tensile strength. Then he said, "If you want some soup, Yell'll heat it. There's nobody in the kitchen."

"No, thank you," Sword said. Even more politely.

Which ended that conversation.

For me. Moke doesn't understand conversation-stoppers, conversation isn't his thing. He makes constructions. He knelt on the end of the pad behind Sword's glooming profile and rubbed the hinge of his neck. He had to do it through the suit but that didn't stop him. I waited for Sword to turn around and kill him. He didn't. He dropped his forehead on his hunched knees.

"That's twice," he said into his thighs. "Nimbus over. I should have got there."

"You haven't learned how to get up warp-speed over two kilometers," Moke agreed. "When you do, tell the Navy and they'll give you five bucks and a medal."

"I got those already," Sword said. "Only I made the bucks myself."

You bet he did. The old recipe, arson, rape and bloody murder. Except I forgot, the guy doesn't rape people. Or not when I'm looking.

Moke acted like he hadn't heard. It's best with Swordfish.

"Yell, we got some soup? With bread. And a steak. That is, it's combed prote. But it isn't bad."

"I won't be able to tell the difference," Sword said, muffled.

"That's right."

Sword laughed, somewhere at the bottom of the register. Blue notes but legal tender.

Moke has these talents.

"What next?" he asked, digging in his thumbs.

"Spaceyards."

"Uh-huh?"

"Your she-twin has inside information. Or so she said. I suppose we got something. All it takes is blood."

I never knew it bothered him.

"Okay," Moke said peaceably. If Sword'd said Hell, or the bottom of the river on Virginity, he'd probably have said much the same.

"A piece of cake," I said. "All we got to do is find a lady named Halo who kills people. Can't be more than three or four million down there."

Yell shoved his head around the kitchen door and said, "Soup. Bread. Steak on the way."

Sword unfolded. He'd quit looking like seven feet of bad road, which was something.

"Do me a favor, Martin. Sit on her head. I can feel old age coming on."

"Any time," Mokey said. He's high on courtesy.

But being Moke he came and cuddled me instead.

The spacers' playpen covers a couple of hundred hectares around the white and green flares of the yards. They have permanent decibels as the lighters land and the big transports take off for orbit and you bring your own earplugs because the guys are immunized. Their normal speech is what passes for howling among humans. They also like light, color and movement. There's people say they can see the neon glare over the port even in daylight and I've seen a colored smudge myself when the cloud cover's low.

The place is laid out for the three Bs—bars, brothels, and beeferies. They have signs from here to there and holo-barkers that dart out and shriek if you get within ten feet. Their spiels are the stuff begot the concept of censorship. Nobody censors them in Spacetown on the supposition anybody wants to be a spacer it's too late already.

Spacers don't belong to Ashton but some get born here. Renegade Aris, outlaw Techs, runaway Umps, an occasional Art with a cosmic consciousness. They can have any education so long as it includes a credit in advanced violence. A lot were born off-planet, like guys from the moons make Sword look normal-sized, blue-black skins made to repel ultraviolets, and the ones come decorated with their symbiotes who're pretty often totally disgusting.

Plus those with a lightsome sense of fun who happen to think it's nifty to be like that. Such as four arms or hands on all four limbs or eyes in the back of their heads. That's thought showy. They almost all have neural implants but not as advanced as Sword's, since they mostly pilot for a living and only kill each other for amusement. The guy's unique. Luckily.

Some are more respectable than others, which ain't saying much. If you're respectable you stay at home. People in their right senses go to a spacers' bar in full body armor. In our case we happened not to have any. These things happen.

The guys who went down in the end were me, Moke, Yeller, Dribble and Swordfish's little friend Lorn, who came around in a heavy-duty copt right after Sword went home and stunk out our apartment with all the perfumes of Arabia. I don't say it didn't need it. We just weren't accustomed. I sneezed.

We had one of these discussions before we left.

Sword wanted to veto me because he claimed I wasn't rational. I wanted to veto Moke because he was liable to get killed. Moke wanted to veto Dribble because he was only a kid and shouldn't be exposed to debauchery, which would have got my vote for different reasons if I hadn't been laughing so hard. Yell, who's an ex-spacer himself, wanted to veto all of us because we were nuts and go alone with Sword, who he said was the only guy among us he'd trust in a fight. That's a slander.

In the end we got stuck with Dribble because he was supposed to protect us, God knows what from. Being mistaken for people maybe. I think Swordfish hopes sooner or later he's going to catch me out in a maternal instinct, which says something about how irrational even intelligent guys can get. Lorn was maybe there because he's a war hero and if someone was rude to us he might fly the copt into them. Provided they let him take it inside.

And Sword went home. He said it was because he was fed up with the lot of us and wanted some sleep but I thought it was pure jealousy and he was just scared of meeting someone even weirder than he is. He also said we could tell him how it turned out in the morning supposing any of us were still alive, which was sour grapes.

Lorn and Yell picked the bar. I wouldn't like to say what system they used. It had a purple neon monkey twenty feet high on the roof that had one cycle where it scratched its armpits and another where it used its paws for purposes unusual in public. The barker was transparent, made up as Aladdin and came out of a bottle, which has to be confused thinking. It said "Boo!" and then went into a spiel I'd rather not repeat with gestures to match. I guess you could hire ladies inside. Also boys, sheep and mutated jellyfish. Take your pick. I passed.

We dumped the copt on the roof and Lorn fastened it to a stanchion with a cerosteel chain which is a waste of time because they just uproot the whole issue. He also took a couple of essential bits out of its guts, which does deter them a couple of minutes while they figure out what's wrong. Mostly you do what he did and bring the heaviest, ugliest thing around so it ain't attractive. Then it only gets stolen if somebody's planning either a holdup or a really major celebration.

The other two copts, both chained, looked like farm utilities from the kind of farm probably breeds mutated jellyfish. They both stank. Most of the boys and girls come on foot or whatever they're using in lieu tonight.

The roof entrance was fixed to be the monkey house or Aladdin's cave, check one or more. It had wavy arcading with lights designed to uncover incipient epilepsy and veiled houris that holoed out. I mean they had veils on their faces. All four were natural brunettes. Lower down they had dancing boys without veils who were natural blonds. Their equipment looked like they'd been sampling the jellyfish.

A curving ramp covered in purple sponge came out in a smoke-filled hole. Most of it was so chemical I hoped nobody was going to strike a spark or we'd all end up in orbit. Everybody was high, which is normal. So were we after we'd had a couple of breaths of what they were using for atmosphere.

It was hard to tell if the joint had decor or not. You couldn't see. Its sputtering neons looked yellow, the tables were covered with dirty glassware and the noise level gave a new dimension to the phrase "cocktail-party deafness." There might have been lewd holos on the ceiling if the meteorological conditions had been better. Some guy in a corner was feeding tokens into a big lighted juke. He had his ear pressed to the speaker so there may even have been music coming out. It had a smell-prog, which was misplaced optimism.

Half the guys were male and half not though not necessarily female and the other fifty percent were God knows what. And yeah, there were at least a hundred and fifty percent of them. In spite of the way they look they're human. Aliens we fight. I don't know why, or even how you can tell the difference.

Lorn found us a table. It was already occupied but since the personnel were dead, unconscious or both, they didn't mind being tipped on the floor. Then he slung their glassware after them on account of at least three were symbiotic. The green fronds behind one's ears grew yellow visual spots and growled at us but the boss man was out so we let it.

A tired-looking mechanical with a lot of stubbed-out-joint burns on its back crawled out of a corner and swept the glass into one heap and the bodies into another. There were several more there already. After a bit the floor tipped and the whole lot disappeared. Maybe a bim in a low neckline was going to appear shortly selling meat pies. I made a note not to eat there.

Their shipmates at the next table practically died laughing and offered Lorn a drink. Then they registered I was the second sex, which wasn't my fault because I'd dressed for combat but there ain't many guys my size, and offered me a drink. Then one took a close look at Moke, said he was cute and offered him a drink. Then the whole lot got a look at the expression in Yell's eye and offered him a drink on principle. The survival one. Dribble was under the table and didn't get offered anything which was good because what most people offer him's a kick up the ass, then he snivels.

Since they were packing enough hardware to start a major international incident we accepted. We also hadn't any drinks.

The barman was an ordinary-type guy with six arms and two trays on each which didn't stop him looking harassed even though he'd an extra leg joint for stepping around customers. Or with unconscious guys on the floor, on. He had a sad introspective face like a horse, the sort often goes with fallen arches. He passed me a glass of green slop and having been brought up heroic I had a gulp.

It tasted like sulfuric acid. It probably was sulfuric acid. When I stopped coughing I found a guy I'd never seen before wrapped around me using all seven fingers to do things I don't accept from unknown male people especially if they got seven fingers. I hauled off to sock him and Lorn looked at me. I changed the sock into a medium-hard slap on the wrist—he only had two, thank God, these guys customize their spaceships and you never know what you're going to find—hauled his hand into neutral territory and thanked him nicely for the drink.

"Thank you nicely," I said.

"Think nothing of it, doll," he said back. "Why don't you and me go upstairs?"

"Because for one thing we just got down here, and for two my friend Moke would be upset."

He looked Moke over careful. "That's cool, he can come too. He's cute."

That made two of them. I began to see it wasn't death Moke was facing, or not right away. Moke hadn't noticed. He was looking around with the look goes with internal filming. I guessed we were going to get pink granite boulders with a lot of legs and seven fingers. Though it rarely translates as simple as that.

Lorn reached over with a sweet innocent smile and lifted the guy into the air with his finger and thumb. When I got a good look I thought maybe I'd acted hastily. Apart from the fingers and his body odor the guy wasn't bad at all. Tall, blond and handsome. It's true he smelled like a hard weekend in a locker room.

"Bim's provided for. You want to sit on my knee instead?"

I guess the guy was used to altitude because he dangled for a bit while he considered.

"Nah," he said finally. "Pass. Where'd you get the neuronics?"

"Third alien war. Know it?"

"Yeah. Spent three years flying around it. You a tech?"

"Hunter-killer," Lorn said with that nice young smile. "What you driving?"

The guy ended up somewhere near his left elbow if not exactly his knee and the conversation got technical. I figured I'd definitely been hasty. Besides, while I personally think Moke's the world's cutest guy, it's kind of humiliating to find two out of three guy people think he's cuter than me.

Dribble had evaporated and I saw his bare rear flirting in a flock of skirts. Since not all the skirts were on females and most of these guys carry artillery I hoped he wasn't going to get killed. Because if he did Moke would grieve and Sword was going to be end-of-the-world mad at me.

A real good-looking bim with long silver hair, low-slung pants and damn-all else apart from a couple of Japanesey lizards tattooed in three-di over her hip bones was leaning over Yell's shoulder whispering sweet somethings in his ear. He looked like he was going to accept. A couple of minutes later I might have been alone.

I put my arms on the table and sighed into my sulfuric acid. Then the best-looking guy yet, a six-foot sliver of carved muscle with hair as thick as the pony's mane and skin-tight leathers, came gliding over like Nureyev in one of his great parts. He had some great parts himself. I gave him the eye like the end of the world and he smiled like an angel. And wrapped himself around Moke. Who looked startled.

The angel likewise took to ear-whispering. It's got to be a local habit. Moke isn't nil on guys, he just prefers girls. Such as mostly me. I don't know what would have happened quite because there was a shatter of glass somewhere near the bar you could hear even above the decibels and the place got quiet. Everybody sat still and a lot of them moved back, crunching into other people who did the same. It made us cozy. I got someone's hip with satisfactory muscle and a reasonably human shape digging into my shoulder but I couldn't see up to know if I was pleased about it or not.

The cleared space showed the bar, which was tridee vulgar and manned by a six-foot-six bim like the Ride of the Valkyries in Eastern veiling and businesslike brass knucks, and two persons I assumed were male for lack of evidence. One was green and porous which says symbiote and the other was white and decorated with chicken feathers. Integral. Mostly around the ass and trailing down its arms and legs. It also had spurs. I don't know what the porous one had but I wouldn't personally have touched it with a branding-iron. I guess Sword's right, I'm a snob. Spacers aren't.

I don't know the cause of the quarrel if any but the two guys were circling like a pair of strange dogs working up to a match for the presidency. There was smashed glass on the ground which they both trod into the purple sponge with real macho airs. The management had to spend on floor coverings. Chicken-feathers had hard scaly feet. Symbiote didn't seem to notice.

Chicken-feathers made the first move with a sharp flash of retractile claws that opened Porous up from groin to jaw. Or should have. The claws were two inches long and looked as sharp as razors. Porous shrugged, gave out a smell like a dunghill and closed right back up. I guess that's got to be disheartening when you just took your best shot.

Chicken drew back but only to give himself leg room. The spur, maybe eight inches of nail-pointed horn, caved in the side of Porous's face. Porous stunk like a sewage farm and pulled his head right back together. You couldn't even see the line.

Chicken had been making all the moves. Now Porous started to get nasty. The stink was awful, seemed to me the guy should get his symbiote in line before we all came down with cholera. He moved forward like an indignant garbage heap and stretched out long arms to grab. They looked a lot longer than arms should, longer than they had standing still. Then I saw the strings of green gloop extending his fingers. They went on reaching for Chicken's face long after the guy's arms ended.

Chicken kicked again, cutting through the strands nearest him, and they fell on the floor with a wet plop. The rest went on reaching. The bits on the floor hump-crawled like slimy caterpillars back to the main mass where they joined on at the feet end and vanished. Porous's whole skin was moving and sliding, going upward to reinforce his lengthening arms. They had to be five feet long and still growing. The rest was getting thinner, you could just about see the shape of a skinny small guy underneath.

Chicken kicked gamely back several times more, cutting off more lengths of green gloop that crawl-humped back and rejoined the battle at the feet. Several guys in the nearer rows began to get the dry heaves and at least one the wet ones. I could see this battle was getting unequal.

Chicken had drawn back about as far as he could and pretty soon they were going to get to real grips.

They did. The long green arms caught up with Chicken and started crawling all over his face. He clawed at the stuff and tore it off in handfuls, which didn't do any good because it went right on plopping to the ground and crawling home. Then he tried reeling the arms in and forcing himself as close as he could get to Porous, who was now very clearly a small skinny guy under a living manure pile. That made him a lot braver than I was because I'd have been yelling for the anti-gas squad. I guess he meant to claw Dumphead's face off before he could reassemble the six inches of porosity he was using as protection.

The end was one of these foregone conclusions. Skinny may not have been much but his symbiote was one mean heap of guck. It let Chicken get to about a foot from the human bit then snapped back like elastic and covered Chicken all over with a green gucky layer. You could see the guy trying to claw the stuff away from his eyes and nose but the smell alone would have knocked out any normal human. He dropped to his knees, then his face.

Porous kept him there long enough to see he wasn't getting back up then he shrugged his jelly around him the way a fancy lady puts on her mink and strutted to the bar. Several guys rushed to buy him a drink. Several more picked up Chicken, who'd got his feathers bent, and tried to bring him around. I'd have said oxygen but they made it with ninety-degree alcohol. Chicken sat up after a while shaking his head groggily, though that could have been the alcohol, and some sympathizers helped him to a table. A lot of people were slapping Porous's back but then I said spacers were hard cases. Wads of folding credit were also changing hands so I guess it was a success for some.

"Ah-huh," said the guy with his hip on my shoulder. He sounded saddened. "Ain't never worth the trouble with a symb. Hell, it make sense. You fighting two guys at once."

I looked up and found it was a high-ultra blue-black, a guy like a weathered ash-tree with a humorous face and hair plaited into a Greek helmet.

"Friend of yours?"

"Guy got licked? Hell, he my grand-brother-in-law. My sister's kid's guy. Lucky he don't get really hurt or I got to go lick Stinker myself. Good way lose a night's drink."

"You noticed."

"How you not?" He made a vile mouth.

"You lick him?"

"Uh-huh." He snorted down his nose. "Me I got good sense wear gas mask. Tell kid so, he know better. Next time he do like I say."

"My father says kids never do like you say."

He looked down at me. He was nearly as tall as Lorn, which said blue sun, light planet unless he was one of the fun-lovers. But blue-blacks tend to be utilitarian.

"He right. What he let nice girl like you do here?"

I jerked my head at Lorn talking ship with three different guys, all pick of the crop though one had a reptilian head peered out from behind his collar I wouldn't have wanted to know and one was another symb, greened over with light glassy fur. "I'm with him."

The Greek helmet turned consideringly in his direction. "We get Aris now and guys talk to them?"

"He was a war pilot."

"No excuse. He done ought take you home."

"We're looking for a lady."

Another snort. I figured it did him for a laugh. "No ladies here. Spacers, hookers, ground crew. She got name?"

"I don't know. I got told Halo, but that ain't necessarily true anymore."

"Is it ever?" he said philosophically. "Know a Halo but she one mean bad bim. You see Halo, run. Stink worse than Stinker."

"I'm looking for one mean bad bim. Where would I find her?"

Another snort. "You won't. Wrong sex, doll-baby. He find maybe." That was Lorn. "Pretty boy, big prick. Halo like that. Maybe you not like so well, he come back maybe less pretty, no prick at all. Halo play rough games. Take advice old man you get nice boy take back home. That way you keep boy and prick. You listen me girl, prove daddy wrong one time, huh?"

He was sweet. I gave him all my teeth. "Thanks. I'll pass the advice to Lorn, maybe he'll take it."

"And I go collect grand-brother-in-law see whether maybe next time he take it too. Why I got feeling neither going to?"

And he waded off into the swarm like a lion in the grass. If they come that color. My mother was always going to take me to the zoo but she put me in the street first.

When I noticed we were short a Moke. Not to mention a Dribble, but Dribble has survival instincts. I grabbed a handful of cream buckskin shirt. Lorn raised his brows.

"Mokey's gone."

"Yeah, sure," one of his war-buddies, the green-furred one, said. "The cute kid? He went upstairs with two guys after the fight. It's okay, neither of 'em's got itch."

"Which had the gun?" Lorn asked looking suddenly intelligent. Like in the copt. Not candy bar at all.

"Didn't see, but it would be Gimp," the one with the reptile collar said. "Don't worry, they ain't violent. Hell, if he says no they maybe let him do it to them. Straight guys, fairly."

"Uh-huh." Lorn rose to the two feet nearer the ceiling than I am that he gets and stretched a hand. "Be seeing you. Where's the stairs?"

"Over there. If you taking the lady ask for Room Three. Bed ain't so gross and somebody's shot the voice out of the genie."

"A benefactor of mankind. Come, Cassandra, let's look at Room Three."

"And likewise One, Two and Four," I snarled. "Weren't you supposed to protect me?"

"And here you are." He sounded hurt. "Dribble had Moke."

"He's probably watching at the keyhole making notes on how it's done."

"I expect he's gone," Lorn agreed. "He's got an oversensitive nose."

The stairs would have been in plain sight if the air had been clearer. They had mind-reaming arches and purple sponge. The side walls were covered with metallic paper decorated with symbols that were magic, phallic, or Arabic swear-words. It must have been repulsive when new but at that stage it also stank of perfume, grease and symbiotes. A lot of dirty hands had felt their way up at arm level and left a crust like third-day soup.

The doors at the top had glimmering arches too and big curlicued numbers. Room One was empty except for the genie, which was in a state of major sexual need and said a string of things I won't detail. Room Two's door was locked. Lorn backed off like they do on the vids and kicked it scientifically over the keyhole. In his case the bastard opened. Life's unfair like that. Maybe the lock was defective.

The two guys inside shrieked, one tenor, one soprano. The soprano had the prick. Considering the position they were in I didn't blame either of them.

"I beg your pardon," Lorn said. "I've lost my giraffe."

"Well, it ain't here, buster," the tenor grunted from between her mate's legs. "Try up the corridor. And shut the door behind you."

Their genie booed us on the way out. It was a different sex and color from the first but made up for it with a bloodred pout the size of a tractor tire and a set of long nails went straight for the crotch.

Room Three opened by itself before Lorn could lift his foot and Yell shoved his head around.

"Thought it was you. You're the only guys I know you get to a joint and they have to call the builders. Shout when you want me, we're winding down."

"Oh, Yell. And you only been here an hour and a half. What's the lady going to think?"

"I said winding." Evil grin. "Shout, right?"

That left Four. The corridor beyond was professional with a curly Eastern pay-booth and a turnstile. Heavily armored. The boys and girls get frisky.

Lorn tried the door and it opened. He raised an eyebrow and we looked in. Like Laurel and Hardy, one head high up, one low down.

"Hi," Moke said.

He was sitting on a glob of blackcurrant gelatin with his legs crossed like an apprentice Buddha. His disciples were at his feet. Lying picturesquely across the rest of the glob, stripped to their skins, one normal with tan belonging to the angel, one scaly with horn-tipped toes and prehensile tail belonging to a guy built like Conan the Barbarian with overtones of Godzilla. The prehensile tail was exploring some of the angel's more intimate anatomy with rapt attention, the angel was responding ditto and Moke was sketching both of them on his pocket slate. All three looked dreamy.

The genie did a belated boo and turned out to be a midget rat-faced kid with bad habits that popped out of an inkwell.

"Fucker's still there," the angel said lazily. "Shrunk but there."

"Guess I didn't use enough charge," Conan agreed in a low deep drawl like somebody talking inside a cistern. "I get it next time."

They went back to posing or whatever it was they were doing. Among the other things.

"Stank in there so we left," Moke explained. "Are we going now?"

"When Yell's finished."

"And when we've found Dribble," Lorn said.

"Right here." A long brown shape rose up as if it had been snake-charmed and yawned hugely.

"He's got a sensitive nose, huh?"

The sensitive nose bared shark fangs.

"Me watch pretty guys," Dribble said contentedly. "Nice-nice. Me learn lot of new things."

"I bet he has, the disgusting little brute. His nose is the only bit that's sensitive. Can we go now?"

"You don't want to fill in time for a while?" Lorn asked hopefully, glancing back toward Room One.

"No."

"How did I know you'd say that?" He sighed. "All right, Cinderella, let's go home. I guess it's midnight. I want you to know I keep your slipper as a precious souvenir."

It was half-past three. We rounded up our mavericks and headed back to the ranch. We ended by having to take the girl with silver hair with us. Seemed Yell hadn't really finished after all.

It was only after Lorn had dumped us at the loft and we were all yawning over coffee except Yell's girl who was licking his neck down toward his belly button that it came to me he had no right to be keeping my slipper as any sort of souvenir.

Because when I wore it and gave it to him I wasn't me at all, I was the Honorable Jocelyn seducing Nimbus. Somebody leaked me. Damn Swordfish. If it'd been me he'd never have got it, I got guys already.

I think.

"Where?" If Sword had been sleeping it hadn't made any difference to his temper.

"A brothel," Moke said. "Guys know her. She has a reputation. Bad."

"Check. Mine thought she'd like Lorn."

"I'll buy her some ketchup. I'm still asking where."

"I get under table, guys talk over head," Dribble squeaked. "Halo brothel on sat. She like spacers, specially rich. Say rich guy get anything. Even me." He started licking his more private parts with a tongue a yard long, a leg cocked behind his ear.

"Don't know who'd have you, pup-face. Anyhow, Moke doesn't want you debauched."

"Debauched?" Dribble asked, looking up from the sanitary operations. "Good nice? Like him guys?"

"Probably," Swordfish said dryly. "Get sense from yours, Yell?"

"Yeah, some," Yeller drawled. "We'd time to talk." He grinned and stretched. "Gotta talk to her again. Knows a couple of things even I never met. Yeah, sat, right. Raissa's pissed off because Halo makes girls pay in advance, 'less they put on a free show. With other girls preferably, though she'll take solo if it's interesting. Issa's stuck on guys. She says Halo got nice specimens but strictly for high rollers. 'Cept the young kids, who're for other guys.

Guys get in free 'cause she figures they're going to buy something."

"What's she selling apart from nice specimens, young kids and free girl-displays?"

"Everything," Moke said. "She's not exactly liberated."

"She sounds liberated as hell. It's the rest of us ain't. All queen bees are the same."

Sword turned a threatening eye. "And?"

"She puts on guy-displays, group or solo, but men she pays. Money or kind. My friends've done shows for her. They're hot together. They took kind. Boys, girls, mutes, animals. Single or in combination."

"What kind of animals?" Christ, animals are for the zoo. Even steak's cloned. If you want to see a cow you got to pay to get in. I sometimes wish my mama had got around to the zoo, I never seen a cow.

Yell looked at me. One of those looks I keep getting like maybe I was short a cylinder. "Mute animals. Lions, tigers, big fluffy things. And woolly ones, llamas, like that. And I heard she got a couple of mutated cheetahs for the high ladies, go this long, Issa says"—he held his fingers about a foot apart—"but you gotta show your credit rating at the door 'cause she takes it all."

"Jellyfish?"

"Small beer, girl. You can get them downside. If you'd gone a couple of doors along you'd've seen one."

"Thanks, I'm the wrong sex."

"They come all shapes."

"Yech."

"But marine animals, yeah. A dolphinarium, filters courtesy of the house. Seals and a male walrus. Couple of killer whales."

Sword whistled. "That must cost."

"She isn't going broke," Moke said. "Not according to Slat and Virgo."

"Which one's Gimp?"

"That'll be Slat. He limps slightly. Had a fight with a symb and lost. The outer layer digested some of him."

"Did he really have a gun?"

"No, why? Told you, it was the smell got to us."

"You coulda took me with you."

"You were watching. Thought you were enjoying it."

I glared at him. "She take symbs as well?"

"Sure she does. Heard she even got a couple of her own in the back shop. Female. Popular."

"Uh-huh," Sword said patiently. "I'm still asking where."

Yell scratched among thick brown hair. He's not ugly these days. "To hear Iss it's an old manufacturing sat, looks a wreck from outside, club inside. It's also a gambling club, you can just shoot craps if you want."

"Don't see the need. You can do that on the Strip."

"Yeah, baby, but you can't buy her hotwire specials on the Strip. Sniff, derm, chew, swallow, smoke, mainline. You want it, she got it. And I ain't talking blue angel."

"Liquor?" Sword asked. With professional interest.

"Yup. All the unlicensed off-planet stuff they take away at the spaceport. Consequently she tends to change profile. And orbit. Which is why where's a delicate question. It's more where now."

I giggled. "The ultimate floating crap game."

"The ultimate floating crap house. Raissa give you coordinates?"

"Yeah, but last week's. She could be anywhere."

"Not anywhere," Sword said. "Moving a sat isn't cheap or simple. She wouldn't look smart if she hit an eccentric and drifted into the edge of atmosphere or put herself where a police cruiser could see her power up. So I'd say a cluster, and creep to the next when it gets hot."

"What's Candy-bar say? He talked the hind legs off the three best-looking guys in the room for an hour." I got one of Sword's nastiest looks. "Then he propositioned me," I added spitefully.

"So long as he didn't proposition the guys," Sword growled. "He got coordinates. This week's. One of the spacers was up night before last. That's why he was spending last night in a dive. Paid two months' work for three hours with a mute mermaid. She could still be there."

"Goody. If Candy-bar propositions me again do I get to say yes?"

"If he's fool enough to ask, he deserves it. I had the idea he was rescuing you from some guy was using your nipples as a keyboard."

"Mmmn. He was cuddly."

"Great. When you get in that position with a mute cheetah I'll ask Lorn to leave you."

"He won't," I said. "Ain't like you. I think I'd like to marry Lorn, he's cute. And rich. Maybe we can share the cheetah. It would make a lovely group. Moke can sketch us."

Cold weather moving in from the Atlantic. Even Moke had turned chill.

"Ship," Yell said, fast.

"Razor's got a yacht. And no, we don't want Hans-Bjorn's luxury job with built-in pilot. Razor has a converted lighter doubles as a gunship. Old, battered, dirty and packs enough power to get you to Pluto. Anyone who goes is a spacer. Yell's advice on clothes. And you're only looking. I don't want anybody trapped in a tank with the killer whales or up to the ears in sentient jelly. You guys are playing the tables, buying the hotwire and vomiting in the potted palms. Don't for God's sake swallow any of it or I'll be paying your hospital bills for the next six months. Don't start any fights. Don't break any furniture. Just get a look at the joint and tell me what goes on there."

"Come and look at it yourself. Don't you usually?"

"But I can't, Cassandra," he said gently. "It's in public. No bushes to hide in. And I'm a monster, remember?"

I find space trips nightside boring. Especially when there were five of us at the front end of a cabin made for twice as many, with Lorn shut in a red-lit pilot's compartment at the front doing technical things with the engines while Moke worked on a set of sketches of entwined lovers with Yell and Raissa as models. The lighter was an old cargo-job and I don't know its qualifications for Pluto but it was short of civilized gravity. Since we were intermittently weightless they struck some poses of gorgeous indelicacy. Since they're both spacers neither of them noticed. Since Moke was sketching he didn't notice. Since Lorn was driving he didn't notice.

Dribble and I noticed, and for once in our lives we hung around each other's necks just trying not to be sick. My semicircular canals are adjusted for high buildings but they don't like low gravity.

"Yow," Dribble wailed dismally. "Not like. Me land dog."

"You can say that again, Fido. Me land bim."

He was gray beneath his tan, his tongue lolling sadly. He looked almost like a kid.

"Why you do this, Drib?"

"Fly space? Sword ask, I come," he moaned, leaning against my knees without even trying to put his nose up my pants. "Now I get sick."

"Sure. I mean be a dog. You could be getting an education or something. You could grow up like Yell."

He turned pathetic boy eyes. "No, Cass mama. I never be beautiful. All my family look like pigs. Live like pigs too. So I dog for Sword. Dog useful. Sword like me."

"Suppose you want to get married. Aren't you scared of frightening the lady?"

"My kids look like pigs. Only me regened, kids come out like rest of family. Poor kids. I don't get married. Sword not married."

"Yeah, that's right, he ain't. Sorry I asked."

He brightened a little. "I look up lot of skirts belong beautiful ladies. That nice. Sword not even see up skirts. Too tall."

"Too true, Fido. Why'm I cuddling a drooling dog-child?"

"Because we both sick?" he whimpered, leaning his head on my knee.

That was too true as well.

Lorn brought the lighter up against a metal hull with a clang and we piled forward.

"Spacesuits, children," he said, coming out of the red-lit closet with the green-lit panel behind him. "We have the technology. Locker's behind you."

I groaned. Putting on a suit in freefall's a thing you like or you don't. I'm a don't. "How about the rest of you go first?"

Raissa hauled out her suit, one bare foot hooked in a handgrip, and started shoving a leg in. Yell was slung casually from the ceiling like a bat and Moke was packing up his slate making frog motions. Dribble hung in his straps and whined piteously and I tried not to do the same.

Lorn, at right angles to the rest of us, grabbed my wrist. "Come up, Cinders. Issa, sling us a suit."

I kicked but he was bigger. He shoved my legs in the bottom half and held a sleeve expectantly. He was anchored by a knee around the edge of the door and looked as solid as a rock. I sulked but I didn't see an alternative. He twisted my helmet, checked seals and did a controlled kick to repeat the job on Dribble. There was a suit to fit him. I guess spacers have things custom-made. I guess they have to.

"What happens if I throw up?" I asked, muffled.

"I got advice for you, doll," Yell said. "Don't."

Moke's a neat mover for a guy looks as if he gangles and when I'd time to look he'd fixed himself. Lorn twisted Dribble's helmet and reached out seven feet of charged lattice for himself.

"Okay, guys. No lines, a spacer would laugh. The entry's about six yards off the lock-port then I guess we follow the arrows. Take Yell's hand, Cassandra, and remember these soles stick on anything. Just move gently. Okay? I've got Dribble, don't worry about him."

Next time I worry about Dribble. I followed Yell onto a rusted plain that extended to the horizon. It was an industrial sat okay and it looked like it been deserted since the beginning of time. And it was in a cluster. Dark shapes hung in stable orbits maybe twenty or thirty nautical miles apart above and below us, their outlines lit around the edges by reflected moonlight. The huge hull was big enough to feel like a floor with the swollen Earth, a dusky globe edged with a bright crescent, leaning on our heads.

A couple of other industrials flanked us, in working order by the swarm of lighters and loaders that clung to their flanks, and two or three reflecting domes nearby said down-market habitation. Some of the older living-sats get bought up by groups, often religious, for whatever variety of abstinence or Satanism they're practicing this month. There was one wheel, small, I'd say an ex-experimental station where they were probably still running experiments but mostly the sort forbidden by law. Body-leggers like places like that.

Not a high-class neighborhood.

My boots rang on the plates and clung. I wavered in midspace trying to get my balance and slid one sole and then the other after Yell, who looked casual. It was supposed to be six yards. I'd have said twelve since that's how many steps it took me, but we got there. Raissa crowded me behind and I could hear her giggling contralto over the intercom. I made a note to reason with her later. And also to get my fingernails reinforced. I'm getting tired of reasoning with dumb bims with my own equipment.

The entrance was a ragged hole leading to black depths that looked as reassuring as a shark pool. Yell's glove tightened on my hand.

"Come on, kid. This gotta lead somewhere."

"If this dame wants custom she should put in guide lights."

"That's what they mean by exclusive, Cinderella," Lorn's voice said in my earphones. "Make the customers work. They pay more in the end. There's an airlock about fifty feet ahead."

He had to have cat eyes. Yell turned his helmet-lamp that way and we swam toward it, ducking through rusted beams and great hanging chains looked like they been used for flensing. Other people's ships maybe. If this sat was inhabited Halo liked privacy.

Yell came up against the port with a minor clang boots first and pulled me after him. If the spacers said it was an airlock it was an airlock. It was as rusted as the rest and I could just make out outlines in the light of my helmet with a wheel in the middle looked locked solid with age. Yell braced himself on the port-rim and gave it a swing. It twirled all the way around and opened on a lighted compartment with a red VOID sign at the back.

This was it. The inside was painted aquamarine with exotic plants that looked carnivorous and stretched blue-purple blossoms that flupped on our helmets and ran over our suits looking for a way in. They seemed to be rooted in the aquamarine walls. Somebody had left a bucket stained with bloody meat floating in a corner that turned lazily on its axis and a few red globules drifted among the leaves. I hoped it hadn't been the last customer.

"It's okay," Yell said. "They're vacuum-structured. They'll cystate as soon as we cycle. Come in and close the port."

Lorn pushed a miserably wailing Dribble in in front of him and twirled the wheel. The sign turned orange to CYCLING and the writhing flowers, big as bicycle wheels, collapsed, shriveled, browned and drew in until the aquamarine wall was marked with a few dry brown nuts clinging to the paint and some more drifting vaguely in the atmosphere.

"She deserves a contravention for biopollution," Lorn said. "This stuff gets in some guy's gymnasium he's going to be eaten alive."

"If he exercises in a force-suit," Yell agreed. "You think this is the kind of district the neighbors complain?"

"No. But I bet the bitch is leaving a trail of these right around the orbit. You want to bet none of them gets into a house sooner or later?"

"I guess that's the least of her worries," Yell said.

The sign turned green to ATMOSPHERE and the inner door slid back. We stepped into artificial gravity and I came to the floor with a jolt. Yell's hand saved my dignity, he'd figured the 45° turn.

There was a guy outlined in the light roughly the size of a male rhinoceros with hide to match and a Navy blaster as big as a cannon in his huge paw.

"Evening, gents. Park your suits over there. You got bims with you? Bims pay at the door. Five thousand creds apiece unless they'd rather perform. Any of you guys any good? The Lady pays for it."

His eyes were on Lorn, who was stripping down to, I admit, seven very nice feet. Raissa shook out her silver hair which swirled around her like a tent.

"Me and my guy perform if you like. He got some good moves."

"Uh-uh. Guy can see that any time. You want to get together with the other bim we take you as a pair. Or either one of you solo, if you got something to show us. Guys like that. Otherwise you pay or leave."

Raissa turned me an inquiring brow, which I negated. We ended by Lorn paying for her and me and having a quarrel with the rhino over Dribble. Lorn declared he was male, which is beyond argument, and the guy claimed he wasn't human. Lorn claimed he was and the guy asked for another five thousand for pets unless Dribble wanted to perform.

I guess that's what he was angling for. Dribble looked like he would have liked it except he hadn't got over being green. They were still arguing when he settled it himself by throwing up on the guy's feet and starting dismally to lick it up. Then he reacted like most people do to Dribble and let us in anyhow just so's not to have to go on looking at him.

I'd thought me and Issa might be overdressed, since we were both clothed below the waist. Bim dress-rule is less means more. She had her silver pants and tattoos and I had iridescent black skins from pubes to ankle and a flower necklace in activated anthracite on an open-spread-die-writhe cycle, plus earrings to match. It made even me crawly when I caught sight of it by accident.

Lorn had gone spacer in black leather jeans and a silver gauze singlet, the kind of outfit produces a strong desire in bim people to relieve the pressure on his privates. Yell had all-over white satin slit to six inches below the navel. The Moke-version jeans showed bits of Moke would have got him arrested on the Strip but he thought they were decent because they hadn't fallen off yet. Yell had lent him a sweat with holos of ladies doing things they'd have paid me and Issa for only we'd already refused. He hadn't noticed that either. He was being grateful we hadn't put him in velvet. Dribble came as he was.

Other people were exotic and I'm talking spacer. Their clothes covered everything except the bits most people think clothes were invented to cover and a lot of it was alive and in some cases joining in the conversation. That was on top of normal spacer abnormality. It was a bit like open day at the zoo crossed with one of the grosser specialty acts from a circus. If we were getting noticed it was for modesty.

An eight-foot black hostess with two feet of silver neck-rings and more of the same on her wrists and ankles, with her personal qualities decorated with nipple and pube jewelry dripping silver fringe, came to meet us and purred basso profundo.

"Clubroom or private?"

"Club," Lorn said.

"You can't take your pet in," she rasped, looking at Dribble.

"I not pet. I sick. You want I show you?"

Like the guy at the door she decided to pass but those vital thirty seconds earlier. I gave her points for intelligence.

"Through to the right. Chips at the door, pick up your winnings on the way out."

Dribble plucked at Lorn's wrist. "Me go private? I awful sick." He leered engagingly. If you got the eye for Dribble's leers. "Nice wet person make me feel better."

"No," Moke and I said simultaneously.

Lorn looked him over. "You going to get digested?"

"You got to be kidding. He does the digesting."

It was the wrong thing to say. Lorn forked out another load of credit would have opened a jewel shop and left change for redecoration and asked the lady to show Dribble something interesting of his choice. Dribble turned

several shades more pink and began to loll his tongue
like his nose had gone cold again. The lady looked at him
with revulsion and took him away. He frisked a little as
he disappeared.

"You didn't have to do that," I said. "He's disgusting
already."

"Stops people looking at us," Lorn said.

With him in the party, that was a hope. All the female
people for yards around and quite a few of the males were
looking at us like we'd brought the good news from Aix
to Ghent.

We found our way into the clubroom, bought handfuls
of chips at the desk, still on Lorn's card—I assumed
Sword was paying in some ultimate way—and sat in
squelchy doughnut-shaped chairs to take in the view.

"Beautiful ass," mine remarked soprano as I sat.

I gave it a hard kick with my heel. "Ah, go on, you
say that to all the girls."

"Only the ones with beautiful asses," it retorted. "My
friend would say the same about your tall friend only I
think he already swooned."

"Thank God for that. What does it take to make you
swoon?"

"You could tickle me a bit around the inside of the
ring," it suggested.

"Yeah? What's that do?"

It went a much rosier shade of gelatin. "Makes me
swoon," it said modestly.

"Lorn," I yelped.

"It's okay, Cinders. They only rape you if you pay
them. There's a notice about it in the hall."

"Thanks," I muttered.

It seemed drinks were free, which was a variation, but
I didn't stay sitting long enough to drink mine. I don't
know what the notice in the hall said but after about five
minutes my doughnut started to get so personal with the

bits in its sphere of operations I got tired of kicking it and went to look at the games.

Half an hour later I'd lost an extravagant amount of Lorn's chips at roulette, won it all back with an unexpected jackpot on a one-armed bandit, which insisted on putting its arm around me and fiddling with my nipples while I played, and lost most of it again at blackjack. I was wondering if this counted as good, bad or normal. I was still in meditation when the lights dimmed and I went to sit on the floor by a doughnut. It rubbed itself against my back like an oversized dog throughout the entertainment but since I had the first one's word its business arrangements were on the inside I didn't pay attention. That didn't stop the floor from humping up and down under me but I figured my pants were watertight so I let it.

Lorn dropped beside me with a plastic sack overflowing with chips, which I reckoned meant he'd been using illegal neuronics unless he'd seduced the machinery. It did act oversensitive. Moke was building something on his slate looked like a hot doughnut a long way gone mixed up with some sort of human shape that when you looked at it turned out to be two human shapes twined together into a long-gone doughnut. I started thinking this stuff was bad for the boy. Moke's never had a dirty mind.

Yell and Raissa had disappeared and Dribble hadn't come back. I leaned on Lorn's shoulder, gave my doughnut a slap and waited for things to happen. Moke leaned on mine and adjusted his slate to show what I'd mistaken for a bad case of doughnut hots was the third person of the trinity like a tadpole with an oversized head growing into the circle between its parents. I felt better about him.

The floor had crept somehow between my thighs and was behaving like floors don't get to. I began to see why so many girl spacers wore pin-heels. I took a handful of it in my fingers and dug my nails in. It made a kind of bubbling noise and went limp. Lorn slapped under his backside and made a wry mouth. A few seconds later Moke closed down his slate with a snap, shoved it under him and hauled me onto his knee. Lorn, who's a quick learner, made a stool of his sack.

The floor seethed a bit and crawled off to annoy the nearest spacer, who ground his heel into it, and his mate, who maybe satisfied its libido or vice-versa. Anyhow, she/he lay around writhing in ecstasy. She/he was a symb with a kind of yellow pie-frill around its neck and upper shoulders that showed glinting spots at all the goffers which got more glinting as the writhing went along and finished by putting out spores that made everybody sneeze.

I began to think I could get to dislike the place.

There was a small not-quite-circular dais at the far end of the room and I guessed we were going to get the cabaret. We got it.

It started with a pink spot in which an incredibly beautiful girl in net skins and sequins did a solo number where she enjoyed herself a whole lot and several guys near us started getting intimate with the floor. Then the spot went blue and we got two boys both overflexible around the skeleton who did things I wouldn't have thought possible and looked like they were having a great time doing it. Then we had a yellow spot and a mixed foursome who were less interesting because once you get into higher mathematics the combinations are limited and after ten minutes you start seeing where they're going. Though as a study in pure math it had points.

Then the spot went bloodred with a ta-ra for the professionals. Two naked guys with their muscles picked out in gilt, especially around the groin, and a delicate white girl like a china doll with a completely expressionless face.

They started quietly with the two guys making ballet movements with the girl, passing her between them to romantic music, sliding her through their legs and over

their shoulders like she was weightless. The girl had about
as much reaction as a sack of flour though she pointed her
fingers and toes a little. It looked to me she was high as a
weather balloon and not about to come down.

The music quickened and the two guys went into an
improved version of the multiple act we'd just seen, a lot
of the same but more artistic and carefully posed, taking
their time and giving the audience their money's worth
of bucks and heaves. Seemed to me after a while the
girl had to be getting sore but she went on playing doll
and showed no reaction at all. If her eyes hadn't blinked
from time to time I'd have thought she really was some
kind of a replica.

After a period of increasing invention from our two
heroes the tempo hotted up and someone offstage threw
a couple of glittering knives which the nearest guy caught.
He passed one to his mate. When the fingers started flying into the audience I retched and turned my head into
Moke's shoulder. Lorn put a hand on the back of my
neck and Moke bent his face to my cheek. The drumming
got faster and faster. At one point something warm and
wet hit my bare back and I bit my tongue and dived
under Moke's armpit. Lorn wiped it off and tightened
his hand.

Finally it rose to a crescendo and stopped. Lorn's hand
slackened and Moke's chin lifted cautiously.

The voided corpse of the girl lay center-stage, truly a doll now. The two guys, glistening from head to
foot, were bowing. There were bits of wet shiny stuff
here and there on the floor which was busy licking it
up.

The girl hadn't made a sound from beginning to end.

A couple of goons with a plastic pearl shell arrived
and removed the remains while the loverboys bowed and
kissed their hands, then the whole lot disappeared stage
left still smiling.

A fresh small drumroll and a woman stood in the center of the stage. She was medium-sized, slender, graceful. Straight toffee-colored hair that must have come to her feet was gathered into a crown of elaborate coils and braids on top of her head, interwoven with strands of threaded gold. Long gold earrings in baroque arabesques hung from the upper whorls of her ears to drape her shoulders and tinkle on her breasts. Her gown—it was no way just a dress—looked like a single length of gold tissue, wrapped around her in a spiral to cover her in a column of sparkle. Here and there the layers of the spiral didn't quite overlap and glimpses of smooth tanned flesh showed through. She wore high gilt sandals on her gilt-nailed feet.

She looked out over her audience and smiled, a cool white smile like vanilla ice cream fresh from the freezer, and a mischievous little dimple played in the corner of her toffee-apple mouth.

"Well, my dears," she said. "That's how it is. I'm Halo, and this is my house. There's lots more where that came from, all you have to do is ask. Don't run, there's plenty for everyone. And"—her eyes were straight on Lorn, who might as well have been bare under his silver singlet—"I'm always around myself. For people who appeal to me. Help yourselves, boys and girls, it's here for you."

There was another small drumroll and she was gone. Enthusiastic applause followed her out. She moved so smoothly and swiftly in her gold wrappings I didn't see exactly how she managed to walk in that skirt and those heels. Maybe she was on a trolley.

Moke lifted a ghastly face.

"Was that real?"

Lorn looked at him with compassion. "Let's go find Dribble. And get Yell's mind out of his crotch for five minutes if we can."

As we walked to the door he bent over and said to me softly, "Well, Cindy?"

"I'd say so. I don't know the dame but I'd bet on her style. I'd say she's a lady who'd throw acid in her costars' faces. And her name's Halo."

"Okay. Now all we got to do is shake her loose."

"And how're we going to do that, killer?"

"I think that's a job for Sword," he said. "Don't you?"

Oh, I did.

Sword heard this story looking like the Maltese Falcon and whistled up Wings. Then he had a long conversation with Hallway. These are both bad signs. Put up storm windows and retire to the cellar.

Moke got sent there—Hallway's, where the magician of the back-of-the-loading-ramp business had laid on a torus of industrial glass insulator twenty feet across was going to give birth to one hot doughnut formed from two lovers and a baby. If I knew my Moke.

I was also whistled, with my dog-child in case I was lonely. For the record, I wasn't.

"I suppose you want to pay your debts. Anyhow I can use you."

"Truth will out. Where's my cute little Lorn? I want to hold his hand."

"He's using it," he snarled. "I'll ask him to send it on when he's finished."

"Not unless he washes it first."

"Get in the fucking lighter."

Sword's temper was getting so rip-snorting I began to think he had to be sickening for something. I've known him since I was fourteen and he's always been calm, if dangerous.

"You had measles?" I asked anxiously.

He made several remarks mostly unrepeatable, polarized his suit and stamped around overturning things. The lighter had to be full of suited guys because the atmosphere got quiet the way it only can when the boss is on board and twenty people are pretending not to be there.

I felt along laps and found a corner of seat with either one double-sized guy or two skinny ones on top of each other.

"Who's that?"

"Hilt," a thunderous growl whispered. "Don't make the man mad when he's working, huh? Me, I want to come home some day. Got my lady waiting."

"Good luck to her."

Sword's pack are genetic mutes and none of them's prettier than he is. Not many even have human outlines. I perched beside Hilt's huge thigh which felt as broad as most people's waists and as hard as a tree trunk and folded my arms. At least he didn't stink, which can't be said for all of them.

"We on the same coordinates?"

"Word is she's shifted. We got to look. I don't think it'll take long, we got good scopes. Nice material, Razor."

"Wings piloting?"

"You're kidding. Sword flies space himself. It's what he's trained for."

"You could've fooled me." I'd thought he was mostly trained for neck-breaking and shooting the eyes out of flies. When nothing better offered.

The red-lit cabin showed nothing but red. But the way we hit orbit I'll testify Sword was pilot. And not in a patient mood. We zipped through the industrio-religious cluster like two spoons of ipecacuanha and came out the other side still making like the Alien War in fast playback. The next cluster was farther out and residential, softly lit with festive reflections and squared landing lights. We skipped it like we were surfing and headed for terminator.

The pale line of dawn was showing on the eastern limb, lighting the atmosphere like a knife blade and turning cloud swirls pink when we hit another group of rusting hulks, red on gray like a mechanical graveyard. Sword slowed. My stomach came back to roughly its usual place, tasted the gravity and took in a reef at the throat end.

"Guess we got there," Hilt growled in my ear.

"How's he know? They all look like garbage."

"Friend Lorn planted a marker," Hilt growled comfortably. "This garbage got its own neon sign."

"Great. So long's he can see it."

"I c'n see it. Big bastard. Hope you know how to navigate in a suit, Cass. Got a way to go."

"Um," I said.

I got suited solo. One, I got my pride. Two, it was damn clear no one was going to do it for me. They did for Dribble but he ain't normal.

No clang. Sword hung off in space maybe five hundred meters from the hull and we got stationary. And weightless. I sent an order down for two more reefs and hung on to my harness.

"Can I follow you?"

"Sure," the hulk grunted. The faceplate of its helmet was void, which is a bit unsettling. "Give you a line 'f you like. Otherwise grab holda my belt. Hell, grab holda my belt anyhow."

It was a webbing sling hung with stuff looked destructive, read lethal. I found a space and grabbed but I guess he didn't trust me because he clipped a sling between us for emergencies.

"Keep ya head down, my exhaust hot," he boomed in my helmet. I ducked.

"Radio silence," Swordfish snapped over the murmur of personal arrangements. "Go."

We went.

That is, Hilt did and I followed like one of those wooden ducks that waggles. He was right about the exhaust. It gave a brief flare like a distress rocket, jerked us forward so fast my stomach did another four-dimensional displacement and we headed for the sat like a tiger shark coming off a diet. I saw why we'd a sling. Damn thing not only nearly took my glove off seals and all, I thought for a minute it had separated my hand at the wrist and left my fingers behind like that campfire story you heard.

I was closing my eyes for the hit when Hilt did another short flare from around his chest and reached out to touch the surface gently. I bumped into his back but he didn't notice. A swarm of spacesuits glided up behind with brief winks of flame. About a third of this lot are bims though I wouldn't like to tell you which offhand. Knowing it puts a useful knot where my throat joins on which helps all of us because it not only shuts me up, it stops me barfing.

Sword's a hot organizer. His method's simple. Anybody fucks up gets their balls cut off. Or whatever, depending on sex. It ain't terminal since they can always regenerate but he has the best-moving gang on the street. Which I suppose is why he's war chief. I'm not sure Razor got his name being a Girl Scout.

Hilt reached for his tools and started on a cutting job Moke would have appreciated. A smaller vaguely human lump that was probably Wings stood by with a force-seal. People guess you're there when they start losing atmosphere. It was neat work. The hiss around the edges was slight, a cloud of dissipating ice crystals that pattered on my helmet like small hail and started forming a crust. I rubbed a window with my glove.

Hilt clipped the cutter and reached for a set of dangling lumps turned out to be the nodes of a small-scale field generator. His minor mate linked them up and switched in. That got us a sealed entry four feet across. It's big for this kind of job but not when Sword's guys got to get through.

Then he reached a big paw to the sling and shoved me inside.

I landed head over heels on a rubber floor, which was lucky or I'd have roused the whole place. This rubber was just rubber or maybe it didn't get cozy with spacesuits. Mine was condensing off frozen vapor, atmosphere and breath-precipitation in a puddle all over so I didn't blame it.

I hadn't figured there'd be staff quarters under the hull after the front entrance, but I guess that was decor. Somebody had put in some wholesale recon. Hilt followed me in and the whole pack after. None of them fell on their faces so they'd either taken note of the gravity or they weren't the falling kind. Sword came last with a spray-bomb and glitzed the hole. The glitz swirled if you looked carefully, but you can't have everything and Halo's patrons are blasted anyhow.

Then he stripped his lattice. So did everyone else so I ripped dutifully at seals. That left a heap of collapsed lattice-work floating around the corridor in a noticeable manner without visible means of support. Dribble sniffed anxiously, ears pricked, and pointed at a cupboard ten yards up. That got his ass kicked by someone I took to be Sword so I guess his recon had been a degree off.

The guy's a perfectionist.

The cupboard contained a pair of resting mechanicals which Hilt deactivated. I'd have jinxed them. He clipped them with the edge of his hand on the bulge they keep their brains in and they split like chestnuts. He's not a great respecter of property. We threw our suits on top and started mushing.

Sword grabbed my scruff three steps later and hauled at the zipper of my coolsuit, meaning take it off. I ended face to face with a suddenly visible Wings, a slender vicious boy with a small mustache and Rudolph Valentino cheekbones, who looked glum. I don't know how I looked but I felt the same way. That made us front-men so we better start being loving and high. We hate each other so it ain't easy. I gave him a glassy grin and he slid his arm around my waist. I could telepath he'd have put it higher only he knew I'd slug him.

"Where are we?" I whispered, going groggy and falling against his ear.

"Hothouse," he snarled back. His voice is like that mostly, he thinks it makes him sound tough. It does, but not if you can see him at the same time. "Back staff corridor. We come out in the works in five steps so choose your poison."

"Why look for more when I got you?"

He did some more snarling, under his breath.

It took six. Sword would have got it right. The door was a door inside, a piece of wall done blue fur with diamond stars out. We staggered in case there was somebody to stagger for but the corridor was empty. Warm breathing piled past.

Dribble came last and shut the door, which vanished. Dribble doesn't wear coolsuits, I suppose it would interfere with his ears and nose. Anyhow he'd drool on it. His nuisance value's high enough without.

"Nice place," he squeaked, pianissimo. "Me visit all over. You want to see mermaid?"

"We want to see Halo, Rover. You visit all over her office?"

"Door locked, but I know where is. Tough guys guard, I get ass kicked."

"Par for the course. Lead on, little Sheba."

"Okay, but you see mermaid anyhow. We go past."

"I think we're getting a lesson in celestial geometry," I murmured.

"We'd better not be," Swordfish said softly. "I'm not in the mood. A straight line'll do."

"No lines straight," Dribble whimpered. "Place all

crooked. I pee all over though, get you there."

He confirmed this happy thought by cocking his leg against the wall.

"Ain't they got cleaners?" I muttered to Sword.

"I imagine so. Clients got to get sick all the time. Drib can tell his own smell down to one part in fifteen million, the only thing's going to stop him's industrial ammonia. Looking at the carpet I don't think they use it."

Looking at the carpet neither did I. Dark blue fur-pile with diamond stars to match the walls. Ditto ceiling. The edges were subtly curved so they didn't quite show. I could see anyone with a load on could get medium confused about which way up they were, never mind which corridor they were in.

Dribble was right, it was a maze. Passages kept coming to an abrupt end in a full-height mirror so you thought you saw a pair of other guys coming your way then realized it was you. Then you'd have to backtrack twenty feet to find the exit. Since the whole place was dark blue and diamond, everywhere looked exactly like everywhere else. Only thing to be said was Dribble has a couple of points on Ariadne.

We met two-three guys in advanced stages of staggers. One was imitating Dribble against the wall but I excused him. The poor bastard probably couldn't find the way to the toilet. If there was one.

"How you find anything here, Drib?"

"Hostess bring. Then you supposed stay. But guys get bored, go walk around, never find nice wet person again. Find someone else though," he added happily. "Then they charge twice if they catch. Me, I run too fast."

"Oh, boy. I'm glad Lorn won something or you guys going to be street-sweeping tomorrow."

"Did he tell you about the return fee on the spacesuits?" Sword hissed.

"Huh?"

"You don't just pay to get in, you pay double to get out."

"What happens if you can't?"

"They have no objection at all to you walking home."

"Oh." Merry lady, Halo. "Lose many customers?"

"Enough to encourage the rest."

I guess they didn't pay much on feeding the floral arrangements at that.

We got to a door curtained in a crumple of silver dewed with brilliants. An invisible finger pulled it back and I got a waft of musk would have laid out an ox plus a sweet singing sigh like a kettle coming to the boil in a helium atmosphere.

The thing inside didn't look like a kettle. More like a sea anemone. It was kind of mauvish-transparent with long arcing tendrils. Two guys were entangled, inert except their functional equipment, which was strained to cracking. Their hands were loosely joined, one left one right, but the rest sprawled. One showed white eyeball under his almost-closed lids. The anemone had each of them impaled, with more tentacles in other interesting places, while it stroked their bellies and thighs with a few left-over limbs. Soft fringes of gently agitated glassy filament along the lower edges looked like they stung because a ripple of muscle contractions followed their caressing touches over the skin. Stripes of red rash marked both bodies as if they'd been whipped.

I figured if somebody didn't rescue them soon what was left wasn't going to be worth much to their captains. Unless they were the captains. That kind of amusement comes high.

"That the mermaid?"

Dribble shook his head. "Siren. Not intelligent. Mermaid talk. Not intelligent either but talk plenty."

A Dribble joke. I didn't know he could make them.

Another hand twitched the curtain impatiently into place.

"Move," Sword said evilly. "You aren't here to get horny. Shift your asses or I'll shift them for you."

We hastily moved on.

Ardent groans were coming from the next door but we didn't get to see what was making them. But the attraction had to be another mute with a strong stench of sea. Water-rippling noises made an accompaniment. The next, around two corners and back on ourselves, Dribble opened himself.

"Mermaid."

I peeped through the crack, feeling Wings peering over my head. When I glanced at his naked torso he was sweating. I hadn't thought he was susceptible.

A bright blue eye as big as an oyster winked back. When I took in the whole lady I thought the eye might be a mistake because the rest was regulation mermaid. Human down to the waist, where she modulated into transparent green-blue scales flecked with neon spots, finishing in a fish-tail that twined ten feet around. It ended in a pair of muscular flukes she'd been using to scratch under her breast. The breast was a double-D cup size with a cute little fringe of scales around the nipple. She had a pointy kitten face under the huge eyes, a pouty mouth painted gold and gold-green hair in rippling waves.

There was a pool behind for if the customers got playful, but right then she was sitting on a rock upholstered in green velvet and painting her fingernails while she whistled an extremely vulgar song like she had more than one tongue. There was some half-finished knitting beside her looked like it was going to turn out a purple sweater or maybe a scarf. She had sexual attributes outlined in scales in much the usual place geographically though she hadn't anything for them to be between, and she greeted us rudely by blowing a string of rainbow bubbles out. She was alone.

"You guys coming in or what?" she trilled, showing

Wings and me a set of cute pointed kitten teeth I'd rather not have got too close to. "I'm bored to death."

She definitely had more than one tongue. She sounded like a recital by the Vienna Boys' Choir.

"Thanks, but not right now," Wings said. More snarly than usual. The lady raised one eyebrow.

"Maybe we call on the way back," I said to be polite.

"You do that, honey," she chanted. "I got special numbers for bims. You'll like it. And you can tell me the latest downside fashions while you're at it. Get practically nothing but guy people. You know why they can't describe a dress so a normal person can imagine it?"

I shook my head. "Nope. Never did figure it out."

"Great. You call in now, doll."

I grinned with all my teeth and pulled the curtain to. Wings was scarlet.

"Hurt bad, guy?"

He spluttered.

"Woman's a monster," he got out at last in a snarl so low I'd trouble hearing.

Sword's voice behind was amused. "Poor boy's shocked. Hadn't you figured he was well brought up?"

I took another look. It could be the truth. He was sweating with embarrassment. Well, you always learn. I put my hand down the front of his pants to console him and scratched his little tummy. He breathed like a walrus all the way to the next intersection. Sword was breathing hard too but whether he was laughing himself hysterical or suppressing a desire to kill us both I wouldn't like to say. It could have been either.

That was Mariners' Beach. According to the sign. When we turned the corner we got Furline Plaza. The smells were animal musk, cat piss, and something dry and powdery was either bedding or flea spray. Sharp yelps and snarls mixed in with heavy human breathing and a bim somewhere was giving out like she was calling from glen to glen. And probably along the mountain side. A purring growl said the mute was having a good time too.

I tried not to sneeze, failed and had to take my hands off Wings to wipe my nose. He looked at me with triumph. The only guy I console successfully is Moke.

"You sure this is the shortest way?" Sword hissed.

"It way I know," Dribble whined, moving his behind farther out of range. "Two more turns. Lady in maze middle."

Sword was grimly silent. We were meeting more people and Wings and I had to play groggy again.

I felt a pressing of bodies against plush walls and a drawing in of bellies as the ladies and gentlemen, mostly men, not all gentle, staggered past. I swear one put his hand right on someone's chest but he was too drunk to notice. Luckily. For him.

Two corners around we heard a shrill human ululation and a cracking sound. The ululation changed to a high short scream and cut off. Wings gave me a spiteful look.

"Enjoying yourself?"

As a matter of fact I wasn't. I was thinking of Dosh and some of the things Moke and me had had to wash and nuskin over when he came home from working the port. And he hadn't got further than the downside bars.

We arrived at Halo's sanctum unexpectedly. It's okay, I looked it up. It was a Holy of Holies, a pair of gilded double doors picked out in diamond flanked by a pair of guys ditto. They were dressed like temple eunuchs on a vid show with little kilts over their business arrangements and gold lamé headbands and they were leaning on a ceremonial scimitar apiece. That wouldn't have bothered me, because Swordfish makes guys eat scimitars, if they hadn't each had a little gold belt above the kilt with an oversized blaster in an open holster and I bet I knew which they used when they lost their temper.

"You again?" the guy on the left said when he saw Dribble. "Thought I kicked your ass last time. Told you what I'd do if you came back."

He hefted the scimitar and Dribble let out a sopranino yelp and hid behind my legs. I didn't blame him. The guy was eight feet tall and six wide and he was one very plain high-ultra from a heavy planet. He was so black he was practically in negative. I thought there was a dimple in the plates under his feet. His mate matched in every detail. Looked like Halo was a traditionalist.

I'm not sure which bit he meant to cut off but in Dribble's place I'd have done what he did, which was edge rapidly backward. The guy had legs to match Hilt's and his big feet looked like they could cover a lot of country fast. I wasn't sure I could outrun him myself and I'm a runner-away of Olympic standard.

Wings did a drunken two-step and caught himself by hanging around my neck. We both nearly hit the floor.

"Wanna see the Lady an' thank her for beautiful evening."

"That so?" the guy on the right throated in a voice had to be manufactured back of his toenails. "Suppose the Lady don't want to see you?"

"Then I go an' knock on the door," Wings hiccupped. Thereby earning my admiration. He'd fixed his chest between me and the blasters, which was heroic but dumb since one bolt would cut both of us in half plus any dozen guys happened to be standing behind us. But I appreciated the thought.

"Take some good advice, boy," the twin with the Toni said. His voice was two octaves higher so just in the lower range of bass. "Go back to the nice clubroom and watch the cabaret. Amuse your bim awhile. Who knows, she may like it."

"She don't love me," Wings whined. He sniveled a bit. "Wanna see Lady."

"Well, son, that could get you hurt," Twin Number Two subsoniced, easing his blaster loose. He didn't need it. "Why don't you go away and fuck yourself or the bim, whichever comes first, and leave the Lady alone? She's engaged right now. When she wants to see people she sends for 'em."

"Then I wait right here till she send for me," Wings said. "Right here on floor. And my bim wait too. You wanna see the Lady, dontcha, doll?"

"Yeah," I squeaked, falling over him. "Him and me both wants ta see Lady. We sit on floor."

He had all his weight on my shoulder and he's heavier than he looks. I could feel I hadn't much choice. He gave a sudden lurch that overbalanced us both and we hit the fur-pile butt-first in a muddled heap. He was on top, naturally. The bastard.

It wasn't bad as a strategy so long as the guys didn't go for their blasters. If they did we were grilled rare. To use their hands or their scimitars they were going to have to come and get us, because we were out of slashing range.

I sprawled against the wall and practiced looking skied.

"Nice floor." I'd learned the giggle from Nimbus in her Mallore phase and it's guaranteed to go through you like a bayonet. I patted the fur. "Cuddly. We wait all night. Lady gotta come out, next time she gotta go to bathroom."

"She got her bathroom right in there with her, bim," said Number One Twin. "Crawl off like a nice piece of gash and pull the chain behind you, huh?"

"Can't. Stupid bastid lyin' on toppa me. An' who said you c'd call me bad names? I tell my guy, he slaughter you."

They liked that. The plates shook.

Wings was flat on his belly across my thighs and his legs sprawled slackly the width of the corridor. No one was coming past without breaking their necks, unless they were set for the low hurdles.

"Beautiful floor. Only will keep moving about. Think I stay till I feel better. Have little sleep till Lady come out."

He laid a sleek brown cheek on the carpet and began to snore.

I let them have another Mallore giggle. "Stupid bastid passed right out. Now what'm I gonna do? When my old man gets in 'n finds he ain't got no breakfast he gonna be real nasty. I bet he come here tell Lady what he think about joint lets guys pass out on toppa his woman 'n keep me here all night. I got one big, big, mean ol' man. Real big."

I stretched my arm high to show big, looking at them reproachfully. "He gonna be one hell mad, my ol' man. He like breakfast on time. You don't wanna come shift this drunken bum offa my legs maybe, let me get home before ol' man come lookin'?"

The twins laughed in unison with a noise like a rockslide.

"Move him yourself, bim," Number Two growled. "He ain't that heavy."

I gave Wings a push and he rolled six inches, belched, and rolled right back. He wrapped an arm around my waist like he was anchoring his copt to it.

"Lovely furry floor. Nice warm bim. Wanna see Lady. Think I'm drunk."

He let his head fall with a thud and went back to snoring.

"Stupid bastid. Can't move him. Too heavy. An' now my legs is funny. When he gets mad my ol' man gets real, real nasty. Nasty ol' man. Nearly's bad 's this stupid bastid here."

I gave Wings another push and got as much reaction as you'd expect from a side of beef. The two guards laughed like a pair of blocked downpipes. I felt almost sorry for them.

"Okay, lady, we come and take the stupid bastard off your legs. Then you can go fix breakfast. Though surprise me if he c'n eat it, state she's in," Number One said. "How about we sling the guy in the leopard pen? Nobody using it. Leopard's kinda bored. Give him a shock when he comes around."

"If he comes around," Number Two agreed. "That's one randy leopard. Better check his credit."

"Yeah, right. Suit money, huh?"

An exchange of leers.

They propped their scimitars on the wall and ambled over. One grabbed Wings by the shoulders and the other by the ankles and they hauled him up like a folded sheet.

The air blurred around them and a sickening crack from the back of Number One's neck sounded like Sword punching rabbits. I'd say it was Hilt took out the other, though it's hard to tell. It was some very blunt instrument. While they were still falling Wings came alive like a galvanized eel, twisted in their hands and brought his fist up from a long way down, a long way up and a lot of hard. I hadn't even seen him pull the knife.

A pair of cold hands hauled me vertical.

"Okay," said Sword's velvet voice. "Let's go see the Lady."

An invisible hand tried the gilt doors. They were locked. I guess he followed up with a kick. Anyhow they vibrated with a metallic clang, buckled and came apart at the join. Silvery scratches opened where the ruined mechanism split, showing the leaves were cerosteel under the paint. Halo guarded her nest. But not against Swordfish.

He gave the doors a shove and they fell back, one crookedly on a broken hinge. A flurry of disturbed air and blurred vision surged through. Wings, taut as a whip, grabbed my hand and jerked me inside.

A soft glimmer of gold-worked fabrics and diamond lamps that picked out gilt splendor in little bright points came to meet us. And soft groans, human.

It was a big room but so hung and padded and layered with richness it looked small. Bijou, like the inside of a very classy jewel box. A bed half the size of a football field draped and pillowed with cloth-of-gold took up a lot of floor. Long drapes tented the ceiling and pooled on a golden-tan carpet, some drawn out at irregular angles for cute. An incense burner was filling the atmosphere with toxic fog.

The walls were covered in dull gold silk paved with paintings in bright gold carved frames. A gilt mirror bordered with cupids and garlands was placed opposite the door. I could imagine Halo looking at herself in it every afternoon after breakfast and asking who was the loveliest of them all and getting the right answer. Or it better watch its ass. It also gave her a view from the bed of anybody came in. Real Design Center. Beauty plus utility.

A chandelier covered with tiny sparkling lights that reflected and re-reflected from its crystal drops hung in the middle and a lot of other little lights glittered here and there among the curtains, hangings, pictures, low carved tables, ornament shelves and other decorator toys such as without which you can't have la dolce vita. Or so I'm told. I think it was meant to look like a fairy forest. It did. A forest of bad, bad fairies.

One of the little sparkling lights was in the hand of Halo. She was ravishing in a shift of plain gold satin slit to the hip bone each side and her toffee-colored hair was wound with gilt cords into a long thick rope. It did come down to her feet. Exactly to the upper tips of the pin-heels of her fairy gilt sandals.

The light was a small red-lacquer table-lighter with a glowing white-hot filament and she'd been applying it to the genitals of a male person stretched on the cloth-of-gold bed under her knee. He didn't seem too conscious but it wouldn't have mattered. His wrists and ankles were shackled with pretty gilt chains to the four corners. Which had daintily carved bedposts for the purpose. He was the one'd been doing the groaning.

The room smelled of incense, roast meat, and vomit.

She turned her Grecian head as we came in—I been told the Greeks had some pretty perverse habits—and the soft rope of her hair slid with a gentle *criss* over the satin. Her toffee-apple mouth, painted with bronze gloss, parted innocently in a sweet kitty-cat smile. She hoisted a curve of artistically drawn eyebrow like she wondered if we'd dropped in for coffee and maybe cookie'd forgotten the cream-cakes.

"Well, come in. When people want to see me as badly as that I'm always available. I'm nearly finished here."

I saw Sword's tall ghost-shadow move among the dainty furnishings to the side of the bed.

"Yes, I see you are," he said, like they were sharing a coffee table. "Hilt, go call a medic and tell him to bring a detox pack. I don't know if this guy's going to die from shock or aphrodisiacs first. You could unlock him now," he added politely to Halo. "He isn't getting up."

She slanted a provocative smile up at the voice, the little lighter balanced. "Oh, I don't know. I think I'd like one finishing touch. Here."

"Here?" Sword said softly.

She squealed like a wounded rabbit and half-raised her fingers to her smoking cheek. For a small lighter it made wicked burns. And it seemed somehow to have changed hands. If you like rough games, Sword's your man. I could have told her that. He stood attentively still, making the little blood-colored thing flip over and under his fingers, watching her cower.

We went on being a picturesque tableau until Hilt got back with the medic. I guess he was personnel because he was dressed got-out-of-bed rather than spacer with his shirt not tucked in at the rear and a pant-cuff folded up over one boot. He was yawning. Hilt was carrying him in one hand and his baggage in the other like a good bird dog by way of seeing they both got there. He put them down and backed off.

Since nobody'd got around to unchaining the guy one of our mates obliged by taking the chains to pieces and a good bit of bedpost along with them. I watched the painted canopy sway and hoped they weren't going to smother the poor bastard before the medic got through with the re-an. Bones himself looked like he'd rather have gone to Halo first, but I'd have said he got a Sword finger in the chest. He did a dramatic backward stagger and changed his mind.

"The lady likes pain," the deep gentle voice said from high up, the little lighter still flipping over and under in midair. "She's savoring it. If that guy dies, I'm going to feed you to the flowers in the airlock."

Bones went a shiny wax-pale and bent hastily over the bed. There were sweaty patches under the arms of his shirt. After a while he said he'd more equipment in his own place and maybe they better get an ambulance. A couple of the Pack stripped the gold spread and folded it to carry the guy and they processed out. The guy wasn't much more than a kid and he'd been good-looking. He still had thick shiny pale hair that fell back romantically from a forehead like polished bone. It flopped over what was left of his eyes as they took him away.

"Good," Sword said, still velvet. "Now we can talk. Shut the door, Wings."

Wings did. He had to be stronger than he looked because the leaf with the broken hinge dragged wickedly over the silky carpet leaving deep ragged grooves were going to need a house call from the decorator. Unless their mechanicals were a lot better than ours.

"Perhaps you know Cassandra." Sword was lazily unfastening his hood on that ruined face. His humorous mouth wasn't smiling and it was only beautiful if you appreciate typhoons. The scar that dragged the left side up looked like a fresh brand and the twinkly lights glistened on the bone of his deformed skull. He carried on downward casually, materializing the twisted ropes of red-blue pucker over his wire muscles, the churned mess of scar-tissue where other people have a heart. He could have been getting ready for bed. "And I do believe you know me. Haven't we corresponded? In a one-sided way, of course. I was sure I knew your style. Tell the lady what we want, Cass, while I get this off."

I told her. Briefly, because I figured she knew more than I did. I explained Razor's point of view a bit because she might not know it.

She listened with careful attention, her head cocked slightly to the burned side, looking like a polite little girl listening to a bag lady. Puzzled but too well-bred to be disgusted out loud.

"Has that anything to do with me?" she asked sweetly when I'd finished.

Sword was bare. He still moved like a dancer, long, graceful and athletic. It was like the corpse and the guy inside were two different people and the one worked the other without even noticing it wasn't perfect.

"Well, it's like this," he said. The voice, coming from that red-striped skeleton with as much hair as a marrow bone, sounded like the same guy did the moving was talking through a micro somewhere in its chest, another throat from another dimension.

He stretched his hand casually to the nearest curtain and gave it a twitch. The material ripped with a fingernail-turning *slissh* and cascaded like a waterfall into a pool at his feet. The weakened bed-post swayed, cracked and began to crumple. The canopy bowed downward at one corner, then another, then the whole thing collapsed with a creaking of wood like a falling forest. A great cloud of dust spumed out and choked us.

One corner of the padded underside fell on the incense burner and turned it over. It began to smolder. So did the carpet. Vile black smoke climbed the air currents in whorls. I put my hand over my nose. Wings didn't but he looked like he'd have liked to.

You can't say Sword's destructions are orgiastic. He's much too cold and meticulous. Halo watched as he twitched down the curtains one by one and added them to the smoldering pile. She gave only the slightest start as he chopped the cable of the chandelier with the edge of a hand and the whole twinkling, tinkling weight arrived with a smash on the carpet, all its little lights shorting out in sharp blue-white sputters and threads of gray smoke.

When he took down the first of the paintings and balanced it delicately between his long fingers, considering the subject—it was some kind of darkish landscape with trees—she spoke once, mildly.

"That's a Corot."

"So it is," Sword said, equally mild. He crumpled it to matchwood. "And this one's a Gauguin. Rather a nice one." The splinters pattered around his feet. "You like destruction, don't you, Halo?"

"It interests me," she said calmly. "Am I guilty of your friend's death? The other matter's academic. As I understand it the woman's dead, probably by suicide, and your only identification's a similarity of name. But you, I admit I find interesting."

"You didn't know Nimbus, I suppose?"

"But of course I did," she said with slightly raised brows. "How could I not? She was my stepdaughter. A boring creature from childhood with a totally infantile desire to outdo her wicked stepmother, even to copying my name. I had to be wicked since I married her father. I admit," she added reflectively, "after a year or two of his company I did see her point. But he had points of his own. A great many. People tended to die on them. We had a short marriage but a very entertaining one. Until he left with some bimbo and dumped his fat plain daughter on me. By the time I'd traced them she was old enough to work for herself, so I let her. I was occupied for a while, in any case. With the bimbo. I do believe her name was Merton. Do you think it possible the adorable Caronne didn't tell you all?"

"All things are possible," Sword said absently. He was dividing a Cubist rendering of a woman's face along the lines of fracture with a sharp fingernail. "I've seen the universe in extremely relativistic terms for some time. I'm only interested in whether you'll testify."

"Why should I do that? We're very old, Jason and I, and we've reached an age when we see less and less reason for being deflected by minor interruptions. The world's full of people who spend their lives complaining. We don't complain. We solve our own problems."

"Then you just got a new one. Me." He stopped in the middle of helping on entropy by turning a rather pretty pink-and-blue Virgin on a panel back into its original wormholes and sawdust. "You didn't think this game was serious, did you? I'm the boss. I play hopscotch while the boys work. Open the door, Wings."

Wings did. I realized he and I were the only guys left. The room had that empty echo. I guess the rest of the Pack went after Hilt and the medic. The door only needed a crack to let in the noise of riot. When he dragged the leaf back you couldn't see the corridor for a confusion like a mess of worms overturned in a jar.

Guys he and she, dressed, half-dressed and bare-ass naked, with and without their pants in their hands, were pushing and shoving, trying to go in different directions at the same time. A greenish type with muscles like King Kong and external gills was swashing through them with the mermaid slung over his shoulder and she was giggling like crazy, her oyster-sized eyes lit like Japanese lanterns. She had her purple knitting in one hand and her nail polish in the other. When she saw me she grinned with forty-eight perfect pearl teeth and three tongues in receding layers and waggled her fingers cheerfully. I guess working for Halo had to be a drag at that. Somebody else was hauling a mute cheetah on a piece of rope and swatting at some other guy was trying to take it away from him. One or two looked like they were just trying to remember where they'd left the exit.

"Close it," Sword said. "It's noisy."

He turned back to Halo and the job of destroying the world's artistic heritage. I was glad she only had about twenty or it wouldn't have had an artistic heritage. If Moke had been there he'd have wept.

"Before I came I left a delayed message for the cops. They'll get it in about an hour. I think I made it interesting enough to catch their attention. Though all they'll get's your staff. The ones are still alive, if anyone's been giving Hilt trouble. He's a bit short, he had a date tonight. Your clients are leaving, as you'll have noticed. I told the guys to let them take any portable property they happened to fancy since you aren't going to need it. I'm having all your nonsentient stuff and the obscener of the talking ones put down. They offend my sense of order. By the time the cops get here you aren't going to have any property and you aren't going to have any clients. The staff have gone already but I'm afraid Hilt jinxed their barge so they'll be floating around. Probably some of them'll talk, somebody always does. It won't matter because the sat isn't going to be here. It goes up in its component particles in"— he took a look at his wrist-display—"fifty-seven minutes forty-three seconds."

Halo was staring at him steadily. Her cheek was puffed like a balloon at one side around a crackled weeping ring but she acted like it wasn't there. She was like her step-daughter. Guts absolutely wasn't what she was short of.

"Just so you don't move on and start again." He snapped another picture, of a hysterical-looking bim with a lot of frizzy dark-red hair, and shivered it to flinders. "Sooner or later you'll get more capital, of course."

He picked up the cupid-edged mirror and held it in front of her face. I guess Snow White was the prettier of the two this time. She took it stoically. Then he dropped it on the floor at her feet. The glass shattered and rang around her sandals. The frame splintered and broke in two.

"I think you're about to have seven years' bad luck. When I consider your mating habits, seems to me you deserve them. But I'm talking business failures. Like any business you touch. However you change your looks, however you change your name, wherever you go to hide, I'm going to find you and put a match to it. Just like here."

He had the last picture, a delicate primitive icon in dark colors and tarnished gilt on a blackened rectangle of wood, in his hands. It had been hanging just beside the mirror.

"Is this your favorite? Or just next after the last one? But then we've time to take care of that problem too. I think you and I may have the materials of a bargain. If we're both intelligent about it. You look intelligent. Are you?"

He crushed the icon to dust and glanced over his shoulder at Wings and me.

"The Lady and I have a bit of discussion we'd rather do in private. Would you like to wait outside? Wings, don't let Hilt get absent-minded and let any filth survive, and watch Dribble minds his manners. If he's laying something, kick him. I want everyone suited up and ready to go in thirty-five minutes. I'm not likely to take that long."

We went. I looked back at the door and they were standing face to face. Halo's eyes were cold, intent, and not even pretending to be innocent. I was glad I wasn't looking into Sword's.

By the time we hit the corridor it was empty. The furry floor was scuffed bare in places and a lot of the diamond stars were missing. A smell of burning came from somewhere past the animal pens in the bit I hadn't seen. It was pungent and greasy, organic and abnormal at the same time. Sea water and some kind of stinking gelatinous stuff had got stamped into the carpet up the maze. The bodies of the guards had gone but one of their scimitars was snapped in two on the floor. There was blood on the blade.

"Come on," Wings said, jerking my arm.

I jerked back. "I'm waiting for Sword."

"He doesn't want you."

"What's that got to do with it? He never has."

He looked at me. Then he shrugged. "If he isn't out in twenty-five minutes I'm putting you into a suit by force and I don't give a fuck if you bite me. I can't hang around here, I got stuff to do."

"So go do it."

He went. I stayed. For two or three generations. I think in the end twenty-three minutes.

Sword came out alone and in his coolsuit. I could feel his grim stare through the filters.

"She'll testify," he said shortly. "I need a bath. Come on, get suited. This place is going up in under twenty minutes and I want clear."

"What about her?"

"She's gone. She has a back way and a private yacht."

"And you let her."

"Yes." The stare was white-hot. "We have an agreement."

"Oh. Fine," I said lamely. I felt about for his hand, caught it trying to avoid me, grabbed it and hung on. After a minute he let me. "Did you really have to smash all those pictures?"

"Yes."

We loped along without saying anything else. In the room where the siren had been there was more slopped sea water and a lot of jelly sloshing around the furniture but no sign of the guys. The place smelled like a stagnant aquarium. Further up there was vomit on the carpet. I hugged Sword's arm and tried not to add to it.

Near the service door he relented. Something dark and flat materialized from one of his pockets and got dumped in my hand. "I palmed this for you. Careful, it's fragile."

It was the little gilded icon. A sad-faced Virgin with her baby against her shoulder, both aureoled with gold, stiff and slightly ridiculous with a painful ancient beauty. Mokey would have died for it.

Swordfish has this habit of reading my mind. "It's yours," he said tightly.

"Yes, Sword. Thank you."

I wiped my nose on his sleeve, which was the nearest, and slid the icon inside my shirt.

"Okay," he said. "Now let's get out before the whole fucking place blows."

We got.

Someone had put the sat on drive because when we got into space it was already drifting quietly out of the cluster toward vacancy. Someone else, Wings at a guess, was keeping the lighter at low speed in position off its flank. We were the last. Sword dragged me after him across the gap, shoved me through the lock, went forward to the controls still in his lattice and took off like a bat out of hell.

The bloom of blue-white flame blanked out even the red cockpit-light before we'd quite cleared the cluster and the lighter bucked on the shock wave.

Most of us were still latticed. Hilt's vast shape next to me patted my thigh with a hand like a mechanical digger and opened its helmet on invisibility.

"Boss cut it fine this time. You get what you came for, Cass?"

"I guess. He says we did."

A grunt.

"Swell, we did, then. Now I go home explain to my lady how I come to stink of bordello some way so she don't kill me before I get through explaining."

And he laughed, like Hurricane Herbert or maybe a high-speed train approaching through a tunnel. I did wonder what she was going to use to kill him with.

Sword and I went back to Hallway's on the supposition Moke would still be there tormenting his doughnut. He was, but looking the more tormented of the two.

"Cass?" he said eagerly, jumping down from Hallway's bench where the two of them looked like they were brewing some particularly scientific and medical coffee. "I'm glad to see you guys." This was only half-true because he couldn't be glad to see Sword, who wasn't visible. "We got troubles."

"Like what?" Sword grated by way of proving he was there and fighting.

Moke made a face. "Friend Cordovan promised Cass and me if we didn't make space he'd set the cops on our tail. For all the world's crimes, past, present and imaginary. He did it. I got a message from Hans-Bjorn, there's been a herd of flicaille tromping over Never all afternoon with warrants a yard long searching for us in the shrubbery and the wine cellar. He got pissed off after a while and phoned the president of the council, who told 'em to clear off. Since they hadn't found us they did but he warns me they're looking down here. Hallway says we better stay with him in case Jason has a line on our loft because he believes he's still clear."

"I think it's time we did something about Mr. Cordovan," Sword said. "He's getting to be a nuisance. Anyhow, I owe him a killing. Hate to disappoint people."

"Yeah, and there's something you'd better know." Moke at his darkest. "Hall got word. Your friend Lorn's going to be upset."

"Haver," Hallway said with his quiet precision. "Had an accident on-set earlier today. In a car-chase where the car was supposed to explode. It did. Only the explosion should have been FX and wasn't. Hospital wasn't taking any bets this evening. It's going to be close."

The silence was so thick you could have rolled and wrapped it.

"You'd better tell Lorn."

Haver was the guy'd been with Lorn the first time I met him. A charming wirehead with a smile like an angel who played comedies at permanent danger to his life. Or so he said. I'd met him once. I guess Lorn liked him. Hell, I liked him.

"I'll deal with it," Sword said. He sounded like the climate on Jupiter and not in one of its quiescent phases. "You guys stay here and do as Hall tells you. If there's trouble he'll get you out. And Cassandra, I mean stay. This isn't the moment to go exploring the subway or whatever amusement you had in mind for tonight. I'll be back."

The door closed on a silent swirl of air. Hallway sighed and put one of the mugs back on the shelf. "Coffee, Cass?"

"Thanks."

"Which was Haver's studio?" he asked, pouring.

"Coelacanth, who else? I'm sorry, Hall. Does Sword ever sleep?"

He made a mild face a couple of degrees more emphatic than usual. "Not tonight, I guess."

"Aurora told me even Coelacanth doesn't kill off comedy stars on purpose."

"Maybe not. Haver was a friend of Lorn's."

And hence of mine. Oh, I'm a broth of a girl.

I humped my rear onto the bench by Moke's side and wound my arm around his waist.

"Hey, look what Sword gave me. I guess it was lying around Halo's place without a chain on. He said it was for me but I'll let you look at it."

He took the little icon reverently and gazed into it like it was a crystal ball.

"At least the guy's got a sense of values."

"Oh, he's got that. He sure has. Does Hall have a spare pad somewhere? I want to go to bed. You better come with me, I think I want to cry on your shoulder."

He gave me a kind luminous smile.

"Okay. Your turn. If we put this on the wall we can both look."

"Yeah. Is there a spell for bringing seven years' good luck?"

"This could be it. Let's try."

When we left Hallway'd cleared off the bench and was wiping it down ready for surgery.

Knowing what he operates on, I didn't think the seven years were starting today.

18

"They're on the Moon," Hallway said, toneless. "Whole pack, plus your friend Dein."

"They've actually started?"

"Seems so. Techs took their stuff out awhile back, Cordovan joined them about three days ago. Got a lot set up out Farside. Comes cheaper. We've a civilization up there."

Moke snorted. "Heard you thought it was us that hadn't."

"We're less tight-assed," Hallway admitted, still toneless. "Sword's collecting a crew. He figures it could get total."

"With Cordovan getting totaled. When do we go?"

"You don't, Cass. I do. He wants backup."

"The hell I don't. Whose boyfriend is this?"

"Lady named Aurora, way I was told it," Hallway said.

"Okay. But it's me owes him."

"Sword's paying."

"He's paying for himself," Moke said. "Caronne stuck in his throat."

"True. She stuck in mine. That's why I'm packing."

"Cass and I have our own debts. Personal. Maybe it's time Sword noticed neither of us is fourteen anymore."

"Maybe you better explain that to him."

"Maybe he could try crawling up his own ass. Am I wrong, or does your civilized civilization have a shuttle service?"

"Last time I heard," Hallway said.

"Great. Then Moke and me'll take it. Sword can get macho on his own. Give him my love and tell him to wash behind his ears."

"He hasn't any."

"Then it's fucking well time he had. If he's going to feel sorry for himself for the rest of his life, count me out. Tell me, Hall. I'm a nasty guy, I didn't send him a postcard. What's wrong with his right hand? Writer's cramp it ain't."

"Maybe you better ask him that yourself, too."

"All he's got to do is wait long enough and I ain't going to care."

"I'll tell him so."

"Do. And tell him if he gets spiteful Moke and me'll bite an ankle each."

Hallway raised a brow. "I can picture that."

"You better. You got no idea how vicious Moke gets if you step on him."

Moke looked amiably vacant, which he ain't. "Check," he said.

The shuttle's low-class, slow but anonymous. Moke and I slid out at dawn in workers' coveralls with a kit bag apiece on our laboring shoulders and walked on our own sneakers to the walkway where we fastlaned into the spaceport. I'd debeaded and delacquered my fake pagoda into a tarty-looking snakes' nest. Medusa the morning after. Nobody looked at us. It's classic Ump garb and the world's full of us.

We stood in line among a whole heap of better-dressed guys with raised eyebrows and let our bellies rumble. They edged off a bit, which can only be good. It wasn't deliberate, we hadn't had any breakfast. Moke bought the tickets with a fake contract-worker's card he got from Hallway who may be Sword's armorer and best friend but who doesn't always follow the party line, and we got to sit in the back of the bus. Or anyhow the shuttle.

After we'd let our bellies rumble a bit more the stewardess deigned to serve breakfast to ameliorate the nuisance. It wasn't up to Yell's standard but you don't expect much of stuff comes in compartments on a little plastic tray. Yell wasn't around on account of Moke sent him back to Never, figuring it might be safer and he and Issa could roll around the furniture as well there as anywhere else. It was one of those meals they give you free sodamints as a courtesy and the courtesy's all on your side.

We got into Lunaport four hours later and came out underground in the famous Lunar gravity makes everybody bound like jackrabbits and gives me a hard time around the belly. It's no use asking about scenery, what they got in the back of the shuttle's no windows. We stopped bounding long enough to give Immigration our fake passports, which was unfair because they're a sovereign state and don't give a shit about Earth APBs. But we did think if Cordovan had an ounce of sense—and he didn't get to be front man for a major company by not having—he'd have a few seeing eyes around the place and there was no point arriving in semaphore. Also, Mokey'd got allergic to signing people's skins. It may not be a Luney custom, sure they got bad habits of their own.

We were shot out of the terminus on an overhead railcar that made like bumper cars and spilled our baggage all over us, causing Earthers to get a lot more physically familiar than most of them quite like to do, and made a noise like a pneumatic door. It stopped abruptly on the closer edge of a dime, explaining the colloid-restraints between seats, and opened all its ports with finality. We fell onto Lunar soil much shakier than we'd started and found a big intersection leading into a whole mess of color-coded tunnels. We stood around looking confused.

"Aurora," Moke said. As a practical guy he's practical. "If they've any sense her phone's bugged."

"But Lunar CI isn't. Unless someone's declared war."

That's a local joke. There's nothing better at dropping rocks on your head than a satellite and guess what the Moon is. It's why they're sovereign and stay that way.

We had a problem with the pay phone, which didn't use Earth credits, until a guy eight feet long and nine inches wide folded down to our level and told us Central Information's free. By Earth standards that ain't just civilized, it's crazy. And I'm avoiding the pun. Luneys are sensitive. Three minutes later we had Aurora's address and were on our way.

The subway was crowded with oversized people who didn't especially look like Hallway except in being oversized and who all seemed good-tempered. I've noticed it's an effect of being underpopulated. Their fashions were very un-Earth, running to float, which floats real nice in low gravity, and balloony layers, which is fine if you're all built like basketball players, which most of them are. There were a few small square people in weird dress around who when you looked closely turned out to be us, I mean the down-below lot. Since we all look weird to them they didn't register our lack of class and were nice to us. They treat Ari VIPs exactly the same, which got to be annoying.

The subway was designed to scare the shit out of you which is a fairly regular feature of subways and shot and swayed through black moleholes like an insane earthworm. It stopped now and then to let more balloony guys on and off then did some more shooting. The Luneys sat around looking casual and discussing real fascinating things like income tax and the price of jet fuel. Ad holos overhead ran to haiku from some local art festival recited

by a kimonoed guyess with a phony Japanese voice and
cuddly toons demonstrating the positions of the Kama
Sutra in full animation.

There's a theory Luneys are a frontier society, so puri-
tanical. I guess about three centuries back they may have
been. Right now their ideas run if you're going to have
kids grow up sexual, which been known among humans,
you might as well teach 'em the details in the hope they
won't want to rape each other. Don't know if it works but
back Earthside they leave us find out for ourselves and
the rape rate on the Strip stays low because of Sword's
fine cutting edge. We do get a few spare genitals about.
It causes clutter. The wastebaskets here are for waste.
Clean, new and detoxified.

We got off in a strip-lit concourse with a lot of designer
jungle to help out the oxygen recyc, pastel-colored balloons for sitting on and three sides of open boutiques. You
could buy replicas of the Soup-Tureen at the Lunar Trade
Center mounted on moonrock plinths, flashing bracelets
set with lava-jewels, floaty clothes in sizes thirty through
ninety-six and coffee and doughnuts in seventeen flavors.
Moke sat on a magenta balloon to orient the tunnel-map
LCI had given us free and it said, "Have a nice day," in a
sweet mezzo-soprano. Luneys have highish voices, it has
to be the atmosphere.

"Same to you," Moke said absently, unfolding the map.
I sat beside him to see if it would say the same to me. It
fooled me. It said, "Welcome to Luna."

"You're lighter than me," he said.

"Uh-huh. I think smart balloons I could get tired of."

"Maybe it only does it for tourists."

I watched narrowly for a Luney to sit down. They
didn't. Maybe they got tired of smart balloons.

"I think we follow the blue stripe to the far end then
we pick up the pink and go three blocks. Houses got to
be numbered. I hope."

"Okay. I'm not sure yet about rabbit-warrens. If you see a passing ferret let me know in time."

He looked patient. "You spent your life climbing through air ducts."

"Right. That's why I'm agoraphobic. Place is too wide for me. I feel like I shrank in the wash."

When we got up the balloon said, "Nice knowing you." I suppose it could have been worse. It could have made like a whoopee cushion. This time I decided not to answer. Maybe it would notice and be disappointed.

There were serious shops on the blue artery for serious shoppers. I made a note to come back and buy a handbag sometime when we weren't on the wanted list. The pink turnoff was residences. And yeah, they had numbers. A lot also had names, fancy carvings, tilework, flower arrangements, and little trees in boxes. They all had polarized windows on the sidewalk, which was wide with patterned cobbles. There were guys wandering up and down it looking like they lived there and a pack of kids playing a hopping game on the patterns.

Aurora's number was partway down the third block and had a painted dragon over the door engaged in killing St. George. Looked like a winner to me, anyhow. Moke pressed the chime and Aurora opened it and fell out all over us.

"Thank God, I thought I'd missed you. That or you didn't want to come. I'll make some coffee, it may make me rational. Dein's on-set and God knows what they're doing. I'm scared to think about it. I'm here all day and some nights and I'm going crazy. He keeps working eighteen-hour shifts and every time I wonder if he's coming back."

I flopped on a pale-blue balloon all set about with Swiss-cheese plants none of which had any remark to make and took off my horrible wig.

"You wanted us?"

She stopped with the coffee machine in her hand. It looked like she'd been rationalizing herself a lot lately. "Didn't you get my cable? Day before yesterday. I thought that was why you'd come."

"Cops are after us. A whim of your employer. It's why I'm dressed like *The Exorcist*, take ninety-two. We haven't had mail for a few days, we had to vacate in a hurry."

"Oh." She looked at the wig. "It's a disguise? I thought maybe it was fashionable. It's quite attractive."

"Only if you're called Perseus. Is Dein okay?"

"Up to date. But I explained about the quarrel. It's the order of takes I'm worried about right now."

"What's wrong with them?" Moke asked.

She shook her head. "You need to know the business. They started at the end. That's okay, they often shoot in reverse especially if there are long-hair shots. You know, the hero starts out cleancut, gets dirtier and finishes shaggy. But it takes a while to grow your hair nicely and it actually looks better if you do it yourself. So they ask the guy to grow a beard or whatever. Then when they've got the scene they shave him and do the cleancut bits later. But they told Dein to stay clean, they'd begin at the beginning and gen his hair up as they went along."

"But they didn't."

"No. And I don't see why they've changed their minds. His hair's a bit flaky, hasn't had time to settle. And they say Cordovan's a perfectionist." She smiled helplessly. "Maybe they just did. Directors get fancies."

"Uh-huh. How difficult would it be to change leading men in midstream?"

Moke looked at me. Brutal, his green glance said. Aurora just looked relieved. I'd figured her for a girl who'd rather come to the point.

"Not so very easy. It would cost money. But it's happened."

"And the earlier the guy drops out the less it costs, right?"

"Yes," she said in a small voice.

Moke gazed blankly out the rear window. It faced on an inner court with what looked like banana leaves and a real fountain.

"Has he sorted out the quarrel with Maranna?"

Her eyes had a salty glaze.

"It's evaporated like it came. Today friends, tomorrow not friends, today friends again. I know it's what people expect in films, but Maranna isn't like that. She's straightforward usually. But I know her and I've a feeling she's hiding something. There are edges. I said she's not vicious, but she's a tough old pro and she fights for things. I think you said out loud what I was afraid to think. Dein playing *High Noon*'s what I don't want to see."

"Which way have they gone?"

"Dein's. All the way back to square one."

"He kills her."

"That's what's in the script."

But if he was slated for removal it wouldn't matter either way. They'd be reshooting with her new leading man in any case. I wasn't quite brutal enough to say that out loud. She knew, anyhow.

"Would she agree to kill Dein?"

"Not in those terms. I'm sure not. But she could be fooling herself. Jason could have agreed with her she's to win really, all she has to do is kill Dein on set. With a prop gun, naturally. She could even think she believes Dein's in on it. Jason's famous for last-minute script changes and pulling surprises on his stars. Then all she has to do is not check. It isn't even her business. It's down to Props."

"A little accident."

"For which Coelacanth's famous," Moke said. "We ran away. And kept running right to Virginity, even though it is the world's nastiest place."

"Dein can't. It's his career. And in some ways he isn't too knowing. He believes in them because he's got to."

"But we haven't," I said. "There's bad weather rising. Could get quite piercingly cold. Can we see these guys? I wouldn't mind meeting Maranna."

"Of course. I'll take you over this afternoon. Would you like some food first? It's morning around the other side and I'm eating Dein-time. I was making lunch."

"Best news I heard all day," Moke said.

Aurora had turned several degrees nearer the sun as if seeing us had done her good. I hoped she was right.

Most places on the Moon you get to by subway on account of it's easier to go under the terrain than over. Since the atmosphere's theoretical, overland means spacecraft. Aurora had one, a small hopper she flew herself.

"Faster," she said as we strapped in. We were crowded, I guess it was built for two, both lovers. "They're filming on surface out at Chaplygin for the space-battle shots and there's a studio for the alien sequences. Jason would rather have been underground but he's using practical lasers for some of the scenes and the authorities won't give him permission. It's something to do with crust stability. Anyhow, there's a major subway artery on the other side of the crater and the starport at Liberty in Mendeleev just over the horizon so they insisted he stay out of the way. Liberty has all the out-system traffic, there's stuff coming and going all the time."

"Practical lasers?" Moke said. "I thought films used FX."

"Not Jason's. He wants authentic externals behind his space battles. They used to mock-up but these days it's cheaper to use scaled-down drones and film them against a real starfield. There's a certain amount of electronic light-and-sound, colored rays and flashes and stuff, and the on-board explosions are controlled from the ground, but he thinks nothing looks like a real laser burst except a real laser burst. Or so he says. I think it's just people find it more exciting if they know it's real. So he has ground batteries and some hand cannon. It's Navy surplus but since it's old the radio controls have been known to fail. The portmaster at Liberty isn't too happy about bits of drone or stray laser fire getting into his landing space. So we're in the wilds. The Lunar authorities are tough about studio conditions."

"That's Luneys. No understanding of our superior social organization."

"They don't have an atmosphere to soak up the bits," Moke said.

"They're just tough. About everything."

"Yeah, well. The trouble about a laser beam is it's like Old Man River, it just keeps rolling along. Would be kind of embarrassing to make a hole in someone. I'm surprised they let him do it at all."

She made a face. "He pulled strings. He's got friends on the Governing Council on Earth and Luna's working up a trade agreement. You push, I pull."

"Sounds like the animal with a head at each end. Except Cordovan's the only guy I know has two assholes and his brains in the middle."

The black-gray surface slid under us, the close horizon sharply curved. Walls of cliff fringed with rubble reared up like theater curtains, ridged and folded over blurred-out crater floors, and drew back as we passed. The sun was a harsh arc that pasted our shadows on the forward port. The stars blazed like lamps, close enough to reach out and pick. The terminator could have been drawn with a compass, a couple of towering peaks catching the glare beyond. It was nearly full moon on Earth so the farside was a sudden fall of darkness like the closing of a shutter as we swung out of sun into Moon-night.

There's very little groundlight showing on the Moon since so much of its life is underground. An array of port-beacons to starboard marked Liberty; landing-grids picked out in rippling bulbs on the surface of a worn ringwall. A shuttle was coming down in an aura of flame as we got level, red and green lamps blinking, from a liner in orbit above. Lines of white riding-lights picked out the immense whale shape dotted with starry sparkles.

The shuttle passed by us, touched on the grid, settled and was drawn out of sight. Pressurized doors closed and the grid lamps turned red. Beyond, a larger ship was warming for takeoff, its vapors voided into space in jets of crystallizing chemical ice. More of the same had condensed and frozen on the rocks, veiling the port in glitter.

Aurora veered south to avoid it and took us over broken lumps of moonscape towards the close curve ahead. At this distance sheer scale made tumbled blocks and eroded ringwalls meaningless, giant shapes dimly starlit, blacker cutouts against black. It was like the Snow Queen's palace with the scattered pieces that spelled ETERNITY. I wasn't surprised Luneys were tough. Seemed to me it needed a special sort of mind to live here at all. Hallway's, maybe.

Aurora was keeping one eye on her radar and the other on her course chart. I was too. Mokey leaned over the seats between us and ground his hatchet jaw into my shoulder, giving me an amicable not-quite-shaved cheek to rub.

"Too big," he said.

Meaning he wasn't finding it sculptural.

"Poor Moke. It'll be nicer on the ground."

"I like it fine here," he said, nibbling my ear.

"Here we are," Aurora said at almost the same moment. "I hate landing in the dark. Of course dark's what Jason's here for."

A green light flashed on the chart and a bright prick echoed it below. A square of white dots sprang up around the edge of the pad and her nose-beacons picked up the luminous cross of a landing marker. We came down quietly on an eroded plain whose ringwall was almost lost over the horizon, near a small collection of geodomes and a pair of pressurized hangars. A cluster of hulls like dead blackbeetles was scattered by the side. An entry belt flipped us toward the dome lock and as the inner doors ground shut behind us a yellow mechanical parker twitched the hopper off the belt and slung it into line. Then it gave us a pressured tube into atmosphere. If Dein and Aurora did this a lot they weren't as sweetly simple as they looked.

She pulled off her leather helmet and tossed her mane over the fur of her Amy Johnson jacket.

"Hello, Parky. Are they still working?"

"You're early again. Friends? Sign in your guests, huh? Yeah, I guess. Mr. Cordovan's the devil when he's in the mood. You want to go wait in the dressing room?"

"I'd like to meet Maranna," I said, making with the big sleaze. Wide bright eyes, look at my fluffy tail. "Is she here? Have they got to the big scene yet?"

"The grand shootout? Nah. Maybe tomorrow. What I hear they done peace palavers all morning and right now Dein's facing-off with Bubba. They been doing it since two-thirty Standard Galactic and the whole pack of 'em's losing their minds. If it goes on much longer one of those boys is going to strangle the other for real. Or so the spear carriers tell me. They went home half an hour ago asking why they worked here. As if I'd know. But if you're hunting autographs you could be lucky. Maranna's still here. Don't know what her temper's like, but you can try her. Decent sort of lady when she ain't put out."

"Thanks." I tried to look like the sort of guy gets my skin signed. "Can I just go in?"

"I'll take you," Aurora said. "Be glad to make the presentations. Then you won't mind if I go look for my mate?"

"Suits me. And find Moke a sculptural view and he'll follow you anywhere."

Mokey gave me the pained green eye. He doesn't follow strange bims, even with rosy-fingered hair. He suspects half of them of cannibalism and the other half of wanting to talk about culture.

"I wouldn't mind looking at your set construction. Like to see how other guys solve materials problems."

"So go sniff their glue, Martin. Only don't get high, I need you."

The dressing rooms were around the side of the soundstage that filled most of the dome. It had the routine red light over the doors and a scampering of busy gray-faced people fussing up and down. The corridor curved around the inside of the dome wall and I reckoned their decorator'd had problems with the carpet.

Aurora stopped at a door with a star and stuck her head around. "Maranna? We aren't disturbing you, are we?"

"You damned well know you are, Rory," the languid throaty blonde at the mirror snarled, turning around. "But if that's Dein's tame genius I'll consider forgetting it. If he has some more pink rocks at hand."

Moke got one of his absent looks. I wondered if we could afford another cut-price garden. It was true we hadn't spent our Caronne bribe-money. Depended a bit if the lady was worth it.

"He's cooking a twenty-foot torus in insulator glass, of two guys making out in four dimensions plus kid. If it talks to you. Right now he's being disappointed. He was hoping the Moon would blow his skull open and it hasn't."

Mokey offered a scarred ragged-nailed hand. Sculpture isn't one of these ladylike jobs, even for ladies. "Tell me where you want it and I'll think."

The blonde looked up at him with turquoise eyes elongated to her temples with glo-paint and a set of lashes you could have used for washing windows. She was still wearing bits of Alien Princess, furry cat's ears, eighteen-inch whiskers and a nerve-controlled lashing fathom of fluff said she had a socket in her tailbone. Which is a major sacrifice because you got to spend the rest of your life sitting on it. They're even more difficult and expensive to remove than they are to put in. Her hands were tipped with retractile claws, FX specials she was in the middle of removing.

She had fine Slav cheekbones and a long narrow mouth with flexible lips suited to smiling sexily or snarling ditto, whichever the part asked for. I could see her as Goneril but not exactly Perdita. But she didn't smell bad. Apart from her makeup, which stank of volatile polymers and sweated fake fur. I figured the reek of jasmine on top was sensorial background.

"Why don't you think and I'll tell you where to put it?" she purred, brushing the hand with long white fingertips.

"He's a fine upstanding lad with a driving license," I said. "Why don't you and me discuss doughnuts? The boy wants to look at scenery."

She grinned, not too nastily. "You paid to protect his innocence?"

"Not exactly. He protects it pretty good himself, only it embarrasses him to say no to a lady."

"He could say yes."

"Not while I'm here."

This time she laughed and waved a claw. "It's okay. At my age I buy pretty boys. Comes cheaper than marriage. Rory, go brood over your man and show the guy some scenery. Maybe he'll get a classy thought for my garden."

She watched them go with narrowed eyes, lazily detaching her cat-lashes. She put them in a jar and began to dismantle the ears. "Okay doll, so what do you want really?"

There was something frank, coarse and experienced about her reminded me of Caronne. I didn't dislike it. She looked like a bim might have gambling debts, love troubles, income tax problems about the three-five million she just forgot to declare last year when she was thinking of something else. And she was at least half honest.

"Dein."

"You can't have him, babe. He's spoken for. You want to watch Rory. She's fiercer than she looks in some ways."

"I think I already had him. In a previous existence. Don't tell them, he doesn't remember. I ain't short anyhow. I mean I want him alive."

"Uh-huh. Meaning what?"

"Look, when I get around to offending you, throw me out. I won't scratch. Your man Cordovan's already tried to kill Moke and me. Since he didn't make it he's trying to put us in jail for a thousand years. If he gets there you won't even have a hot doughnut. Spiteful man. He doesn't know we're here. If you feel like revenge, tell him."

"He's a sweetheart." She'd got one ear off and put it on a stand. Her own beneath was basic elegant but red and bent with weight. She rubbed cream on it tenderly. "So what can I do, kid?"

"Heard there was a contract fight about who kills who in the climax. Which you let drop. And they're shooting tomorrow."

"God willing, and if our lovely Jason ever gets finished tonight. Those boys going to be gray in the morning. So?"

"I'd like the shooting to stay on film." I caught her second ear as it peeled and put it on the other half of the stand. She massaged reddened gristle. "If I were Cordovan and I wanted rid of Dein, you know what I'd do?"

"Does he want rid of Dein?"

"Maybe I didn't explain to you properly. What Dein remembers happened in his careless childhood ain't exactly what happened really, and if how he got that way ever went public it'd open a can of worms the size of boa constrictors. And it's Cordovan who could end up strangled."

"That's Jason. So what would you do, sweetheart?"

"I guess I'd make a separate agreement with each of my stars and tell each of them the other had given in. I'd tell the guy he was shooting the lady and the lady she was shooting the guy. With fake guns, naturally. Then I'd give each of 'em a working blaster and stand out of range. Dein's not much of a shooter, or he wasn't when I knew him. So chances are his costar might kill him. Or not, of course, since he thinks he's supposed to kill her. Except he's a terrible shot. But it would go over fine. Accident, professional jealousy, whatever. Whichever way it turns Jason wins. Big scandal, real gun on set, somebody kills costar, everyone knows there was a messy scandal. Bet neither of you's any idea just how messy it's going to look when the scandal sheets get through with it. One of you gets killed, other gets the blame. Whichever, Dein's either dead or disgraced so even if this story about the little muddle in his head gets out, say by somebody like me, who cares? The guy's over. And I'm not sure Jason'd mind if it worked out it was you got the charge. He believes in the values of thrift and self-help. And I mean self."

She sat still in the act of brushing glitter out of her hair. Her eyes had darkened.

"And if somebody had a plan like that, what suggestions would you make, doll?"

"Can you tell a real laser from a prop one?"

"Can you?"

"Probably. But I'm not here. I'm the Invisible Woman, or Rory's little hopper could just depressurize on the way home. With us in it."

"Straight answer: no. Guns ain't my thing. I take what I'm given. All I know is they all shoot colored light but with one the smoke and flames is fake, with the other they ain't. Can Dein?"

"Not in my day." I leaned over to help detach the platinum bristles over her brows. "You know Haver?"

"Sure. Cute kid. I'd have had him for my third husband if the little bastard hadn't got a fit of self-preservation."

"You heard he got hurt couple days back? An exploding car that really exploded. He's a friend of a friend. The friend knows too much about this story or someone thinks he does, and he talked to Haver or someone thinks he did. There's a guy herearound who don't wait for proof. Anybody touches us gets bad luck. I liked Haver. I don't think he knew a thing. Now they don't know if he's going to make it."

Turquoise eyes looked out of the mirror, calculating and troubled.

"Listen, bim, Rory tell you I can't throw this film?"

"She said you're a bit short. Creditwise."

The eyes flickered. "Worse, baby. My contract's on the line. Coelacanth's hit white water and they're slinging ballast. I'm borderline. If I can stay aboard another couple of years I can sort out this mess and think retirement. Host a vid-show, take a trip off-planet, you name it. They ditch me now and I'm up to my neck. The IRS is going to take me for everything I've got then a couple of little Houseboys going to come around break my arms for not having more. If they don't throw acid in my face."

I looked at her Slav cheekbones. I'd already seen Caronne.

"I can cover you for acid."

She raised a brow. "Twenty-four hours a day for the rest of my life?"

"No. My contact goes to the root of the problem. He meets guys carrying acid on his territory, he got this habit of pouring it down the front of their pants. You've no idea how discouraged they get."

She almost smiled. "You got rough friends. Why was I getting that idea? But you see, sweetie, being a pauper ain't easy. I'm not as young as all that. I hear what you say. Maybe I believe it. But I got to think. Why don't you go talk to Dein?"

"Okay. But if . . ."

"Listen, bim." She caught my wrist with an unexpectedly strong hand, the tips of her fake claws digging long rose-prickles into the meat of my palm. "I done a lot of things, but I never killed anyone. Not even by accident. I got to think. Go talk to Dein."

"Yeah, sure. Thanks for listening."

She made a half-stripped cat face. "Thanks for talking."

I left her detaching whiskers all over her dressing table. She was thinking, all right. As I closed the door she jerked a little too hard and the long wire came loose complete with glue and cuticle. The last I saw she was plastering nuskin with a shaking hand and saying things ladies mostly don't.

I closed the door and headed for the soundstage.

Dein came off-set grimed, sweaty, and got up as Flash Gordon in designer stubble. He looked as if he'd have liked to relieve his mind of some classic phrases usually reserved to the Navy and guys dig holes in the street but he saw Aurora and didn't.

"Twenty-seven. It's got to be a record. Harran and I are so hoarse we've run out of scream."

"It's probably what he was waiting for," Aurora said.

"Guy's a sadist." He cracked her ribs a bit and looked at Moke and me like he'd found us in his personal linen. "You again? You want more measurements? Going to build a crater or something?"

"I invited Martin and Cassandra," Aurora said. "They've been talking to Maranna."

"Maybe she'd like a crater," Moke said. He sounded tired. Dammit, the guy had been his lover, had loved him. Maybe he was finding what I'd found already. Dosh was dead. "Be a change to build down instead of up."

"Sorry," Dein said grudgingly. "Bit tense. Every take Harran has to throw me on the floor and I have to get up and knock him across the table. Floor's dirty."

"One of those routine diplomatic meetings," I said. "How's Harran?"

"Hasn't spoken to anyone in an hour apart from screaming lines, but his throws have been getting more and more sincere. He's worse off than me, he's in those damned cat ears. Hope he's got a sympathetic makeup girl or he's liable to scalp himself."

"Maranna's doing her own."

"She's a hard woman."

"Her poor little ears were red."

"Nothing to what Jason's are if he's on Harran's wavelength. Let's go, woman, before I start chewing you. I need meat."

"Go wash up and you can have some nice combed prote," Aurora said.

He groaned.

"You get to shoot her after all," I said, watching him shed Flash Gordon and some dirt. He kept the stubble. I could see Aurora had a hard night coming.

"That's the idea."

"What do you do if she arrives with a gun in her hand?"

"She's got to. It's in the script. That's why I shoot her. She arrives in armor with gun to say she's decided to renounce her people and fight to the death on our side, I see the gun and mistake her for Brother, bang. Wailing and gnashing of teeth. Gnash."

"Do something."

"Like what?"

"Let me take the magazine out before you start."

"If you do that it won't flash." He sounded like Jerry trying to reason with that cat. "It's a prop gun, it shoots light-beams."

"Then it won't matter. I want Maranna to see you're unarmed. The crew can think it's a misfire."

"Please," Aurora said.

"What's the matter with you guys?"

"We're psycho. Call it a joke. On Jason. The lady said please."

He shook his head, tired. His mixed-color eyes were eroded to pink. "We'll have to redo the take."

"Judging by today you're going to have to redo the take anyhow. Twenty-six times."

"Tonight I'll promise anything just so's I can go home."

"Thanks."

"Anything for a quiet life." He didn't sound convinced.

Neither was I, but I wasn't going to say so. Aurora was looking like she believed in me. I hate to disillusion people.

Apart from twenty-seven takes, which seems to me perfectionism carried to lunacy, film people get up at hours aren't on the clock. I don't know what Moon-time said when Aurora's domestic arrived with coffee but my metabolism said it was the middle of the night. Mokey didn't notice, he gets up in the middle of every night to commit works of art. He's the only guy I know doesn't suffer from jetlag.

We stumbled in the hopper and headed out to Chaplygin. Dein looked like he was still asleep inside his eyes. He didn't even take time out to insult us. But Aurora was springy in a green flying-suit and a cap labeled SPACE CADETS. Of course she hadn't been working. I find not working's harder.

The lot was still black except for the grid markers but a space battle was in progress over it. A couple of fleets of blackbeetles were shooting each other with blue and red lights and pretending to blow up. I guess it was a practice run because none of them actually did.

Dein disappeared to get redirtied, which was hard on him since he'd just had a shower, and Aurora took us to the canteen to eat. My metabolism sat up and looked around and I nearly forgave everyone. For whatever it was. Short nights get to me but I knew it was someone's fault. I remembered after a bit. Jason's.

The confrontation was being played in the big pressure-studio at the far end. We went out in a kart-train reserved for the stars. In the back. The segmented caterpillar rattled through four or five geodesics done up in alien decors including a swamp-forest and a banquet hall with half a roof. We slammed in and out of sets of double pressure-doors every couple of minutes for a mile or two until I thought we were coming out at Liberty.

Dein in front looked like an actor being a spacer and Maranna was in full ears and whiskers. Her twin slumped in the opposite corner had to be the tough guy Harran. He was almost the same size and fixed in a blond wig could lead to misunderstandings if any of the techs pinched bottoms. Maranna's tall for a bim but he was the fragile-actor type. From the front he was male and embittered, because he was working on the mood, because he hadn't gotten over yesterday or because he was naturally mean. The rest of the train was full of extras and techs with grav-cartons. Cordovan wasn't there, which was lucky because it saved us getting into manslaughter before we'd seen the acting.

The set was two sides of Flash Gordon's room with a carved table covered with the sort of charts they used in sailing ships, red-plush chairs from Designer Cheek and weird lighting arrangements to make unearthly. Dein stood around having his face fixed and Maranna got fitted into the faceplate of her armor, which was steel-blue, glittery and picked out with Cyrillic obscenities by way of alien decor. Then somebody handed each of them a glitzy-looking shooter and they made aiming motions around the scenery. It's how it takes people who know squat about guns.

I got a gap in my self-confidence when I saw the shooters. It looked like if either one shot anything more than Halloween sparks I was a ringtailed tree-rat. Then I asked Dein if I could look at his and found I had a ringed tail. That fucker was a gun. A nice lightweight laser-pistol with an easy balance and a good weighty mag to balance it. The trigger and muzzle were business, the ziggy bits were icing. I squinted down the barrel and found a red targeting-spot. Hoo-boy.

"Mag, okay?"

Dein had his punch back but he didn't quite like to break my arm in public. "Dammit. It's a dumb joke. The thing's a toy."

"Say I've numb brains. I'd like it as a souvenir."

I sprang it and weighed it in my hand. Maybe it shot Christmas glitter. I didn't think so.

Maranna's mask glinted on the other side of the set. It covered her face leaving only the fur ears and a couple of blond locks showing under the helmet. If she'd really been fighting I'd have advised her against, getting shot in the ear ain't as amusing as advertised. But since it was a fairytale I could see dumb ol' Flash might mix her with Bubba.

I couldn't tell if she was looking or not. The eye slits were narrow, slanted and edged with sparkle. They were turned roughly in our direction. I'd been trying to catch her eye all the way and succeeding so badly I figured she didn't want it caught.

I raised the gun, sighted at her, then switched it around and winked at her through the hole where the mag ought to be. The mask shone blankly back. Then she turned deliberately away.

I gave Dein back his shooter and they took positions. People were moving around and someone was yelling directions through a bullhorn. That said the big man had arrived and Moke and me better fade into the scenery. Aurora was there whether Dein wanted her or not and she joined us in the outer darkness and fastened on my arm like a remora. Or maybe a teenage mutant killer squid.

Whatever, she was cutting off my circulation.

"Is it okay?" she whispered in my ear. "It's my imagination, right?"

"Sorry, doll." I'd been checking. If I ever saw a practical mag with full charge, that was one. I wasn't happy. My options seemed to be, in order, trust Maranna and if she shot Dein say awful sorry, my mistake. Let Maranna have a knife in the gut right now before she had the chance to shoot, and if she turned out to have a real toy gun say much the same thing. Or stand still and pray. I didn't like any of them.

Option number four was stand up and let Cordovan have the knife in the gut before anybody did anything, but that wouldn't necessarily stop Dein getting shot and it would guarantee me an appearance in court on a Murder One. I wished like hell I had an effective tool myself, plain or disguised as a Christmas-tree ornament. Unluckily you can't get on a Moon shuttle tooled, especially if you're being Ump. They got this smart little barrier takes it away from you. While simultaneously calling the cops. I'd had to fake my ya as a screwdriver to get a lady's basic defenses.

The guys on the set were getting down to work while I jittered. Dein was being knowledgeable with the sailing-ship charts. Maybe he was planning his summer vacation for when this dumb flick was over. Sets of techs on various-level grav platforms took pictures of him doing it.

Then Jason didn't like the lighting and they all stopped while they fixed some of the spots to show up the hollows in Dein's cheeks more hollowly. After which he got to do it again.

This time it was okay, he picked the Virgin Islands, rolled up the chart looking like a guy got something settled at last and gazed idealistically into the air. That got filmed too, from several different angles and in closeup.

Then he made a thing of admiring a ring the size of a fortune cookie in real fake solid gold with glass inlays and registering pain and anguish. I guess it was his engagement ring or something. It didn't say a lot for the Princess's taste but they did that several times from all the way around likewise.

This had taken an hour and I was vibrating. Also, if Aurora didn't let go soon I was going to get gangrene in my fingers. If there was an answer I still didn't have it.

Maranna was sprawled in a canvas chair with MARANNA written on the back and her mask was turned away like she wasn't going to look at me even if not doing it killed her. I tried willpower and it didn't take. Harran was leaning on a piece of scenery looking more embittered than ever, but I guess he was an actor and they weren't filming him until later, which very few of them actually care for.

Finally Maranna was called. She settled her mask, got up and vanished behind the set and Aurora's nails nearly met through my biceps.

"This it?"

She nodded like she'd lost her spit. I loosened my ya, God knows what for, and waited. Moke looked unhappy which made three of us.

Somebody outside kicked open the practical door at the back of the two-sided room and Maranna stood, as they say, framed in it. She was fur-eared, armored and glittering. Her laser was aimed straight at Dein's head.

Dein snatched the gun from his belt and pointed it. Naturally, nothing came out. I saw her finger tighten. Then several things happened at once.

Harran, who'd been lounging behind us, did one guy-type dive like a top-grade linebacker, caught Dein above the knees from the rear and brought him down for a clear personal foul.

Maranna's gun spat a line of white light dead across set to a dangling light-unit maybe ten feet above anyone's head-level and severed it neatly from its cable. It hit the ground with a noise like a small earthquake.

And a blue-white flash from somewhere to the side caught a quiet-looking tech standing near one of the cameras a few feet away and cut him in two, along with the laser he'd been leveling to finish off anyone who was left.

From which I made some hasty deductions. One, Maranna was straight. Two, Harran was left-handed. And three, Swordfish had arrived.

Cordovan caught on fast. I guess you don't keep your hide intact as long as he had without, even if it's bronze. He rose up like the statue in Don Giovanni and lifted his boss-man's bullhorn.

"Lasers!"

The crew had frozen in place. They ungelled in one flash thaw.

Harran and Maranna dragged Dein to his feet by an arm each and hauled him staggering toward the practical door. Aurora took a huge gulp of breath to have hysterics, had a look at where she was and took another to swallow them. I remembered she was an actress. Moke was leaning urgently on both our shoulders trying to get us on the floor.

A subterranean voice shuddered the air over my head.

"Cass? Boss says will you get these guys on that little bitty train-thing and clear 'em all outta here before somebody gets hurt? And he says will you for godssakes go yourself while you still breathing?"

"Hilt." I was really happy to not see him. "Can you drive the damn thing? I think they might need help getting to their hoppers. I don't know how many of the guards are Cordovan's. Take Rory and I'll collect the guys from the back."

I took off before he'd time to argue and shot out onto the studio floor weaving like a hare. Dein's ziggy gun was under the table where someone had kicked it, less magazine. Which I had in my hand. I ducked to grab and slapped the one into the other on the run. I caught a steel-blue glint and almost landed on top of them.

It looked like half the techs were Cordovan's and the other half were scared out of their panties. They were getting a lot in each other's way. Laser beams fizzled above and below. I wouldn't have said it was healthy. Sword had picked his place. The big studio left more room for imbecility than any of the geodomes, where the first stray shot would get you explosive decompression, but there are still better ways to collect your interment allowance. Diamonds are forever, but atmosphere's for as long as you don't have a hole in the roof.

I grabbed a steel-blue arm with fur ears above and snarled at it.

"Kart-train, there's a guy going to drive it for you. He growls but he's cute. Then grab your hoppers and don't stop till you get to Lunaport. Take Dein, Rory's waiting. Go."

The blond head jerked acknowledgment and leaned over to shout at its twin. Then it took off past me like a hundred-meter hurdler and shot back onto the set. Arclight glinted off its sequined mask and rococo laser.

"Not that way," I yelled. "She lost her fucking mind?"

"He's trying to draw them while we get out," Maranna said over my head. "Dein took a knock on the skull there and he's woozy. Come on kid, get it together, huh?"

His eyes were unfocused and there was a rising lump on one temple. He struggled to wobbly legs and wavered against her shoulder. She put an arm around his waist and hauled. They look fragile and ain't.

Hilt had Aurora in the kart-train plus a couple of scared-looking script girls and two or three camera crew with their heads well down. Moke had vanished.

Harran zigged across the set like Douglas Fairbanks taking on the Three Musketeers, vaulted the table like the big sword fight and made for the open. His blond hair flew and the helmet glittered.

A red shaft from the gallery splashed dead in the middle of his breastplate. My own ribs tightened. He faltered a single second, picked it up and kept running. I remembered only some of the lasers were practical. A lot were FX. The trick was knowing which. A tech stepped in front of his latest zag holding something chest-high looked exactly like a laser and all hell practical.

"Stay right there, bitch."

Maybe Harran didn't care for the name. Maybe he'd seen Maranna's lamp-trick. He hoisted her prickly pistol and let the tech have it like the OK Corral. It was wild but it did the job. The tech screamed and hit the floor. Harran hurdled him and zagged again towards the train.

The next red shaft got a makeup trolley right ahead and cut it in half. Harran jinked around and Hilt's invisible hand grabbed his collar and hoisted him bodily into the kart.

"Fucking hero," the tunnel voice rumbled.

"I've always wanted to do that," Harran said in apology.

The little train left like a rocket in a shower of sparks. The pressure-iris opened and thunked shut behind. They were gone.

The rest of the fight had spread all over. Cordovan's guys had the lasers, real and make-believe. Since you couldn't tell them apart the only thing to do was try to avoid them all. Sword's Pack had invisibility, organization, and experience.

Somebody with a lightweight rollup reflector-shield was dug in behind discarded scenery systematically taking out the gallery crews with a sonic bazooka. It was hard on the ears and a bit severe on techs manning fakes. Only as

I said you couldn't tell which. Someone else, or maybe more than one, was playing hoopla with the grav-platforms and winning kewpie dolls with a series of well-placed gas capsules. The air high up was getting kind of green and most of the platforms had quit firing and were drifting peacefully, bobbling on the air currents.

I dodged light-stands and cameras back of the set. Harran's run had scared me. The fake room was solider than I'd expected but cables and piles of half-finished carpentry behind were real easy to trip on. The lights were strobing madly.

I ran into a skinny tech coming the other way and clutching what looked like a flare pistol. I raised my practical raygun. The tech gave a squeaky female yelp and dropped its artillery. I grabbed it by the belt buckle.

"You playing fights?"

"I want to go home," it wailed.

"There an emergency door?"

"Two. Jason just went through the far one, he wouldn't take me with him. There's another this side."

"Then go through it, kid. And leave this sucker behind, the guys don't shoot unarmed shes. In general."

She scuttled off, sobbing a bit and trying to hide among scenery. An invisible hand caught her by the scruff and ran her squeaking to the lock door. I hoped there was an adequate supply of spacesuits in there with directions for use.

Moke materialized from semidarkness and took my arm.

"Cass, Sword says get behind the shield, they're almost through. He's looking for the boss-man."

"Rear exit. Tell him. Bet the fucker's got transport like little friend Halo. Me for me and all for one. I'm going after him."

"Cassie, I need you," he shouted in my slipstream.

"I need you too," I yelled back. "Be careful."

Moke's intellectual in a real physical trade. When he saw me disappearing one way he disappeared the other.

The rear door didn't open onto a lock but onto a smaller studio cut off by pressure doors. They spiraled when I leaned on them, so it had atmosphere. The outer lock must be on the other side.

The place was in darkness. When the second iris whooshed behind me and took the last drop of light with it I might have been swimming in an ink-bottle, Japanese black. I felt around the wall for switches and found nothing but slick plastic sealer.

There was wood under my boots, echoey hollow boards over something. I stood still to kill echo and felt with my toe. It was a narrow footway with a light metal rail separating it. From God knows what. The other side dropped but there was no way of telling whether it went down inches or feet without sliding into it.

I didn't like the idea. I'd seen Jason come in and I didn't think he'd had time to get out. One thing I was sure of, he wasn't going to stand around like Little Jack Horner waiting for me to catch him. More likely he was three inches away in the dark with a gun in his hand about to go bang.

The monster came at me out of the middle while I was still stretching whiskers.

It was green, semiliquid and luminescent. It looked like a heap of animated seaweed built up around the outlines of a rotting corpse, it was ten feet high and it stank like the Okefenokee Swamp on a bad day. Assuming it has good ones. It leered at me out of the dark with a pair of rolling eyes that weren't exactly in line and reached out with arms as long as twin rope-walks. A couple of its fingers dropped off and it sniggered.

It had to be some kind of symbiote. I thought of Porous back at the bar and it gave me right-to-the-backbone shivers. Dammit, Porous had been repulsive at ten feet, and this thing was walking up on me googling with its drapy arms going drip and waggle, stinking bad enough to make a mule puke, so near you could reach out and touch it. Or contrarywise. If I didn't do something it was going to reach out and touch me and I didn't think I could stand it.

Hell, what did for Chicken would do for me. I slid out my ya and slashed at its yellow-nailed fingers. They were maybe eight inches from my eyes. I saw the blade flash in green luminescence and the thing vanished abruptly into dark.

I waited poised, holding the ya point up. I didn't know where it had come from or if it was still out there. I had the other hand spread in front of my face in case those long yellow fingernails were still groping somewhere in the blackness.

Nothing. Then I heard its wet bubbling snigger from farther away and the sound of sucking mud. A smell of marsh gas drifted back. Now that was weird. Marsh gas?

I'd figured the answer before the dragon came zooming down from the upper reaches screaming like a kamikaze and billowing flames and smoke, its breadknife talons aimed at my face. With sulfur stench that was almost visible.

The flames were even useful. I saw the shadowy roof above, metal tie-beams across the pressure shell supported by diagonal cross-struts and a loop of cable only a couple of feet above my head hanging from a pivoted arc lamp. I jumped for it before the dragon got to my level and made all the use of the light I could while I had flames to see by.

I shoved the ya back into my sleeve, got a hand to the loop, and felt it hold. I got a leg around and started monkeying. The dragon was going too fast to brake. It screamed through the space where I'd been and carried right on through the wall.

Back to Japanese blackness. But I knew where I was, and where Jason was too. There was a high catwalk the length of the side wall and he was standing near the far end with a little flat box in his hand. The control. For the smells and holos.

Because we were in the holo studio where they manufactured space beasts and other delights for the use of the goonoes. I guess Flash-Dein had been getting the benefit of the Swamp Thing and maybe the dragon. And whatever else our Argonaut had on his mini-control board.

I got an arm over the beam followed by a knee and hoisted myself over the rough blunt edge. Advantage me. Jason had blinded himself with his own dragon and now he'd lost me. I squinched flat on my belly the length of the girder and started a slow quiet crawl across the roof toward the other end and the airlock. I still had the tricked gun and if I could get there before him I'd cut him off.

The floor was a dark grid, probably metal, six or eight feet below the level of the walkway and I supposed it had something to do with setting up the holos. Only reason I was taking the high road was I thought he was less likely to see me there. I found the other reason it was a good decision by accident.

Jason was standing still, whiskering around in the ink. I could hear his breathing, hard and held-in. Then the cautious scrape of a foot. He was moving. I speeded up my crawl and came on something light and hard that skittered. A loose bolt somebody'd left up there mounting it. I thought a couple of swear words. The noise would locate me.

The bolt hit the metal below with a light thunk and a sheet of blue flame rose six feet in a storm of sparks.

That sucker was electrified. I froze and the flash from
Jason's disruptor cut across the studio and pulverized the
walkway.

He took a couple of running steps then I guess he
worked out I wasn't where he'd thought and slowed
down. He didn't want to meet me in the dark any more
than I wanted to meet him.

A gleam of yellow light fell across the floor as the inner
pressure-iris opened, and a blurred shadow moved swiftly
across before it could shrink shut. I heard a clink from
the catwalk.

The air burst into a whirl of colored fire. Columns of
sparks walked across the grid, swirling as they went in
smoky spirals, and a series of whistling catherine wheels
screamed from one side to the other in midair with a
sound like twenty chainsaws. A whole fleet of blue
tadpole shapes moved slowly in the other direction,
undulating.

The light dazzled off the shiny plastic that coated
the walls and filled the studio with glare. I knew what
Cordovan was doing. He was hoping to blind Swordfish
with his firework display long enough to throw him off
balance while he ran for the lock.

A magnesium fountain grew out of the floor, rose up
and up and turned into a waterspout. Golden light cascaded down to meet it and they coalesced in a tornado
of flame. Up on my beam my eyes were in shadow. I
lay still above the flaring light-shapes and tried for
bearings. Cordovan was nearly at the far end of the catwalk, his little demon-box held out like a weapon. He
had a gun too but he couldn't quite see where to use
it. But if he could get into the lock and start it cycling neither of us would be able to open it until it was
through.

And if he wanted to be really smart he could try putting
a disruptor bolt through the roof before he quite closed

the door. The thought made my hair prickle. I hoped Swordfish was moving the faster.

In the light of a flowering sunburst Sword's shadow flickered up over wall and roof. He was about halfway along the catwalk, moving so easily with his fast smooth grace it hardly swung under his weight. And I saw something else. My inside suddenly screwed into vacuum and turned inside out.

"Sword! Under you!"

For a second his outline hesitated, flung like a blown candle by the crazy lights. Then the shadow was gone as if it had never been and there was only the gap in the boards Jason had made and the catwalk swaying like a broken bridge. The river on Virginity.

A mushroom of fire from the electrified grid lit up the whole studio like a nova, followed by the blue-white flare of an exploding magazine. For a moment I couldn't see anything at all. Then through bitter water and whorls of rainbow light I saw Cordovan reach the platform at the end and jump up onto it.

There was a big gimbaled spot mounted in the center pointing to the middle of the studio and he dropped the control box to turn and swing it. The wheels and tadpoles died. The beam of the spotlight sliced the darkness and played in white circles over the plastic.

He'd figured by now I had to be high up. The white circle fingered lazily among the roof beams.

"Come out, Cassandra," he called gaily. "I know you're there. Your friend wasn't as clever as he thought. I've got you."

The light felt across the roof and came to rest on my face. I grinned into it with bared teeth.

"Why, Jason. So you have."

I lifted the little fancy gun in the same movement and fired straight into the center of the spot.

"You fucker, you killed my guy."

The lamp shattered and went out. The rest happened almost too fast to follow. The studio was still lit by the licking blue glare of Sword's fall and everything showed in uncertain undulating shadow. I saw the big light, destabilized by the impact, swing around on its gimbals. It was heavy and the platform was small. It caught Cordovan just under the ribs and flung him off into space.

His foot hooked a trailing cable as he went over and a loop of it twitched around his ankle. It ran out three or four feet, jerked and held. He swung there, head-down over the grid, and screamed.

I think he screamed to me. I think maybe he even screamed to Swordfish. There wasn't a damn thing I could have done. I was halfway across the room and fifteen feet above. I could see what was going to happen even before it did.

The cable was only snagged, there was plenty more up back. Cordovan's own struggles were pulling it free. He screamed some more, tried frantically to double himself up to get a grip on the loop above him and the snag gave way.

The cable jerked again, swung and pulled smoothly loose. I watched it run out to the blue flare from below and the sudden stench of burned flesh that went with the final shriek. Then I covered my face.

"That was my kill, Cass," a warm velvet voice murmured in my ear. "You made me disappoint the guy."

His hand on the back of my pants was all that kept me on the beam.

"Sword?"

"Was coming out after you to borrow your gun. Lost mine when I fell through the boards there. Thanks, bim, I almost didn't see that. Got a hand up just in time. Let's go, this is a nasty place."

He could say that again. I caught his cold hard grip and we went.

• • •

In the main lot occasional flashes still cut through thickening smoke. The gas capsules, tailored to produce fumes that rose, had finished off the lot on the gallery and the blue-green smog was probably going to leave them all with bad cases of bronchitis. The ones who didn't already have terminal sonic bazooka. Most of the firing was at ground level.

"Please, Cassandra, will you just once remember you're a cat burglar, not the goddess Athene in full armor, and get behind a reflector?" Sword growled, leading the way through the clouds.

"You're kidding," I said, coughing. "That's you. Sprung full-grown from somebody's head."

"Wrong. I got born. But I owe you, kid."

"I couldn't bear to see you fall in the river."

"I never seem to have time to hear that story. Got to go."

He dropped me in the smoke and evaporated. I stumbled over the edge of a reflector-shield and landed on a pair of warm bodies that giggled. Or one did. Soprano.

Moke and Dribble in each other's arms like Beauty and the Beast. Moke was on his back aiming at arclights with some gadget with an odd flat barrel. The lights were going out all over the set.

"Hey guy, take care. It's vacuum out there. You go through, we go with it."

" 'S okay, it only works on lights. Guy dropped it on his way past when Wings or someone caught up. It's a kind of control-thing. He was putting lights on and I'm putting them off. Ought to shorten things. The Pack can see in the dark, the techs can't." He grabbed my hand and squeezed. "Run off again and I whack you. Even if it ends by debauching the kid."

"Nice cute Moke."

"We come through space battle," Dribble trilled. "That one dumb space battle, all light and no whump. Real dumb ships with spiky bits. Hall put spiky bits on us too and fix we lights, we make dumb flashes too, nobody notice. Razor going to be mad about spikes, nice lighter make everybody laugh. Sword send me find you, I find. Me get kiss you now?"

"Not until I got a bathtub handy, Fido. I like to wash under the shower, habit I got. But I'll kiss you, I'm twisted."

I grabbed an ear, found a bit of forehead and gave him a wet smack. Hell, I really felt like kissing somebody.

"Knew you like me," he squeaked smugly. "Why you crying?"

"Shut up."

"Cass?" Mokey said, finishing off the last light and dropping his gadget. "I got an idea."

We were huddled in a corner behind our reflector like the three kings of Orient waiting for star-rise while soft padding steps moved past in the dark. Mopping up, maybe. If there was anything left to mop.

"Yeah?"

"A cube. House-size. Gray-metallic with red burn-marks in streaks, maybe some rust. And holes all over like Swiss cheese, big ones and little ones, with ringwall effects. Then you look through them and it's going to be matte black in there with a light display. Crossing beams in different colors with diffraction rings where they hit the wall, all rainbows. I think it'll be nice."

"Attaboy."

Dribble giggled like a whole raft of piccolos and slobbered in my ear. I'd have whopped him but I couldn't see the little bastard.

We sat in a heap and waited for daybreak. The artificial kind. You don't get anything else in the middle of Lunar night. It was a while coming.

I wondered what Hallway saw in the place.

With a bit of ill will these cases been known to take years. Hans-Bjorn asked Yell and Issa to dinner until he got the whole story, and ours came up within the month. It's an advantage of Ari friends. I think he was pissed when he heard what had been happening to Moke, he likes the boy. Apart from his money value. Razor spent the waiting-time munching his old law-books, or maybe he just sat on them the old-fashioned way. The opposition wasn't too violent. Coelacanth had other things on its mind and somebody in high management decided to throw Jason's memory to the wolves and concentrate on Operation Skin-save.

Sword caught us at home where Moke was working, sat on the edge of Hallway's bench with an attack of neutrality so extreme even his voice was transparent and zoomed in for the barbecue.

"Well, Moke?"

"Well, what?"

"You wanted to tell Dein the truth. Now's your chance, his career's hanging. Maybe he ought to know what he really is. It's in your hands."

Not one of his gentler days. Moke sat with bent head, a sheaf of sweaty hair hanging over his face. He looked at his fingers. His knuckles were tight.

"No," he said at last. "Cass was right. Dosh is dead.

284

This is Dein, a guy I don't know, and he has a nice lady I do know, and there's no point spoiling things. For Dosh's sake. His life got spoiled enough."

Sword said nothing. He rarely points out he's won.

Dein and Aurora finished their films and went back to Divine and we had dinner with them. Dein was gracious. The occasion was to celebrate the opening of the Edo rock, product of the authentic Moke sweat and tears, which the artist had just given him free. I wasn't at all sure he knew enough about art to be properly grateful. The horizon hadn't improved and I looked at the sky a lot and tried not to get vertigo.

Aurora kissed me as I was leaving. "Thank you," she said.

Nobody kissed Moke. Dein did follow him down to the pad as we were leaving and offered an awkward handshake. I think to show he was sorry for thinking we were cheapskates. When he had Moke's hand in his he paused and held it for a moment, looking into his face with a little puzzled line between his brows as if he felt maybe he ought to know him from somewhere and couldn't quite figure out where. Then he let go and waved goodbye with a good-riddance air. It wasn't his fault really, I guess. The stem-brain isn't a good communicator.

I tried to make up for it by licking Mokey's ear in the yacht but it took him a long time to lift his head and when he did he had pink eyes.

"It would've been wrong to tell him," he said at last. "Dosh was in love with me. He's dead. It's not a bad afterlife, maybe."

He always loved the better of the two.

The big case was in the Hall of Justice in Hampton-of-Argos and drew a record audience, the holonews hit top ratings three nights in a row. Moke and me told the story of Dosh and Nimbus. We were careful not to look at Dein, who was in court but strictly as a spectator. Even

Razor couldn't prove Coelacanth had tried to kill him, the confusion after the fight was so total nobody could identify Maranna's laser anymore or find a live witness that the charged magazine wasn't an accident. Looked to me he'd decided none of it happened. Maybe it would let him sleep better. I thought it might not do that for Aurora, but she was looking out from now on. Sword and Hall stayed invisible, which is business as usual for them.

We had to make a deal for immunity before Halo would sing but we cut it and she appeared as billed. In a serene black suit with discreet fur around the collar and her toffee hair braided into an innocent aureole would have debauched a whole regiment of choirboys. She gave neat clear evidence in a neat clear voice and when she'd finished the wainscot was full of the scurry of sinking rats taking to the lifeboats.

She made most of it Cordovan's fault since he wasn't there to argue, but the list of arson, rape and bloody murder would have filled any number of red revolutions. Seemed her stepdaughter hadn't been a nice lady too. Big surprise. Nobody said a word about her own career and the Merton sisters had sunk without trace but we felt we'd done what we could for Caronne. Nobody remembers minor film stars thirty years on in any case. They're lucky if they last thirty minutes. The film industry was condemned in five flats and several fat cats became thinner and were locked up. The Earth government got the message and sent in the rodent operators.

A lot of bit players in our personal drama had their own personal dramas sorted. Moke and I got our charges canceled again. Marchand rose clean and new out of the ashes of Coelacanth and picked up various people's contracts. Dein's space-pic had had such rip-roaring publicity it was sold out on all networks before they'd even finished filming. Haver came out of hospital limping slightly and raring to throw himself out of more windows and

Antonia Ottery Lopez and the other survivors of her group shuffled home from the plague block and went back to slaughtering Stan Getz. Lorn came around once to see me in the most indecent pants yet and drank toasts out of each of my best boots in turn. I had to buy a new pair. A number of people on and around the Strip got the chance to go on making their own way down the black-brick road toward whatever paradise they imagined was at the other end instead of ending in an organ tank, though none of them knew it so they weren't grateful.

It's how things are.

I met Halo in the corridor after the final spiel and she smiled coolly.

"Satisfied?"

"Thank you." I was a little surprised she recognized me, but I guess I was the guy pulled her stepdaughter's hair. I wasn't sure if that put us on the same side or different in her book. I hadn't known we were speaking.

"Then you can give me my icon back."

I'm usually fairly honest. This time I looked her in the eye.

"What icon?"

She laughed. "I misjudged him then, he kept it for himself. I knew he liked it." She ran an amused eye over me. "You should tell him. Breaking my pictures hurt him a lot more than it did me. There are plenty more where those came from."

"That's because you value the prestige and the money. He valued the pictures. I'll tell him, though. Next time he'll know to save them and give them to Moke."

"There won't be a next time. We have an agreement."

"Then he'll keep it. If you do."

She smiled again, vanilla ice cream gilded with toffee. "I understand my best interests."

"I think he's betting on that."

We moved apart. A few steps on she turned back.

"He's good," she said. "In bed. Damned good."

"I'm glad. I'd hate him to give up so much for nothing."

The smile widened. "I'm glad you're glad. I could like you, Cassandra. You're nearly as vicious as I am."

"Not quite," I said. "I get sorry for people sometimes. I'm not sure you do. I'm sorry for you as well. You sounded as if you once rather liked Nimbus's father. Maybe you used to be human."

Her smile went out for one second and came back up like a kick in a generator.

"He was the biggest shit I ever met. But it's a kind thought. Good-bye, Cassandra. Shame about the icon, I'd say he's your type."

And this time she was gone, gold and straight and lacquered as an Egyptian goddess.

"Thanks for nothing," I muttered. But strictly to me.

Swordfish had been around just once since the Pack evaporated out of the ruins of the film studio and faded off the Moon like ice off a crater. It was the longest I'd ever been in the same bit of space without meeting him somewhere and I'd begun to worry. Mokey'd been up to the ears, or wherever he keeps his operating instructions, polishing Dein's rock, working on the doughnut for Maranna and making sketches for his Lunar cube. His slate was practically red-hot.

He'd been subdued since the grand giving of evidence and I figured he was tired. Though Moke's been tired all my life and it's never made much difference. I kept licking his ear but it didn't seem to console him anymore. I began to think I was a failure.

About a week after the verdict we were lounging around the workshop of our loft, or I was, both drinking beer and contemplating a materials hitch on the doughnut baby.

The couple were no problem, apart from the normal ones inherent in rendering four dimensions in insulator glass, but the baby had to be done separate and grafted on and Moke had been trying out different solutions on spare bits of material all night. It was a nice baby, very like a tadpole with a rude face and the question was how to graft it without melting its salient parts with the heat torch.

"No use," he said finally. He sat on a carton and looked depressed. "I've tried it five times over and it doesn't get any better. I think I'm just going to have to take the risk and go ahead. Maybe I can re-form the melted bits later."

"Put it down, Moke. I love it, I don't want its rude little thingy cooked. Come to bed and let's have a day out tomorrow. You're getting too tired to think."

He gave me a pale smile. "You go up, Cass. I want to meditate a bit longer. Don't worry, I won't cook its thingy while you aren't looking. I'll come before long."

"If you say so. Don't take all night, guy. That muse of yours rides you too hard. You need to housetrain the bitch before she finishes you."

"That's what makes her a muse, Cassie. If you break her she stops performing. Go on. And don't use all the hot water."

"Slander. When did I ever?"

He gave me an abstracted wave. I climbed the new inside stair we'd got built by our landlord's brother-in-law—having relatives who can do everything in the world between them's a Gooder specialty—and headed for the icebox and the shower in that order. I was expecting Moke up before I'd finished, but I got to swallow prote sandwich with kelp dressing, wash and crash in perfect tranquillity. I didn't mind too much. I was tired too. I had a vague idea he got in beside me sometime in the smaller hours, but if he did I was too asleep to ask if he'd made it.

When I woke up with routine morning sun coming
through the batten blinds in yellow stripes and the landlord's parakeets quarreling like half a jungle under the
window, he was gone again. That's often a good sign. It
tends to mean the answer came with the dawn and the boy
rushed off to do it before it faded. The kitchen was tidy,
but Moke's a tidy person. I made coffee sleepily, shoved
a couple of slices of real bread into the toaster and yelled
down the stairs.

"Moke? You want some coffee?"

No answer. When I leaned over the stairwell there was
no noise either.

"Mokey?"

Echo said the doors were closed. He usually works with
them open, it lets the fumes out. And a bit more light in. I
went down barefoot, scratching my ass vaguely under his
shirt, which was the first thing I'd picked up when I fell
out of bed. The doughnut gleamed like water in a shaft
of light from one of the high windows and its sharper
angles sparkled. I wandered over and looked again. I
can't stop looking at Moke's things sometimes, if I had
enough money I think I might buy them all. Except he
likes to see them in public places where people can rub
them. The baby was in the middle, perfectly joined, the
graft invisible. The whole construction shone joyfully. It
was beautiful.

And that explained that. He'd solved his problems,
worked himself flat and gone out to stretch somewhere.
I was a bit put out he hadn't wakened me to look at it.
He usually does. But I guess I was crashed. Maranna was
going to be happy, anyhow. I creaked back upstairs to my
cooling toast.

I dumped the dishes in the washer, took a celebratory
shower and picked some nice-to-Mokey clothes. This was
going to be a wander-around-parks day with a lot of beer
in it. It's how we usually celebrate. Tomorrow's always

another Lunar cube. Then I parked my butt in one of the new improved wicker chairs we'd imported and waited for the return of the hero.

Quite a while. I noticed after I'd picked up the mail and drafted some answers and looked at the news on the mini-vid we keep in a corner not to look aboriginal to see if Dein or Aurora were giving any more interviews, that it was after half-past ten, I was sitting around in blue silk pants with sequins and there was nobody to go out with. I got up and walked around the room a little. Then I wandered back down to the workshop to have another look at the doughnut, just in case Moke had sneaked in while I wasn't looking. Though he hadn't, I'd have heard him. Then I walked around some more.

Finally I went out front past the parakeets and hollyhocks and broke in on the landlord's coffee break. He's called Gordon and is nicer than he looks.

"Good morning," he said, looking a bit startled. We usually only bother him for bread and beer and it wasn't one of our times.

"Hi. Has Moke been through this morning, either way?"

"Why, yes. He went out around seven, just as I was opening up. I'm quite surprised to see you, I thought you must have gone in advance."

"I was asleep. I been waiting for him to come home."

"Oh." His sad beagle face was blank. "I thought perhaps he was on his way to the spaceport. He had his kit bag, you know. I must be mistaken."

"What did he say?"

"Only good morning, as he always does. And then Mr. Allen went out after him about an hour later. I really believed your house was deserted."

"Well, I guess it is. Nobody here but this chicken. Thanks. See you around."

I went back in, truly puzzled. Mokey takes rambles

around the streets now the local vigos know him, and he goes looking for inspiration in the city parks. Sometimes he just feeds the pigeons. I've never known him do it carrying a kit bag. I supposed vaguely it was something to do with Moon-cubes. For some reason I had a bad feeling around the middle of my middle. Anyhow I hadn't straightened the bedpad, which is the job of the last guy out of it, so I figured I might as well fill in time. Especially since Yell had vanished too. I'd thought the place was quiet. I climbed back up to the loft, put on a pair of jeans since the blue sequined pants seemed premature and went to tug at the quilt.

The folded paper fell out. Moke must have propped it on his pillow for me and I'd heaved the quilt over it getting up. My gullet gave a hitch. Moke's never had a single thing to say to me he couldn't just shout in my ear. It took me a moment to get the courage to open it.

I was still standing looking dumb when crashing steps thundered up the outside stairs accompanied by hilarious male and female whoops. The door banged open and Yell fell through in a tangle of long silver hair, kicking she-legs in skin-tight leathers and an undulation of tattoos. Issa was back in town, and it looked like he was carrying her over the threshold. I had some idiotic idea I ought to congratulate them or something when it came to me it was our threshold and neither Yell nor Issa's the marrying kind.

They got a look at my face and sobered abruptly. Issa came to ground-level and Yell looked concerned.

"Cass?"

I held the letter dumbly out toward him.

Cassie,

I'm sorry, this is supposed to be a girl thing. It doesn't get better when it's me. I think it was seeing Dosh walking around dead but I can't go on. Our fami-

ly's through. I think it's been that way a long time and
I didn't want to know. I've slept with Sword's ghost for
two years knowing you'd have to go back, he's always
been the other half. I know. I fell in love just once too,
only I was older than you. I hadn't realized what kids
you both were when it began. He's your real family and
maybe he needs you even more than I do. I respect that.
I guess I got my old muse. She doesn't lick as nicely
as you but we'll make out. I'm not your twin brother,
Cass, it's the one thing I can't do for you. This I can.
Be happy and wish Sword luck for me. And ask me to
the christening.

Watch yourself.
Moke

Yell looked at it blankly.

"What's it mean, Cass?"

I shook my head. It felt like wood. "You can see what
it means, Yell. Mokey's left me."

"But he loves you."

"I know. I guess that's why."

Guys are dumb and bims are dumber. I couldn't stand
Yell's shocked face and seeing Issa wonder whether she
ought to hug me or offer me alcohol. I ran down the
stairs and out into the street without even stopping for
a handbag.

I'd walked five blocks before I even noticed I hadn't
any shoes on.

21

Hallway was in his cellar in his usual posture but he clipped the arteries when he saw me, unsocketed his wrist-jacks, dumped his helmet and let the poor little mechanism alone.

"Cassie. Long time no see."

I'd bought some boots and spent long enough walking around to get a bit of cool back. I was working at keeping it.

"Whose fault's that? Have a good time back home, Hall? Never did get to see you."

He gave me a small rueful grin. "It was . . . nostalgic. So long since I've been there I was finding the gravity too low. That says it all. But maybe I'll go again. I find I've missed it."

"Don't know why you haven't been before."

"Disgraced myself. I've been trying to pay. It's a custom."

"I don't believe it."

He sat on the edge of the bench, pushing his little patient out of the way.

"Has Sword ever told you about himself?"

"That bastard never tells me anything."

"How he got here?"

"I met him with Razor."

"Right. He was a freelance gun on Razor's territory

when he was nineteen. And good. Razor doesn't tolerate competition. He pulled him in and gave him a choice. Join the Pack or the lost-in-action file. He joined. But Razor had some kind of gap to fill. Shaped like a son, maybe."

"Sword is his son."

"He became so. Razor saved his life, I think. He'd have killed himself if the old man hadn't kept hold. But Razor'd had a son who left. When his dad stopped being respectable. He must be quite old now. Became a schoolmaster."

"Holy hell."

Hallway smiled. Pale. Maybe it was catching. "No, just an ordinary Gooder. Razor turned one way, his boy turned another. Generations. I've known Sword a lot longer. Since we were both kids. I killed him."

"You may not have noticed, Hall, but the guy ain't dead."

"The boy I knew is, Cassandra."

"I wish I knew what people were talking about today. I knew I was old but I'm getting senile. Nothing I hear makes sense anymore."

"The Third Alien War began when he was thirteen and I was fourteen. We met at the Naval Academy. He was training as a pilot and I was on technical maintenance. I chose it, his father sent him. I don't think he objected. We were kids."

"Chose? You're a pacifist."

"I am now."

"I suppose Sword's a pacifist too?"

He sighed. "He's what things have made him. He tries to keep order."

"It's a way of putting it. Didn't know you knew each other so long."

"We did. I was his tech. I think they paired us because we were ridiculous. Teeny and Meany, the Tin Twins.

The only two guys in the world higher than windmills."

"Hilarious. What a thing it is to have a sense of humor."

"You didn't see us," he said, grinning a little. "Maybe you'd have laughed too. I doubt if the aliens found it funny. Sword had the highest kill record in the Corps."

"He got bad habits young. He still has it. Must be running out of places to notch."

Hallway's kind wide mouth hardened. "It wasn't a joke, Cassie. The Navy was using children back then. Faster reflexes, no conscience, no understanding of death. Killing geeks. Like a fucking vid. Bang. When our friends disappeared I'm not sure we understood they'd gone. It was like being out in a game. Dead, lost your third life, come back and play tomorrow. We didn't understand people."

"Yeah. Tough, I see that."

"Toughish. Everyone we knew. Sword flew his first combat mission the day after his fifteenth birthday and two years later he led the group took out Top Gun. Our name. Their major battle-cruiser. Thirty hunter-killers to engage while they got the heavy armor into place. All flown by children. Sword was the eldest. Five came back. The crew of the cruiser must have been thousands. They wanted specimens so our techs kept fishing alien corpses out of space. But they were spoiled. Explosive decompression."

"Big men."

"Real big."

"I meant the Navy, Hall."

"I know." He looked hard at the wall. I couldn't see anything but white paint. "The average life of a hunter-killer in the battle-zone was three weeks. Sword lasted three years. He was eighteen when they finally got him. He'd a chestful of medals. Back then he was proud of them."

"Back then."

"Look at him, Cassandra. They came expensive. They often do."

"That was the aliens?"

"No. It was me. The tech set up the plane. The pilot had implants to mesh with his computer. In flight-mode he and his ship were one organism, neurally linked. They couldn't tell each other apart. Sword was on a minor mission, the kind he'd done hundreds of times. Maybe that's what went wrong. He got the backflash from a laser hit someone else. He was hurt but not seriously, he'd started back. Then the systems blew. Took out the inboard computer and him with it. They were one. His whole motor nervous system. He ought to have died. Physically, pretty much, he did. But he had a mechanical heart. That's another naval joke. They take the hearts out of fourteen-year-old children and put mechanicals in their place. It was supposed to be needed to stand the stresses of battle flight. The kids thought it was an honor. Boy kids, girl kids. They competed for it. His kept him alive long enough for a lift-ship to pick him up."

"And you got the blame."

"It was my fault. Failure of hygiene. I let something, a dust speck, a bacterium, get into the circuits. I take more care now." He glanced around the spotless lab. "Escaped horses. Sword insists it was the setup was oversophisticated. It's true more kids died from systems failure than alien fire."

"Our noble rulers. Remind me to send them a Christmas card."

"Not just them, his family. The last conscious thing he did was try to exonerate me. I could have stayed on, but I didn't want to. Seen too much. Sword was the end. And the end was bad. You don't know how bad. You didn't know him before."

"Too bad for his folks? After all, they knew him."

"It must have been a shock. Their son the hero. They

came to take him home and there was nothing human to recognize. Or to recognize them. He was mutilated, he had as much control as a retarded baby. Deaf, dumb and blind. A driveling imbecile outside. But I knew the implants and I knew his intellect had to be intact, it was just his body he couldn't control. He was going insane. He'd been beautiful. Girls went crazy over him. The family couldn't stand it. His father put him in an asylum for incurables and left him there. And made his sister the heir."

"Platinum-plated dog turds."

"It was hard, Cass," he said patiently. "I had trouble handling it and he was my best friend. And they hadn't seen the things I'd seen."

"Couldn't they have got him doctors or something?"

"Could, didn't. He calls it puritanism. It had to be black medicine with all the gear in his head and his family's too holy to touch it. Easier to forget him. He could be oversimplifying. The mutilation he learned to handle, I think it was the desertion was too much. Maybe they just didn't know how. I don't know."

"He really has a sister?"

"He has a whole family. He's stayed in touch with the women. Not to meet with, you understand, just call with a blank screen. I think he may have seen his sister in Face a couple of times, she doesn't know how badly carved up he is. He still blames his old man."

"And you took over."

"It was a debt. And I loved him. My little brother, we grew up together. That's why I'm here. Black surgery comes high and the only way I could pay was sell what I knew. I'd spent five years in the Navy, I was fully trained, I had contacts. The Strip wanted to know me. When Sword got back on the team they wondered what had hit them. I guess the aliens already knew."

"If he was the same at seventeen, I just bet they did."

He smiled a little more. "He was a wild kid at seventeen. Now . . . he's Sword. And we're still a team. The Tin Twins. I bought him basic movement and eyesight. It was all I could afford. He paid for the rest himself. At what he knew how. It made him Swordfish."

"Maybe he should have bought more."

"It was his choice. His family found him monstrous. He chose to stay that way."

"He has a hole in the head," I said violently.

"Perhaps. Do you blame him?"

"Yes. Where is he, Hall?"

Hallway looked at me. "He's been in the hospital all month."

"And nobody told me? He got hurt in that fight?"

"No. Since we came back. Razor sent for him."

"And put him in the hospital? I don't believe it. Not a word. Where can I find him, Hall?"

He scratched among his hair. "He wanted to be left alone."

"When did I do what he wanted?"

He hesitated. All the guys I met had something wrong today. No, amend that. Yell and Issa were okay. Hell, amend it back. The last glance I got at Yell he looked like a used lightning conductor.

"Hall, Mokey's gone away. He's left me."

He raised startled eyes.

"He thinks Sword and me are married or something. I don't know what week it is. I got to talk to the guy. Please?"

"Are you married or something?"

"How do I know? I been walking around for hours thinking about it. That's why I need to talk to him."

He sighed and reached for the city directory.

"Cassandra, be kind. He's my brother."

"And mine."

"No," Hallway said. "That's exactly what he's not."

• • •

The space under the walkway was the garden of frozen time. Once, before things changed and we got new lamps for old and the entire world lost its job, it maybe was smart. Broken towers reached up under the belts with browned-out daylight reflected in their windows. Wildlife rioted over them. Straggling trees trailed in entries and stooped over what was left of boutiques and the façades of phantom bars. The flowers that had lived in boxes in the plazas had escaped and gone back to type, throwing the slabs up in heaps. Vines climbed the glass walls. The holes behind had got rounded off and grown into caves where small things clicked and skittered. The flares of the walkway threw rippling lines of light and shadow. There was nothing human left, not even the wild dog packs that go with deserted buildings. These were too old to have anything left worth scavenging.

I don't know what the pink crystal arrow had been called originally but now it had the letters ANH TA LTO over the doors like a Chinese invocation. A wild rose as big as half a forest clumped over the front and white cabbagey flowers hung where the windows had been. The steps were carpeted with fallen petals. Nobody had trodden on them.

The doors were jammed. A turnstile arrangement hung back with a creak when I leaned on it, then swung suddenly and let me nearly fall on my face inside. The place was full of pigeons that rushed up in circles and flew around and around above my head.

In a lobby as big as a cathedral a desk shedding marble facing was falling apart in front of a honeycomb of worm-eaten pigeonholes. There was a single yellow envelope propped in one, wrinkled with damp. I wondered who it had been for and if it had mattered to them they didn't get it. The real pigeons had homes in the ceiling fixtures and they'd been there a long time. The place was frosted with droppings. A curved staircase rose at the back with its rail hanging and the curve had a swaybacked slump like if you climbed it you might walk around a corner and find yourself in outer space. Without a helmet. A row of rectangular holes could have been elevators. Anyone took one would end in the oubliettes.

I found the ballroom beyond the desk, hysterical pigeons dive-bombing all the way. Clouds of dust puffed up into the patches of light from the walkway. The doors were opaqued with ice-ferns of dirt and marked with black hieroglyphs where their gilt had worn off. They stuck on the floor and I had to heave to squeeze through.

The light inside was wavery like under water. Acres of floorboards felted in dust stretched ahead, sloping up and down in hills and valleys with holes where you least expected them. The wall mirrors were vertical skating rinks mapped with blotches. The dim light greened by rose leaves reflected from one to another.

I walked like I was floating without making a sound, leaving a line of deep clear bootmarks. They followed me like a glass shadow, a person made of air walking behind me treading where I trod. Something crunched under my boot and broke into glittery edges, the remains of a faceted luster like a dry icicle. I looked up at a frozen waterfall of chandelier covered in cascades of spiderwebs. My vibrations had disturbed it and a shower of powdered grit fell into my hair. Another crystal hit with a light thud and kicked a crater in the dirt. I got from under.

The wreck of a big old musical instrument like a horse's coffin knelt on two legs in a corner surrounded with wilted music stands. It had yellow gappy teeth at one end and some writing that said STEI and stopped. There weren't any musicians, not even drowned ones. The place looked like the ballroom on the *Titanic* and all you needed were sharks. I circled a hole that could have swallowed an asteroid, headed for a service door, and met one.

"What d'you want?" A low snarl from the shadows.

Well, now. Life.

"Swordfish."

"Ain't no such animal."

"Nuts. Go tell him I want him."

"Get lost, bim, before you get in trouble. There's nobody here."

"I can see that. So shift your ass, Nobody, and yell me up the boss-man."

"Get lost, I said," he snarled, getting nasty.

I slid the ya down my sleeve and shoved it moderately into his invisible belly. I leaned a bit. I wasn't in an accommodating mood.

"I'm getting and you're losing. Push and I'll get some more. If you're no good for anything else go call me Hilt. At least he talks English."

There was a pause. Then he sulked.

"Hilt'll kill you."

"I doubt it. But it's possible I may kill you. Move it, Lassie."

I got that alone feeling. I stood around and admired the wall sconces to see if they were going to stretch out their arms and hold up lighted candles. They didn't.

"Hi, Cass," the underground voice rumbled suddenly over my head. "Sorry about the guard. Nobody comes this way so we put the kids here keep 'em out of our feet. Sword don't want to see anyone. Shut himself in day before yesterday, ain't talked to anyone since. He gets blues after surgery."

"Is he real sick, Hilt?"

"He acts it, kid."

"Nobody told me he was hurt."

"Ain't, that I know. Had a run-in with his old man. Old guy won."

"That's what Hall said. I can't believe it. Sword's never run in with Razor. Razor'd give him anything."

"Yeah, well, maybe he did," Hilt said like an avalanche in the mountains. "If I let you in you promise you tell him you did it over my dead body?"

"Sure. He'll believe that right away."

"Knowing you he just might. Long enough to keep my body alive till tomorrow, anyhow. Come down, girl."

He meant down. The service door opened on a grav-elevator as deep as a well that went down like the journey to the center of the earth. Bowels, as they say. I hoped it wasn't digesting.

I was worrying about maybe coming out in Australia when we landed in a lighted corridor that ran in both directions with a common modern floor and rows of doors like the girls' dormitory in Juve Hall but bigger. There were fire doors each end and the entries to more elevators.

"Boss down here," Hilt said, turning left.

His big feet padded away and I loped behind. A door cracked as we passed and I caught the crackle of laser fire and the sharp ozone smell of a firing range. Farther down someone had left theirs open on a room with an emperor-sized divan, colored posters in bright holo of the world's more gorgeous dancing stars, male, and some lace underwear in luminous silks would have fit a hippopotamus, female. Hilt's invisible hand delicately pulled it to. He has a strong sense of propriety.

A double door in the middle crashed back as we got level and someone large, smelly and not too sober rebounded off the far wall. Then he, she or it made another rebound as its superior officer caught up, and did a noisy gut-suck to let me past. I guess that was the common room. Whatever was happening inside sounded like the Teddy Bears' Picnic at too few revs per minute. Deep, growling and not sober at all. To the accompaniment of deuterium rock on a top-quality sound system. I could see if you were feeling fragile you might want to be alone. I hoped the place was soundproofed.

At the end was a single plain slab. Shut.

"Right here," Hilt rumbled. "If he asks, you teleported. Remember you never saw me."

"How could I, guy? You're all invisible."

He laughed like falling forests and went away. To join the picnic, by the fresh blast of sound that made the roof shake.

And left me with Sword's closed door. Seemed to me I'd been standing outside Sword's doors since I was fourteen, and they'd always been closed. I'd just had to get the habit of opening them. When I needed him. Thinking back, I'd needed him a lot over the years. Even over two years when he wasn't there and insisted on playing out my game of sending his best friend postcards. Determined to make me send them to him in person. Dammit, he knew better. He'd always known. As well as Moke did.

I used my fist on the doorphone and when that didn't draw any immediate reply I added a couple of kicks for emphasis.

"Sword! Open up or I'll kick the bastard in."

He knows I can't but he also knows I'll try real hard.

The inner lock clicked and it opened the smallest slit.

"Okay," his voice said, tired and slow. "Come in if you must."

It looked the way Sword's rooms have always looked. Basic monastic with books. Not religious unless you worship literature. I knew a lot of them. When I was a kid he made me read his library from end to end. He called it education. Guess it worked. I learned to hate Tolstoy for all time.

The iron cot was covered with an imitation Navaho blanket I bought him in the market just after I was fifteen to stop him sleeping on military gray. It was almost gray itself by now. You could just about see it once been red, yellow and black. I hadn't much money back then.

From the indentations he was lying full length with his head slightly turned. That worried me. I've almost never seen Sword lie down to meet people. His eyes were filtered out and there was nothing to see but a dent in the blanket.

"Hey, mec. You sick? Real sick?"

"No," he said in that slow tired voice. "Thought you'd gone."

"Of course I went. I been testifying. Was your and Razor's idea. You didn't tell me you were in hospital."

"I'm not now. Thought you'd taken off for the open spaces with Moke."

"Well, you were wrong, I'm here. Moke's gone away. He's left me."

Pause. Pregnant. Ain't natural for a guy. I sat on the side of the cot where most people his size have ribs.

"Good for him. I didn't think he had it in him. What exactly would you like me to do? Kill him for you, or just drag him back chained to the tail of my copt?" He sounded wearily ironic.

"You want me to leave? I mean really?"

"It's what I've told everyone. It doesn't seem to have taken. Since you're here, I suppose I can play big brother one more time. I've had the practice. You know the way to my shoulder."

"Sword, you're scaring me. It ain't the first time I've lost both my guys at once. It is the first time each of them's left me because I love the other. I came to tell you about the river on Virginity. The one you don't have time for."

"Oh, yeah. That one." The head-dent shifted.

"Right. You fell in it."

"With my usual tact and delicacy. It's okay. I can swim."

"Not there you can't. Nobody can. It's semisolid. Kind of a running quicksand. And it seethes. Nasty green things grow up and gel back down again. It's vile. Saw a little mole-coney fall in it once and it took the sucker five minutes to drown. Nobody could get to it. Local people go out in hovers but not near the bank, you can get overturned, it's where the humpy stuff grows. Moke had to take me away. I couldn't listen to it crying."

"Tough Cassandra." An invisible arm got around my waist. "The bim of steel. So why did I fall in?" His voice had warmed to something I almost knew.

"Dunno. Perversity? Anyhow I thought you were dead. You shit. I saw you fall and I couldn't stop it. And there was something you wanted to say to me real bad, only it was too late."

"When are you coming to bed with me?"

I almost didn't hear. It was a murmur from far away.

"Do you want me to?"

"No. What you heard was an echo. Ignore it."

"It sounded like an echo from halfway down a three-mile cliff. I've lived with Moke for five years, Sword. And Dosh for three of them. I'm not quite the Sleeping Beauty."

"I didn't have sleeping in mind. You didn't say when."

"Now. Why the hell's it taken you nine years to ask?"

The other arm joined the first and tightened. "I'm an imbecile. I was proving something to my father and he didn't even know. Then I missed my chance and let that asshole Doshchenko get away with you. Finally I took my clothes off to see if you could stand me and you couldn't. Who could? Can you stand me, Cass?"

"No. Who could? Moke's right, damn him. He always is. I been in love with you since about the third day we met. I got natural bad taste."

"I laid Halo."

"I know. She took care to tell me but I knew anyhow.

How else could you've got that perverse bitch to agree? If you do it again I'll kill you."

"No way." The arm tightened some more. I heard my ribs creak. I pretended I hadn't. "Listen, Cass, I'm what appeals to perverse bitches. You know the girl in the story who kissed the monster and he turned into a man. Did you ever think maybe she was disappointed? Going to all that trouble. To kiss his dirty slavering muzzle out of love. And finding herself with the prince next door. There's a glamor in monstrosity."

"Never thought of it. I just can't stand to see some guys fall in the river."

That's what education does. Makes you think stuff like that. I could tell he was sick.

"How many's some?"

"You and Moke."

"Moke. Right."

"Sorry, mec. He stayed with me. A damned long time."

"When even I didn't."

"You always did. Does it matter, Sword?"

"No."

"I came for you. Mokey told me to."

"The boy's intelligent. In a dumb sort of way. You want to see Razor's handiwork?"

I took a deep breath. "Why not? I seen Mark One, guess I can take Mark Two. You know the girl and the monster? It was his catchy conversation she liked. She probably didn't even notice the prince next door. What did you do to Razor? You must've really annoyed him."

"I really annoyed him. I played with the affections of his daughter."

"Oh. Well, you can stop. Get out of the suit, I seen you."

"Not like this," he said. His hands moved to the zips.

I breathed. He was right. I never had.

• • •

"You didn't like it," he said gently into my hair some-time later.

"Sure I didn't. I make these noises for all of the guys. Did any of your previous perverse bitches tell you making love to you's like wrestling an anaconda?"

"You were doing the wrestling, I thought you enjoyed it. We don't have to, all you've got to do is not chew me to death. Don't you like anacondas?"

"I adore them. I gnaw their ears wherever I find one."

"Then why are you sniveling?"

"I never snivel."

"You snivel constantly, like a public fountain. It's a wonder your face isn't green."

I gave up eating his shoulder and took a long noisy snuffle. "Moke left because he thinks you and me are married. He says he'll come to the christening."

Sword paused with his hand halfway down my spine. I guess he's been rubbing it in moments of crisis for a long time now. "Nice of him. When are we having it? And can we be clear in advance whether it's a boy or a casting?"

"Please, Sword," I said on a gulp. My conversation was beginning to have a shortage of words. "I need you. You could have answered my postcards."

"I did. I sent you a film-chip."

"Five minutes before I came back anyhow."

"Damn. I wish I'd known."

"Mokey did. I don't quite know how to live without him, either. And he's trying so hard to be a gentleman."

"That's his trouble. He doesn't understand you. The poor misguided boob's been trying to be a gentleman all these years. Did you know you're dripping in my armpit?"

"Moke isn't nasty to me."

"More fool he. If someone isn't, you're going to be dripping in people's armpits for the rest of your life.

Almost certainly mine. In fact it had better be mine. Who bought that underwear that's all over the bookshelf?"

"You did."

"Uh-huh. I could see it was indecent. It's what I said. The boy's got one fault. He's short on imagination."

"*Mokey?*"

"Right. He's shit-hot on sculpture but zero on panties. It's all a question of the direction of one's creativity. When we get through I promise to talk to him."

"I wasn't through."

"Neither was I. If you're really hungry I can call out for steak. I think the bit you're on's undercooked."

"When Issa did it Yell got all dreamy."

"He's a spacer, they're psycho. I'll probably get used to it in time. I see why Moke hasn't any meat on his bones."

"It isn't funny, Sword."

"I know it isn't, you damned convoluted bim. I said we'll talk. Tomorrow. Or maybe the next day. Give the stupid bastard room to find out how well he does alone."

"Maybe pretty good. He's got his fucking muse."

"Fucking a muse could turn out to be thin entertainment in the long run," Swordfish said. "Getting on alone's something I know about. I haven't talked yet. Got business on hand. You'd be surprised how good I am at talking. Among other things."

I'll speak for the other things. Talking, what was to say? But maybe it really was a question of creativity.

Sword can be all hell creative. I've seen him.

It was two days before we got around to sorting our problems. We'd nine years of time to make up. We took possession of the loft to get away from the deuterium rock, since we were losing our minds with it on and the Pack might lose theirs with it off, and rolled about all over it. Nobody else showed, which was maybe as well. Lorn came out of some high-fashion limbo and took me to an uptown precinct to buy a celebration ring, a daffodil-colored diamond bigger than the Ritz. It was indecent. When I said so he laughed like a drain and told me everyone would think it was glass. They didn't. They thought I'd stolen it. Then we strolled through the lower Strip goggling in windows and he had his backside pinched twice by skaters. It would have been oftener but I kicked a couple.

"If you will wear those pants, you're going to get raped before we get home. And if you do I'm not going to rescue you, I'm just going to stand here and die of shame."

"Would you like me to take them off?" he asked innocently.

"No!" I yelped.

"I've very nice legs," he said, with a kind helpful air.

"I know. So does everyone in the street. I won't list your other virtues, they're all on public display."

"You're jealous. Can't stand competition."

"I'm not accustomed to being one half of a specialty exhibitionist act."

"I thought you did it with Doshchenko all the time."

"That was different."

"Ah." He turned the idea around. "You're a snob."

It was true the difference between his pants and the tightest ever worn by Dosh was about seven hundred credits.

"Let's go visit Mokey," I said grimly.

"As you like. So long as you remember my mechanical half flies space. It has faster reflexes."

"I'll bring a blindfold. And a prayer book."

"You won't be able to use both of them at once."

"No. I'm going to use them one after the other, according to circumstances. I remember what happened to my pants last time you were in charge."

The ship was the latest luxury short-course racer with a custom bar in back. I looked around it and shuddered.

"Where do you get these things?"

"I borrowed it. From a friend of . . ."

"A friend. I know. When are they letting him out?"

"Not until they're quite sure he's cured," he said reassuringly. "Would you like some champagne in lieu of the prayer book, since I don't seem to have one on hand?"

"I'd rather have some good hard moonshine, but I guess any kind of anesthetic'll do. Unless you're sharing it, in which case I think I'll stay on the ground."

"It's all right, I don't drink. Not unless I take anti-alk pills first. My metabolism's specialized."

Oddly enough I felt safe in the racing job, maybe because we were strapped in, maybe because for once we didn't have to slot a lattice. He flew a lot faster than Yell, but then Yell has normal instincts of self-preservation. We zoomed in on Never like a bullet. He didn't bother to call for landing permission until it was rushing up at our eyeballs and then did it with an air of lackadaisical arrogance I've never seen on anything human, not even him.

"MacLaren DeLorn calling on Hans-Bjorn Eklund. Give me a grid."

No "please."

"You don't think maybe you should ask nicely?"

"I have it on good authority his man Henry's a shit. Yours."

"Sure he is. What if he doesn't open the screen in time?"

"Sweet Cinders. First, shits are impressed by rudeness, it's what they'd do themselves if they were rich enough. Second, this screen's only atmosphere-retention and micrometeorites. The macro-belt's outside the satsphere. The Government does it. If I hit this screen at speed in this ship, all I do is punch a temporary hole and heat my skin a little. He'll lose a degree or two of pressure, not enough to hurt him with an atmosphere this size. It could get Henry a scolding."

"I'd just hate that."

"So should I. It would spoil my paint job."

Henry made it, though the radio gobbled a bit while he came to terms. Lorn's sometimes hard to come to terms with. We settled on the grid with his ordinary terrifying precision, swung neatly on our axis and ended facing back out.

"I don't blame you for wanting a quick getaway after that display," I said sourly.

"I always cover my rear."

"But only just."

"Cassandra, has anyone ever told you you bear malice?"

"No. Why?"

• • •

Our—Moke's—compound is among a grove of trees a few hundred yards from the house, made up of a main cabin in cedar boards with a shingled roof, with his workshop at right angles, and a smaller cabin where Yell can retire for privacy if he wants. He very rarely does but today Issa was in residence. I wasn't surprised to see them. With Moke and me both AWOL it made sense he'd come where he knew he'd find people. They were sprawling in loungers on their terrace with several pieces of clothes on, or nearly, drinking beer and bronzing. They looked as if they'd had a hard happy night. They waved limply with big white smiles and didn't get up.

We gave the cabin a miss and headed straight for the workshop since it was where Moke was most likely to be. I scuffed my boots in the grass and trailed. Lorn strode right in like a shark with a reluctant pilot fish.

"Good morning, Martin."

The workshop was full of iron sheet that had to be areas of Moon-cube, a lot of plexifoam containers labeled CHEMICALS, DANGEROUS, heavy machinery in poised attitudes and Moke. He was sitting on one of the containers with a switched-off cutter in his hand gazing at the ground and his hair looked as if it had died in the night. His pants weren't just dead, they'd come back from the grave and were waiting for a stake through the heart. I've never seen him look so ill in my life, and shimmering health's never been his thing.

He looked up as we breezed through the door, ran a reddened eye over each of us and cracked the faintest echo of a smile.

"Hi, Sword. Was expecting you."

"Then you got me. What the hell is this?"

"I'm working. It's a concept you understand."

"I understand the concept," Sword said. "Well enough to see that's exactly what you aren't doing."

"Dammit, Mokey. You knew this guy?"

"Sure I did. How could I not? I'm a specialist in shapes and volumes. Recognized him the first time I saw him. Apart from, would Sword ever let you out of his sight if it was dangerous? I'm surprised you didn't."

"I'm not clever," I muttered.

"You were in love with the original. I wasn't. I didn't have the same impulse to use the one to annoy the other."

"Is that what I did?"

"Always. With Sword. He's the only guy you've thought rated it. What did you come for?"

"You," Swordfish said. "We find your procedures a little arbitrary. I seem to remember a couple of years back you were about to lose your mind because you thought Cass had run out. You didn't think you might upset her or something?"

Moke flushed. His red eyes pinked toward blood color. "Dammit, Sword, I'm the invisible man. One of my talents. Ironic, isn't it? You've been behind a suit where no one could see you and Cass has seen you all the time. I've been right in front of her and she's never really seen me at all."

"Be careful, Martin. It was me she cried on all night. Why do you think I've protected you for five years? Both of you. Cass needed you. I know why you pushed her away, but you're taking a risk. She sees you. You could lose something you need badly. Unless there's someone you like better in the cupboard?"

"You know there isn't. There's only one person I want and without her I don't care what I do."

"Then drop the fucking heroics, isn't one horse's ass in the family enough? Let's talk."

"I've told Cass. My family's over."

"Bullshit. We're your family. Doshchenko's over, is that her fault? You were kids. Now you aren't. Is she to pay for your bad conscience? Razor saw through Dosh, it's how he convinced me."

"I know," Moke said. "She wanted you and when you weren't available she fell for the first very tall guy who spoke to her. I figured it too. Of course she couldn't know you were dark, she hadn't seen you."

"Her crush on Dosh was a kid thing, Moke, it couldn't have lasted. What do you think I stuck around for? The hell with it. I want help. Dribble needs an education, he's getting impossible. You're the only guy I know can handle him."

Moke didn't answer. There was a salt rime on his lashes and his eyes were focused on space. Or on Swordfish, or through him. I followed his stare.

That piece of murderous marine life was standing in the entrance, framed against the bright light of a midday sky. He really looked as tall as a windmill. One hip was shot in an elegant slouch, his head slightly tipped to the side. He looked beautiful, vulnerable and dangerous. A couple of thousand creds of designer leatherwear was shaped over sleek bones. The dark blue-purple atmosphere edged and defined him.

Moke's gaze had concentrated. His right hand was scrabbling, but only for his slate. "That's it. Keep still, will you? No. Don't move your head."

"What are you doing?" But Sword held the pose. Only the edges of his lips lifted slightly.

"War memorial. Public competition, Hampton-of-Argos. I had some ideas but this one's it. Six meters of polished steel with holes where its heart, brain and guts ought to be. Looking at the sky and carrying a dead child in its arms."

"That child was me," Sword said.

"That's why I'm going to give it your face."

"If you must. Can't we . . . ."

I squeezed his arm. "It's no use. When he gets one of

these turns he just stops hearing. You want me to get you a beer? You could be here all day."

The only reason we weren't was Hans-Bjorn. His owl-eyed mechanical Henry II spidered up in the middle with a message in upper B-flat and a bad case of mechspeak.

"Mr. Eklund presents his compliments to the son of his old acquaintance Cameron DeLorn and would be delighted if he would care to come for a drink at the house especially if he's brought Cassandra because Mr. Eklund's been missing her."

Meaning Hans-Bjorn had noticed his Moke wasn't up to the Moke mark. Henry stood hopefully around waiting for an answer and since Mokey was too busy to talk and Sword simply raised an inquiring brow I gave it.

"Thanks, Henry. Moke's making a sketch but I'll twist his arm and we'll be there. Please tell Mr. Eklund Mr. MacLaren DeLorn is delighted to have the opportunity of talking to his father's old friend, and give him my love and kisses."

Sword waited for Henry to get out of earshot before being offensive. "I hope this family isn't going to get overstretched. Do you love and kiss all Moke's clients or is this a special occasion?"

"She thinks he's her uncle," Moke said absently. "Because he acts like it, I suppose. Could you turn maybe a quarter southwest?"

Hans-Bjorn's met our friends and being a nice guy he tries to act as if it didn't matter. He set about setting Lorn at ease, which is a waste of time. Then he took a second look and stopped bothering.

"Cameron DeLorn to the last detail," he said. "Incredible. I've known your father a long time. United Space."

"That's my mother. The MacLaren half. My father's Interplanetary Engineering Inc. The merger ought to be called Pirates of Space but they prefer DeLorn-MacLaren

Enterprises. My father was under the unhappy impression I'm heir to both."

"Moke wants to make him into a war memorial," I said hastily, before the conversation could go really downhill.

"I like that. Your war record's famous." H-B also has an eye. He turned the subject on a dime. "You must keep pretty busy, I believe your father's into heavy deals. What do you do with your leisure?" It isn't a wise question, the beast's liable to answer. And you're happier ignorant.

Lorn studied the seams of his boots. "I'm a caretaker."

"Yeah," I helped. "He takes care of people."

Moke stared into the depths of his beer glass. Maybe he hoped to find the answer to life, the universe and everything in the bottom. If he did, it didn't seem to make him feel better. Lorn gave him a sideways glance.

"I've taken lots of pills," he said wistfully. "Was someone offering a drink?"

Hans-Bjorn couldn't not have noticed the atmosphere, it was within a spark of setting off the sprinklers. But he's spent a long time coping with guests. He got Henry II passing flutes around and salted bitty things on porcelain saucers. He saves our skins with over-classed clients. I took Moke's beer glass away by force and he looked at me woodenly. I got a flush of water to the eyes and nearly missed the table.

"What do you think of the war rumor? As an ex-pilot?"

"You've heard it," Lorn said, interested. "It's going around. My banker says the market's jumpy."

"He's right. The Coelacanth scandal hasn't calmed things. One or two other people are tottering, I hear. Of course, your father's above that sort of worry."

"Armor-plated." He stretched his legs a yard or two over the terra-cotta tiles and held his glass to the light. "This is nice."

"All princes next door are the same. You quit drinking out of my slipper already."

"Forgot to bring it with me, Cinders. Remind me next time. That boot's got holes in it."

"Not to mention her foot," Moke said in a voice from the next dimension. Lorn didn't seem to notice. He was gazing peacefully into the purple-blue sky.

Then I saw his face go blank and got one of those feelings. The kind that raise your neck hair down to your tailbone. I hadn't seen that sweet narrow smile since we'd gone chasing around the shopping mall ten yards ahead of a gunship. I didn't know how I could have known him so long and not recognized it. Because if the long girl's lashes were Lorn's, the taut spine and coldly concentrated gaze were all Swordfish. His eyes were fixed and they were pools of frozen mercury.

"Do you have a shielded room anywhere in the house?" he asked gently. I know the tone. Its name's trouble. "One with separate life-support?"

"Yes, of course." Hans-Bjorn was surprised. "Standard for artificial environments. Why?"

"Well, I'd say you have maybe eight minutes to go and get in it. If there's any heavy furniture, like a table, get under and protect your head. Take the kids with you and shout for Yell. Oh, and call your pilot. If he shifts he could just get clear. I suppose your field controls are inside?"

Hans-Bjorn's mouth was open. "The main generator . . ."

"Good. Get Yeller to deal with it, he understands. You want all the screen power drawn into a single bubble around the house. You'll lose your terraforming but if it can hold the worst for a few seconds you'll save yourself and possibly some of your belongings. Got to go. Give me five minutes to make the pad." He saw Hans-Bjorn's blank look. "It's okay, I can. Go on."

He was on his feet and moving, hauling on my wrist with one hand and Moke's with the other. My eyesight isn't boosted but by that time I could see them too. Five little shining points, pricked out above the terrestrial equator like a flight of glittering flies.

"Coelacanth's dead!"

"Body-legging's House business," Sword said. "They don't forgive easily. All of us in one basket. What a chance. Move it."

"Sword—"

"I can turn most or all of them aside. They'll follow me at close range. I'm trained for it, Cassandra. Go!"

Hans-Bjorn had risen, his face pale. "What happens to you if they do?"

"With luck I'll outfly them. Call your people. You're liable to shed environment fast. Take the kids away. Me, I'm paid for it. Career caretaker."

"You can't," I shrieked. "Five of them? Not even you. Sword, we waited nine years and we've had three fucking nights."

"Yeah, it was great fucking. Look after Genius, he needs you."

I opened my mouth and he grabbed my shoulder and flung me violently into Mokey's arms.

"Martin, take her away."

Moke caught and held me.

"The guy's in love with you, Cass."

"That's love? Swordfish, you shithead!"

But I got his turned back, poised to run. I'd never seen him in action out of a suit. The hyped muscles stood out like wires under the leather. Moke pulled Hans-Bjorn's arm and dragged us both towards the door.

As Sword blurred to move an intolerable light snatched our linked shadows and pinned them to the wall. Moke's and mine hand in hand and his stretching the width of the terrace like a steeple falling over both of us. The shield whited out and I stopped being able to see anything but spires of flaring color.

Never shuddered to its roots and for an instant we lost gravity. I felt my feet leaving the floor as planters and tables floated loose. Then the field cut back in and everything, us, plants, glasses, furniture, settled back in place with a grinding and smashing of valuable fragile things and we were gasping in an atmosphere like the summit of Everest.

Somewhere in the planted groves there was the crash of a falling tree. Damp earth and crushed geraniums spilled over the tiles. I found myself on my knees with Moke wrapped around me and splinters of shattered crystal under both of us. Hans-Bjorn had fallen back heavily into his lounge chair, his cracked flute in one white-knuckled hand and a foaming-over bottle in the other.

Sword was half across the lawn, balanced in a crouch, his hands spread like a wirewalker. Behind him mechanical Henry lay on his back in a wreckage of biscuits and caviar kicking feebly, a silver tray bent in one claw. Then Lorn straightened, paced back like he'd come off the golf course, and held a hand to each of us. We crawled shakily into human postures. Moke had a wrist to his mouth that dripped bright thick drops.

The emergency generator cut in with a subterranean thump and oxygen began to hiss out of ducts in the floor. Yell was staggering across from the studio, Issa clinging to his arm, with the look of the old spacer who's been here before and didn't like it last time and I could see Henry I's panic-stricken figure windmilling among the trees.

I looked up at the sky. Five overlapping flowers of dark smoke were spreading outward from a center just above the equator and dissipating slowly into space like the tail end of a firework show. There was still a sparkle of falling debris hitting the edges of atmosphere. Somebody down there was going to be hellish annoyed. Letting off nucleonics in sovereign space is more than usually illegal.

"What was that?" Eklund croaked.

"A present from my stepfather, at a guess," I said weakly. "He got to have one empty garden."

Lorn smiled, his eyes gray, clear and beagle-warm, flicking dusty specks off the sleeve of his black leather vest.

"You'd be surprised what grows in Razor's garden. I'd say the second flight was labeled Return to Sender. He tends to take 'em out at ground level. Stops them making the same mistake twice."

He prized the bottle and glass out of Hans-Bjorn's hands and laid them on the table. The top was cracked. Then he gave Henry II a heave and deposited him on his claws. Henry whirred and clicked, shrugged his owl-eyed shoulders and got into mode.

"Would Sir like another bottle?"

"Yes, please, Henry," Hans-Bjorn said in a very good fake of his normal voice. "Make it two. And would you send the gardener to take care of the broken pots, please?"

There's a lot to be said for an upbringing if you happen to have one. I sure hoped his art-collection had survived. He's one guy who'd rather go with it.

We lay on Mokey's terrace in the sun and drank beer and gazed at the woods which looked more natural with traces of weather. Like some brown leaves and a few crooked trunks. The gardening mechanicals were going crazy but that's mechanicals. No esthetic sense.

Moke hadn't said anything while Henry gelled his wrist, and nothing while we walked back, and he hadn't said anything more while he got the cans and glasses out. But I knew the pinched look around the nostrils. It's only happened once but it was memorable. The explosion was heard all over Ashton.

I hadn't stopped shaking. I probably wasn't talking to Sword but I was hanging around his neck anyhow until I got back the spit to swear at him. He was cuddling me with an air of innocent sweetness as if he didn't know he was about to get slaughtered by both of us. Which he did. I did wonder what kind of expression he'd had under the suit all these years. I'd be surprised if that was it. Moke went on pouring beer. The air above his head looked like a smoke signal.

"So," he said finally, whacking down a glass like he meant to ram it through the table and and planting himself between Sword's feet. Sword gazed across with limpid eyes. "You're the guy who lectures me. On responsibility."

"I do my best," Lorn said modestly.

"I leave you alone with Cass three days and the first chance you get you try to kill yourself."

"It's okay, Moke," I said, wet and squeaky. "Give me five minutes and I'll do it for him."

Neither of them paid any attention except Sword leaned his chin on my head and breathed.

"I didn't want to scare you," he said. "That screen hadn't any chance against a direct hit with five warheads no matter what Yell did. Someone had to take them out in space and I'm the only guy with the know-how. I didn't have time for an ethical debate."

Moke's eyes flamed. "Career fucking hero."

"Gave that up at eighteen. It's simpler." Sword looked down. His brows were ridged and he laced his fingers carefully together and put pressure on the knuckles. They whitened.

"I'm sorry, Cass. You're both right, it's a hell of a way to prove love and you deserved to know. I've never known how to tell you. Razor tried to convince me to have radical surgery when I was nineteen and if I'd done it I might have had something to give you. Only you don't know what it's like to be a hype. You get into it and afterwards everything's faded. There's no taste or touch or smell to it. I don't know if anyone ever rehabilitates, all the guys I knew who tried either quit or killed themselves. It's irreversible. You think it's natural for guys to do what I do? My metabolism's fucked. Everything I do uses me up a bit more. I shouldn't have touched you. I tried not to. But I needed you too much. I don't think at bottom I'm as strong as Moke. Only if someone has to dive into the river on Virginity it's me. I'm halfway there already."

My jaws had tightened until my teeth ached. I pried them apart. "How long?"

"I don't know. A year? Ten? Very few of us live over forty. Very few live as long as I have."

"Doctors . . . ?"

"No. You remember the old guy completely worn out at a hundred and eighty on his fourth rejuve? He's three hundred years my junior. I haven't any lives left, Cassie. Every time I go over a wall I use another ten years. You counted the walls I've jumped?"

"Razor . . . ?"

"He wanted me to have something. He hasn't any problems, he's a partial and his metab's adjusted. I'm total. It was you used to say I wasn't human. The latest doc did a bit of new work that could add a year or two. I'd like to have a kid and see him . . . her, whatever, grow up a bit. Avoid some of my father's mistakes. If I can. And I don't want to leave you alone."

"You want to hand me off to Mokey. Today or tomorrow?" I didn't even care I was crying. "You're a shit, Sword. You had nine years to love me and you let me go. You can't die now."

"It isn't voluntary, Cass. I held off for a lot of reasons and I was wrong. You had to go before I really knew my weakness. Arrogance. I've paid. I am paying. Not enough, I know."

"Do you think Moke deserves this? Dammit, I like him. I won't be handed around like a parcel. By either one of you. Him to you, you to him. Pass the Cass. Who do you guys think you are? Can anyone play? Why not call Yell and Hans-Bjorn to have a turn?"

"Cassie," Sword said. "I've survived the last ten years for you. Don't kill me now."

"How about me?" I yelled. "What makes you think I need either of you?"

Moke had slumped. He dropped his arms around my shoulders and rubbed a wet scrubby cheek against my ear.

"The way you're crying? I'm here, Cass. Hell and damn you, Sword. What made you think I'd really leave? I've a sculpture to do. Two, with the plaza in Hampton-of-Argos. You guys need someone to keep you straight or this could run forever. Then there's Dribble. I guess I'm the only person around here who's actually grown up."

"Not since the other day," I snarled.

"Right. But I've had three days to reach adulthood. I think I just made it. No parcels, Cassandra. I'm here when you need me."

I put a hand around his strong skinny neck and twisted to look into Sword's eyes. I don't know what Halo saw. What I saw was the guy I'd known half my life and needed since I was old enough to know what needing was. And he looked like he was burning up. "I hate you," I said.

It's what I've been saying in emergencies for years. He wrapped his long arms around my waist and creaked my ribs.

"I know."

Mokey straightened and reached for Lorn's shoulders, digging his fingers into the muscle. Guess it was easier with leather. "Relax and have a beer, guy. It isn't for today. Aren't we having a celebration? I want to drink to it." He flicked a wry smile. "I understand you, Sword. It's my damnation."

"And I understand you. It's mine."

"Damn the pair of you to hell," I said. And managed to drip down Sword's shirt and Moke's hand at the same time.

Square One. My favorite place.

Sometimes I ask myself if this board has ladders or if it's joke-shop material clear through. The snakes I've met. Can you climb an anaconda in flight? It looked like I had a handful of years to try, if nobody started a war in the meantime.

Love is the Aphrodite clipjoint, step in and get taken. You can't fuck with the gods. Ask Cassandra.

Who is

signing off.

December 1990–July 1991

**EXPLORING NEW REALMS IN
SCIENCE FICTION/FANTASY ADVENTURE**

By the same author

CRASHCOURSE

In the cybertech world of tomorrow, the rich get their kicks
from watching films with emotional implants – the viewer
feels whatever the actor feels. For heightened realism the
actors aren't given a script – they simply react to whatever
happens to them. For all they know this is real life – not *reel*
life – and the film hasn't even started yet. Dangerous, maybe.
But the money is irresistible.

When Cass, Moke and Dosh sign a movie contract, they
reckon they've got it made. Work a few weeks, run a few
risks, and they can finally get off the planet. But the script
turns out to be a real killer, and their female co-star has some
plans of her own . . .